NEVER CALL IT LOVING

The tears filled her eyes again.
'It isn't that I'm not proud of you. Seeing the
way they reverenced you, I was so proud I
couldn't bear it. When I read your speech at
Ennis I cried. I know what you have to do, and I'll
try never to stop you. But I can't promise always
to be calm and sensible.'
'Nor can I,' he said. 'Nor can I.'
'I'm so afraid one day you'll hate me.'
'For what?' he asked in amazement.
'For tearing you in half.'
He made no answer to that. Instead he said, 'But
you're with me, Katharine?'
He only called her Katharine when he was most
deeply serious.
'Yes,' she said reluctantly. 'I have to be.'

Never Call It Loving

Dorothy Eden

CORONET BOOKS
Hodder and Stoughton

To another Irishman

Copyright © 1966 by Dorothy Eden
First published in Great Britain 1966
by Hodder and Stoughton

Coronet Edition 1968
Second impression 1969
Third impression 1970
Fourth impression 1973
Fifth impression 1976

Printed and bound in Great Britain
for Coronet Books,
Hodder and Stoughton, London,
by Hazell Watson & Viney Ltd,
Aylesbury, Bucks

ISBN 0 340 02927 7

CHAPTER 1

WHEN Katharine twice changed her mind about the dress she would wear for dinner that night, Lucy lost her patience and spoke with the familiarity of long service, her voice tart with disapproval.

"Really, Miss Katharine, anyone would think you were entertaining royalty."

"I suppose in a way I am, Lucy. I believe that Mr. Parnell is called the uncrowned king of Ireland."

"Well, if he hasn't yet got his crown he won't object to your old blue silk."

"That's the trouble," Katharine fretted. "It is old. It's quite two years out of fashion."

"You haven't minded before. You've said you don't need new gowns, buried in the country. It's not as if the Captain likes to see his wife getting shabby."

Katharine gave a small shrug, dismissing that argument. Willie hadn't noticed for a long time what she wore, and Lucy knew that well enough, if age hadn't dimmed her faculties too much. But the old creature had always been stubbornly devoted to Willie, and wasn't likely now to admit that there was anything in him to criticise.

"Anyway, from what I've heard," Lucy went on, "you won't care for Mr. Parnell. They say he's a dour sort of a man."

"Where have you heard that, Lucy?" Katharine asked in amusement. "Who have you been gossiping with?"

"I read the newspapers, Miss Katharine. Especially since the Captain went into politics. And a fine lot of braggarts that Irish party seems to be. Always trying to upset poor Mr. Gladstone. It's a good thing they'll have the Captain to teach them manners, Now then, which dress am I to pack?"

"The brown velvet, I think, and I'll wear my topaz brooch. You're quite right, Lucy. I don't want to be dressed up for Mr. Parnell. He works so much with the poor that I don't believe it would be in good taste to look richly dressed."

"But you do pay for dressing, Miss Katharine," Lucy said wistfully.

Katharine smiled, half in amusement, half sadly.

"What, and me over the thirty and with three children! Besides I had enough of that when Willie bought me clothes he couldn't afford. And don't pretend you don't remember."

Lucy chose to ignore that and asked: "Who is to be at this grand dinner party?"

"Only a few friends. Willie and I decided not to have too many on this first occasion. The O'Gorman Mahon, of course. It was his idea. Colonel Colthurst, Colonel Nolan, Justin McCarthy. And Mr. Parnell, if he comes."

Lucy looked up, the half-folded gown in her arms.

"You mean you don't even know for sure if he's coming?"

Katharine fastened the topaz brooch in the lace at her throat, regarding it critically, then took it off and handed it to Lucy to pack.

"Mr. Parnell is an unknown quantity, Lucy, as you yourself seem to know. Perhaps he does need to be taught manners, because he hasn't answered my invitation. But I'm sure that was merely an oversight. He's a very busy man. He'll be there. After all, Willie and I are giving this dinner for him."

Why should she be so anxious to look well for a man she had never met, dressing up her over-thirty charms for him? Especially since she didn't even know if he would come. He was becoming one of the most talked-of men in the Government, and already, although he was so young, was a brilliant Parliamentarian. Yet no one seemed to know what he was like as a man. He was elusive, anti-social, an enigma. Charles Stewart Parnell. Born in Ireland thirty-four years ago, growing up at the same time as she was, he at Avondale in County Wicklow, she at Rivenhall, in Essex.

She slipped into a dream, thinking that now Rivenhall seemed like a place where it had always been summer. The swing under the yew tree, the strutting bad-tempered peacock, the white dresses of herself and her sisters sprouting like mushrooms when they had a picnic on the lawn, Lucy in her immaculately starched cap and apron coming out in the summer dusk to call that it was bedtime, the sky yellow and the trees black and the air full of the scent of roses.

Although summer had stopped the year that Papa had died. The year that Captain O'Shea, the dashing young Irish Captain in the 18th Hussars, had come courting.

He had scarcely waited for her father to be buried before wanting her to marry him. He was good-looking, charming, witty, and the best horseman in his regiment. His mother and his sister Mary were his remaining family. Although the O'Sheas were Catholics, and Katharine's father, Sir John Page Wood, had been an Anglican clergyman and Royal chaplain, none of Katharine's sisters and brothers, or her mother who had also had royal connections—she had been a Lady of the Bedchamber—had thought Captain O'Shea's religion an obstacle. Dear Katharine did not need to embrace the Catholic faith. She merely had to promise to bring up her children in it.

Dazed by her beloved father's death, she was the youngest of thirteen children and her father's favourite, Katharine had been so thankful for Willie's kindness, comfort and generosity that she had failed to distinguish between gratitude and love. She had been very young, only eighteen. But she had soon enough begun to grow older when she had discovered Willie's own immaturity, the recurring financial crises that seemed to be a permanent part of his life, the tendency he shared with a great many of his countrymen to drink too much and rely too much on his charm and wit, and, most trying of all, his quarrelsome nature. She had been completely mature by the time her third baby was born, and when it, too, had been taken by Willie and his mother, a frail old lady wrapped in exquisite Cashmere shawls and piety, to be baptised with great ceremony in the Brompton Oratory. This time she refused even to go inside the church, but stood outside, a lonely woman in her fashionable clothes, watching the pigeons wheeling and strutting, waiting for her children to be returned to her.

She had heard that Charles Parnell was a Protestant. He must be a remarkable man to have succeeded in becoming such a power in a Catholic country.

It was only recently, however, that Katharine had be-

7

come aware of his existence. Although always interested in political affairs (her father had encouragèd her to have a social conscience, and her uncle, Lord Hatherley, who had been made Lord Chancellor now that Mr. Gladstone's Government was back in power, frequently invited Willie and her to dinner parties), she had not followed the Irish question with deep interest until Willie himself had decided to begin a serious career at last and had stood for election at County Clare.

She knew that the Irish party had been leaderless since Mr. Isaac Butt's death, and that Charles Stewart Parnell had recently been elected in his place. Mr. Parnell had been Mr. Butt's protégé, and the old man, who with his amiable affable manners had been as popular as an Irish politician could be with the English, had written of him some years ago, "We have got a splendid recruit, an historic name, young Parnell of Wicklow, and unless I am mistaken the Saxon will find him an ugly customer though he is a good-looking fellow."

Since then young Mr. Parnell had created a new slogan which called the three "F's", fixity of tenure, fair rents and free sale of the tenants' interests, and had passionately supported Michael Davitt's Land League, an organisation formed to protect tenants against unfair landlords. The English hated the Land League, the Queen who had no patience with her Irish subjects, called it "that monstrous land league", and Willie complained that it was becoming positively dangerous to be a landlord in benighted Ireland. The Land Leaguers were getting out of hand, burning down a landlord's house and asking him questions afterwards, driving off his livestock, setting fire to his haystacks. They did everything, Willie said bitterly, except put poison in the poor fellow's tea.

Anna Parnell, Charles' sister, had made herself notorious by forming a Ladies' Land League, and by writing inflammable seditious articles, but she was an hysterical unbalanced creature. Her brother was another matter altogether.

At least that was what The O'Gorman Mahon had said when he had accompanied Willie to Eltham after Willie's successful campaign in County Clare.

The two of them, flushed with success, filled the house with noise and laughter. Katharine had never seen an Irishman so much larger than life than The O'Gorman Mahon. Tall, white-haired with a handsome craggy scarred face and a torrent of picturesque language, he had been a famous duellist and soldier of fortune, friend of kings and emperors. In his old age he had turned to the comparatively milder amusement of Irish politics.

He and Willie boasted that they had kissed every girl in Clare and drunk with every man.

"And your poor husband, Mrs. O'Shea, detests Irish whisky. But he drank it like a man."

"And admired every baby in every filthy cabin from Clare to Limerick," Willie put in, wrinkling his nose distastefully. "What with the babies and the latest litter of the pig, I couldn't tell which was which."

The O'Gorman Mahon roared with his tempestuous laughter.

"Faith, and they thought Willie too finely dressed to be a true Irishman. But his kisses brought them round."

"I'll strive to bring a little sartorial decency to the Irish party if I do nothing else," said Willie. "And I'll make a bet that that has more effect in the House than all Parnell's eloquence. Let the English know that some of us are civilised."

"Ye'd be more than civilised, if you'd do something for Parnell. They tell me his begging expedition to America has nearly finished him."

"How do you mean?" For the first time Katherine spoke.

"He suffers from a delicate constitution, but never mention it to him. He's an aloof reserved creature and gets hostile if his health's mentioned. He's got no woman to take care of him, poor fellow. That might be something you could do, Mrs. O'Shea."

"Me?"

"For the sake of the party, woman," said Mr. Mahon, drinking deeply, and indicating that he would like his glass refilled. "He's got a powerful following and we just might whip the English with him. Isn't that so, Willie?"

Willie might want to shine in politics, but he had no

9

desire to quarrel with his sophisticated English friends. Ever since his army days, where he had incurred debts amounting to fifteen thousand pounds which had nearly bankrupted his father, he had had a love of social life. He had always sought friends who were influential and rich, although in living up to them he had several times reduced his wife and children to penury.

Katharine had been unhappily aware for a long time that Willie cared more about the cut of his suit, and that she should be expensively gowned as befitted his wife (who was, after all, only an extension of himself), than that they had a permanent home and he some useful position in life. That was why she had been so pleased when he had decided to take up politics.

But already he was in a dilemma because he didn't want to offend his sophisticated English friends by taking up the unpopular and boorish Mr. Parnell. Nevertheless, he didn't want to offend The O'Gorman Mahon either, for with his colourful and overwhelming personality, all doors opened to him.

He compromised by saying that he and Kate would give a dinner party in London and ask Mr. Parnell, but he was quite sure the fellow would not come.

"He has no manners. I hear that he simply ignores invitations."

Katherine was aware of the piercing black eyes of The O'Gorman Mahon on her.

"That's a thing no woman of mettle would allow to happen. Isn't that true, Mrs. O'Shea?"

"How can I stop it happening?"

"Don't ask me. Use your feminine wiles." He looked at her again, thoughtfully and appreciatively. "If I make no mistake, you have plenty of them. You might do your country a service."

"You make a mistake, Mr. Mahon. I am not Irish."

"But you're married to an Irishman. That makes the poor ould country, for better or worse, your own. Don't do her any harm, Mrs. O'Shea."

Katharine had to laugh.

"Does all this come out of a simple dinner party? Ireland's fate?"

"An oak grows from a seed, Ma'am. Anyway, no one ever told me that Charlie Parnell didn't like women. He was reported to be pursuing one in America. But she escaped him, or he escaped her, I don't know the rights of it."

Willie said he objected to his wife being expected to become Parnell's nursemaid. The two men began a slightly drunken wrangle about what could or could not be expected of a politician's wife, then found themselves too comfortable and too tipsy to argue. The O'Gorman Mahon swallowed a half-tumbler of neat whisky, rolled a remarkably bright and lascivious eye, and said slowly and deliberately, "You could get any man at your feet, Mrs. O'Shea. Even that old puritan Gladstone. I'm only asking ye to be a wee bit kind to a tired man. Is that beyond your ability? Say it is and I won't believe you."

She didn't intend to say it was, for she was looking forward, with some curiosity, to meeting Mr. Parnell. She would place him beside her at the dinner table and, if he did prove to be unsociable and difficult, she would do her best to draw him out. Of course it was not beyond her ability. She had helped her father in his parish too much, and talked too much to all kinds of people, both rich and poor, and had too much sympathy with the wretched and the underprivileged, not to be able to find a great deal to say to Mr. Parnell.

Although she had never been to Ireland herself. She had wanted Willie to take her there on their honeymoon, but he had refused. That had been thirteen years ago in the year 1867, and things were pretty wretched, with another famine, and Kate might be upset if she saw a corpse lying in a ditch, or they encountered one of those numerous black-clad processions making its grief-blinded way to the church-yard. It was extremely tiresome the way the Irish were always starving, as if they enjoyed their misery, as if they willed the potato crops to blacken with blight. From the Queen down, the English nation was sick and tired of its awkward quarrelsome vociferous illogical and irrepressible neighbour.

As a landlord himself, even though his estate in Limerick was heavily mortgaged, Willie allied himself with the English against the constantly troublesome peasants.

Of course, if he and Kate had confined their visit to Dublin, and had had invitations to balls or receptions at Dublin Castle, they could have had a fine time. The great reception rooms at Dublin Castle were the setting for some of the finest gowns and jewels in Europe. One didn't need to know anything about the stinking candlelit cellars in the slums where three or more families lived in one room, one could avert one's eyes from the out-thrust skeleton hand of a starving child, or the anonymous bundle of rags lying in eternal stillness in the shadow of an alley.

But could Willie have trusted his new wife, with the tiresome social conscience she had inherited from her father (which she would soon grow out of, he trusted), to dress in her pretty elegant trousseau gowns and ignore the prevailing fashion in Dublin for black threadbare head shawls, frayed skirts and clogs, or, for the children, one ragged garment through which the wind blew, and from which a skinny shoulder or buttock stuck nakedly?

He seemed to doubt if he could. So he had taken her to Paris where they could be as gay and extravagant as they pleased.

From Paris to the racing stables in Hertfordshire which had failed, to the miserable little house in Harrow Road where Katharine's first baby, Gerard, had been born, to the much grander house in Beaufort Gardens, where both Norah and Carmen had been born, and where Willie had indulged in a social life he couldn't afford, to this ugly large Victorian mansion, Wonersh Lodge, in Eltham, which belonged to Katharine's aunt, and by whose courtesy and generosity they lived there . . . It had been a journey that had taken thirteen years, and that had become increasingly painful as all her affection (it had never been love, she had long ago realised), for her charming weak untrustworthy self-indulgent vain husband had died.

"Miss Katharine!" That was Lucy's voice prodding her. "You look as if you're miles away."

"I am, Lucy. At least not miles, but years away." Katharine gave herself a shake, bringing herself back to the present. "I was thinking of my wedding day, I don't know why."

12

Lucy's lined and shrunken face softened. She dearly liked to talk of weddings, and that of dear Miss Katharine, who had been her charge from infancy, most of all.

"You wore that white lace bonnet trimmed with pink roses that the Captain admired. You looked like an angel. And then you nearly ruined your looks by crying and thinking you might be making a mistake. I was ashamed of you. Imagine if the Captain had seen his bride in tears."

"He's seen her like that often enough since," Katharine said briefly.

But Lucy was having none of that. She had brought up her charges, Katharine, and her sisters, Emma, Clarissa, and Anna, to hold their heads up, keep their backs straight, and not to indulge in self-pity.

"Now, I'll not listen to any grumblings. You with a good-looking husband who's a member for Parliament, and three lovely children. Shame on you, Miss Katharine! And am I to pack your night things?"

Katharine went into another daydream, this time about her children, Gerard, her handsome son who was now at preparatory school, and the two little girls with their rosy faces and their soft bright delphinium-blue eyes. Aunt Ben called them her butterflies, but they were more like flowers, a delicious nosegay of pink, blue and white. Her children were the good things Willie had given her.

She had to rouse herself to answer Lucy.

"My night things? Yes, Lucy. I don't care to travel alone late at night. I'll stay at Thomas's Hotel."

Lucy could make no comment about that, because it would have to have been derogatory towards the dear Captain. She knew that he had rooms in London, and seldom came to Wonersh Lodge on any day but Sundays when he took the children to Mass. He would be unlikely to accompany his wife home after a late night in town. He insisted on her doing a certain amount of entertaining for him, but she could hardly complain about spending the rest of the night at Thomas's Hotel, where they had known her since her childhood. She must enjoy escaping from the boredom of the country now and then, although she professed to like living in Eltham, and playing the part of unpaid companion

13

to her old aunt. Though it couldn't exactly be called unpaid, since the old lady had provided the house, the servants, and a good deal of their expenses. She had done this because Katharine was her favourite niece and she liked to have her near. She was very old, very rich. Katharine knew that Willie found a great deal to commend itself in the present situation, though he did not intend it to be thought that his marriage had failed. So Katharine, looking well-groomed and attractive, must make an appearance in society now and then.

Katharine had not lived with Willie for thirteen years without knowing exactly how his mind worked. He had no more surprises for her. She had long ago decided that her happiness must come from her children. But she could still enjoy an interesting dinner party. Willie had always admitted that she was an accomplished hostess. She was looking forward to this evening and the challenge it presented. She had met plenty of Willie's Irish friends, most of them hearty hard-drinking talkative men like himself. She had a distinct feeling that Mr. Parnell would be stimulatingly different, that his cold and unapproachable manner would be just a façade which a perceptive woman could penetrate.

"Now, Miss Katharine, I've spoken twice," said Lucy severely.

"I'm sorry, Lucy, I wasn't listening."

"I asked what train you mean to catch."

"Oh, the five-thirty will be early enough. I promised I would go and see Aunt Ben first, since I'll be late in the morning. I'll pour tea for her, and be back in an hour."

Aunt Ben had young Mr. George Meredith there when Katharine called. He read to the old lady every afternoon. She had always had an interesting literary and political circle, especially when her husband, who had been a Member of Parliament, had been alive. A great many celebrities had passed through her famous tapestry room. Now she was old, almost ninety, and there were no more large parties at the Lodge, but she still liked to cultivate young writers. She enjoyed listening to Mr. Meredith because he had a pleasant voice, but this did not mean he had freedom to read anything he chose, particularly his own works. She found them not to her taste at all. Perhaps when he was an accomplished writer and had stood the test of time, like her old friend, Mr. Trollope, she would enjoy his work. Only, by that time, of course, she would be dead and buried. It was a pity, but infinitely better for their friendship if he confined himself to reading Miss Austen, Mr. Thackeray and Mr. Trollope.

When Katharine arrived, Mr. Meredith seemed glad to escape. He bowed himself out, taking care to step only on the rugs, as another fad of Aunt Ben's was that she did not like the highly polished parquet floor to be walked on in anything but soft slippers, of which she kept a supply handy for callers.

Aunt Ben put up her face to be kissed.

"It's nice to see you, Katharine, but I wasn't expecting you until the morning."

"I told you I would come and have tea with you before going up to town."

"Oh, yes, of course, how forgetful I am. You're giving a dinner party. That's nice. It's time you had some gaiety. You're too much with an old woman and children. I don't deny it's nice for me and the butterflies, but you want the company of men occasionally. And I don't mean only Willie. You have great assets, Katharine. It's time a man discovered them."

Katharine looked sharply into the gentle unfocussed eyes, as dim and faded as yesterday's bluebells.

"I mean a real man, my swan. You know my opinion of Willie. I am sorry to say I have never considered him anything more than an overgrown schoolboy. It's only because he is your husband that I receive him at all."

"But, Aunt Ben—"

"I am eighty-eight years old and permitted to be outrageous. I don't say you have to fall in love. That would make excessively awkward complications. But enjoy mature conversation and companionship with the opposite sex. I have been fortunate enough to have that privilege all my life. It's something an intelligent woman shouldn't have to do without. You're still young. There's time. Life doesn't end in Eltham."

Katharine was laughing. Aunt Ben's perspicacity constantly amused and surprised her.

"This is only a small political dinner, Aunt Ben. Willie thought we ought to entertain Mr. Parnell. We may find him very dull."

"Dull!" The old lady leaned forward to tap Katharine with her fan. "It's not like you to be so stupid, Katharine. How could a man who seems to be wielding more power than Daniel O'Connell—I met him once, and a most fascinating eloquent noisy creature he was, he swept me off my feet. I remember feeling quite stunned afterwards. Ever since then I've decided a little leaven of the Irish in the world is an important thing. But what was I saying?"

"About Mr. Parnell."

"Oh, yes. If he is greater than Daniel O'Connell, then being dull is the last thing to expect of him. You are more likely to feel stunned, as I did."

"If he comes," Katharine murmured.

Aunt Ben looked at her in surprise.

"Good gracious, do you think he might not come? My dear child, I think I can trust you not to let him escape with a display of bad manners like that."

Katharine was dressed in her town clothes before she went to say goodbye to the children.

They rushed at her with cries of joy, in spite of Miss Glennister's attempts at restraint. Katharine wondered again if this young woman were quite the most suitable person to be the little girls' governess. She was not good at keeping order, and there was something wistful and sullen beneath her prim exterior. However, one had to remember the unsatisfactoriness of a life such as hers and realise that she could have had worse faults than her affected cheerfulness and her furtive looks of envy.

"Mamma, are you going to London?" Norah demanded, and Carmen added, "To see Papa?"

"Both. We are giving a party. Lucy has packed my bag. So Miss Glennister will read you your bedtime story tonight, and I expect you to be good children."

"Mamma, who will dance with you? Papa?" Carmen asked.

Norah, with the superiority of the elder sister, said scornfully, "She will dance with a lot of gentlemen. Won't you, Mamma?"

"Not nicer gentlemen than Papa?" Carmen asked anxiously.

"Silly, how could there be nicer gentlemen than Papa, or Mamma wouldn't have married him. Would you, Mamma?"

"Or had him for our father?" said Carmen. "You have to have a father for babies."

Norah forgot to look superior and said eagerly, "Mamma, couldn't you get us another baby? Carmen and I would so dearly like one."

Another baby? The children didn't know what they were asking. How could she tell them that there would never be any more babies. She had resolved that that part of her life with Willie was over the morning six weeks ago when he had come to her at Thomas's Hotel. The morning indeed, when he had been supposed to call for her there the previous evening to take her to Lady Londonderry's ball! Dressed in her ball gown, she had sat waiting from ten o'clock to midnight. Then in a rage she had torn off her clothes, dropped them on the floor, and gone to bed.

Shamefacedly Willie had appeared after breakfast, saying that he had completely forgotten about her until less than half an hour ago. The ball, the fact that he had persuaded her to come up to town for it and that she would be dressed and waiting for him, had entirely vanished from his mind. He had been detained at his club. Some friends of his had arrived from Ireland. She knew what the Irish were.

She did. One of them stood before her now. In the bright morning light she saw all too clearly the marks of dissipation on Willie's handsome face. She saw, too, his pleading eyes, his deliberately humble smile. She knew that he was expecting to talk his way out of one more misdemeanour, one more intolerable slight. She was certain, too, that it had not been any of his countrymen who had detained him last evening. For some time she had known as surely as she could without having a detective follow him, that he was far from being a faithful husband.

She had never known him to be anything but importunate in his desires, caring little whether he was sober or drunk, or whether or not she welcomed him into her arms. Far less

17

did he reflect on the possibility of giving her pleasure. What a dangerous idea that would be, having one's wife actually enjoy sex. Leave that to the women whose business it was.

Willie, Katharine knew, would have regarded himself as an average husband, perhaps a little better than average since he had good looks and charm. What he did not see, at that moment, and was unlikely ever to see, was that his charm for her had vanished forever. She had tried not to think about the other women so long as none of them ever crossed her path, so long as Willie was discreet. Anna, her sister, had long ago warned her to expect this sort of thing. A wife was exceedingly lucky if her husband never strayed.

But to come to her like this straight from a woman's arms, giving his appealing boyish smile, expecting to be forgiven for this final humiliation, wanting to kiss her! Katharine, shivering with distaste, had backed away from him, saying that from this moment their marriage was over except in name, and that if he attempted to touch her she would scream.

She knew that he would not have his wife screaming for help in that hotel where she was so well-known. His face went dark, but presently he managed to control himself, and observed that she had a perfect right to be angry. She would get over it. She had at other times. Had he behaved so much more badly this time?

No, she said wearily, it was just that she had finally grown tired of forgiveness. In future, it was a word that didn't exist for her. And now, if he would oblige her by seeing that a cab was called, she intended returning to her children.

Willie had made one last uneasy attempt at peace before she left. "Tell the girls I'll be down on Sunday. You might try being in a better mood by then. You can't ditch me like this, you know. After all, I am your husband."

Yes, he was her husband, and she was his wife. And Aunt Ben was gently telling her to find other interests, and the children, with their absurdly hopeful faces, were begging for a baby in the house. It was a situation that should have made her weep. But one couldn't go on weeping for the rest of one's life.

So here she was smiling and kissing the children, telling them that if God wanted there to be another baby He would send one, and that it was not a ball tonight, but a dinner party. And wondering in what style she should do her hair. And who she would put on Mr. Parnell's other side at dinner . . .

CHAPTER 2

IT was eight-thirty, and Katharine could not any longer postpone going in to dinner. She left instructions that if Mr. Parnell arrived he was to be shown in at once, and then led her guests into the small private dining room at Thomas's Hotel.

She stubbornly kept the chair on her right hand vacant. A busy man like Mr. Parnell might have been unavoidably detained. He could very well have much more urgent business than a dinner party.

"We will forgive him," she said gaily, "if he arrives by the time we reach the sweet."

But the chair remained vacant. Sitting there with her head held high, the topaz brooch sparkling in the lace at her throat, Katharine found it almost beyond her ability to remain a serene and competent hostess. She was so unreasonably disappointed. And angry too, although she hoped that she concealed her anger. How dare Charles Parnell be so rude as to completely ignore her invitation!

Willie, unlike his wife, didn't attempt to hide his offence.

"The fellow has no manners."

The O'Gorman Mahon gave his great roar of laughter, highly amused, and Anna, Katharine's sister, with slight maliciousness, wanted to know why Katharine imagined she would succeed when other hostesses failed.

"Perhaps he's ill," Katharine suggested.

"Ill, bejasus!" Mr. Mahon was even more amused. "He talked in the House from two till half-past four this afternoon. Does that sound like a sick man? Deuced eloquent he was, too. Words flowing from him like a fountain. If ever ye want to set eyes on him, Mrs. O'Shea, I expect ye'll have to go to a session of Parliament. To be telling the truth, I'd recommend it. The man's worth hearing. And he's not one of your uncouth codgers, Willie, waving a blackthorn stick, even if he thinks he can dispense with the social graces."

A visit to the Houses of Parliament was exactly what

Katharine was planning, although not in the way The O'Gorman Mahon had suggested. She was developing the greatest curiosity to see this controversial man. She had gone to great pains to arrange her dinner party, inviting guests whom she thought would interest Mr. Parnell. She felt humiliated in front of them.

But her voice was smooth as she said, "I promise you I won't disappoint you another time. Mr. Parnell will be here."

She quietly made her plans. In the morning she did not return to Eltham, but persuaded Anna to accompany her on her errand. They hired a cab and drove to the House of Commons. There, Katharine sent in a card requesting Mr. Parnell to come out and speak to them in Palace Yard.

Anna, for once, was awed by Katharine's audacity.

"What do you think you're going to achieve? He'll only hate you for exposing him like this."

"I don't intend to expose him," Katharine said serenely. "I only intend to meet him."

"He won't come out. He'll send an excuse."

But he did come out. A tall spare figure, very upright, walking without haste across the cobblestones. And young. Or young for all they said he had done. He was bareheaded, his thick dark brown hair brushed smoothly, his beard neatly trimmed and glossy. His handsome aristocratic face was very pale. In contrast the eyes which he turned so directly and inquisitively on Katharine seemed almost black, though, as he came near, she saw they were a deep brown that glowed. Eloquent eyes. Her heart gave a curious flutter.

"Mrs. O'Shea?" He bowed. His voice held a question. He was not angry about being interrupted in important business. He was interested. She knew that at once.

She held out her hand. "I am Mrs. O'Shea. This is my sister, Mrs. Steele. I have called to enquire why you didn't come to my dinner party last night. My guests were disappointed."

"Your dinner party? Last night?" He frowned. "Oh dear, I'm afraid I knew nothing about it."

"But didn't you get my invitation? I sent it to Keppel Street where I was told you were staying."

"And where no doubt it is at this moment. I must confess to a bad habit of never opening letters."

His eyes seemed to burn as he looked into hers. There was no doubt now about his interest.

"But if you will ask me again, Mrs. O'Shea, I promise to come."

"I believe I will hold you to that promise."

The banal words meant nothing. They were merely polite sounds. Their instant deep awareness of one another needed no sounds. The O'Gorman Mahon's flippant words, "Nobody has ever told me that Charlie Parnell doesn't like women" were merely an echo. She was certain he had never looked at another woman like this. Just as she had never looked at a man, even her own husband . . .

Anna, making some casual remark, stirred her to reality.

"We mustn't keep you from your business, Mr. Parnell." She leaned forward, holding out her hand. As she did so the white rose she had tucked in her bosom when dressing fell out. He swiftly stooped to pick it up. But instead of handing it back to her he touched it to his lips and then tucked it in his own buttonhole. He smiled faintly, gave a small courtly bow, and left them.

"Gracious!" exclaimed Anna. "He's quite a lady's man after all. He was certainly taken with you."

"Do you think so?"

"Well, if he wasn't he was a very good actor. Did you drop that rose deliberately? Really, Kate. I wouldn't have thought it of you."

"No, I did not," Katharine said indignantly. All the same a smile trembled on her lips. "It was quite accidental."

"A fortuitous accident," Anna said, not entirely convinced. "After that little touch of gallantry he'll hardly refuse to come to your dinner party. Who will you ask?"

Willie had left for Ireland that morning. He was to be away for two or three weeks. Katharine didn't intend to wait for his return. By that time Mr. Parnell himself might have left London. Anyway, she didn't want a large formal party. It meant too many people to look after and not enough time to devote to the one man to whom she wanted to talk. Had he gone back into the House with her rose in his buttonhole? She was agitated, as much in a dream, as a

22

girl in her teens. This was nonsense. And dangerous. It was one thing to be out of love with one's husband, but to fall in love with another man would be crazy.

"I don't think Mr. Parnell would care for a large party. He needs relaxation, not a lot of people bombarding him with questions. I think we ought to have a quiet dinner, just you and I and Uncle Matthew Wood and Justin McCarthy, and after dinner take a box at the theatre."

The idea had come to her in a flash. She thought it brilliant. But Anna was looking a little shocked.

"Before Willie comes back? He won't like it, Kate."

"Why not? He entertains often enough when I'm not there."

"He's a man."

Katharine's mouth set.

"Don't be so strait-laced, Anna. There's no harm in my plan, and I intend to do it exactly. By all means refuse to come if it bothers your social conscience."

But Anna wouldn't stay away, she knew. Neither, this time, would Mr. Parnell.

Although he gave her another fright by arriving very late. She was so relieved to see him that she welcomed him warmly. She thought how tired he looked, but his extraordinary eyes were brilliant and alert, and he proved to be a charming guest, quiet, courtly, and with an ironic wit. That he was boorish and unmannerly was completely untrue, and the element of ruthlessness, the criticism most frequently made about him, showed only once. That was when, as was inevitable, the talk turned to politics.

"I hear you are filling Mr. Butt's shoes very well," said Sir Matthew Wood.

"I hope that I am."

"Poor Mr. Butt," Anna said. "I always thought him so nice, so amiable."

"Amiability, Mrs. Steele, is not the quality to right my country's wrongs."

All eyes were on the handsome face, now coolly aloof, of this man who called himself Irish and spoke like a well-bred Englishman.

He said with cold precision, "In politics, as in war, there are no men, only weapons. I intend to use each man in my party for exactly what he is fitted. To hold a breach or to fire a broadside, or to infiltrate within the enemy's lines. We are not on the defensive any longer. We are on the offensive."

"You have some good men for those tactics," Sir Matthew said. "I've noticed Mr. Biggar's eloquence."

Mr. Parnell gave a flicker of a smile.

"You mean his talkativeness, I presume? Or what we call 'the gift of the gab'. Yes, he's a useful man. He commended himself to me by one remark. He said, 'Why should Ireland be treated as a geographical fragment? She is not a geographical fragment. She is a nation.' And there is our whole campaign in a nutshell."

"He's an ugly-looking devil, I must admit."

"He isn't the first crook-back England has contended with." Again Mr. Parnell gave his faint derisive smile. "He won't do murder—I hope—but he'll be devilish useful in our policy of obstruction."

"You're not making yourself very popular by that," Sir Matthew said. "I hear Mr. Biggar was on his feet for three and a half hours yesterday, and that even the Speaker protested."

"The Speaker said he could not hear Mr. Biggar clearly. So Mr. Biggar obligingly moved his chair nearer. That was all."

"He was wasting the House's time with a lot of irrelevant nonsense."

"But I have just been telling you, Sir Matthew, that is our policy. If England won't make fair laws for Ireland, then we don't propose to allow her to make any laws for herself either."

"You're really going to pursue this aim of Home Rule to the bitter end?"

"To the bitter end."

There was a brief silence. Then Mr. Parnell said courteously, "I'm afraid we're boring the ladies. It's not my fault. When I begin to talk politics I can go on for much longer than even the famous Mr. Biggar. But I am devoted to the theatre, Mrs. O'Shea. I am looking forward to it immensely."

Katharine scarcely realised her deliberate choice of a chair in a dark corner of the box until Mr. Parnell sat beside her. With the lights turned down and the other members of the party leaning forward to watch the stage, she had the illusion that they were completely alone. She had wanted this. Her heart was beating quickly. She tried to pay attention to the show, but the man beside her seemed much more in her line of vision. She kept glancing sideways at him sitting relaxed, his hands folded in his lap. She had thought her glances unnoticed until she encountered one of his, bent on her in quiet scrutiny. She gave a half-smile and it was returned. There was an extraordinary exciting intimacy about this exchange of glances in the dark theatre box.

When the lights went up for the first interval, Anna and the others proposed refreshments in the bar. Katharine said she was a little fatigued, she thought she would remain where she was, and, as she had known would happen, Mr. Parnell instantly said that he would keep her company.

They were alone.

"I have kept your rose, Mrs. O'Shea."

"Mr Parnell—do you always attack subjects so directly?" She was laughing. Then she said in a low voice, "Why?"

"Because it reminds me of you."

"You are a flatterer as well."

"As well as what?"

"You are not married, Mr. Parnell. Everyone says you love your country so much that you have no time for more frivolous interests such as parties and women."

"If you hadn't said that so seriously I would believe you were making fun of me. Am I not here this evening?"

She laughed. "But I shamed you into it."

"No one could shame me into anything. Believe me." His eyes glowed in his pale face. She was aware again of the quiet intensity that pervaded him. She imagined that he brought it to everything he did, every subject he discussed. He must have nerves of steel, or he would wreck his health by his ardent way of living. It had been an irrelevance to think that a man like this could give all his emotions to a country. He must be highly aware of women —as indeed she knew he was at this moment. Her skin tingled. If he were to put all his intensity into being a lover ...

"I'm glad you came," she said quickly, casually. It was better to make conversation, even provocative conversation, than to indulge in these thoughts.

He made no answer to that beyond giving her that quiet curiously intimate caressing smile.

Then he said without any preamble whatever, "I imagined myself for a while to be in love with a young lady in America. But then she gave me a verse of poetry, carefully written out, and asked me to read it, and I knew that if she expected me to live up to all it said, I would disappoint her cruelly. So we said good-bye."

"What was the poem?"

"Shall I recite it to you?"

"Please."

He did so, in an undertone that yet did not take the eloquence out of his voice :

> *"Unless you can muse in a crowd all day*
> *On the absent face that fixed you:*
> *Unless you can dream that his faith is fast*
> *Through behoving and unbehoving;*
> *Unless you can die when the dream is past,*
> *Oh, never call it loving."*

"I think that's Elizabeth Barrett Browning," Katharine said after a moment.

"Yes, I believe so."

"One would need to be very dedicated to the object of one's love to do all that." Katharine thought of Willie and her lips twisted wryly.

"It could be possible for a few people."

"A very few."

"You look too sceptical, Mrs. O'Shea, for a young and beautiful woman. Surely you still have illusions?"

The bell had rung and people were beginning to come back to their seats. Katharine was glad of the interruption. They had advanced dangerously far in such a short conversation. She was frightened and highly elated at the same time. What was happening couldn't be true. And yet she was deeply irrevocably sure that it was true. A woman's instinct in these things never failed. Perhaps a man's didn't

26

either. For he had the temerity to lay his hand briefly over hers as the lights went down.

"Perhaps it's even possible to turn illusions into realities," he said, under cover of the orchestra beginning to tune up. "I have never believed anything impossible." He paused a moment and then asked abruptly, "Are you ever in the House? Do you ever sit in the Ladies' Gallery?"

"No. But now my husband is in Parliament, perhaps I will."

"Then I will look for you. Well now, what have we in the next act?"

The next act . . . Aunt Ben accepted as perfectly natural and admirable Katharine's sudden intention to take an interest in politics. She should, of course, be interested in her husband's new profession. It might even happen that Willie surprised them both and proved himself an able politician. He had always had wit and a sharp, if lazy intelligence.

"It's time someone did something for that tragic Ireland. It will have to be an Irishman, since no one in England will. We did begin to get a little interested during the great famine. I organised funds for soup kitchens myself. But then people said the stories of so many dying from hunger were exaggerated. The Irish always did exaggerate. So we began to forget about them again, to our undying shame. I think perhaps we English have always found them too excessive in everything, their religion, their poverty, their legends, their martyrs, even their dying. So tiresome, turning a perfectly natural event into a melodrama. Remember, Katharine, I want no fuss. No candles, no mourners. I just want to disappear, like a little melting snow. But being excessive in their ways doesn't excuse us for neglecting them." Although Aunt Ben seemed to ramble, flitting sharply from one subject to another, none of her remarks was idle. Katharine had learned to listen attentively. "And if they're disorderly it's only because they need a strong leader. Someone not disorderly. I suppose that would be too much to hope for, from that country."

"Not too much at all, Aunt Ben. I believe they already have one."

"I expect you mean young Mr. Parnell. But he was very rude, not coming to your dinner party."

"He hadn't opened my letter. I told you that. And he did come the next time."

Aunt Ben gave her her bland gaze. "Ah, yes, I see you have forgiven him. Mr. Meredith was reading to me about him yesterday. He's being very provoking in the House. How splendid. Willie must take some lessons from him. Perhaps you ought to encourage him, Katharine."

Katharine said quietly, "That's exactly what I intend to do, Aunt Ben. One day I'll bring him to visit you."

"Yes, do that, dear. I always remember Daniel O'Connell's fine presence. Has Mr. Parnell a presence, or is he still too young?"

"I think he has an exceptional presence."

"How very interesting. Do you think he has the ability to get the better of Mr. Gladstone? I confess I would enjoy that. Mr. Gladstone, in my opinion, is too conceited by far. I am glad the Queen sets him back occasionally. Katharine dear, are you going?"

"I must, Aunt Ben, if I'm to see the children before they begin their afternoon lessons. And then I thought I might slip into town to listen to the debate on the new Land Act. I believe you may realise your hopes, Mr. Parnell may well get the better of Mr. Gladstone. If not this year, certainly the next."

"How nice, dear child. It's plain whose side you are on. I expect it's simply that you don't care for poor Mr. Gladstone's white hairs. Run along then, and tell me about it tomorrow."

On her first visit, looking down from the Ladies' Gallery, she thought she would have to search for him on the Irish benches. But by some uncanny instinct her eyes went directly to him and at the same moment his unmistakably met hers, for he half-raised his hand in greeting. She gave a small non-committal nod, then realised that her hand was pressed to her suddenly accelerated heart, which must have completely given away her emotions if anyone had been observing her closely.

Fortunately the speaker at that moment was the Prime Minister himself. With his famous presence, his crest of white hair, his fierce eyes and his boldly jutting nose, he held the attention of everyone except, apparently, the Irish member who had been more interested in the movement in the Ladies' Gallery.

Katharine wondered how many glances he had cast in that direction before she had come. She felt her cheeks glowing, and was glad there was no one here to recognise her. The only visitor she herself recognised was Mr. Gladstone's daughter Mary who was deeply devoted to her father, and often came to listen to him.

She tried to pay attention to the matter being discussed. It was about the dangerously primitive condition of the Welsh coal mines, and the employment of children who were no better treated than pit ponies. It was a distressing subject and Katharine should have been moved by it. She should also have been interested in recognising other prominent figures, Mr. Joseph Chamberlain, tall, sallow-faced, with his bland but acute glance, the Honourable Charles Dilke who had a gleaming roving eye, young Lord Randolph Churchill fixing a glassy gaze on the speaker, Mr. Disraeli, now Lord Beaconsfield, putting a hand to his black carefully-arranged ringlets.

But she only noticed that in the middle of the Prime Minister's speech Mr. Parnell had unfolded his long legs, stood up, and unobtrusively left the chamber. Presently there was a muffled disturbance behind her. Someone said, "S'sh!" A tall form slid into the seat beside her. Under cover of some scattered applause which Mr. Gladstone had earned for himself, the already familiar voice said, "I just came up to say good-day to you, Mrs. O'Shea. It's nice to see you here."

She noticed that he was wearing a white rose in his buttonhole. If it meant what she suspected she was deeply pleased.

"Is anything interesting happening this afternoon?"

"No. The Prime Minister will go on about coal mines for the next hour or more."

"You won't be speaking?"

"Not today. Unless something comes up later this evening."

Someone said, "Hush!" and they had to be silent while

29

Mr. Gladstone's eloquent voice rang through the House. Mr. Parnell stood up.

"I shall look for you here again," he whispered.

Then he was gone, and she spent the next half-hour convincing herself that such an exchange of words had been completely without significance. They could have been shouted to the whole house.

What was not so insignificant was the way her cheeks burned and her heart raced so that the lace on her bodice fluttered. It was absurd to feel like that simply because he had taken the trouble to come up and speak to her. If she were going to behave like this she would have to give up this absorbing new interest in politics.

It would never do for there to be a scandal involving the leader of the Irish party.

Yet, on her next visit, when Mr. Parnell made his greeting, this time casually touching the rose in his buttonhole, but did not come up to speak to her, she was acutely disappointed. It was no use telling herself that Mr. Biggar was in the midst of one of his interminable rambling speeches that was making the House yawn and fidget, and that no doubt Mr. Parnell was anticipating going to his assistance if the flow of words failed him. The Irish party was engaged in one of its celebrated obstructive measures that would probably keep the House sitting until midnight. She was selfish enough to think Ireland as tiresome as everyone else did, and wondered only when Mr. Parnell would be free to come up and exchange a few words with her.

For two days after that she was unable to come to town. Carmen had a feverish cold which Norah caught, and the little girls wanted their Mamma. Neither Lucy nor Miss Glennister sufficed at a time like this. Then Lucy went down with the cold which settled on her chest. No one knew exactly what Lucy's age was, but suddenly she looked very old, almost as old as Aunt Ben. Katharine made her stay in bed and was impatient with her when she rebelled, the silly independent creature.

Aunt Ben, too, was particularly demanding. Reluctant to begin the long dull afternoon of the old and enfeebled, she delayed her dear Katharine as long as possible, wanting last minute things done or some small problem discussed at length. It only needed Willie to come home with one of his attacks of gout, Katharine thought, and she would be virtually a prisoner. She was restless, frustrated, irritable with the servants, unable to eat or sleep.

She was crazy. She was developing an obsession. It surely was not normal to see nothing but that pale face with the compelling eyes, to hear nothing but one voice.

She must forget him. She must not see him again. She must tell Willie that Mr. Parnell was all the things people said of him, unmannerly, unsociable, ruthless, cold, and she preferred not to entertain him again.

But the little girls recovered. Aunt Ben decided to detain poor Mr. Meredith instead of herself, and she was driving to London on a cool sunny afternoon.

She had scarcely taken her seat in the Ladies' Gallery before he was beside her. There was going to be a long dull debate which didn't require his presence, he whispered. Would she care to come for a drive? He needed some fresh air before getting back for the more important business of the first reading of a Compensation for Disturbance Bill which was being introduced by Mr. Forster, the Chief Secretary for Ireland.

She rose without a word. Her frustration was over. She had so much wanted to be alone with him and at last he had created the opportunity. She might have known that he would.

Mr. Parnell told the cab driver to drive down the Embankment in the direction of Kew. At first he was full of the new Bill being proposed later that day. Forster, he said, was hated in Ireland as much as he hated the Irish. No good would come out of any Bill he proposed.

"I abhor violence," he said. "We must find more effective and more subtle ways to get what we want."

"What causes the violence?" Katharine asked.

"Evictions, evictions, always evictions," he said passionately. "You won't travel down a road in any county without meeting a pathetic little group of outcasts, the baby in its mother's arms, the older ones, and never a shoe among the lot, walking weary miles, their bits of belongings in the handcart. Nowhere to sleep that night, no bit of land of their own. They're hungry for land, Mrs. O'Shea, just an

31

acre, just ten square yards. But they've no rights to anything they till, and if the potato crop fails and they don't pay their rent, out they go."

"If they refuse?"

His profile was hard, pure, dedicated.

"Their wretched cabin is burned down—over their heads if they're too stubborn to move out. I've seen a woman begging English soldiers to wait just an hour until her dying husband breathed his last. I've seen a mother thrown out to give birth to her baby in a wet field. I've seen—" he paused, wrenching himself back from his bitterness. "Forgive me, Mrs. O'Shea. I didn't intend to harrow your feelings. I only meant to explain that I don't have much faith in a Compensation Bill made by the English. Who has ever compensated my people for their children who have died from exposure or plain starvation? But I hate violence. Burning down the landlord's property only leads to prison or the gallows. We'll find a better way to win. And we will win, don't you doubt it."

"I don't doubt it," said Katharine. "But look! It's a lovely day. You're not prejudicing your cause by enjoying it."

She threw back her veil, letting the sunlight fall on her face. And suddenly he gave his slow sweet smile.

"That's better. Now I can see you. Ah!" He sighed. "This is what I needed."

"Why do you care for Ireland so much, Mr. Parnell?"

"Because I hate injustice. I hate suffering. I hate and loathe and fear premature and unnecessary death. I do love Ireland. I was born there and its mists and its soft air and its grief are in my bones. I will give my life to it. I made that vow some years ago. But don't imagine," again he smiled, looking directly in her eyes, "that Ireland takes all my emotions. Are you happy?"

"At this moment? Very."

"So am I. Sunshine, the horse jogging along, no hurry, nothing in the world but ourselves. I wish it could last."

The small coldness settled on her, and was resolutely banished.

"How can it, when you have such an enormous job to do, and I—"

"And you?"

32

She said lightly, "I am becoming quite a politician. My husband will be pleased."

"Shall we not talk about your husband?"

She gave him a startled look. He said, "I prefer, at this moment, to indulge in a daydream that there is no one in the world but ourselves. I like you in blue. And that little fur tippet. Do you know that I have thought far too much of you since our evening at the theatre."

"But that is—" She stopped, and amended her protest to a simple, "I have thought of you, too."

She was thinking how mistaken people were to say that he was cold. The tenderness in his face was making her heart stop.

"I should like to see you a great deal. Is that possible? I know that you have a family to look after. But it would mean so much to me if it were possible, now and again, like this. I work too hard because I'm lonely. I go from one hotel to another, one meeting to another, one country to another. I spend a good quarter of my life on the Irish mail steamer."

"You should marry. You need a wife."

"I suppose you had to say that." His eyes lingered on her for a long time. "But what do you say to the present situation? I have no wife and I want to be with you on as many occasions as possible."

"You scarcely know me."

He smiled with that unnerving tenderness.

"But I do, Mrs. O'Shea. You would be surprised how well I know you. Or is it presumptuous of me to think so? I'm a clumsy fellow sometimes."

"I'm sure you're not." Her answer was so emphatic that he laughed, his eyes glinting with amusement and pleasure.

"I may be, or try to be, a master of strategy in Parliament, but I fear I'm not that with the opposite sex. I make far too many blunders. I would hope very much not to blunder with you."

His lightning changes from light riposte to deep seriousness shook her poise. She was moving into a commitment she had not intended by saying:

"I have three children. I couldn't let them be hurt by any scandal."

"Would it be scandalous if we were to drive together

occasionally? I suppose the world would think so." He looked wistful. "You see what I mean by being a blundering fellow, Mrs. O'Shea."

She turned swiftly to face him. The impulsive words were out before she could stop them.

"For myself I wouldn't care."

His extraordinary deep dark brown eyes seemed to flicker and burn. He laid his hand over hers but did not immediately speak. His touch and his look were eloquent enough. When he did speak his voice was deeply troubled.

"Think carefully, Mrs. O'Shea. Hurting you would be the very last thing I would want to do. Now I fear we must return, if I'm to be in time for the debate."

He slid up the window to give orders to the driver. Then he settled back and took her hand again. It lay in his all the way back to Westminster and the Houses of Parliament. She only took it from his clasp once, and that was to remove her glove.

CHAPTER 3

WILLIE came home on Sunday. He bounced into the house, shouting in a loud voice for the children.

"Where are they, Lucy? Are they ready for Mass? Kate—" He watched Katharine coming down the stairs. "You're looking extraordinarily well. I hear you've been going up to the House. Are you taking an interest in politics for my sake? That does surprise me."

"I'm finding the debates interesting," Katharine said. "I was getting dull down here. My brains need sharpening. I hope to hear your maiden speech before long," she added.

He was pleased. "Yes, I must work on that. I fancy they'll find me quite literate compared with some of our members. By the way, I hear that you persuaded Mr. Parnell to come to dinner. You've had quite a social success, haven't you? Clever Kate. What persuasions did you use?"

"None. Mr. Parnell isn't the misanthrope he's reputed to be. He refuses to go into the houses of the English because he feels it weakens his case against them. He says this is one of the tricks the English deliberately play—they entertain the Irish with lavish hospitality and then expect them to have the good manners not to bite the hand that feeds them. But Mr. Parnell won't be caught that way. He came to my dinner party because I'm your wife. He's counting on your support in his campaign. I hope you'll give it to him."

"I daresay I will, if he doesn't get too extreme. I certainly don't agree to cutting my English friends. I'll dine with them if I please. But I'm glad you got him, Kate. It's quite a feather in your cap."

There was no time to say more for the children came hurtling down the stairs to greet their father.

"Papa, you came! Carmen said you wouldn't, but I said you would."

"Thank you, Norah darling, for your faith in me. Then

are we ready? Is Miss Glennister coming with us? Splendid."

Miss Glennister, dressed for church, had followed the little girls down the stairs. She was looking animated, too, her sallow cheeks quite flushed. She admired Willie who no doubt said flattering things to her because he had a compulsion to make all women like him. She was full of coyness and arch remarks when he was in the house.

"I hope you haven't anyone coming later, Kate," Willie said. "Let's have the day to ourselves. I believe I'll stay overnight for once. I have no urgent business in town tomorrow."

She did not miss the familiar and very unwelcome gleam in Willie's eye as he looked at her in her freshly laundered morning gown with its snowy collar and cuffs. He suspected nothing, he only thought her good looks due to the country air. Couldn't he see the way her eyes grew secret and her lips were inclined to tremble? She must be careful. Willie had had the grace not to make any demands on her since their last disastrous quarrel in Thomas's Hotel. She had thought then that any further lovemaking from him would be excessively repugnant, but now she regarded it as quite impossible. The fact would have to be made clear to him.

There was disappointment and a look of outrage on his face when later he came into her room to find her lying with the curtains drawn against the sunshine.

"Dammit, Kate, you can't have a headache on a day like this. Anyway, you've never been the type for headaches."

"I am now," she answered in a low deliberate voice.

He was not slow to get her meaning.

"You've never been angry with me for as long as this before. What's happened?"

"Nothing's happened except that I never was so angry before."

"I wasn't with a woman that night! If that was what you'd caught me at—" He saw that he was not believed and had the grace to colour and avoid her gaze. And hearing at last the thing she had suspected for a long time gave her no sensation except a wry relief. She knew now, indeed had known since that other hand had lain over hers, that she could never bear Willie to touch her again.

"Oh, dammit!" Willie exclaimed. "Every man sins a bit now and then even if he loves his wife." He grew resentful, looking at her recumbent figure. He had expected anger, not indifference. Had she been shocked into a stupor? No, not clever Kate. She was playing a game with him, making him suffer a bit. He didn't like it. He turned on his heel.

"I'm not coming begging to you. Now you can come to me when you return to your senses. And I warrant that won't be long. You're a healthy woman." He was smiling coarsely. "So you'll have to climb down from your high horse, my lady."

Lucy came fussing in when he had gone. She was puzzled and distressed.

"The Captain said he was staying, but now he's changed his mind. You didn't do anything to upset him, Miss Katharine?"

She scanned Katherine's face for signs of tears. She knitted her brow at Katharine's expression of half-smiling peace.

"You don't look as if your head's very bad, I must say. But I'll tell cook to prepare a light supper. A little soup and a lightly boiled egg?"

Katharine sat up. "That wouldn't satisfy a baby, Lucy. Anyway, I'll be coming down to supper. I feel almost quite recovered. I think I had a little too much sun this morning, that's all."

But how long could she go on like this, subterfuge, excuses, long absences that became more difficult to explain to the children who were acutely hurt if Mamma missed kissing them goodnight? Amends could be made for everything but one person's disappointment. She noticed how eagerly his eyes sought hers across the space that separated them, he on the floor of the House, she in the Ladies' Gallery.

She had begun to call him Charles and he called her Katharine or Kate, or when he was particularly tender, Katie. They had several more afternoon drives in hansom cabs, taking care never to engage the same driver twice. Sometimes they scarcely talked at all. He sat beside her, their hands touching, and simply relaxed, the peacefulness taking the lines of tension out of his face until he looked what he was, a man of only thirty-four years of age.

Sometimes he was in a gay mood and they laughed a lot. She suspected this was a side of him that he usually showed only to his own family, of which he was very fond. He talked about his home, Avondale, in the misty blue Wicklow Mountains, which had been left to him by his father.

His eyes glowed as he talked about the house, with its hall large enough to take a coach and four, the carved oak minstrel's gallery, and the railings hung with memorials of Parnell ancestors. There were huge wood fires, and dogs, and devoted servants. He had always tried to treat his tenants well, with the result that there was seldom trouble on his land.

Avondale stood on the River Avon, not far from the beautiful vale of Avoca. There was a shooting lodge at Aughavanagh and this was where he went when he most needed relaxation and peace. He and a keeper and his two dogs stayed in the lodge and no one came near them. There was sun and misty rain, and the grouse in the heather, and blue glimpses of water and the peace that he dreamed all Ireland should have.

His father had died when he was a boy at school in England. His mother, who was American, was on one of her restless jaunts to America, and he was the only one to follow his father to his grave. He had been full of resentment that his mother had left his father to die alone. He had stood, a gangling boy of thirteen, watching the earth being tipped into the grave, and clenching his fists to prevent the awful ache in his throat turning into actual sobs.

He hated death. He found its enormous aloneness something too terrible to contemplate. Even if his mother had been there he might not have felt any better. But she was in Philadelphia talking Fenian rebellion to Irish immigrants and sympathetic Americans who, like her own father, had fought the successful War of Independence against England.

He thought that his hostility towards the English had probably been engendered by his mother, although his father and his grandfather even though of English descent had been notable advocates for Ireland's rights.

But his mother was a fiery patriot. She boasted of her husband's remote kinship with the romantic young martyr Robert Emmet, and was certain that the blood would come out in her sons. She made the boys read the histories of the Irish martyrs, and the speeches of the great Daniel O'Connell.

She was constantly in trouble for her seditious statements, and on one occasion the English militia actually raided her house. But all they found to take away was Charles' sword, the one he had used when he was a cadet in the Wicklow Militia.

That had angered him as much as it had his mother. "Damn their impudence!" he had said, and his mother, with the familiar fanatical gleam in her eye, had applauded, and urged him to say it to their faces, to do something to end their tyranny.

His mother, he feared, was a little unbalanced because, while still reviling the English, she had taken the greatest pleasure in attending functions at the Viceregal Lodge in Dublin. An invitation from Lady Carlisle, the Lord-Lieutenant's wife, would make her get out all her party finery. Perhaps she wanted to know the enemy, or perhaps she simply loved a party.

His sisters—they were all beautiful, particularly the dark-eyed Sophia—loved gaiety, too, although Delia, the eldest, was touched with melancholy, and Anna had an obsessive militant tendency that she had inherited from their mother.

They loved him to come home to Avondale and join in their balls and parties. There was nothing like a ball in an Irish country house with fiddles playing, the swish of taffeta and silk over the old polished floors and the shine of a hundred candles in the beautiful Waterford glass chandeliers. Dawn would be breaking and waterbirds calling over the river before the music stopped.

The balls at Avondale were never marred by hungry faces at the windows, or scarecrow figures lurking at the kitchen door hoping for scraps to take home for famished children. No one starved on Charles Parnell's estate, and he would not rest until the same could be said of all other landlords in Ireland.

When Katharine asked him what had eventually made him take up politics he replied that no one thing had done it. He had always known that it would be his life's work. Perhaps it was because he had been born in the year of the Great Hunger and some precocious memory of it had stayed in his heart. But he had at first shied away from the sacrifices and the enormous expense of physical and mental energy involved. He had had to grow older and gain courage and dedication. Ireland had a way of consuming and eventually destroying her great men. She demanded nothing less than their life, their bones to lie in her unhappy soil. She loved and revered bones.

Katharine shivered at that. They looked at one another and the sun was shining on their faces and suddenly they both laughed. His words were not prophetic. They were merely another bit of Celtic extravagance. His mother might be American and his father Anglo-Irish, but he, in his thought and speech and emotions, was entirely Irish. So of course he used poetic melancholy.

And anyway he grew younger all the time he was with her. He admitted, reluctantly, that he sometimes suffered from poor health, but now he had never felt so fit.

"You're good for me, Kate. How I wish yóu could always be with me."

She couldn't tell him how much she was beginning to wish the same thing. When she was with him Willie, dear Aunt Ben, even her children, to her shame, were shadows. She told herself that his magnetic personality, used with such effect in the House and on platforms throughout Ireland, was affecting and overpowering her too.

But it was more than that. Their only embrace had been his hand laid over hers, yet she felt weak and dizzy with the sweetness of it. Once, when he smiled with particular tenderness, tears came into her eyes. When he left her his tall elegant form with its proudly held head remained printed on her sight for minutes afterwards. She knew, soberly and sadly, that she had never been in love before. Indeed she was learning to know herself for she was also fully aware that she had something of his single-minded dedication that counted no cost. Only hers was to a man, not to a country.

Could all this have happened in such a short time? It had happened, she knew with illogical certainty, in that one moment when he had stooped to pick up the rose that had fallen from her bosom.

Anna was giving a party. She wondered if Katharine would persuade Mr. Parnell to come to it.

He agreed when he knew that she was to be there. Their private meetings were of necessity brief and infrequent. He never saw nearly enough of her, and meeting her in public now had a special titillation. Their polite words hid all their secret thoughts. He could say, "I hear you are devoted to living in the country, Mrs. O'Shea," while his eyes met hers with a scarcely repressed twinkle. Besides, he enjoyed seeing her dressed for a party. He looked at her bare shoulders with frank admiration. He said, in full hearing of everybody, "May I compliment you on your dress, Mrs. O'Shea?" He himself was meticulously dressed, and made a favourable impression on the ladies. They had heard he was unsociable and uncouth, but instead he was quite charming. And so good-looking.

"Be careful. You are going to be in great demand," Katharine whispered under cover of her fan.

"Am I?" His look of alarm made her laugh merrily. "Then I must display my boorish side at once."

"There's no need for that. I'll rescue you. I must leave early to catch my train. Will you drive with me to the station?"

Since Willie was not there—poor Mrs. O'Shea so often had to go out alone—no one thought it anything but good manners on the part of Mr. Parnell to offer to accompany her to her train. Charing Cross was on his way home, anyway. He would drive on to Cannon Street where he was at present staying.

As it turned out the brief drive, to which she had looked forward all evening, turned out to be much longer. For on arrival at Charing Cross she found that she had missed her train.

"Then we'll drive down to Eltham. What did you say the

distance was? About eight miles? That's nothing to a good horse. Let's pick the best horse on the rank."

Laughing with merriment, they earnestly studied the merits of each horse, until Charles settled on the glossy over-fed one at the end of the rank.

"He'll be a little slow, he's much too fat, but we don't want to hurry, do we?"

After a short discussion, he arranged a fare with the cabbie, and handed Katharine into the dim slightly odorous interior of the hansom cab. The driver whipped up the stout horse, and with bells jingling merrily, they set forth.

Even then, the drive was too brief. As Wonersh Lodge in all its ornamented ugliness loomed in sight, Katharine realised that they had hardly said a word the entire way. They had sat in the most complete dreamy happiness, their hands touching, her head not quite on his shoulder. Now they were there, and he faced a lonely journey back to London.

Moonlight shone on the fields and hedgerows. The air smelt sweetly of clover blossom and new-cut grass. There were no lights in the house. It was after one o'clock and everyone would be in bed.

Katharine let Charles help her out of the cab. He told the cabbie to rest his horse a few minutes, he would not be long. "So this is where you live. Now I will be able to think of it."

She led him down a side path, saying that she liked to go in through the conservatory door when she arrived home late, so as not to disturb anyone. They felt their way beneath hanging creepers to the door. On the doorstep they were out of sight of the road, in a sweet-smelling cave of leafy branches.

Suddenly he took both her hands.

"Let me stay."

Before she could answer he had taken her in his arms and kissed her. It was a long kiss. When it ended there were tears on her cheeks and he was saying, "If you knew how I have longed to do that."

She pushed him from her, gently but firmly.

"No, Charles, you can't stay. I'm sorry, but the children, the servants—"

"I would leave before daylight."

"It won't be long until daylight. No, it's too big a risk for you to take. Besides, Miss Glennister has ears like a faithful hound."

"Who is Miss Glennister?"

"She's the children's governess. I'm not sure I could trust her. She admires Willie." She laughed unsteadily. "I think she might have a secret passion for him. Anyway—you must go."

He took her face in his hands, holding it up so that the moonlight fell on it.

"I've fallen in love with you."

All laughter had left her. "I've wanted to hear you say that, and yet it frightens me. What are we to do?"

"I don't know, Kate. I don't know. All I can tell you is that I won't be content to live on scraps."

"But you must know that is all we can ever have. It's not only my children, it's your career. What would your party say if they knew what you were doing?"

"Let them say what they choose."

"No, no, that's just moonlight madness. You'll see sense in the morning. You're not going to throw away the whole good of your country for a woman. And a woman you can't marry, at that."

"If it came to the test—" he muttered. He suddenly shivered violently. He lifted his head and his face, in the dim light, was all at once austere and curiously pure.

"Somehow the one half of me must be made to meet the other," he said, as if to himself. The bells jingled on the waiting horse. The cabman was getting impatient. Charles gave a small, courtly bow, not attempting to touch her again.

"Then will you have tea with me tomorrow? If you come up on the four o-clock train I'll meet it."

She nodded, feeling that already she had a reprieve, something to make her feel better about the long drive he must take alone. She wondered how she was going to live if she were going to worry about him every moment he was out of her sight.

But perhaps it would get better, easier, more acceptable.

43

It never occurred to her to have the good sense to bring a dangerous friendship to an end.

She knew at once, the next day, that something was wrong. He greeted her almost abstractedly, his gaze brooding.

"I had meant to ask you to stay up to dinner," he said, "but I have to catch the night mail to Ireland."

"Has something happened?"

"There's trouble. An innocent woman has been killed. And on her way to church! Her husband was shot at, but the bullet hit his wife sitting beside him instead."

"Oh, Charles! How terrible!"

He looked very pale, his lips set.

"And I shall be blamed, of course. This crime was committed by one of my followers. I must keep them in control." He smacked his clenched fists together. "I won't have violence. The objects of the Land League are to protect, not to kill." He repeated, "Not to kill," in a whisper.

He had led her off the station platform, and beckoned to a cab driver.

"I'm sorry, Kate. Don't let this spoil our tea together. We'll go back to my hotel."

Before they reached Cannon Street he had made an attempt to shake off his gloom.

"You're looking lovely, Katie. And after such a late night, too. Did you have to spend the morning with your aunt?"

"Oh, yes, darling Aunt Ben. She was so understanding when I yawned and dropped things. She said she was glad to see I wasn't wasting too much of my youth in sleep. There was plenty of time to sleep when I reached her age."

"And what is that?"

"Nearly ninety, bless her."

"I shall adore you when you're ninety."

They were both laughing when they reached the hotel. Katharine had thought they would sit in the lounge having tea quietly in a secluded corner, but as soon as they entered another contretemps occurred. There were several tweed-clad gentlemen sitting in a corner drinking stout, smoking, and talking.

44

Charles, giving a brief look in their direction, took Katharine's elbow and quickly steered her towards the stairs.

"Members of my party," he muttered. "I won't have them staring at you. We'll go to my room."

There was no opportunity to protest. Did she want to? It was so much nicer to be completely alone with no anxiety as to who was watching them. One could face the implications later.

Charles rang for a maid, and asked that tea be sent up. Then at last he relaxed, taking her in his arms, and pressing his face into her shoulder.

"Kate! You don't know how much you're beginning to mean to me."

And he to her, she thought silently, her fingers in his thick smooth hair. His half-packed bag on the floor, the bed bearing the faint impress of his form—he must have been resting before he came to meet her—his silk dressing-gown hanging from a hook on the door, his brushes and toilet equipment on the dressing-table gave her a feeling of greater intimacy than she had ever had.

"I won't have Healy and Dillon and the rest staring at you. Papists! They have rigid cast-iron consciences. Kate?"

"Yes, love." The endearment came naturally and sweetly to her tongue.

"There's something I must ask you."

"Of course."

"I can't help it, I'm beginning to think of you as mine. But you have to live with your husband." She could feel the rigidity of his form and answered the question he had not put into words.

"He doesn't touch me. Even before we met, I no longer loved him. I'm like the wife in a melodrama—I lock my bedroom door." She looked serenely into his tormented eyes. "I'm not being facetious. You don't need to fear."

His fingers pressed cruelly into her shoulders.

"You can't go on with a marriage like that."

"Divorce?" She tested the word. "That would ruin you."

There was a knock on the door and abruptly he released her.

"Come in."

45

A waiter came in with the tray of tea. He set it down, paused to look curiously at Katharine, and left.

Katharine sat down composedly at the table.

"Let us have tea and talk quietly. What time does your train go?"

"Six o'clock."

"Then we have only an hour. And you have to finish packing. This is too big a question to discuss in an hour. In any case, there's nothing to discuss. You're the leader of your country. They say that you're called the uncrowned king of Ireland."

"Celtic extravagance!"

"Perhaps. But the people worship you, isn't that true? They look to you as their saviour."

"Sometimes that's an impossible burden."

"I'm sure it must be, but it would also be impossible to have it ruined by a woman. You would hate me. And I'm no Helen of Troy. I don't intend to be a woman who changes the history of a country. Because that would happen. I believe in you that much."

"You're too intelligent, Kate."

"Apart from that, we're wasting time even discussing this subject. Willie is a Roman Catholic. He would never tolerate divorce any more than those papists, as you call them, downstairs."

She poured the tea, her hand miraculously steady.

"There. Drink that. Thank goodness tea is one thing the English and Irish have in common."

He smiled faintly, and obediently sipped the tea. She thought he looked a little less drawn though his face was still tormented.

"Charles, already you're a man of history. If you never did anything else, you would be that. But you're going to do so much more. How could I have it on my conscience to stop you? So let us postpone this conversation for a year or two."

"It will be a bitter road this way," he said soberly. "Do you realise how bitter?"

"Yes."

"Then don't you want to leave me now?"

The tears rushed to her eyes.

46

"No. Oh, no."

"You said you didn't want any scandal for your children."

"Neither do I, but even that I have to risk."

He smiled at last.

"Then why are we even speaking of it? Ah Kate! All at once I feel better. You do that for me, you see. You banish nightmares."

"I hope I will always be able to do that."

"You will, never fear." He looked at his watch. "The devil take it. I must pack."

"How long will you be away?"

"A week. Perhaps two. May I write to you?"

"Oh, please."

"And will you promise to answer my letter. Address it to Avondale. Will you wait now and drive to the station with me? Or do you hate railway stations?"

"I hate being left standing on them alone."

"I told you it would be a bitter road."

"I know," she said sadly.

She was alone even before the train had left. His body was beside her, certainly, but his mind was far away, his eyes shadowed with the tragedy of another newly-dug grave in a country with far too many graves already. She wanted to pull him back to her by telling him that she was wretched, too, it wasn't only in Ireland that people could be unhappy.

Then she was ashamed of her weakness. If she were to deserve his love she must be as strong as he was. She must smile as the train pulled out of the station. His last memory of her must never be one of a lonely woman in tears.

Anyway, tears were an extravagance, for he would soon be back. She knew that he would always come back.

CHAPTER 4

THE summer wore on, and it seemed probable that Mr. Disraeli was glad to be elevated to the House of Lords, to watch Mr. Gladstone battling with the difficult and increasingly insoluble Irish question. The Land League seemed to have got entirely out of hand and not a day passed without some fresh outrage being perpetrated. The toll of arson, terrorisation and even murder rose daily. It was all very well for Mr Parnell to say he was against violence, the Fenian element in his followers was growing unmanageable, even for him.

But, despite the anger and dismay in England and despite the Queen writing, "Something must be done about these shameless Home Rulers", there was the occasional English sympathiser. General Gordon, who was by all accounts reliable, and British to the core, wrote, "The state of our fellow-countrymen in Ireland is worse than that of any people in the world, let alone Europe." He described them as "lying on the verge of starvation in places where we would not keep cattle."

It was forced upon the Government to think again. Mr. John Morley talked picturesquely of "the wild squalor of Macedonia and Armenia not being less wild than the squalor in Connaught and Munster, in Mayo, Galway, Sligo and Kerry". Since the House of Lords had contemptuously thrown out the Compensation for Disturbance Bill, there was nothing for the Government to do but fall back on the detested coercion. If anyone cried out with hunger or protested that his children were starving, kick him, beat him, throw him in jail, but silence him for his impudence.

As for Mr. Parnell, who had had grandiose dreams of bringing the English to their knees, if he could not be arrested as the peasants he incited to violence could be, there would be other ways of dealing with him. Lord Cowper, the Lord Lieutenant, and Mr. Forster, the Chief

Secretary, put their heads together. But while they were still plotting Mr. Parnell made his triumphant speech at Ennis.

And it was not an incitement to violence. It was a very different affair altogether.

He stood easily on the platform, his hands clasped behind his back, and asked a quiet question.

"What are you to do to a tenant who bids for a farm from which his neighbour has been evicted?"

As was to be expected the wild tattered hungry crowd roared, "Kill him! Shoot him!"

Mr. Parnell waited until the tumultous applause had died down, and then said with his quiet reasonableness:

"I think I heard someone say shoot him, but I wish to point out to you a very much better way—a more Christian and a more charitable way—which will give the lost sinner an opportunity of repenting."

The crowd stirred restlessly, but such was the man's magnetism that no one interrupted.

The voice, with its devastating logic, went on: "When a man takes a farm from which another has been evicted, you must show him on the roadside when you meet him, you must show him in the streets of the town, you must show him at the shop counter, you must show him in the fair and in the market-place, and even in the house of worship, by leaving him severely alone, by putting him into a moral Coventry, by isolating him from his kind as if he were a leper of old—you must show him your detestation of the crime he has committed, and you may depend upon it that there will be no man so full of avarice, so lost to shame, as to dare the public opinion of all right-thinking men and to transgress your unwritten code of laws."

The eternal soft misty rain was falling, shining on the uplifted faces, blurring the distances. When Mr. Parnell had finished speaking he wiped the moisture off his cheeks and no one knew whether it was rain or tears. All they knew was that this man with the pale face and eloquent dark eyes was the man they would follow and on whom they would lavish their untidy emotional but total love.

The speech at Ennis was no pointless meandering in the House of Commons designed merely to obstruct business.

There was nothing negative or defensive about this. It was oratory in the best parliamentary tradition. It merited comparison with Mr Gladstone. The seventy-year-old Prime Minister was forced into an uneasy new contemplation of the troublesome Irish question. If Parnell, a man of only thirty-four, could command his audience so effectively now, what would he do in ten years or twenty years, or when he had the white hair of his Prime Minister?

Stories began to drift across the Irish Channel about the adulation the young man was receiving; people mobbing him in the street, kissing his hand, carrying him shoulder high. If it didn't ruin him, and they said it wouldn't because he was too calm and level-headed, then he was becoming a force to be reckoned with. The Irish party would no longer be amiably dismissed as a fairly negligible factor in the government of the British Isles.

Of course the Celts made everything larger than life, especially a man like this, composed, proud, unknowable. They could invent romantic stories about him, they could already see in him the making of one of their revered martyrs. So the English had better be careful in their treatment of the new Irish leader. Should there be signs of martyrdom, a fire would be kindled in the emerald isle that might smoulder and burn for a century.

It was all very well for the Queen to sigh with exasperation and say that she found her tiresome Irish subjects becoming too tedious with their constant rebellion. How could the people expect mercy when they defied all laws, and drove poor Mr. Forster distracted? He must make an example of more of them. The gallows was a terrible thing, but perhaps a few judicious hangings would at least put the fear of God into the rest of the populace, since it was too much to hope that they would ever learn good sense. No, the Queen had never seen the Dublin slums, or the disastrous cabins that housed the poorer of her subjects, but she believed the descriptions of these places to be greatly exaggerated. And anyway couldn't the people do more to help themselves?

The troublesome thing was that they did, incited by Mr. Parnell, and in entirely the wrong way.

The famous speech at Ennis had been taken to heart, and

was put into practice three days later. Captain Boycott, an Englishman, agent to Lord Erne in Connaught, was offered what was considered a just rent by the tenants on Lord Erne's estate. He refused it contemptuously and ordered the usual eviction notices to be served on the unruly tenants.

The notices were not served, because the process server, by what intimidation no one knew, was persuaded to desist from doing so. One morning Captain Boycott got up to find his house, dairy and stables empty. His servants had left him in a body. What was more, no shopkeeper would serve him, no mail was delivered, he could persuade no one to come and milk his cows or look after his horses. He was abandoned. And he must have been haunted by the thought of the whole county chuckling evilly and gleefully at his fate, for, although later fifty men, under the armed supervision of police and soldiers, were forced to gather his crops, he himself could not stand the awful isolation. He left Connaught, never to return, unwillingly leaving his name to be used in quips in every public house and tavern in the country.

The new policy had a name. Boycott.

At first Katharine, waiting impatiently for Charles' letters, was a little disappointed with them. They were warm and friendly, but gave no account of the tremendous work he had been doing, or what had been happening to him. They said both too little and too much.

> "Morison's Hotel, Dublin.
> "Dear Mrs. O'Shea,
>
> Just a line to say that I have arrived here and must go on to Avondale this evening where I hope to hear from you. I may tell you in confidence that I don't feel quite so content at the prospect of ten days' absence from London amongst the hills and valleys of Wicklow as I should have done some three month's since. The cause is mysterious, but perhaps you will help me to find it on my return.
>
> Yours always,
> Charles Parnell"

But he was going to tell her nothing about what he was doing and planning, and, above all, when he was coming back?

If he loved her, why did he leave her alone so long? He had said he would be a week and instead it was nearly a month. Why must the affairs of his country be quite so absorbing?

Katharine looked soberly at her face in the mirror.

She couldn't understand how it showed nothing of her inner turmoil. She still looked serene, good-tempered, even generous. And she was not generous at all. She was beginning to think herself more hardly done by than the three million struggling people across the Irish Sea.

Now that he was away from her, had he had second thoughts about the dangerous unwisdom of their friendship? Had his other side, his deep driving obsession to free his country, absorbed him completely? How well, or how little did she know him? Should she be grateful if he stayed away and left her to sink back into the peace of her quiet life, with her children, the garden, Aunt Ben, and an occasional visit to London to do some entertaining for her husband?

Sometimes for a whole hour, when she romped with the children or drove sedately through the park with Aunt Ben, she persuaded herself that this was the best solution. Then, without warning, shatteringly, his face would come into her mind, the sound of his voice into her ears. Her hand would tingle as if his lay on it. And she knew he had only to whisper a request and she would fly to him, utterly reckless, utterly willing.

Willie was in London, living in his rooms at Albert Hall Mansions. He sent a message to Katharine asking her to come up. He was giving a dinner party for Mr. Joseph Chamberlain whom he counted as one of the most influential men in Mr. Gladstone's Government. So Kate must be sure to come. Whatever their differences she had promised to help him in his career. And he was sure she would agree that his conciliatory tactics were far more effective than the hostility and arrogance Parnell displayed.

Katharine agreed that more than ever now the façade of their marriage must be kept up. Anyway, she was curious to meet Mr. Chamberlain, and there might be news of Charles. She sent a message to Willie saying that she would come.

The conversation at the dinner party was about the new word that had been coined, "boycott". Mr. Chamberlain thought it a cheap trick, something to get popular publicity. But Willie, who saw the stature Parnell was acquiring, was torn between his powerful English friends, and his necessary allegiance to the leader of his party. Who should he cultivate most? Could he successfully take the middle of the road?

Katharine could read what lay behind his handsome face. Long familiarity had taught her the working of his mind. He despised his countrymen as a whole, so was angry that one of them should prove so supremely effective. He was jealous, too. And yet the honesty he had compelled him to admire Parnell, perhaps more than he did Chamberlain. He would like to be friends with them both.

"My wife has a great admiration for Mr. Parnell," he observed.

Mr. Chamberlain let his appraising glance rest on Katharine.

"I didn't know he was a ladies' man."

Willie laughed, his blue eyes alight with amusement.

"Oh, it wouldn't be for that that Kate admired him. Would it, Kate? She likes his courage, and his gifts as an orator."

"Well, don't let the man become a legend, Mrs. O'Shea," Mr. Chamberlain said, a trifle irritably. "Then we'll never get down to real business."

"So you are going to do business with him?" Katharine enquired calmly.

"It looks as if we have no alternative. Isn't that so, Captain O'Shea? I'd be glad to know, if it could be found out in advance, what sort of a reception Mr. Parnell proposes to give the new Land Act. I think it's as good an act as could be devised, but he doesn't trust us an inch. He's got an unshakeable belief that every law we make is biased in our favour."

"Or perhaps that you won't keep your word," Katharine said.

Willie darted her an angry look, but Mr. Chamberlain laughed in his dry way and said: "Oh, I know Mr. Parnell bears no love for us. He's convinced no good will ever come out of England. So I'm afraid we've reached an impasse with him. Unless you can sway him to your more generous view of us, O'Shea."

When Katharine reached home that night she found all the lights on and Miss Glennister waiting for her in a state of extreme distress.

"Oh, Mrs. O'Shea, something terrible has happened. Lucy—"

The silly woman began to cry and Katharine had to take her and almost shake the words out of her.

"What? Is she dead? Where is she?"

"Not dead, Mrs. O'Shea. But she can't speak. She tries, and it's awful."

Katharine was halfway up the stairs.

"Has the doctor been?"

"Yes. He says she's had a stroke. She won't last long, he thinks." Miss Glennister was in fresh tears. "I've told the children she's poorly. Poor lambs, they'd be so frightened if they knew the truth."

"They must learn not to be frightened," Katharine said, and didn't wait for Miss Glennister's tearful rejoinder, for she was already halfway to Lucy's room.

She scarcely recognised the poor distorted face. The doctor had sent a nurse who said softly to Katharine, "Speak to her, Mrs. O'Shea. I don't think she sees anything, but she can hear. She's been waiting for you."

Katharine took Lucy's hand, and felt the gnarled fingers moving feeling for her rings to identify her.

"It is me, Lucy. Don't worry about anything. I'll stay beside you."

Lucy—the faithful figure that had been beside her all her life. There had never been a time without her. She had been growing old, one realised, but not this old. She had never complained, never said she was getting tired or feeling ill until she had had that nasty chill a little while ago. Katharine sat beside her, fighting tears. Lucy who had shepherded her through childhood, been like a rock beside her when Papa had died, rejoiced in her wedding, and the

54

birth of her babies, loyally poured out her savings for the dear Captain when he was temporarily embarrassed, as was natural to a gentleman who enjoyed a gay life.

"I'm here, Lucy," she said at intervals during the long night, as the shrunken figure on the bed breathed with more and more difficulty.

And in the morning there was a letter from Dublin.

"My dear Mrs. O'Shea,
    I cannot keep myself away from you any longer, so shall leave tonight for London. Please wire me at 16 Keppell Street, Russell Square, if I may hope to see you tomorrow, and where.

Yours always,
C.S.P."

She crushed the letter in her hands. Her face was distraught. She had promised not to leave Lucy, she could not leave her faithful old servant who, bereft of all other senses, could yet feel to grope for her hand and cling to it.

But she hadn't seen him for so long, and how was she to bear the thought of him waiting for the message she could not send. He would pace up and down the hotel lobby, hoping that perhaps, instead of the message that never arrived, she would arrive herself.

This was torture. She was suffering every moment of his disappointment and perplexity. Would he think she had decided to give him up, that the price of loving him was too great and she was too mean-spirited to pay it?

Lucy died late that night, and in the morning Katharine, saying she must tell Willie personally, took the train to London. Her first call was at the Keppell Street Hotel. Heavily veiled, she enquired at the desk for Mr. Parnell, only to be told that he had left for Dublin less than an hour ago. But there was a forwarding address. Had it been left for her?

So at least she could write and know that within twenty-four hours he would have an explanation and the assurance that he had not been deserted.

Willie came back to Eltham with her. He shed a few emotional tears over poor old Lucy, the loyal soul she had been, and took her to be buried at Cressing beside Kath-

55

arine's mother and father, where she would have hoped to lie. He behaved very nicely, and offered to stay longer if Kate would like him to. She saw that he expected to use Lucy's death as a basis for a reconciliation. What better time for Katharine, weeping and forgiving, to seek his arms? She was dismayed and disgusted, and very relieved when, thoroughly bored with a house in mourning and an aloof wife, Willie could stand it no longer and went off to seek gaieties in London.

After that the house was very quiet. But at last the longed-for letter with the Irish postmark arrived. Katharine cried when she read it, for Charles was full of sympathy for her loss. She could hardly imagine his happiness at receiving her letter. But matters were tense and he could not get back to England for a few days. Did she know that Captain O'Shea was suggesting his coming down to Eltham to visit, and what did she think of that?

This was the first she had heard of such an idea. Willie must have been in touch with Charles since he had been here. It was typical of him not to have discussed the matter with his wife.

She walked about feverishly trying to imagine how she could hide her feelings if Charles were actually in her house, sitting in her drawing room, and Willie was expecting her to play the part of a gracious hostess. It would be an impossible situation! She must plead all the excuses she could think of, Lucy's death, the shabbiness of the house, Aunt Ben's demands on her time, Willie's own dislike of the country.

"Katharine, my bird, you look so sad." That was Aunt Ben, looking up from the froth of shawls with which she protected herself from draughts in the tapestry room. "You mustn't grieve for Lucy. She had a quick and merciful end. She wasn't left cooling her heels as I am. Now don't sit at home brooding. Bring the children over this afternoon. I haven't seen them for a long time."

Norah and Carmen loved going to visit Aunt Ben. They were awed by her great age which Norah guessed to be two hundred years at least. They pleaded with her to tell them stories about her childhood, which she obligingly did, describing the kind of clothes she used to wear, poke bonnets, long skirts and petticoats, white stockings. No little girl then would have dreamed of wearing the hideous black stockings of nowadays, and what was more, showing her leg almost to the knee. The little girls giggled merrily. They could not possibly imagine Aunt Ben in her poke bonnets and white stockings either. She could never never have been a child.

"Could she, Mamma? Mamma, aren't you listening?"

Katharine aroused herself and smiled. Dusk was falling and the owls were beginning to hoot. In a moment the maids would come in to shut the windows and light the lamps. It was time to go back to the empty house and her secret worry.

Did Willie really mean to invite Charles to the house?

He did. He broached the subject when he came down on Sunday.

"Will he come do you think? You must add your persuasions to mine. You seem more successful than me in snaring him."

"Snaring! What a horrible word."

Willie looked surprised at her vehemence.

"It expresses exactly what I mean. You're a bit sensitive, aren't you? What's worrying you?"

She walked about agitatedly, twitching back the faded curtains, pointing to the carpet where it was worn.

"The house is too shabby. Mr. Parnell is the leader of the Irish party. It's almost like entertaining the Prime Minister. And we haven't enough servants."

"Then engage more."

"Willie!" She rounded on him angrily. "With Aunt Ben already paying all the household expenses, how dare you suggest being extravagant like that. Have you no pride?"

Willie, sensitive about his pride, was instantly aggrieved.

"There's no call to say a thing like that when can't you see I'm trying to do the thing to advance my career. You can't accuse me of liking Parnell. He isn't my type at all. But I've wit enough to see the way things are going. He's going to become a major power in the Government and I've no doubt his friends will come in for some notice. Besides, I'm getting some influence of my own that he'll hardly have the bad sense to ignore. And he isn't coming down here to look at the state of the furnishings. He's been slaving himself to death in Ireland, rushing from one end of the country to the other. He needs a rest. We'll have him down next weekend when he arrives back in London."

"Will he come?" was all Katharine could ask weakly.

Willie fixed his cool blue gaze on her.

"Didn't I suggest that you add your persuasions?"

"If they're worth anything."

"Oh, they are, I assure you. It's getting around that he admires you."

"Is—it?" Her hand, halfway to her throat, stopped, by sheer effort of will.

"Thinks you're a fine-looking woman. Well, that's what he told Tim Healy." Willie, his point gained, had picked up the newspaper. The dangerous moment had passed. It hadn't really been dangerous at all. For he was quite pleased that that cool and fastidious politician, Charles Stewart Parnell, should admire his wife. He liked to have his possessions admired.

Mr. Parnell was due to arrive on Saturday evening. The house was in a flurry because Willie was supervising everything. The cook had already been in tears, and Miss Glennister had the little girls dressed in their white muslin party frocks quite an hour earlier than necessary. Katharine had objected to the children being dressed up so obviously, but Willie was proud of his pretty daughters and wanted to show them off. It was a pity Gerard was not home from school so that he could show off his son, too.

Katharine sat in her bedroom hesitating a long time over her own toilette. Willie would be pleased if she took the greatest pains with it.

She wanted to look beautiful for Charles, but only for him. Why must he be put in the intolerable position of watching the woman he loved playing the part of the well-groomed and apparently cherished wife? She toyed with the thought of putting on her least attractive gown and coming down looking crushed and colourless.

Vanity won. She spent a long time brushing her hair and coiling it round her head. She put on a low-necked dress that showed her shoulders to best advantage. She was very pale, but her eyes were bright with tension and excitement.

She patted a little rice powder on her nose, and sprinkled a few drops of perfume on her handkerchief.

When she heard the wheels of the cab, she flew to the window to draw back the curtain and peer down.

There he was stepping out of the cab. The sight of his tall figure, so immediately familiar as if it had never for a moment been out of her sight, made tears spring to her eyes. She clenched her hands, resisting an impulse to go running down the stairs, and flinging open the door to welcome him.

She had firmly decided not to do this. Willie was to greet Charles (she must guard her tongue so she did not call him by his first name publicly) and take him to his room. This would give him a chance to adjust himself to the house and the circumstances before meeting her. Not that she wasn't absolutely sure he would carry off any situation with complete aplomb.

She lingered in her room, giving Charles time to change. Willie would have told him that dinner was at seven.

She went down precisely at that hour, and found Miss Glennister bringing her charges down at the same time. So the greetings were easy after all. Willie was exuberantly showing off his daughters, and Mr. Parnell was courteously giving them all his attention. When he turned to Katharine, it was with the greatest ease and simplicity.

"Mrs. O'Shea. Forgive me for being quite absorbed in your little girls. I see they have your husband's eyes, but your smile."

Katharine bent swiftly over the children, kissing them on their rosy cheeks.

"To bed now, angels. Kiss Papa goodnight."

In the resulting small flurry she had regained her poise and was able to say without a tremor: "How good of you to spare time to come down to us, Mr. Parnell. You have been working much too hard, my husband tells me."

He gave her his grave considering gaze. He was very thin, with deep lines engraved on his cheeks. He looked as if he needed weeks of rest. No sounds would disturb him in the bedroom overlooking the garden except the early cawing of rooks, or the wind in the trees. He could rest or work as he pleased.

"If you find it comfortable here, we hope you will come again."

Willie didn't see the light leap in Mr. Parnell's eyes for he had his back turned, pouring sherry.

"Yes, I've an idea you might find it useful to make this place your headquarters, Parnell. It must be inconvenient moving about so much. How does your mail ever catch up with you, for instance? And how do you snatch a bit of rest without being besieged by all and sundry? But we'll talk of that later. Kate and I are eager to hear all about the latest developments in Ireland. Aren't we, Kate? My wife is developing quite a taste for politics."

"Yes, we do want to hear everything," Katharine said calmly. "But after dinner, Willie. Mr. Parnell must be hungry as well as tired. Shall we go in straight away?"

And that was almost the only remark she made to him for the entire evening. Willie began to talk politics before they had finished their soup, and the discussion went on, growing more and more absorbing to the two men, until Katharine excused herself, saying that she would like to go on talking but not, she begged, until the small hours.

They both sprang up. Charles contrite, Willie perfunctory. Willie kissed her on the cheek, saying, "Sorry, my love. This is pretty boring for you."

"Yes, you've been very patient with us, Mrs. O'Shea. As you see, I get carried away with my schemes. But this idea of preparing test cases to prove the value of the Land Act, when it goes through, is the only way to be sure that it is a fair act and the English mean to stand by it. I think it would have far more chance of being a fair act if only we could deal directly with the Prime Minister while it's in preparation. But he'll never be seen conferring with any of the Irish members. That would damn him in his own party's eyes. What we need is a go-between, a person not connected with either party."

"Preferably," said Willie, "a woman."

Charles shot him a sharp look. "Had you someone in mind?"

"My wife."

Katharine made a startled exclamation.

"It isn't as preposterous as it sounds," Willie went on,

and it was clear that Mr. Parnell didn't think it preposterous either, for he was giving Katharine a contemplative look that made her remember his remark that he treated men as weapons. Women, too? Even one he loved?

"Kate is very good in political circles," Willie was saying. "Joe Chamberlain was quite impressed with her the other night."

"She would only need to carry messages," Charles said thoughtfully. "Would you care to do it, Mrs. O'Shea, if we find the opportunity?"

Willie, pleased with his idea, broke in to say that Gladstone, who was supposed to be a rigid puritan, cherished a secret weakness for good-looking women. Look at his reputation for saving prostitutes. One can hardly be expected to believe that he was only interested in their souls.

"Mrs. O'Shea's business with him would be strictly political," Charles said coldly.

Unabashed, Willie said he was only emphasising that Gladstone would be unlikely to refuse to see Kate.

"The point is," said Charles, "whether Mrs. O'Shea would mind doing this. We seem to be merrily arranging her part without consulting her wishes."

"Certainly I will do it if it serves a useful purpose," Katharine said unhesitatingly. The idea was beginning to excite her. It would be tremendous to play an active part in the coming struggle. Whatever anyone said, a woman with an active mind found keeping house an unsatisfying and frustrating occupation. She would enjoy meeting Mr. Gladstone and that enjoyment would be heightened by knowing she was helping the Irish cause and Charles. Besides, might it not give them more legitimate opportunities to be together?

"Thank you Mrs. O'Shea," Charles said gravely. "I think this may be a most useful idea. We'll be grateful to you."

She went upstairs and undressed and lay down in bed, but it was impossible to sleep. When, much later, she heard the men come upstairs she lay rigid for a long time, fearing that Willie, in his present affable mood, might decide to test the feelings of his wife in much the same way that he was planning to test the reaction of his countrymen to the new Land Act. But mercifully he stayed away. She knew that their state of armed neutrality could not go on for ever. Perhaps he meant to keep his threat that she would have to come to him if ever she wanted him again. And that eventuality would be most unlikely, she reflected, and suddenly fell soundly asleep.

She awoke to a state of great happiness, as if she had just realised for the first time that Charles was under the same roof as herself.

Even if she had no opportunity to see him alone, he was here, safely. She didn't have to worry whether he was hungry, tired, cold, lonely. She had only to tap at his door and hear his voice answer, and know that, for this short space of time at least, she could look after him as well as she looked after the rest of her household. He was in her care.

But her good fortune was not limited even to this. For Willie was taking the children to Mass, and suggested that while they were gone Kate might take Mr. Parnell for a drive and show him the countryside. A breath of fresh air was what he needed. He looked as if he had been out of the sun and burning midnight oil for much too long. Aunt Ben would allow the use of her dogcart, as she often did when Katharine wanted to take the children for a picnic. How would Kate enjoy driving the King of Ireland, no less!

Katharine looked demurely at Mr. Parnell, trying to keep the amused sparkle out of her eyes.

"Will you trust yourself with me, Mr. Parnell? You will be quite safe. Prince is so sedate and elderly that Carmen could drive him."

"You don't need to assure me of that, Mrs. O'Shea. I am sure you would be capable of driving the most spirited horse."

Willie waved them off with his blessing. For one moment Katharine was positively angry with him for his stupidity. Did he never realise that she might be truly unhappy and not his possession forever? Then, because he was so blind, a great wave of intoxicating freedom swept over her, and she whipped up Prince, beginning to laugh gaily as they moved briskly down the drive.

"Isn't this wonderful? Where would you like to go?"

"Wherever you take me, my darling."

His voice was as full of happiness as hers. She turned and

their eyes met in the first full glance they had been able to exchange since he had arrived.

"It's a miracle," she said. "Shall I make Prince gallop for joy?"

"Poor old Prince. He would probably collapse between the shafts, and I think it's better for us to get back uninjured. You look very well, Mrs. O'Shea."

"And so do you, Mr. Parnell." She slowed Prince's reluctant trot to a walk. "Charles!"

"Katharine. Katie."

"You look better this morning, as if you had rested."

"So I have. I thought at first it would be impossible with you just down the passage. I had only to get up and walk a few yards to be with you."

"You mustn't!" she breathed.

He gave the faintest shrug. "I didn't, did I? I'm still clinging to a few vestiges of good sense."

"At least we were under the same roof. I thought that was an immense thing to happen to us. I had never imagined it would."

"But I wonder how wise it is."

"Oh—wisdom! On a morning like this. It's a forbidden word. Let's be reckless, let's toss our bonnets over the windmill as Lucy would say. Poor Lucy. I miss her so sadly, and yet now you're here beside me I'm quite heartlessly happy."

"Was it very bad, Lucy's death?"

The morning was not quite shadowless after all. Katharine repressed a faint shiver. "Yes, it was bad. And yet— how can I confess that it wasn't as bad as thinking of you waiting for me that day? Alone, without a message. You must have thought I had deserted you. I almost wanted to die with Lucy. It was natural and peaceful for her to go, but thinking of you coming so far just to see me, and then unable to, not knowing what had happened—I made a resolve then that I would never do this to you again, no matter whom I hurt. I'm not a ruthless person, but for you I would be. Do you believe me?"

"Yes," he said, his face deeply troubled.

"Did you think I had deserted you?"

"No, not that. But I was immensely relieved to get your

63

letter." He took her hand, paused only to strip off the glove, and held it between his own. "These things will happen to us, Kate. The next time it might be me not able to get in touch with you. In that case, would you think I had deserted you?"

"Only for Ireland."

Her words were so wry that he burst out laughing.

"At least it will never be for another woman. That I promise you."

"Then perhaps you had better give me back my hand in case Prince decides to bolt. Neither I nor Ireland intends to lose you. What do you say to Willie's suggestion?"

"That we use you as a messenger to Mr. Gladstone? I think you could be very valuable to us. Gladstone is sure to admire and trust you. But what are your true feelings about this?"

"I would enjoy it. I wouldn't feel so left out. I'm constantly being told that politics are not for women, but I'm sure women could have far more influence than anyone suspects."

He was looking at her with his gentle ironic glance.

"Would you like to be a woman of influence, Kate?"

"I believe I would."

"Then be careful. I may come to depend on you entirely."

"That's impossible. You're much too strong and self-sufficient."

"Am I Kate? Is that as much as you know me?"

"But you've been alone so much. It must have made you strong."

"Then I wonder I've never stopped thinking about you since I met you. What am I to do about that?"

"How can I tell you since I have the same problem? And anyway—I would like you to depend on me. For everything! I'm beginning to hate people who keep us apart. I can safely hate all your troublesome peasants in Ireland, but Willie, dear Aunt Ben—even poor Lucy dying—" her voice was low with shame, "I almost hated her. I know that you can be ruthless in your work. Are you ruthless in loving? As I am beginning to be. One of us must keep sane, Charles."

64

He stopped her deeply troubled monologue by saying lightly: "We shall take it in turns to keep sane. Today it is my turn, tomorrow yours. The day we both are mad together—", he smiled a little, "—that will come, too. At the right time. Now, what about this plan of your husband's that I use your house as my headquarters. Providing he is home, of course."

"Would it serve a good purpose?"

"Oh, it would do that. It would be a great help. I could have all my mail directed here, I would have a permanent address at last. And an escape from London when I need to get away. Besides, I'm beginning to think that Captain O'Shea could make a very useful contribution to our campaign. That is, if he is genuinely for us and not for his English friends."

"Oh, he has useful connections," Katharine said, not wanting to say that Willie was, first and foremost, for himself. But Charles was too intelligent to be taken in by any show of patriotism on Willie's part. He himself admitted to using men—and women, herself, too, as it suited him. Politics were not for the sentimental or the unduly scrupulous.

"But what do you think of it, Kate? My being here?"

"It frightens me. It seems as if fate is forcing us to be together. How can it end?"

"Why should we talk of endings?" he lifted her hand, and kissed her fingers, each one separately. "Why not beginnings? I'm in an optimistic mood. And you were talking a moment ago of tossing bonnets over windmills."

"So I was."

"I shall be content to see you with the children—look at you across the table—watch you coming in from the garden—hear your voice from another room."

She looked intensely into his eyes.

"Will you, Charles?"

"Well, not entirely content. But content."

She sighed and smiled.

"Then it's settled. Do you think we should turn back now?"

"Go just another mile, if Prince is equal to it."

"Prince has no say in the matter."

Katharine flicked the lazy horse with the tip of the whip,

and he jogged on peacefully, stirring a small dust. The road led through hop country, and all at once a boy on the roadside stared intently at them, then sped barefoot across a field shouting. Almost at once, from nowhere, the dogcart was surrounded by excited ragged sun-burned people. They surged forward crying, "The Chief! The Chief!" Some tried to clamber into the dogcart. A child fell, almost under Prince's hoofs.

"Who are they? What are they doing?" Katharine asked, dragging on the reins. Her heart was beating rapidly in fright. She thought they were about to be mobbed.

But Charles leaned forward lifting his hat and giving his grave smile. A woman snatched at his hand to kiss it. Someone shouted, "God keep your honour!"

"Thank you," he said to the uplifted faces. "Thank you. I'll talk to you when I'm back in Ireland. Now if you will be good enough to let us by."

Their farewells rang out. "God bless you! God bless the Chief."

"Some of my people over for the hop-picking. Did they alarm you?"

Katharine didn't answer.

"I'm afraid their love is almost as dangerous as their hate. Kate?"

She whipped up Prince, keeping her face averted.

"Kate, You're not crying! You *were* frightened. But that was nothing to what they can do. Last week they carried me on their shoulders for half a mile through Dublin and I was never so scared in my life. I thought I would fall down among their loving arms and have their loving feet trample me to death. All with the best intentions."

"Must I share you with them?" she asked passionately.

"Ah, Kate! So that's what it is. But what you have is entirely separate from what they have."

"Is it?"

"My darling, how can you even ask?"

She faced him sombrely, her tears dried on her cheeks.

"Whatever we separately have, it's all housed in the same body. And I'm afraid."

He didn't, as she expected, remonstrate with her. He just said, in a low voice, "I know, Kate. I understand."

66

The tears filled her eyes again.

"It isn't that I'm not proud of you. Seeing the way they reverenced you, I was so proud I couldn't bear it. When I read your speech at Ennis I cried. I know what you have to do, and I'll try never to stop you. But I can't promise always to be calm and sensible."

"Nor can I," he said. "Nor can I."

"I'm so afraid one day you'll hate me."

"For what?" he asked in amazement.

"For tearing you in half."

He made no answer to that. Instead he said, "But you're with me, Katharine?"

He only called her Katharine when he was most deeply serious.

"Yes," she said reluctantly. "I have to be."

CHAPTER 5

THE lamplight shone on her hair and her face as she bent over the letter she was writing.

"Dear Charles,
   I have received your letters (both of them). The second was so much more precious than the first . . ."

She paused to re-read the two letters that had arrived that morning.

"Dear Mrs. O'Shea,
   I must thank you again for all your kindness which made my stay at Eltham so happy and pleasant. I enclose keys which I took away by mistake. Will you kindly hand enclosed letter to the proper person and oblige,
                              Yours very truly, C.S.P."

She smiled faintly and tenderly as she read the second letter, the one that was to have been handed to some hypothetical person had Willie been home when the post arrived, and insisted on seeing what Mr. Parnell had written.

"My dearest love,
   I have made all arrangements to be in London on Saturday morning, and shall call at Keppel Street for a letter from you. It is quite impossible for me to tell you just how very much you have changed my life, and how I detest everything which has happened during the last few days to keep me away from you. I think of you always . . ."

They had made this arrangement about the letters when he had stayed at Eltham. It had been a sensible precaution, for, with many separations ahead of them, neither of them had been content to receive the kind of letter that said nothing loving or personal.

Willie, who did happen to be home, read the one intended for his consumption, and said carelessly:

"The arrangement seems to be working out very well, Kate. I'll let you know when he intends to come again."

As if she would not know herself! She repressed a smile, and made a comment that Mr. Parnell had not seemed to mind the shabbiness of the house.

"Good heavens, no! If you were to see some of the places he spent nights in. He has no pride about that. He'll happily stretch himself out on a straw pallet in a peasant's cabin. I'm damned if I would. But that, I suppose, is how he gets his popularity."

"And yet they call him cold in England. They just don't know him. The servants worshipped him. Cook is wearing a locket with his likeness round her neck. But she comes from Tipperary, so I suppose it's understandable."

For a moment Willie was looking at her a little too fixedly.

"You seem taken with him yourself."

"I think him a charming and thoughtful guest." She thought her voice sounded too defensive, so she went on enthusiastically, "I'm becoming very sympathetic with his cause. I would like to help it, if I could, apart from carrying messages to Gladstone."

"You'll help sufficiently by seeing that Parnell is made comfortable when he stays here."

"Certainly I will do that," she replied with deceptive meekness.

But she could do more than that, for now that Charles's mail was directed to Eltham, she had taken it on herself to attend to it. His dislike of opening letters and answering them was now well-known. After a week or two of reading them herself she was not surprised. They included everything from adulation to virulent hatred. There were begging letters, invitations to every manner of function, gifts of money, or more personal gifts. Every week a box of eggs arrived. It gave no clue as to the sender.

On the first occasion Charles was in the house, and instantly told her to have the eggs buried in the garden. She looked at him in surprise.

"They may be eggs or they may not be," he said cryptically. "We won't bother to find out. Don't let your dog be poisoned." A cold shaft of fear struck through her. For the first time she realised the danger that he walked in daily.

"Charles, how terrible!"

"Terrible? Not at all. I told you that politics are war. You can't have a war without shots being fired. Besides, that would be exceedingly dull."

After his second stay at Eltham he wrote from Dublin:

'My stay with you has been so pleasant that I was almost beginning to forget my other duties, but Ireland seems to have gotten on very well without me in the interval."

He had not been idle, however, or the Land League had not been idle on his behalf. But by persuading tenants to stop paying rent it had overstepped the mark and Mr. Forster, the Irish Secretary, whose rage had been simmering ever since the boycott affair, had taken an extreme step. An information was sworn against the Land League. There was to be a trial by jury of Parnell, and fourteen others.

There was no word from Charles. Katharine waited in an agony of anxiety, day by day. She read his speech in Dublin, with its echoes of cool irony, when he expressed regret that Forster was degenerating from a statesman into a tool of the landlords, but for more news she had to wait.

Willie could give her little, for he was furious about the whole affair. He was a landlord himself, with his property at Limerick, and this was one thing about which he did not see eye to eye with Parnell.

"He may be able to afford to give up his rents, but I can't. He's letting the Land League get away with too much altogether. He'll regret it."

"But what about the trial? What will happen?"

"What do you think? Will any jury in Ireland convict them? You may be sure they won't."

Parliament reopened and the Queen, in her speech from the Throne, said, "I grieve to state that the social condition of Ireland has assumed an alarming character." She lifted her pale blue eyes and looked round the floor of the House, hoping perhaps that her indignant royal survey would arouse remorse in the breasts of the recalcitrant Irish members. Perhaps she was thinking of the exploits of Captain Moonlight.

This was the latest outrage. A band of men would go silently about their evil errands at night, to maim cattle, burn landlords' homes, even to dig a grave at the doorway so that the appalled owner would look into its mocking macabre black depths when he opened his door in the morning. These crimes were attributed to the mythical Captain Moonlight who was never visible, never in the same place twice, but who had instituted a reign of terror that must be brought to an end.

Mr. Forster was to urge the suspension of the law of Habeas Corpus so that suspected evil-doers could be thrown into prison without all the expensive and slow machinery of a trial. If he could convict the organisers of that villainous association, the Land League, he would have scored a real triumph. The whole of the English Parliament was on his side. The Land League was responsible for a conspiracy to impoverish landlords, and they must pay for their audacity.

Christmas went by and all that Katharine knew was that Charles was spending it at Avondale. He dared not leave Ireland in this state of crisis, and anyway his sisters Anna and Fanny begged him to stay and the servants were delighted that Master Charlie was home. He was there so little nowadays. Even his dogs had almost forgotten him.

Katharine herself tried to be gay for the sake of the children. Gerard was home from school, lording it over his sisters, and naughtily making fun of poor Miss Glennister behind her back. Aunt Ben had one of the young fir trees cut in her park, and brought into the tapestry room to be erected in a tub and decorated. Willie found, at the last minute, that he had urgent affairs in London. Was it simply a grander Christmas party, or a small intimate one with a female friend that kept him, Katharine wondered, and was enormously relieved to have him away.

Aunt Ben had made an exception of Christmas this year. Usually she liked to sleep through it. She was too old for festivities and left such foolish junketings to her servants. But dear Katharine was there with the children, and since it seemed that Willie intended to do nothing about them, she must. So candles were lighted on the tree, and there were gifts, and the younger house-maids were encouraged to romp with the children.

It was all gay enough, and Katharine hoped no one noticed her abstraction. She sat at the window watching the early dusk beginning to fall, and wondered incessantly what the new year would bring.

"Katharine," Aunt Ben called, "why are you looking out into the dark? Are you watching for someone?"

"No, Aunt Ben." (Only the person I can't expect to see, that tall straight figure with the high-held head . . .)

"Then come to the fire. There's only ghosts and goblins outdoors on Christmas Eve. I believe that's what you've been seeing. You look quite stary-eyed. Pour a little of the mulled wine, and let us wish ourselves a happy new year."

Katharine obeyed, and drank the wine, and smiled, and thought that it would be a miracle if her wish came true.

Willie came down on Sunday and she asked as casually as possible when the Land League trial was to take place.

"Soon, I daresay. Why do you want to know?"

"I was wondering when to expect Mr. Parnell back in England."

"Oh, that's hard to say. He may be clapped in jail. There are plenty who would dearly like to jail him on one pretext or another."

"But they couldn't!"

"My dear Kate, if Habeas Corpus is suspended they can do what they like."

"You don't seem to care!"

"Well, you seem to be doing a lot of worrying on Parnell's behalf," Willie said aggrievedly. "I wish you'd start doing some on mine. I've been troubled with gout on and off since Christmas."

"I expect you ate too much plumduff and drank too much port."

He glared at her angrily. He liked to have his indispositions taken seriously.

"You've got hard, Kate. I don't know what's happened to you."

"Don't you?"

72

"Oh, yes, blame me for changing your nature, of course. But you used to be sympathetic and kind. You've still got the same gentle face. It doesn't seem right. To look at you, no one could guess how hard you've got."

Katharine turned away rapidly to hide the tears in her eyes. Was it true that she was getting miserly with her sympathy, saving it all for one person? But where was Willie's, except for himself? He had over-indulged and now wanted to be petted. Because his foot hurt, he could not spare a thought for anyone else.

He ended by going back to London in a huff. It was very cold and had begun to blow a gale. After the children had gone to bed Miss Glennister excused herself, saying she had letters to write. The two women often spent the evening by the fire together, although Katharine found Miss Glennister dull company, and was always glad when she had gone upstairs.

But tonight the house seemed particularly lonely. It was probably because the wind was crying outside, and she kept thinking of the same gale blowing across the sea and battering at the poor dark miserable cottages and cabins in Ireland. She prayed that Charles was safely at Avondale, and not sheltering in one of the comfortless cottages himself. Would he be put in jail, as Willie had so blithely suggested? She could not bear the thought. His last letter had been written before Christmas. There hadn't been a word since. Where was he? Why didn't he write?

Ellen came in to ask if the mistress would like a hot drink before going upstairs. It was such a cold stormy night, a body froze going from one room to another.

"It's going to snow, I feel it in my bones. Then shall I just be getting you a wee drop of hot milk, ma'am—" She stopped abruptly as the front door bell rang. "Mercy, who can that be at this hour?"

Katharine started up. Was it Willie back in a more congenial frame of mind?

"Now, ma'am, don't you come out in the cold, I'll see to it."

But Katharine, possessed by uneasiness, followed her, and was standing just inside the hall when Ellen flung open the

73

door to reveal the tall figure with the first flakes of snow on his shoulders.

"Charles!" Katharine whispered.

She would never know how she stopped herself from running into his arms. Probably it was because Ellen, belatedly realising who the visitor was, had fallen on her knees and impulsively kissed his hand. It was Mr. Parnell, praise be to God. She had his picture hanging round her neck, and now there he was in front of her, escaped from all those courtrooms and trials that the bloody English had devised.

"Close the door, Ellen," Katharine heard herself saying calmly. "Mr. Parnell, what a surprise. Do come in to the fire. You must be frozen, travelling on such a night. You haven't crossed the Irish Channel?"

"I have indeed, and it isn't a thing I would care to repeat in this weather. May I trespass on your hospitality tonight, Mrs O'Shea?"

"But of course. Your room is always ready, as you know. Willie was here earlier but went back to town. And I was sitting alone by the fire wondering how the trial was going. They let you free?"

"You see me here."

"Yes, I do." Ellen was still gaping. Katharine said, "Ellen, tell Jane to light the fire in Mr. Parnell's room. And prepare a tray. Something hot."

Ellen bustled off and she drew him into the sitting room, closing the door, and, with a sigh, going into his arms.

"Oh, my love, you're safe. I've worried so."

He kissed her, holding her closely.

"Kate! Let me look at you. Are you a little thin?"

"It would be no wonder."

"But I was never in danger. You should have known that."

"I feel as if you're always in danger. And anyway jail would have been bad enough."

"But there was no likelihood of jail. There may be later. But not this time." He laughed. "Did you think a jury of my own people would convict me?"

"Then what happened?"

"The jury retired, and when they came back after a very

74

long time the clerk of the crown asked, 'Have you agreed to your verdict, gentlemen?' 'No,' said the foreman. The Judge then had to have a word. 'Is there any likelihood of your agreeing?' 'Not a bit, my lord. We are unanimous that we can't agree.'"

Katharine laughed helplessly. "You Irish! So what happened?"

"The Judge said that he couldn't force an agreement, and I was only grateful that I had time to catch the steamer. I had been willing the jury not to embark on their usual long discussion of politics and hold me up unnecessarily."

"But what did people say?"

"I didn't stay to listen. I only wanted to get back to you. Oh, they were jubilant, of course. I believe there were going to be bonfires lit on all the hills. We won't let the English forget this mistake." He sighed deeply. "I'm tired. It will be so good to have a rest. But am I to stay, Kate?"

"What else would you do?" she asked in reproach.

"You said Willie was not here. I was afraid he might not be. But I couldn't stay away. Just for tonight, Kate. Tomorrow I must be in the House. Forster is carrying out his threat to introduce a Bill suspending Habeas Corpus. We've got to fight it with every means we've got."

"But you look so tired. You need rest."

"Just tonight, Kate."

"Food, shelter, rest. You treat me like an innkeeper."

"You know me better than that."

She nodded, ashamed of her moment of pique. He had been away so long, he was to go so soon. Although he looked ready to drop, she was going to grudge every minute he spent in sleep.

As it happened he was not inclined to want to sleep either. When the servants had gone to bed, he told her to stay with him, by the fire.

She sat on the floor, her head against his knees. She felt his fingers in her hair as he began to talk.

Presently he was telling her everything. The winter rains in Ireland were very cold. They found their way through thatched roofs, through windows stuffed with bits of sacking and straw. The children who never minded running barefoot in summer were pinched and frozen. If they were

75

turned on to the roads with their evicted parents they were so cold, hungry and miserable they didn't even cry any longer. To dry up tears was the worst thing of all. There was the mother dragged to watch her son hanged. He was a skinny undersized lad of only sixteen, he had been found near the barracks with a loaded gun. When questioned he had been perky, cheeky, defiant. But on the gallows he had no defence left. He had gone into a kind of catalepsy of terror, and his watching mother had the horror of it written on her face for ever.

A grand ball had been given in Dublin Castle. There had been enough food to feed a regiment. Statistics showed that over a hundred had died that bitterly cold night in Dublin alone, of cold, malnutrition, and the attendant diseases, typhus, consumption, lung fever.

In the country people who had never locked a window or bolted a door now did both at nightfall, and were fearful to stir outdoors not only because of the military but because of the depredations of their own kith and kin who had lost all reason and nightly, by their forays, risked the gallows.

Yet there were the immense crowds who listened and hung on Mr. Parnell's words as he begged them not to throw away all that was being achieved, to have patience, to trust him to make a fair but peaceful settlement with the English. He hated the English, too, but he did not intend to slaughter them one by one, he would defeat them without bloodshed in their own Houses of Parliament in their own city . . .

He will stop soon, she thought. It's good for him to talk, but he will stop soon and kiss me again, and the servants have all gone to bed. It's as if we were alone in the house . . . Is this the night that neither of us is going to be sane?

The heat of the fire was making her cheeks and her body burn. She felt languorous and heavy limbed. As his fingers moved in her hair she trembled.

"Gladstone will have to do something with his Land Bill this session," the weary voice was saying. "If he doesn't I won't be responsible for my men. I'll have to make him, Kate. I'll have to use every ounce of my strength—and that —isn't as much—as it was . . ."

76

His hand had slid heavily off her head. She turned sharply. She thought he had collapsed. But he had only lost consciousness. He was sound asleep!

She had to throw off her languorous feelings and be practical. She was half-laughing, ruefully, as she lifted his long legs on to the couch and settled his head on a cushion. Even then his eyelids remained firmly closed.

Such a seduction scene, she thought, as she hurried upstairs to get rugs.

But her amusement and regret left her and she could only stand looking down at him tenderly and lovingly after she had covered him warmly against the cold night. His cheekbones were too sharp, with hollows beneath them. The bones showed in the fine rounded prominence of his temple. He had extraordinarily long dark lashes, like a woman's. She wanted to touch them. But his face, for all its pleasing shape, looked empty and extinguished with the dark eloquent eyes closed. It looked far away, remote, unreachable, as if infinitely more than the Irish Sea were between them. She found that she was shivering slightly, then realised it was only because the fire had gone down and the room was growing chilly.

She banked it up again, intending to wake and come down every hour or so to replenish it.

But in the end she slept, and opened her eyes only to find an excited Norah and Carmen peering into her face, willing her to wake.

"Mamma! What do you think? Mr. Parnell is asleep on the couch in the sitting room! In all his clothes! Miss Glennister is scandalised." Norah began giggling wildly and Carmen, her faithful imitator, immediately followed suit.

"But it would be more dreadful if he were in his nightshirt," Carmen said, and they were off on another wild attack of giggles.

"It's not dreadful at all," Katharine said, sitting up. "Mr. Parnell arrived late and was very tired and fell asleep by the fire, and I know all about it. Pass me my dressing gown, and then go down and tell Ellen to prepare a large nourishing breakfast."

"Why, is Mr. Parnell starving, too?" Norah asked.

"Of course he isn't, but in this cold weather we all need

77

to eat nourishing food. And Mr. Parnell has a train to catch so tell Ellen not to dawdle."

She dressed hastily and went downstairs to find Charles laughing merrily with the children.

He looked up when she came in and gave his peculiarly radiant smile.

"Good morning, Mrs. O'Shea. I had a capital night on your couch. I didn't stir until these two young ladies came in. I couldn't think for a minute where I was. You were exceedingly good to a wayfarer last night."

That last sentence was for the benefit of Miss Glennister who stood primly in the background, her eyes bright with suspicion. Bother her, now Willie will have to be told. But what was there to tell? She had given food and shelter to the Irish leader. Would it have been less reprehensible to turn him away?

"Come, children, off to your lessons," she said briskly. "Mr. Parnell, there is a train to Charing Cross at nine thirty-five. You have ample time for breakfast. I'll walk across the park with you on the way to my aunt. It's stopped snowing, thank goodness, but it's bitterly cold. I hope the House is adequately heated."

"I hope so, too, since we're assured of a very long sitting today. Perhaps you may come up to hear a little of it, Mrs. O'Shea. It will be interesting, I promise you. Mr. Biggar has some fireworks, and so have I. I can't be sure we'll get to bed tonight at all."

At least in the park, with the wind like ice on their faces, and a glitter of frost on the dun-coloured grass, they were alone.

"What am I to tell Willie?"

"Simply that I took him at his word and came down to my headquarters. Surely he isn't going to mind that?"

"I wouldn't tell him at all if it wasn't for Miss Glennister. But she will. The children will, too. It's nothing, Charles. Only that I don't want any silly servants' gossip to spoil our friendship. We'll tell what we have to, and be silent about what we don't."

"Sensible Kate." He seemed to be in fine spirits this morning. "Will you be up this afternoon?"

"If I can."

"If the debate looks like going on all night I'll slip out. I'm going to book a room at the Westminster Palace Hotel in the name of Mr. Preston. Will Mrs. Preston be good enough to come and enquire for her husband—say half an hour after she sees him leave the House?"

"Charles! Is this wise?"

"No, but nobody knows me there. It's safe enough. And I intend to see you for a little while alone, without either a suspicious governess, two charming but inquisitive children, an Irish cook who embarrassingly wears my picture round her neck, or any other odd person lurking round corners. Come, Katie. Who is to be sane today, you or I?"

She caught his hand, laughing.

"Both of us, but I expect I'll be there."

He kissed her under the leafless oak at the corner of the park where the path led to Aunt Ben's house. He said it was because she looked so captivating in that furry hood, like a bright-eyed squirrel. Then he strode away, lightly and briskly, and she stood a moment feeling the most perfect happiness. She wondered how to quench it in her glowing face before Aunt Ben's acute gaze rested on her. From now on she would grow secretive, devious, expert at lying, jealous of emotions expended on other people, absent-minded. People would begin to notice. Aunt Ben didn't matter so much. She was old and extraordinarily tolerant. But what about sharp-eyed Anna whom she saw most of her sisters? What about Miss Glennister and the servants? What about Willie?

She dismissed these problems airily as she walked towards Aunt Ben's house, the grass crackling beneath her feet, the trees bent by the harsh north wind. There would be ways to overcome all the difficulties. This afternoon she would see Charles again. Mrs. Preston would meet Mr. Preston. She skirted an icy puddle, climbed the steps to Aunt Ben's front door, opened it, and went in, calling good morning to the maid dusting the hall, and walking upstairs, her head high, carrying her happiness inside herself like a light.

CHAPTER 6

THE House was packed that afternoon. It had been rumoured that the Irish were going to make a lot of trouble over the Habeas Corpus bill, and this proved to be all too true.

Mr. Biggar, looking in the rudest of health, had embarked on one of his marathon speeches, ranging with relish from subject to subject, and with many Irish colloquialisms which the bored English members found incomprehensible. When he at last began to falter Mr. Healy sprang up to take his place. Mr. Healy who was very young, and an ardent follower of Mr. Parnell, had a caustic tongue and a breast full of overcharged emotions. But perhaps he was more bitter today because news had come that Michael Davitt had been arrested for violating conditions of his ticket-of-leave. Poor Mick was becoming a jailbird. The long term he had already served as a political prisoner in Dartmoor had not succeeded in teaching him caution.

This news had obviously upset Mr. Parnell, too, for when his turn came to speak, although he maintained his tantalising politeness and polished wit, there was an undercurrent of deep anger in his words. If this disgraceful Bill were to be passed, a man would have less freedom even than his friend Mr. Davitt had. There wouldn't even need to be a trumped up charge against him. He would be thrown into jail and perhaps six months later someone would have the courtesy to tell him his supposed offence. Yet the British were a nation who boasted of freedom. On any occasion when an audacious foreigner had jailed a British subject a war, no less, was started. Why should not the Irish start a war for the jailing of Michael Davitt?

So it went on and on, the tall pale-faced figure, slender, erect, his voice sometimes ringing with scorn, sometimes low with compassion, penetrating to every corner of the House.

Mr. Gladstone leaned back in his seat on the Front Bench,

apparently relaxed, his great nose jutting towards the ceiling, his keen gaze fixed on nothing in particular. Sir Charles Dilke fidgeted a little, he didn't care at all for Mr. Parnell, he thought he behaved like a foreigner, with his posed aloofness, and his undisguised hatred of the English. Mr. Chamberlain listened impassively, thoughtfully. Mr. Forster, whose Bill it was, was anxious. He had professed himself most reluctant to introduce such a Bill, but his anxiety to have it passed disproved his reluctance. The Irish members sat in a huddle on their benches, occasionally whispering to one another, or chuckling at a telling point. Everyone knew that they had no manners. If they got angry and began shouting each other down they could reduce the whole sitting to a shambles. It seemed likely that this would happen before this Bill was passed, if anyone had any energy left by then.

Katharine could see Willie sitting slightly apart from the rest of the Irish members, as if he would have liked to deny association with them. He was dressed in his usual dandyish manner which served to heighten the untidiness and strange profusion of styles worn by his colleagues. But he was listening intently to the debate and no doubt meant to take his own part in it when the opportunity came.

Katharine hadn't been sure at first that Charles had seen her enter. The Ladies' Gallery was crowded today, in spite of the inclement weather.

After a little while, however, Charles' eyes unmistakably met hers. There was no hesitation in the flow of his speech. He continued to relate England's centuries of misrule, caring little that all these things had been said a hundred times before. They could be said another hundred times, until the English were weary enough of the relentless voice to listen and agree, if only because of an overpowering desire to escape to the warmth of their firesides and food and rest.

At last Mr. Parnell sat down and William O'Brien, the Dublin journalist, sprang up to take his place. The debate was young, if debate it could be called when the Irish members intended to hold the floor, and keep the English sitting until their bones stiffened to the hard benches.

Mr. Parnell lifted his gaze to the Ladies' Gallery, touched

the handkerchief in his breast pocket, and quietly left the chamber.

Katharine waited an interminable half-hour before also getting up to leave. Willie did not seem to notice her departure. If he did he gave no sign.

It did not prove difficult to get a cab. Wrapped in her warmest cloak, and heavily veiled, she enquired at the desk of the Westminster Palace Hotel for her husband, Mr. Preston.

He was in the small sitting room on the first floor, the clerk said. He had come in only a few minutes ago, and asked that his wife go up when she arrived.

Dear Charles. He so carefully paved the way for her so that there was no embarrassment about their meeting.

He was sitting by the fire in the sitting room, and as luck had it, there was no one else there. They could ring for tea and have it uninterruptedly, while they talked and quietly enjoyed each other's company.

"Ah, Katie. I have many ideas of heaven. This is one of them."

"Is it going to be a long sitting?"

"Very long." He chuckled. "I'll make a wager that we're still there this time tomorrow, and perhaps the next day, too."

"You mean that no one will get any sleep?"

"Only what he can snatch by slipping away for an hour or two like this."

"Then you should be resting now."

"Which is precisely what I am doing. I have begun to think that I never rest unless I am with you."

"Oh no. You mustn't let that begin to happen, or I shall never stop worrying about you."

"I like to hear you say that, which I suppose makes me a very selfish man. Can you meet me here again tomorrow?"

She nodded. Only a snowstorm that made the roads impassable would keep her away.

"Bless you, my darling." His face looked extraordinarily alive, the excitement and tension of the drama in the House still possessing him.

"Do you mind an hotel like this? It isn't very grand, but it's safe. No one will look for me here."

"Then that's all that matters. Actually," her own eyes were bright with excitement, "I think this is enormous fun."

"So do I. But it isn't a game, Kate."

She refused to hear the sober note in his voice.

"Let's make it one. Then—"

"You'll forget that it's a little sordid, a little dangerous?"

"I didn't mean that."

He smiled at her tolerantly, as if she were Norah or Carmen.

"Very well, it's a game, my dearest. And you're perfectly right, as always, for I don't doubt it will turn into some sort of treasure hunt. We can't always come to the same hotel, or meet on the same railway station. But I can be very ingenious. Can you?"

"I've never tried. But of course I can be." She was laughing with eagerness. "I can do everything you can do except oppose Mr. Gladstone in public."

"You shall do that in private, and before long. And with the greatest success, if I know anything about it. We'll lose this present fight, there's no alternative to that. But we'll make it such a poor victory for the English that in very shame they'll do something. Well, that's for another day. Will you tell me when it's six o'clock, Kate? I must go back then."

They were quiet after that. Charles lay back in his chair, half dozing, and she was content to sit looking at his face in the firelight, imprinting it once more on her memory. Six o'clock was not far away. But there would be tomorrow.

That sitting of the House lasted a marathon forty-one hours before the Speaker intervened, announcing that he had resolved to stop all discussion on the Bill, and that it should be read forthwith. So, with considerable difficulty, and still protesting that it wrung his heart, Mr. Forster got his bill passed. Mr. Gladstone, not making any attempt to hide his relief, said that it was a welcome end to a session remarkable for the speeches of the Irish members, some of whom "rose to the level of mediocrity, but more often grovelled amidst mere trash in unbounded profusion".

Immediately, Mr. Forster jailed without trial hundreds of Land Leaguers. But the Land League remained and would do so unless its leaders were arrested. No one quite dared to arrest so powerful a man as Mr. Parnell was becoming. It was decided to wait, as he himself was waiting, to see what the effects of the new Land Bill would be.

Immediately after the House rose from that interminable sitting Charles had to go back to Ireland. He had managed to send a message to Katharine telling her he would be catching the night mail, could she be at Charing Cross to see him off?

She could, although it meant not being at home to say goodnight to Norah and Carmen. They were becoming used to Mamma being away a good deal. Carmen sometimes wept a little, but Norah scoffed at such weakness. Hadn't Papa said Mamma was in the country too much, and mustn't she go out to dinner parties and balls?

"But she isn't wearing her ball gown," Carmen sobbed. "She had on her green coat and skirt. She can't dance in that."

"She keeps a ball gown at Aunt Anna's," Norah said, which was true. Carmen was a baby and had no sense.

And Katharine, in her green coat and skirt, with a cloak over that, and her small velvet hat with a thick veil, walked up and down Charing Cross station waiting. Trains went in and out and people gathered and melted away. She was always left, a lonely figure pacing up and down. The railway porters looked at her curiously, she was well-dressed and obviously a lady. It was odd that she was there alone. They were quite relieved when at last she was joined by her husband, the tall handsome man with the neat brown beard.

He came striding on to the platform, his arms held out to her.

"Kate darling! I was quite unavoidably detained. Are you angry with me? Are you frozen?"

"Neither." She was so glad to see him, how could she feel any emotion but pleasure. "But you've missed the last train to Holyhead."

"I know. I shall have to stay in London until tomorrow."

"Come down to Eltham."

She said it unhesitatingly. Why should he not spend another night there? He couldn't go looking for lodgings at this hour, and in the cold.

"May I, Kate? What about Willie?"

"Willie would be furious if he knew you were without lodgings on such a cold night. Besides," she tucked her arm into his, laughing, "the porters are quite convinced I was waiting for my husband. Don't let's disappoint them."

They crept into the house long after midnight, going through the conservatory door. Katharine lit candles and went to the kitchen looking to see what food Ellen had left in the larder. She found soup which she heated, and a good-sized leg of cold lamb. She prepared the tray and carried it into the sitting room where Charles had coaxed the embers of the fire into a blaze with fresh wood and coal.

It was one more period of uninterrupted time together. Charles said that it too late to go to bed. He must be off at daylight. Anyway, time was too precious to waste in sleep. There were so many things he wanted to talk about. Would she listen? She was such a good listener, attentive and intelligent. Besides, if he didn't talk—She looked at him questioningly when he paused, and saw the flames deep in his eyes. Flames that were no reflection of the fire on the hearth.

"I don't know how much longer I can wait for you, Katie. Have you noticed that I never even kiss you now?"

"Yes," she said in a low voice. "I have noticed."

"I don't dare to. I must try to remain a gentleman, damn it all."

"Why?" Her voice was no more than a whisper.

"Yes, why?" he said harshly. "I suppose because we must keep some sort of hold on ourselves. And anyway I won't have any kind of snatched affair with one eye on the clock and the other on the door. We need time. Time, time, time. I won't have you lightly, you're too sweet, too beautiful. If you knew how I want to look at your body . . ."

She couldn't look at the strained face above her any more. She put her head in her hands and began to weep.

"Ah, now, my dearest!" His tenderness made the ache in her throat unbearable. She could not stop her tears for several moments, and when at last she did, he lifted her face, and kissed her wet cheeks without passion, but comfortingly, as he might a child's.

"Don't cry, Kate. It hurts me too much."

"I'm sorry."

"This was not such a good idea, missing my train. All the same, I'd like to be able to come again, late at night like this. Is it too dangerous? It would be wonderful if I could. Something to dream of all day."

"If you tap at the conservatory window—don't rouse the servants. I'll hear you. My bedroom is just over the conservatory."

" 'Unless you can die when the dream is past, Oh, never call it loving . . .' " he quoted dreamily. "Come, sit beside me, Kate. Rest a little until daylight."

He left the house before anyone had stirred, and she had the long lonely day to face, rings of sleeplessness round her eyes, her attention constantly wandering from Aunt Ben's or the children's demands.

"Was it a nice ball, Mamma?"

"Ball?"

"The one you were at last night. Norah said you were at a ball and that's why you couldn't say goodnight to us."

"Oh yes, my darlings. Only it wasn't a ball, it was just some people at dinner."

"Was Papa there?"

"No, not last night," said Katharine, seeing Miss Glennister's sharp attentive eyes on her. "He had other affairs. Grown-ups' business."

"It's a pity grown-ups have so much old business," Norah said. "Are you going to London tonight, Mamma?"

"No, I shall be home to say goodnight to you. I shall even read you a bedtime story if that pleases you."

"Oh, yes, dearest Mamma!"

Miss Glennister's face went a little pinched and sour. She was really not the nicest of young women, but she was a sad lonely creature, one must try to be kind to her. So long as she didn't slip into that trap that existed for sentimental unloved governesses and nursemaids, and develop an unhealthy and possessive love for someone else's children.

86

Willie came home on Sunday, as usual. He talked about the sitting in the House, but his mind was on other things. He thought he would pay a long overdue visit to his relations in Madrid. His gout had been troubling him and he would like to escape a part of the English winter. He scarcely bothered to ask her if she minded. Why should she mind, the cold way she treated him nowadays?

"I'll be back in a month or so." He winced as he moved his foot. "By the way, how's the old lady for a bit of cash?"

At first Willie had pretended reluctance about having his expenses subsidised by Aunt Ben. But now he had come to see it as his due. Wasn't she practically usurping ownership of his wife, tying her to the country whether he needed her or not?

Katharine promised to ask. She knew Aunt Ben would refuse her nothing. It would be easy enough to get Willie his money. And to have him away for a whole month . . . She was already forming the letter she would send off to Dublin that night.

But why had there been no news from Charles? She had waited for interminable days, fretting and worrying. She knew she would never get over this anxiety when he was away. She would walk about like a ghost watching for the postman, and when the longed-for letter came she would have to restrain herself from embracing the postman for bringing it.

At last the letter did come and it had a Paris postmark. Why was he in France? Katharine's heart leaped in dismay. She tore open the envelope and read rapidly,

> "Hotel Brighton,
> 218 Rue de Rivoli,
> 27th February, 1881.

My dear Mrs. O'Shea,

There was no letter for me from you at the usual address. I fear something may have gone wrong. I have been warned from Dublin that there is some plot afoot and that my arrest was intended for passages in my Clare speech, and that bail would be refused. I think, however, that they have now abandoned this intention, but will make sure before I return.

Yours, C.S.P."

The letter fluttered to the table, as she unfolded the one enclosed beginning:

"My dearest love,
  You cannot imagine how much you have occupied my thoughts all day and how very greatly the prospect of seeing you again comforts me. Can you meet me in London at nine p.m. tomorrow evening anywhere you say. I send one or two sprigs of heather I plucked for you at Avondale, and have carried in my pocket to France . . . I left Dublin hurriedly without a chance to let you know. But I think things will have calmed down by now. If not, I will have to make other plans. But I can't go away longer without seeing you . . ."

His reference to something going wrong meant that perhaps Willie had become suspicious. It was their constant fear. She had written, but he must have left for France, before her letter had arrived. His arrest! She had heard the talk about it, as everyone had, but she had thought it merely another threat of the Irish Secretary, Mr. Forster, who was never short of threats. To see the words in Charles' own writing filled her with terror. He had had to go to France to be out of the way. So it was really serious.

But he was coming back this evening. Was it into danger?

CHAPTER 7

SHE drove up to London late that afternoon, and left a message at the Keppel Street address that they always used in emergencies. She would be at Thomas's Hotel. He could call and ask for her there. She carried the heather he had sent her inside her glove for luck. She had a feeling that from now on they were going to need a great deal more luck than they had already had. She was burning with anger for Mr. Forster, Lord Cowper, and all their confederates. To imagine that a man like Mr. Parnell could be arrested! It would be the most disgraceful act yet of the British Government.

She was waiting restlessly and uneasily when he arrived.

He greeted her with a simple startling question: "Can you hide me, Kate?"

"*Hide* you!" She felt as if the words had been shouted, as if all the hotel staff had heard them. But there was no one within hearing. They stood together in the foyer, a well-dressed man and woman apparently exchanging polite greetings. She was on the verge of hysterical laughter.

"Are you having a joke?"

"Far from it, unfortunately. I've been warned privately to disappear for a few weeks. I should have stayed abroad. Instead I've come back. Am I mad?"

"Oh, Charles! Hopelessly. It's true that Willie's in Spain, but all the same to hide you—it would be impossible."

"That's not a word in my vocabulary."

"But with the children rushing everywhere, the servants —someone would talk."

"The servants mustn't know. Nor the children."

"You mean—hide you completely? For weeks?"

He nodded, watching her, waiting. He always looked thin and tired after an absence, but today he was much more than merely tired, he was disturbingly haggard.

"Have you been ill?" she asked sharply.

"I did have a chill. I stayed in bed a day or two in Paris. I visited Delia there. But she's just like my mother, she's on a hectic social round from morning till night. So I came home."

He said home. And what was she doing, being a coward?

"You need rest."

"Yes."

She looked round uneasily.

"We can't talk here."

"If you can't do it, Kate, there's nothing to talk about."

His voice was courteous, as always, but for the first time she heard its implacability. She remembered the things of which he was constantly accused, ruthlessness, cunning, a remorseless use of people to suit his own ends. Was he using *her* this way? Her eyes flashed with indignation.

"You must be able to find a much safer place, somewhere where no one knows you."

"Yes, I daresay I can. I'm sorry to have embarrassed you, Kate. We did call our meetings a game. I suppose I should have realised the point comes when they're no longer an amusing one. Well, I must be off."

He gave his grave bow and turned away.

"But where will you go?"

"Back to Paris, perhaps. I'll write."

She tried to detain him. "Charles, it would be utterly rash. You must see that. If you were found in my house, you would be ruined."

"Yes, my darling. You've convinced me of that. I was merely indulging in a dangerous daydream. Goodbye."

He was gone. She stood staring after him, unable to believe it. He had come and he had gone in the space of a few minutes, a few disastrous minutes in which she had failed him, completely,

Oh, she had been completely sensible, completely level-headed.

But who wanted to be those things? Who wanted to be left alone while the man one loved disappeared, became an outcast, perhaps lay ill and neglected somewhere.

He had looked ill, his face marked with fatigue. He had

90

come instinctively and intuitively to her for help and she had failed him.

But didn't he see how impractical, how dangerous, how impossible his scheme was?

Or had he known about the little boudoir off her room to which no one ever went but her? It was over the conservatory so even footsteps moving about would not be heard from below. If he were to rest in the daytime and she smuggled him food at night . . . Better still she could pretend to be feeling unwell and keep to her room, and have all her meals brought up. Ellen, having a large appetite herself, was supremely pleased when other people could be persuaded to eat well. There would be plenty of food to share, and, late at night, she could cook over the fire in her bedroom.

They had always longed for time together. In this way, they could have almost limitless time.

But she had refused him. She had let him go. She had made him all too well aware that their fascinating game had become too dangerous. Now he would believe that she had never regarded it as anything but a game.

The realisation appalled her. She rushed to the door, pushing it open in such haste that the doorman Thompson, another of her old friends, looked at her in surprise.

"Do you want a cab, Mrs. O'Shea?"

"The gentleman who just came out—there was something I forgot to tell him—which way did he go?"

"He's just this minute driven off in a cab. I didn't hear the address he gave. Perhaps he'll be back and I can give him a message for you, Mrs. O'Shea."

The cold settled into her heart.

"No, I'm afraid he won't be back. He wasn't staying here. Yes, get me a cab, Thompson. Ask the driver whether he's willing to go to Eltham."

The house was silent when she arrived. Too silent. Everyone had gone to bed except one of the maids, Jane, who was in the hall, turning down the gas.

"Is there anything you want, Ma'am?"

"Yes, light the fire in the downstairs sitting room. I drove all the way down and I'm frozen. I have some letters I want to write."

"Yes, ma'am. Would you like something hot to drink, ma'am?"

"No, nothing, thank you, Jane. Just light the fire and then go to bed."

"Unless you can die when the dream is past . . ." The words kept running through her head. *"Never call it loving . . ."*

She would like to be dying now, she thought. She knew that she would never sleep tonight. Even though Jane had left the fire burning brightly, she piled more coal on, and sat back to wait for the tormented hours to go by. Perhaps by morning she would be convinced again of her good sense. Now she could only think of Charles, cold, tired, roofless, friendless, and that there was no way for her to let him know how intensely she regretted her lack of courage.

He would still love her, she supposed, but not so much. And he would never ask her for anything again . . .

If only he had given her time to think.

But how did a man in imminent danger of arrest have time to spare for the social niceties?

Of course he had been selfish, unreasonable, audacious, expecting her, English to the core, to be a martyr for his miserable country, if necessary.

But he was worn out, he would no longer be thinking straight, he had come to her instinctively, so certain of a welcome and a refuge . . .

She got up restlessly, and lighting a candle, went upstairs and tiptoed along the passage to the children's bedroom. Standing shielding the light from their sleeping faces, she whispered: "I did it for you, my darlings. Do you care? Will it make you happier? Am I a good Mamma?"

By the fire again, she felt so desolate that the tears began to fall down her cheeks. She was crying, with her head in her hands, when the gentle tap came at the window.

Charles! Could it be?

She flew to pull back the curtains an inch. It was so dark, she could only see a hand, a tall form. But it was enough. She was through the conservatory and had the door flung open in seconds. Almost before he had time to tiptoe down the gravelled path and be ready for her welcome.

She drew him inside. His cheek was cold against hers. His arms crushed her.

"Katie, my love, how could I leave you like that?"

"I only refused to help you because of the children."

"And I would have thought less of you if you hadn't."

"But if you knew how I regretted it. You're cold. Come in by the fire."

"No, I mustn't stay. It was only that I couldn't bear to leave you in the middle of a quarrel."

"It wasn't a quarrel. And of course you're going to stay." She had drawn him into the sitting room and was taking off his overcoat. "Sit down and get warm. When did you last eat?"

"I don't remember. Let it be. I'll eat tomorrow. I've decided to go back to Delia in Paris."

"You're doing nothing of the kind," she said serenely. "I have everything planned. You shall have the little room off my bedroom. I'll keep the door locked in the daytime. Can you sleep by day? I'm afraid you'll have to, but at night it will be perfectly safe to sit by the fire in my room. I've decided to be something of an invalid for two or three weeks. I'll keep mostly to my room. Aunt Ben can manage without me temporarily. She knows I haven't had a rest for more than three years. And the children mustn't be allowed to worry me. It won't do them any harm either. But it might be as well if you had your meals during the night. No one else uses my bathroom. You can safely bath at night. We'll simply be turning night into day."

All he said was, "What an organiser you are. You've left me with nothing to say." But there were those flames burning deep in his eyes again, and suddenly she knew this decision she had made was as momentous in its way as the one she had made that day now nearly a year ago when she had gone to Palace Yard and demanded that he come out to speak to her.

At this moment, she had no fears, no regrets. She was only amazed at how quickly despair could turn to happiness.

"I intend to send you back to Ireland looking a new man."

"Your regime sounds so pleasant, I may not go at all."

She laughed happily. "Then let me show you your new quarters. Have you a bag?"

"I left it with the cabbie. He's waiting at the end of the lane. I wouldn't let him come too near and wake the house. I had to bribe him to wait to take me back to London."

"Then bribe him to go away. Quickly."

It was a game again, exciting, utterly irresistible. But more than a game . . . Making up the narrow bed in the little sitting room Katharine found her hands trembling. She had to keep active, shaking out lavender-smelling sheets and blankets, putting out towels, (she must be careful not to let them hang in the bathroom), arranging a table and chair by the window where Charles could work.

By the time he had come quietly upstairs the room was ready, and she had built up the fire in her own room so that they could sit there until they grew sleepy. For complete safety, she would turn the lock in her bedroom door. Presently she would make toast over the fire, and boil a kettle.

He came into the room, closing the door softly behind him. He stood looking round, and then asked to be forgiven, but he had never seen her room before and he had often imagined what it would be like.

He studied the photographs of her father, and of her children, Gerard, Norah and Carmen, on her bedside table. Then he looked at her nightgown and fleecy dressing gown laid across the bed. He picked up the dressing gown.

"Put this on, Katie."

In his quiet voice he made it seem such a reasonable request. Her heart began to race. "Now?"

"Yes, now."

He crossed over to her, and began to take the pins out of her hair.

"I've waited too long to see this down."

The loosened locks fell on her shoulders.

"And this."

His hand was on her breast, and suddenly she thought she would faint, her heart was racing so madly, and her breasts seemed to be starting out of their covering.

Amazingly, he was not trembling. His fingers, as he unbuttoned her bodice, were capable and sure. He was not going to fumble. He was going to undress her quickly and skilfully. She was not even going to feel naked, but perfectly right and natural.

"You must begin with my waistcoat buttons, Katie. I think they are possible for a woman to undo—though I have never proved that fact—until now." In between phrases his lips were on her hair, her forehead, her throat. He lifted the heavy mass of her hair and kissed the back of her neck. "This is one place—I have always wanted to kiss. And this." The hollow between her breasts was especially vulnerable. She again felt as if she must swoon, and whispered, "Let me lie down, Charles."

He almost carried her to the bed. When she lay in it he covered her and stood looking down at her, her spread hair, her face on the pillow.

"The light?" he said at last.

"Put it out. Just the firelight—and lock the door."

Her voice was slurred, as if she were a little drunk, or half-asleep. The firelight made shadows dance on the ceiling. The flames whispering, and the faint rustle of his clothes falling to the floor were merged. She closed her eyes, letting the tremors that ran up and down her body take complete possession of her. So this was adultery, she was thinking dizzily. No, this extraordinarily sweet waiting and anticipation was not that ugly word, it was love. Her adultery had taken place long ago with Willie, with a body she didn't love.

He had slid in beside her, and she was instantly intolerably aware of his body beside her.

"What are you thinking, Kate? Katie? My love, my dearest, my only one?"

"Only that—" Her voice trembled too much, and it didn't

95

matter for his mouth was on hers, dismissing her unnecessary words. Anyway, there were no words for what was happening. It could be pleasure for a woman, after all, she was thinking incredulously. Sweet, shattering, cataclysmic . . . She thought she was going to die of it . . .

CHAPTER 8

SHE was reluctant to disturb the dark head on the pillow beside her. He had slept so soundly, without stirring, as if this were his first deep sleep for weeks.

But there were movements downstairs and the grey light of a February dawn was showing in cracks behind the drawn curtains.

"Charles!"

At her first whisper he was awake. There was startled recognition in his eyes, then an instant alertness.

"I must go."

"Just into the next room. The bed's ready. Can you sleep again?"

He kissed her lingeringly.

"I want to stay awake and look at you. But if I must."

"You must. I'll have to unlock the door. The children may come up."

"Kate—"

She laid a finger on his lips. "Don't talk now. Tonight. I'll bring you some food shortly. Part of my invalid's breakfast."

She felt extraordinarily light-hearted. She had never felt less ill, but illness was not difficult to simulate, for her completely sleepless night had left her eyes shadowed and her face drawn. She was over thirty, and not so resilient about late nights. When she rang, and Jane came it was easy to pretend tiredness and headache.

"I haven't been feeling well lately, Jane. I've decided to keep to my room for a week or two."

"Oh, ma'am! Shall the doctor be sent for?"

"Certainly not. I said I was only tired. But I want a message taken to my aunt. I'll write it presently. And ask Ellen to bring up my breakfast."

"Yes, ma'am. What would you be wanting, ma'am? Something light?"

"No, Jane, there's nothing wrong with my appetite,"

Katharine said a little sharply. "I told you I was only tired. Completely fatigued. I don't want to see anybody. I intend to rest."

"What about Miss Norah and Miss Carmen, ma'am?"

"Not even them, Jane," Katharine sighed realistically, passing a weary hand over her brow. "Tell them Mamma is a little poorly. But she'll be better in a few days."

"Yes, ma'am." Jane bobbed, her simple face completely convinced. "I'm ever so sorry you're poorly. Shall I take the message to the Lodge?"

"Yes. After breakfast. And try to do the fire without bumping and banging. My head won't stand noise."

Ellen, bless her, believed in feeding an illness. The breakfast tray arrived laden with toast, honey, two boiled eggs, a plate of freshly baked muffins, and a large pot of tea.

Katharine enjoyed the sparkling fire, the wintry scene outside, the warmth of the bed, and above all the knowledge of who lay not ten feet away from her.

Immediately Jane had left the tray she got silently out of bed, locked her door, and then carried half the food and a steaming cup of tea into the next room.

"Drink it quickly, Charles. I must put the cup back on the tray."

She watched him drink it thirstily, and eat a slice of buttered toast.

"Can you manage now until this evening? I promise you a good meal then."

"I can manage. I'll sleep."

"So shall I."

Their eyes met in their new intimacy.

"How am I going to look ill?" she whispered. "I feel—"

"How do you feel, my darling?"

She put her finger to her lips. "I'll tell you tonight."

After all, the day went quickly, for she, too, slept. She woke as it was growing dusk to find Miss Glennister at her bedside.

"I'm sorry to disturb you, Mrs. O'Shea, but the children are upset. They think you're really ill."

"I've explained that I'm not ill. Only tired." Katharine peered at the thin permanently suspicious face of the governess. "Don't stand there in the dark, Miss Glennister. Light

98

the gas. And the children must understand that their Mamma can't always be at their beck and call no matter how much she loves them. Surely you're capable of making them realise that? I need a complete rest from everybody."

"I understand, Mrs. O'Shea. I thought you were doing too much, with so many late nights."

"That's none of your business, Miss Glennister. Just attend to the children."

And now I've offended her, and she has eyes like a hawk, Katharine thought, and surprisingly was not in the least worried. No worry was going to touch her in this blissful state of suspended time.

She rang for Jane and asked that the fire be replenished, and plenty of coal brought up as the weather was so cold, she would want to burn it all night. Also, Jane might bring up a kettle, and milk and sugar and tea, as this state of exhaustion left her feeling in constant need of nourishment. She might like to make tea during the night. No one was to be alarmed if they heard her walking about.

Jane, looking pop-eyed, enquired again if the doctor shouldn't be sent for. Old Mrs. Wood had asked the same question, and wanted to send her doctor.

"No, I've told you I don't need a doctor," Katharine said sharply. "All I need is solitude and quiet. My aunt will understand that."

"Oh, yes, she does, ma'am. She says you're not to hurry back. It was just cook and me wondering—"

"Then cook and you must stop wondering," Katharine said. "I appreciate your thoughtfulness, but just do as I say."

Jane still lingered. "We was wondering should the master be told."

"Certainly not. On no account. Anyway, by the time a letter reached him in Madrid I will be fully recovered. I won't have this fussing, Jane. I'm not in a state to tolerate it. Just obey your orders and tell Ellen to do the same."

It took a great deal of patience to wait until eleven o'clock when it was safe for them to move about. And until midnight before she dared go down to the larder, and load a tray with food.

Fortunately she had never scolded Ellen for keeping a

lavish table. One could always depend on finding cold cuts, remains of pies and puddings, fruit and the bread that was baked fresh each day.

They sat like children in front of the fire having a midnight feast. Even after only twenty-four hours he looked amazingly rested, his cheeks smooth, his eyes bright.

"You told me you would send me back to Ireland a new man, Kate."

"If I let you go at all."

"And if I will be able to tear myself away."

"I expect you will hear your country calling."

His face tightened and she wished she hadn't made that quip. She hadn't meant to be flippant.

"Will you believe me if I tell you I'm trying to shut my ears?" he asked.

"Yes, I believe you." (For now, she thought privately. For this evening and perhaps tomorrow.) "But let me warn you, you're mine now and I can be very possessive. I won't always behave well."

"Darling Kate, I will adore you when you are bad."

"You must know what I mean."

"Yes, I know. You're a brave and beautiful woman, and I now regard you as my wife." His voice had a low vehemence. "So I won't always behave well either. But we must do as well as we can." He held her hands tightly. "I want to tell you—what happened last night—I hadn't intended it when I proposed coming here."

"Oh, I wanted it to happen," she said, with honesty. "Now I suppose I'm an adulterous woman."

"Kate! *Never* say that!" His eyes blazed. "You're my wife, and never think anything else."

"That isn't what the world would think."

"The world won't know." He continued to look so angry, that she said challengingly, "Are you sorry, then?"

"Sorry! Presently I will show you how sorry I am."

She had picked up a knife from their supper plates. "I would kill you if you were."

"I believe you would. You're a very dangerous woman."

She began to laugh, her face merry in the firelight.

"What are we doing, loving or hating each other?"

"I know what I'm doing," he said soberly. "But you've

put me in front of everyone, Katie, even your children. How can I keep you happy?"

"Just by never stopping loving me."

"As easy as that?"

"You don't believe that would make me happy?"

"I think you would be superhuman if it did. Oh, my darling—" he held her in his arms, putting his head against her breast, "—if I could forget—" He stopped, and said, "Oh, my darling," again, and was silent.

"If you could forget all the goodbyes and separations?" She said. "Well, who knows whether there are to be any more. We have tonight, and tomorrow night and the next night. I do believe," she said, searching his face, "that you're a pessimist."

"Perhaps I am. But not tonight. As you say." He was feeling for the fastenings of her gown. "Can I see the fire-light shining on you? Will you be cold?"

"In spite of what you say—" Her voice was as fierce as the flames that beat on her bared skin, "—as long as you love me I will be happy."

The next day Anna came.

"Kate, what's this about you being ill? Does Willie know?"

"No, and you're not to tell him. I won't have him coming home because I've decided to be lazy for a week or two."

"It's not like you to be lazy." Anna's eyes had grown sharp in the last few years. She was very good-looking, very smart in her green velvet costume with the neatly fitted waist and flowing skirt. But she had a restless dissatisfied look. The kind of look Katharine supposed she herself must have had before meeting Charles, and even up until last night. Poor Anna, she thought, and all the other deluded nice women who thought that sex was to be endured, not enjoyed, who didn't know about making love with firelight playing warmly on one's body, who stiffened and closed their eyes when their husbands approached.

"Kate, what are you smiling about? You look like a cat full of cream."

"Was I smiling? I suppose I feel rather guilty lying here when I'm not really ill. But I was dreadfully tired. I haven't had a rest for longer than I can remember."

"Then why didn't you pack up and take the children to Brighton for some bracing sea air?"

"In February? Don't be ridiculous. I prefer to rest in my own bedroom. Did you come here to criticise me?"

"No, but I took the trouble to drive out from town when I heard you were ill. I must say you hardly look ill at all, and Ellen says you're eating much better than you do when you come downstairs."

"So you see there's no need to worry about me," Katharine said smoothly. "Ring the bell, and ask Ellen to send up tea. Must you hurry back to town?"

"Yes, I must. I have a dinner party tonight. John expects me to do more and more entertaining. I declare I'm the one who needs a rest. You're lucky Willie leaves you alone so much."

"Am I?"

"Well, you don't look too unhappy for a neglected wife," Anna said waspishly. "If you ask me, Willie's mad to be away at a time like this if he wants to make a name for himself. The Irish party is in a mess. Did you know that Mr. Parnell is to be arrested when he is found?"

"Why can't he be found?"

"Don't ask me. The man's wily as a fox. Anyway I thought he was your friend. Hasn't he told you where he was going to lie low?"

"Would he trust a woman with a secret like that!" Katharine said. "Anyway, I think the whole thing is scandalous. How can the Government put itself in such disrepute as to arrest one of its own members?"

"It *is* for sedition," Anna said. "I must say if I were the Prime Minister I would want to suppress someone like Parnell, too."

"I thought freedom of speech was one of our privileges."

"Oh Kate, now you're just being superior. You won't be drawn because Mr. Parnell is your friend. I do agree that he has a most romantic melancholy air. I wonder why he doesn't marry. He would do so much better with a wife, only she would have to be in sympathy with his cause otherwise she'd die of loneliness."

Dear Aunt Ben sent to enquire each day how Katharine was, and made Katharine weep a little when the baskets of fresh fruit, oranges and bananas and hothouse grapes kept arriving. She sent some of them down to the nursery, but kept a good supply for those midnight meals by the blazing fire.

By the end of a week Charles looked immensely better. He said he had slept so much he had quite overcome his tiredness. Now his brain was active again, and he was beginning to formulate new plans. Soon he would have to leave.

It was an idyll that could not have gone on for ever. They were lucky that it had gone on successfully at all. Katharine, by a supreme effort of will, hid her grief at the thought of the coming separation.

"Must you really go? Will it be safe?"

"I think so, Forster will have simmered down by now. There'll have been too much of an outcry for his liking."

"But won't this state of affairs happen again?"

"Very likely. Later it might be useful to be arrested. But not now. I have too much to do. Could you get me some writing materials, Kate? I must begin to work. I promise to be very quiet about it."

So the misty green and turbulent country across the sea came into her peaceful boudoir, and haunted their last evenings by the fire. It was the shadow behind them all the time, and she could not send it away or she would send half of this man she loved with it. It was reflected in his eyes all the time now, making his expression troubled, absent, sad.

Once he said, "It's a pity Mick Davitt couldn't have had as comfortable a prison as I have."

He was working on his principles for Home Rule. The new Land Act, he said, might be a better one than they had expected. He had reason to believe that Gladstone was growing sympathetic towards their cause. But even if it were a good Act, he had to oppose it, with his objective the much more important one of Home Rule. He could not afford to admit that anything the Government did was entirely good.

He also had reason to believe that Gladstone would welcome some form of negotiation with the Irish party, so long as it were kept secret.

"After I've gone I want you to call on him at Downing Street. Wait a few days and then send a note asking him to see you. Will you do that for me?"

"Supposing he refuses to see me?"

"That's a risk you will have to take—as you took one that day when you came to Palace Yard. Do you remember?" His eyes were twinkling and she had to smile.

"Mr. Gladstone is over seventy. One can hardly expect him to be so susceptible to a message from a strange woman."

"And let us hope that strange woman is not so susceptible to Mr. Gladstone."

"When do you want to go, Charles? And where?"

"If I speak the truth, I don't *want* to go at all. But I must. On Monday, I think. I shall take a train to Harwich and go to France. I can return to Dublin from there. It's much safer to be thought I was hiding in France than in England."

"But what a long journey!"

He stroked her hair. "It will give me time to get used to being alone again."

"Charles—another thing I had thought of—supposing I—supposing we were to have a child."

His fingers in her hair were still.

"I had thought of that, too."

She looked up fiercely.

"I should want to have it."

There was a long silence. Too long.

"Dear Katie. So should I."

All the things it would mean must have flashed through his head, disgrace, ruin, the sacrifice of his ambitions, the betrayal of his people.

"Don't worry about it," she cried swiftly. "I should manage."

He looked at her, his question unspoken.

"It would have to be Willie's, of course," she said calmly.

"There would only be one way to arrange that!"

"Yes. That's what I'm telling you."

He looked so outraged, so stricken, that she had to speak briskly, almost coldly.

"You make plenty of other sacrifices for your country. This would be just one more."

"But this is *you*, Kate. And you're mine."

He pulled her to him so savagely that she exclaimed in pain.

"It hasn't happened yet. It's only hypothetical. But this had to be said. And now, whether you like it or not," she struggled in his cruel grip, "I'm going to pray to have your child."

His hands slackened. She saw his tormented face.

"One has to be practical," she said.

But when the tears shone in his eyes, making them black with pain, she wavered and lost her aggressive self-control.

"I want something, too," she whispered.

"You have me."

"I share you with three million other people." She smoothed back his hair, seeing his high bony forehead, his beautiful brows. "We have so little time left. Let's be happy every minute of it. But Charles—"

"Yes, my darling?"

Her voice was low, stubborn. "I'll still hope for a baby."

He kissed her forehead. "Then so shall I."

The whole plan had been astonishingly successful. There was only one problem left, and that was how to get him safely away.

In the bitter cold just before dawn he stood in his overcoat and muffler, his bag in his hand.

"I'm off now."

They might have said goodbye a hundred times in the bitter early dawn, they behaved so casually, not even touching hands. It had been arranged that he should walk to the station and wait for a train. The important thing was to leave the house unobserved.

"I'll come down," she said.

"No, stay where you are, I can let myself out."

"And bump into a hundred things en route? I'll go first. For heaven's sake be careful not to make a noise."

The journey down the stairs was safely accomplished. In the sitting room Katharine thought it safe to light a candle to guide him through the conservatory.

"Are you sure you have enough clothes? Is your overcoat heavy enough?"

"I'll be fine. Just let me out."

The wind that blew in their faces when she opened the door leading into the garden was icy, the dawn a faint grey light over the lowering sky. It was dismal beyond words. Katharine was shivering violently. The candle in her hand had blown out.

If she had wanted to have a long sentimental farewell they would have frozen to death.

"Charles, take care."

"And you, Katie. Go and see Gladstone next week. Write and ask for an appointment."

"Yes."

"I've told you, you can always reach me at Morison's Hotel in Dublin." He pulled his muffler closer. "It's like the north pole. Don't catch cold."

"Nor you . . ." But he was gone, striding towards the gate, his long dark form melting into the grey of the winter.

The idyll was over.

CHAPTER 9

THE house came to life when the mistress was up and about again. To her distress, Katharine found Carmen peaky and thin. She had been only picking at her food, Miss Glennister said. She had really been very difficult and had had to be punished on two occasions.

"She thought you were going to die, Mamma," Norah said, and Carmen rushed to bury her face in Katharine's skirts.

"But what nonsense! I was only tired. I only wanted to be very quiet. Norah understands that. Why didn't you, my angel?"

She lifted the child's face, anguished and wet with tears. It was so young, and yet too old in its apprehension of grief. She could hardly bear to look at it, thinking of what she had done.

Aunt Ben was another matter. She said querulously that Mr. Meredith had had a cold, and she wouldn't allow him near her, sneezing his germs about. And she had gone driving and caught her servants doffing their caps to that woman who lived on the other side of the park.

"I've told them I'll dismiss them on the spot if I catch them doing that again. I remember the Peninsular War and Waterloo." She set her mouth grimly. "My dearest friend, Annie March, lost her husband at Waterloo, and I could name several others. It was a terrible time. And all caused by that mad Corsican who should have been shot rather than allowed to start a royal line." Her querulous eyes rested on Katharine. "Surely you know who I'm talking about?"

"Yes, the Empress Eugenie. I've seen her out driving occasionally."

"Empress indeed! She's nothing but an ambitious Spaniard. Widow of an upstart. He didn't even make any memorable history. I can forgive a man who makes history. He is entitled to foibles, eccentricities, what you will."

What was going on in her remarkably shrewd mind? The dim blue eyes looked at Katharine with nothing but peevishness.

"You don't find me in the best of tempers, I'm afraid. I've only been outdoors once this week, and I've had no one but the servants to talk to. Conversation with them only makes me feel that I or they are suffering from rapidly failing minds. I'm glad you're better, Katharine. Stand in a good light so that I can look at you. Anna tells me you were just being self-indulgent." Katharine waited nervously for the result of the long scrutiny. But Aunt Ben seemed satisfied with what she saw, for she said, "You look a bit delicate, I believe. Anna tells me you don't manage your husband well, letting him go off without you so much."

"But Willie and I find—" Katharine stopped, thinking angrily that Anna must mind her own business. "I won't have Anna discussing my marriage."

"Quite right. But ill health is a refuge that only weak-minded women take."

Katharine, about to deny indignantly such a suggestion, abruptly closed her mouth. Silence was wisest. Aunt Ben subjected her to another close scrutiny, as if something puzzled her. But, to Katharine's relief, she dismissed the matter by suggesting that they wrap up warmly and take a short walk on the terrace. Then perhaps Katharine would be kind enough to unravel her knitting which had got into a terrible muddle. If anyone were to ask for her opinion, Katharine had overtired herself by all that sudden intense interest in politics.

"It's supposed to be Willie, not you, who's the politician."

"That's true. But Willie and Mr. Parnell have decided that I might be useful as an intermediary between them and Mr. Gladstone. I've written to Mr. Gladstone asking if I may see him."

Aunt Ben gave her a long look.

"Well, that's something a bit different to winding wool for an old woman."

February turned into March. Snowdrops in the garden at Wonersh Lodge and one deep disappointment. There was to be no baby. And an answer had come from Mr. Gladstone at last.

Non-committal, it said simply that Mr. Gladstone would see Mrs. O'Shea at Downing Street on Wednesday afternoon at four o'clock.

A fire burned in the well-polished grate, its reflection flickering in the panelled walls. Mr. Gladstone stood in front of it. Katharine crossed the red turkey carpet to let him take her gloved hand. He bowed over it for a moment, then lifted his head to subject her to an intense scrutiny. She had dressed with the greatest care. She had had no new clothes for some time, but her dark green coat and skirt with its neatly fitting waist and fashionable bustle was still smart, and she wore her fur-trimmed cloak and small fur hat. It was a costume Charles had admired her in. He said it made her look exceptionally handsome, and Mr. Gladstone's assessment suggested that he had reached the same conclusion, for he smiled and his deepset penetrating eyes actually twinkled.

"How do you do, Mrs. O'Shea. Your letter intrigued me. I must confess I wondered what kind of a woman to expect."

She relaxed. The interview was going to be a success.

"I hope I don't disappoint you."

"It's the matter of your visit that may or may not disappoint me. Can you hold your tongue?"

"Indeed I can."

"Then you're a remarkable woman. Sit down. Over here by the fire." He watched her settle herself in one of the leather armchairs, then sat opposite her. "Now tell me what the Irish party means to you. I never saw anyone look more English than you do, if I may say so."

"But you must know that my husband is Irish, and the member for County Clare."

"Oh, aye." Mr. Gladstone leaned forward, never removing his disconcertingly sharp gaze from her face. He was like a fierce old eagle with his crest of white hair, his hooded eyes and his tremendous nose. "But it isn't your husband who sent you to me."

"Mr. Parnell asked me to come," she replied calmly. "He believes you have sympathy with his aims."

Mr. Gladstone grunted.

"He's an extraordinarily troublesome fellow. But he's right that we're all heartily sick of the Irish question. It will have to be settled one way or another. There must be some meeting point. Has he got one to suggest?"

Katharine took the papers from her bag.

"He's been working on his formula for Home Rule. He thought you might like to study his proposals at your leisure."

"He's a bit impatient, isn't he? We haven't got the Land Bill settled yet."

"He's looking beyond that."

Mr. Gladstone took the papers, muttering, "It takes time to roll this stone uphill. I've begun to think of Ireland as a great stone that's likely to roll back and crush any-one who tries to move it. Tell Mr. Parnell that the first thing he must do is stop his policy of obstruction. It's serv-ing no purpose except to make us all lose our tempers. A deplorable and undignified situation." He tossed the papers on to his desk. "Very well, I'll have a look at these when I get some time. I don't promise anything. This kind of dealing may get us nowhere. When are you seeing Parnell again?"

She could not stop herself saying, "Is the danger of his arrest over?"

The dark sunken eyes sparked beneath ferocious brows. Mr. Gladstone's fingers paused on the bell he had been going to ring.

"That will depend on the activities of your friend."

Not Mr. Parnell. Your friend.

"But—"

She was showing too much anxiety. His fierce expression relaxed subtly.

"We are not barbarians, Mrs. O'Shea." The bell pinged. A door behind them opened. Mr. Gladstone rose.

"Good day to you, Mrs. O'Shea."

She duly wrote a long letter reporting this interview and at the end of March, there was a reply postmarked Galway. "Can you meet me at Prior's Hotel in Bloomsbury at six p.m. or thereabouts on Thursday? Ask for Mr. Preston."

She had liked Mr. Preston, she thought radiantly. He had been delightful to her at the Westminster Palace Hotel on a previous occasion. She was impatient all day with Aunt Ben, the children, the train that was unbearably slow, the cabman who seemed unable to bring himself to give his horse the slightest flick of the whip.

Then she was too early, and Charles was late, and she had an hour to spend in a dismally dark and chilly lounge. She had taken pains with her appearance, and looked much too smart and fashionable to be in such a place. She pretended to read a magazine, and wondered how long Charles intended to be in England, would he be able to return with her to Wonersh Lodge, would she be able to bear it if he couldn't? Could they ever recapture the ecstasy of that stolen fortnight? This dismal place, with people giving her suspicious looks, was a most unlikely place for a lover-like mood.

Her apprehension proved correct, although it didn't seem as if Charles noticed the prevailing gloom. He was preoccupied, abstracted. He was delighted to see her, but still too near to whatever he had been doing in Ireland to throw off its memory.

"Katie, I had to see you. But I have only an hour."

"An hour!"

"I'm sorry, but it can't be helped. I've called a meeting which is likely to go on until the small hours, and first thing in the morning I'm off to Liverpool to speak to Irish workers there, and then back to Ireland. Don't look at me like that."

"How should I look?" she asked stiffly.

"At least as if you're pleased to see me. Even this was most difficult to arrange. I was travelling with Dillon and Kenny. I had to make an excuse to get rid of them."

Her face was rigid.

"This is the first time we have met since—"

"Do I need to be reminded?"

"I don't know."

"Kate! Kate! This is the way it is. If you hate it you must let me call a cab to take you home." Suddenly his eyes shone with tears. "But don't please!"

It might be wrong, it might be weak, but she knew she was never going to be able to resist him when he pleaded. She took his hand, saying warmly, "I haven't the least intention of doing such a sensible thing. Have you time for tea, at least—Mr. Preston?"

"If you will pour it for me—Mrs. Preston."

As quickly as that the coldness and disappointment had gone. When the waiter brought tea to a table in a quiet corner even the dark dreary lounge seemed cheerful.

"But you will be in London again soon?"

"Very soon. And when the debate on the Land Bill begins I will be here constantly."

"Is it safe for you now?"

"In the meantime. I'm going about quite openly. We all feel as if we're sitting on a powder barrel, but that has its stimulating moments, too. How did you get on with Gladstone?"

"I wrote and told you."

"I know, but I want to hear it from your own lips. Did you find him a very intimidating old gentleman?"

She smiled, thinking of that almost cosy chat by the fire.

"I'm sure he could be intimidating, but he wasn't to me."

"So Mrs. O'Shea can do what the Queen can't."

"What do you mean?"

"Tame the old eagle. You're a wonderful woman, Katharine."

Looking at her like that with his own special tenderness, he made this snatched meeting worthwhile after all. There were so many things she wanted to talk about, but in the end they said very little. They drank the tea, and she studied his face closely for signs of fatigue or ill-health, was fairly reassured by what she saw, and was quietly conscious of the extraordinary happiness of just being in his company, even discreetly, with a table between them and the eyes of strangers on them.

Then it was the end of April and Willie was home from Spain. He was leaving almost immediately for Ireland. The trouble about Parnell's arrest had blown over, but no one knew for how long. The man wasn't idle, and if his speeches weren't seditious they were dangerously near it. Willie would be seeing him, so if she had a message for him, she had better say what it was. Katharine looked at him sharply, guiltily.

"He wrote and told me you had seen Gladstone. You didn't tell me this."

"You have only been home an hour."

Willie acknowledged this impatiently.

"Well, tell me what happened."

"I took Mr. Gladstone Mr. Parnell's notes on Home Rule, and he agreed to study them when he had time."

"Surely he said more to you than that."

"Oh, yes, he asked me if I could hold my tongue."

"Which you can do very well," Willie said sourly. "I never knew a woman who could hold her tongue as you do. Norah and Carmen tell me that you've been ill. I never heard a word about that. Why wasn't I told?"

"It wasn't serious. I didn't want to worry you."

"If you go on behaving like this, the time will come when I won't be worrying even if you're at death's door. I don't know what's come over you. You were never a cold woman once. I'll wager old Gladstone wouldn't have thought you were."

Katharine's eyes flashed angrily.

"That was scarcely what would have been in his mind on a purely business visit."

"Don't be an innocent. It's in every man's mind, all the time, when the woman is young enough and good-looking. I wouldn't put it past being in Charlie Parnell's mind, either. I don't suppose the man's a monk."

"Let us talk of something else."

"Oh, very well, let us talk of the garden, the weather, your aged aunt, Gerard's school holidays, what we're having for dinner—anything that might distract me from thinking what a damned unsatisfactory wife I have. I tell you, Kate, I won't put up with this much longer. Don't you know that what you're doing is a cause for divorce. Refusal of conjugal rights. Don't wince. You're not as nice-minded as all that."

"Keep your voice down," Katharine pleaded.

"I don't care if the whole household hears," he shouted, growing dangerously red in the face. "I might get a little sympathy then."

"Then perhaps you had better divorce me."

He looked at her in outrage.

"Would you like me to do that? Is that what you're up to? Then I'm going to disappoint you. I'll never divorce you. You're mine, and that's all there is to it." His mouth began to droop. "Damn it, Kate, you don't hate me as much as all that?"

Her heart had been beating violently in mingled hope and fear. A divorce so that she and Charles could marry? But the scandal would ruin him. Apart from the cold disapproval in this country, the Catholic population in Ireland would hound him into obscurity, if not into his grave. No, it must never never be thought of.

She made herself touch Willie's arm in a gesture of friendliness.

"Of course I don't hate you. I'm very fond of you."

"Fond of me! Like a sister!"

"Leave it now, Willie. I haven't been well."

"You look in the pink, if a mere husband might be permitted to say so. Well, I've told you before I'm not coming crawling to you. I'm off to Dublin tonight, and I don't know when I'll be back."

April into May and May almost at an end. Carmen was still looking peaky, and since Aunt Ben was to have an old friend to stay Katherine decided to take the children for a short holiday to Brighton. She intended to go ahead of them and find a suitable place for them to stay. But before this could be done the telegram arrived from Dublin. *"Meet me at Vauxhall Bridge Station nine-thirty tonight."*

It had always been Charing Cross before. Did Charles think the porters may have been too observant of the lonely lady waiting for her husband so had made a new meeting place? If he had thought so, he scarcely took care to protect her from observation tonight, for she was still waiting when it was time for the lights in the waiting room to be put out.

The porter was apologetic.

"It's the rules, ma'am. But it's cheerful in the firelight. I'll put another shovel of coal on the fire. There's nothing in the rules about that." The replenished fire smouldered. The porter looked curiously at Katharine with her fur tippet and her fashionable hat. "Your party got delayed, ma'am?"

"Party?"

"The party you was waiting for, ma'am. Missed his train, perhaps?"

"Yes, I think he probably has. But he'll come."

And he did, almost before the fire had settled down to a good red glow. His tall form in the doorway made Katharine spring to her feet.

"Kate, why are you sitting in the dark? Are the railways so poor that they can't provide lights?"

"The rule is that lights are to be put out at midnight. So the porter tells me."

"It can't be that late!"

"Look at your watch."

He didn't believe her until he had pulled the watch from his pocket and consulted it by the light of the fire.

"Good heavens, how can you have patience with me?"

"I suppose I know you will always come."

"And so you wait. I would wait for you, too." He kissed her on the mouth, careless that the porter had come in, apparently to keep a watchful eye on the fire. "Are we getting a cab home?"

Her heart leaped.

"If there's one on the rank."

He had tucked her arm in his, leading her out of earshot of the too inquisitive porter.

"Then your husband isn't home?"

"He was, but he's gone over to Limerick to look at his estate. How long can you stay?"

"I must be in the House tomorrow."

She was determined to spoil nothing this time by disappointment or resentment.

"I had hoped you might stay in your room for a day or two."

"Not this time, my love. But soon. We might think of some other arrangement less dangerous."

"Then you must leave before dawn," Katharine said equably. "And dawn begins awfully early nowadays."

"If we can find a fast horse we'll have a full three hours."

"Yes." Katharine leaned her head on his shoulder.

"I believe I can see a sleepy cab driver over there."

Charles lifted his arm to hail the man. "Don't move your head, my darling. The fellow can see that you're my wife."

She hadn't dared to sleep for fear of oversleeping. But it gave her the greatest pleasure to hear his quiet breathing beside her and know that he was resting, however briefly. She felt calm, deeply happy, deeply satisfied. She would like to have a baby from this night. It would be a happy and perfect child, conceived in love and tenderness.

But dawn was getting near. A sudden thought came to her, and she slipped carefully out of bed, put on a wrap, and groped her way downstairs. The french doors in the downstairs sitting room led into the garden. As she opened them the scent of roses came to her. It was not yet light, but the setting moon shed its faint illumination over the garden. She tiptoed across the dew-wet grass to the rosebed, and saw the just opening white roses glimmering. She cut one with her manicure scissors and returned swiftly upstairs.

It was time for Charles to wake.

Lighting the lamp woke him instantly. He started up, at first not knowing where he was. Then he saw her bending over him, and a look of the greatest happiness came over his face.

"Katie," he said softly.

She held out the rose. "Look, it's just opening."

"White. Your rose."

"No, yours. I planted the bushes for you last year."

"And they've bloomed already! I count this the happiest augury."

"Yes, but now you must get up. It will be light in another half hour. The summer is all very well for roses, but it does have short nights. Where did you put your clothes?" She looked round and picked up his jacket lying over a chair. "This needs brushing and pressing. It will have to make do with a brushing. The next time you come to stay—properly, I mean—"

"As opposed to improperly?"

"When Willie's here," she said severely. "Then the servants can attend to all your clothes. You need a valet. What are these things in your pockets?"

116

"Take them out. I get all kinds of queer trophies thrust at me when I'm campaigning."

She spread the quaint collection on the table. There were religious medals, handkerchiefs embroidered with shamrocks, and other sundry strange objects.

"What's this?" Katharine asked, holding up an extremely dirty frayed bit of rope.

"That, I'm afraid, is a gruesome relic. It's supposed to be a bit of rope that hanged a martyr. And I believe there's another equally gruesome object there, a bullet that's gone through a man's heart. I imagine it's supposed to have gained some mystical power. Throw it away."

"And this?" She was looking at a shiny coloured stone.

"The children give me things. 'A quare bit of a stone' or 'a farden me mither give me'. Keep them for me Kate."

The room seemed suddenly to be filled with the faces and the thrusting hands of the people who pressed about him on his journeys. The dirty tangle-haired children eagerly giving him their small treasures, their parents donating their more sophisticated and horrible holy relics. Once again the dark hungry land had come into this peaceful English bedroom.

"They must love you," she said reluctantly.

He sat on the edge of the bed pulling on his trousers.

"They do. Too much. They're insatiable."

He came to stand by her. "You keep my sanity."

Her throat was aching.

"I hope I always can."

A bird twittered in the garden.

"You must hurry, Charles."

He was dressing rapidly. "Put the rose in my buttonhole with your own fingers. When are you going to Brighton?"

"On Saturday, but only to find rooms. I'll come back for the children."

"Perhaps I'll see you before then. I'll let you know."

The lamp was growing pale as the early daylight filtered through the windows. He bent his head to kiss her. His lips were gentle now, different from their hungry passion in the night.

"Bless you, my darling." He turned at the door to look at her with twinkling eyes. "When I'm thrown out of politics

I'll take up burglary. The most silent enterer and departer of houses in the country."

She laughed, although her eyes were wet.

He had left in such haste that he had forgotten the portmanteau he had brought with him. Katharine stared at it in dismay. Then she smiled. It would bring him back, perhaps sooner than he had intended.

She removed it to the bedroom at the back of the house where he slept when Willie was home, and put it in the wardrobe out of sight. The servants wouldn't see it there. Then at last she went back to bed, to sleep a little before the day began.

The next day she went to the Ladies' Gallery and sat there for two hours, but Charles did not appear. She could see several other members of the Irish party. But the House might have been empty when Charles was not there. She left, and carried out another plan, taking a cab to Hatton Gardens and going into a jeweller's shop which she chose for its reputable but inconspicuous appearance.

She wanted a signet ring for a gentleman. It was to have an inscription engraved on the inside. Could it be done quickly?

"If it is a simple inscription, by tomorrow, madam."

"Yes, it is a simple one. Just the letters K and C intertwined."

"Ah, yes. A nice sentiment." The jeweller was elderly, and appreciative of his well-dressed customer. "A charming gift for your husband."

"I hope he will think so." Katharine had a pleasant warm feeling in her heart. She loved all these anonymous people, hotel waiters, cab drivers, shopkeepers, who shared her secret. They cast their benevolent eyes on a happy couple. What did it matter if the rest of the world did not?

CHAPTER 10

JUST as Katharine entered the hotel on the Marine Parade at Brighton someone tapped her on the shoulder. She turned sharply to see a stranger wearing a white muffler well-wrapped round his throat and jaw. He had the ragged remains of a beard. He looked gaunt and quite unfamiliar. He was Charles.

In the first moment her surprise was greater than her pleasure.

"What have you *done* to yourself?"

"I cut off my beard in the train with my pocket scissors. Do I look unrecognisable?"

"You look horrible!" But she was beginning to laugh. "Oh, Charles! Did you know I was on that train?"

"You said you were coming down on Saturday so I watched all trains until you arrived, and then followed you here. Shall we register?"

"We?"

He wrapped the muffler disguisingly round his face, and marched to the desk, to ask for a room for Mr. and Mrs. Stewart. The manageress looked at him with deep suspicion. Katharine was trembling. They had been recognised already!

"I hope you're not suffering from an infectious disease, sir?"

"No, no, only a bad toothache."

"Oh, that's all right sir, I was afraid you might be catching." The woman smiled in the friendliest way and handed him a pen with which to sign the register. "I can recommend a dentist if you wish."

"That's very kind of you. But I have a little laudanum which I find very effective. Is this a room with a good outlook?"

"Over the sea, sir. I'm sure your wife will like it."

It was a very nice room with a flowered carpet and a

119

large double bed. Safely in it, Katharine collapsed with laughter.

"Really, Charles. That was the most audacious thing! And I haven't told anyone at home that I will be away all night."

"Send them a telegram. Say you find the sea air so bracing." He threw off his hat and coat and muffler. "Isn't this wonderful? Don't you enjoy being audacious?"

"Not with you looking like that. Oh, Charles, your beautiful beard. Where is it?"

"Decorating the Sussex hedgerows. Luckily I had a compartment to myself."

"Take a look at yourself in the mirror. You look like a tramp. You must go to a barber and get properly shaved."

He studied himself critically, fingering the stubbly whiskers.

"I'm afraid you're right. I'll go at once."

"No, not at once. I can bear the sight of you for a little while." She was beginning to realise the marvellous thing that had happened. They were to have a whole day and night together. But already she was grudging the time he must spend at the barber's.

"Look at the sea. It's even blue for us. And I have a gift for you."

"Then you must have known I was coming."

"No, it was only in my bag for the next time I saw you." She took out the box that held the ring. "See if it fits."

She watched him slip it on his little finger. Impatiently she made him take it off to look at the inscription inside it.

"It's our marriage lines," she whispered.

The flames burnt deep in his eyes.

"I'll wear it to the last day of my life."

They walked up and down the front, her arm tucked in his, quite openly, like any other married couple. They had tea in the Palm Court and even danced to the music of a piano and two fiddles. Katharine wished she had brought a prettier gown. Then they would have made a good-looking couple, she and her tall clean-shaven romantically pale partner.

"What will your friends say about your beard?"

"Let them say what they like."

"Charles, do they wonder where you disappear to?"

"They can mind their own business."

"But do they?"

He grinned.

"Oh, they have trouble in tracking me down sometimes."

"Then do they suspect anything? About us?"

He frowned slightly. "If you must know, they suspect I have a woman somewhere. But they don't know it's you."

"Have a woman somewhere" . . . The words jarred.

"Kate, have I said something to upset you?"

"No. No, of course not."

"You asked me those questions."

"And you answered them."

"Then why are you looking like that?"

She had always to tell him the truth.

"I was suddenly seeing us as the world would see us."

"And you didn't like what you saw?"

"Charles, don't speak in that cold voice."

"If you hate this, Kate, I'm not forcing you to stay. I'm not forcing you to do anything. I only thought that you were as happy as I was."

Was . . . "But I *am* happy!" she cried. "It's only that—it would be so wonderful—why isn't it complete?" Her words were clumsy, stumbling, inevitable, and she hated herself passionately for bringing that look of cold withdrawal to his face.

"I shouldn't have said that, Charles. After all, it's my fault. It's I who am married."

"We could go to Europe if you would leave your children."

"Now you are blaming my children, when you know very well you would never desert Ireland!"

"But, Kate!" He was intensely hurt. "I thought you were with me over Ireland."

"Sometimes I am. Sometimes I hate it, with all its misery, coming between us."

"Then let's leave it to its misery, and go off and save our own happiness."

"Then you would begin to hate me. I've told you that before. No, we're caught. Hopelessly."

"I never intended you to think this a trap that you're in."

He stood up. "Come, my love. I think we'd better go home."

"You mean not stay here?"

He fingered his chin. His voice was humorous but his eyes were not. "It seems I sacrificed my beard for nothing."

She was acutely distressed.

"Oh, no, don't go. We have our lovely room. I'm sorry for those things I said. Tell me you're sorry, too, and let's be happy again."

"Even in your cage?"

She stamped her foot. She was almost in tears.

"Don't *be* like that! I'm not in a cage. I'm with you, and I love you."

He sat down slowly. "Then perhaps a plush-lined cage? For it's no use protesting. It is one, and we're both in it, and I never saw it so clearly before."

But he didn't apologise for the things he had said. She remembered now that he had once told her, after an argument with some of his party members, that he could never keep his rabble together if he were not above the human weakness of apology.

Well, she was not above it. She was deeply warm-heartedly repentant for the mood that had come over her. She wished he would take her up to their room and kiss her and laugh, and let the strain ebb out of his face. Then it would be a good thing that these things had been said openly, and not merely brooded silently over.

But, although now friendly and courteous again, he remained a little aloof. Even in bed the shadow remained. She hadn't thought his love-making would ever be without tenderness. She went into his arms willingly, and he took her hungrily, passionately, but his eyes blazed almost as if he hated her already. Perhaps, for a little while, he did. She was getting too deeply into his life. She was even threatening his beloved country.

Two weeks later, after she had returned from her holiday at Brighton with the children, the package arrived at breakfast time. She opened it unthinkingly, then surreptitiously covered the photograph it contained with the wrap-

122

ping paper. The note that had fallen out she could not resist reading immediately.

It said simply, *"I had this taken wearing the ring you gave me."*

She realised that this was his apology for their quarrel. She wanted to go to her room immediately and study the photograph in solitude and cry for happiness.

But the children were at the table and demanding her attention. They had been discussing whether they might begin going to dancing classes.

"Do let us, Mamma."

"Let you what, darlings?"

"Go to Mademoiselle Brancone's," Norah said. "Mamma you're not listening."

"Yes, I am. Yes, I do think it might be a good idea. We'll discuss it with Papa on Sunday."

Miss Glennister's observant eyes were on the wrapping paper Katharine still clutched. She quietly put it on her lap, and went on, "Dancing lessons could take the place of drawing in the meantime, Miss Glennister. Or perhaps you think that could be fitted in, too. But I don't want the children's playtime cut short. I don't believe in long hours of study, especially in the summer."

The warm July sunshine and the scent of roses was drifting in the open window. Katharine felt the heat, even this early in the morning, a little trying. She hadn't felt very well just lately. With mingled fear and joy she thought she might be pregnant.

"Mamma, I said could we go to the village this morning?"

"This morning? Don't speak rudely like that, Norah."

"But you were not listening again! What are you *thinking* about?"

"I was thinking perhaps you ought to have piano lessons, too. If Papa thinks we can manage it."

Papa, indeed! If dancing and piano lessons were arranged, it would be Aunt Ben who paid for them. But the façade of a father who provided for his family must be kept up. As must the façade of a mother who constantly had her children's good at heart . . . Was she being a very bad mother, forgetful, inattentive, absent too frequently?

"Then may we, Mamma?"

Both children, in their white pinafores, with their hair tied with blue ribbons, their gingham skirts growing a little too short on their long legs (remember to go to Debenham & Freebody's and order more clothes for children, Katharine noted), stood impatiently in front of her.

"Why do you so particularly want to go to the village this morning?"

"Oh, Mamma! We'll have to tell her, Carmen, if she doesn't remember herself. It's your birthday tomorrow, Mamma. We want to buy our present."

Tears filled Katharine's eyes. She gathered the soft slender bodies into her arms.

"I'd *quite* forgotten! That shows how old I'm growing. Of course you may go to the village. If Miss Glennister doesn't mind accompanying you."

"Certainly, Mrs. O'Shea," said Miss Glennister primly. "Will you be going to London today?"

"Why do you want to know?"

"I noticed in the paper that there was to be a debate on the new Land Bill for Ireland." The young woman's voice was perfectly polite and expressionless.

"I was aware of that, Miss Glennister," Katharine answered smoothly. "It's a Bill that interests Captain O'Shea particularly. But I think it's too hot a day to go to the city. I intend spending the afternoon in the garden, and catching up with Mr. Parnell's mail. There's a great deal to send on to him."

She would like to have been in the House for this particular debate, but to tell the truth she really didn't feel up to it. She wanted to lie in the garden chair out of the sun and dream, and make plans. If there were to be a baby she must begin facing what had to be done . . .

Perhaps it would look like that aristocratic high-browed dark-eyed face in the photograph she studied so intently and lovingly in the privacy of her bedroom . . .

In another two weeks she was as certain about the baby as she could be without seeing a doctor. She was in a state of alternate joy and despair. In a very short time she would have to take some definite action, but at present she couldn't shake herself out of her dreamy indecision. She didn't once go to the House although she knew that Charles would be looking for her and wondering what kept her away. The progress of the Land Bill and Ireland's future were temporarily of little concern to her. She was going to bear the child of the man she loved. How could any other thought be in her head?

But one other thought had to be there, and that urgently. Willie.

She had quite coldly and ruthlessly to take steps not only to protect her child, but also her lover.

Humiliation, distaste, treachery, would have to be emotions she ignored. She had to go to bed with Willie as soon as possible. Her purpose was dedicated. Guilt scarcely came into it.

The event finally happened very differently from the way she had intended.

Willie burst into the house one afternoon and scarcely listening to her exclamation of surprise that it was not Sunday, he made his way to the stairs.

"I know very well it's not Sunday. Are you alone?"

"Except for the children and the servants. Why? Who did you expect to find here?"

"I'll soon tell you."

He went leaping up the stairs, leaving her to follow more slowly, even then conscious that she must avoid hurry or agitation for the sake of the child she carried.

Very red in the face, his hair dishevelled, not at all the picture of sartorial excellence that he usually liked to be, Willie moved swiftly about her bedroom. He opened wardrobes, and even looked under the bed.

"Willie, what *is* this?" she asked incredulously. "Are you expecting to find a man under my bed?"

Not answering her, he left the room and went along the passage to the back bedroom which he himself had suggested should be put to the use of Mr. Parnell.

Katherine's heart stopped. She was suddenly remembering the portmanteau Charles had left after his last visit. It was still there. He had forgotten to come for it.

And that was precisely what Willie was looking for. He dragged it out of the wardrobe and said with angry satisfaction, "So it is true."

"*What* is true? I wish you would pay me the courtesy of telling me why you are behaving like a bull in a china shop."

Willie kicked the portmanteau viciously, then looked at her, breathing heavily.

"It's all over London that you and Parnell are seeing each other frequently. As usual the husband is the last to hear. I find I'm a laughing stock. A cuckold! What a damnable thing to do to me!"

Katharine heard her own voice speaking with a miraculous icy calm.

"Willie, what malicious nonsense is this?"

"And this isn't Parnell's bag? Why, his own initials are on it. Can't you read? Are you blind as well as untruthful?"

"I know it's Mr. Parnell's bag. He left it here for convenience, just as his mail comes here. And if you forget that the whole thing was your suggestion, then there must be something very much wrong with your memory."

"And the bag walked here alone?" said Willie, heavily sarcastic.

"Of course it did not. Mr. Parnell left it after calling one day—for his mail, and to see if you were at home."

"And was very glad I was not, so that he could stay all night."

"Who says this?"

"I don't need to tell you who says it. Isn't it true? What about the morning the children found him sleeping on the couch? Are you going to deny that?"

Miss Glennister, Katharine thought. She had always suspected the young woman had sly ways, and a foolish admiration for Willie. Probably she was in love with him. Probably she had been looking for something concrete, like the portmanteau, to report to him. She must have found it when Katharine was at Brighton.

"No, I'm not going to be so stupid as to deny something that actually happened," Katharine said calmly. "It's perfectly true that Mr. Parnell spent a night on the couch. He had crossed from Ireland in a gale and was exhausted. It was just after the Land League trial. He fell asleep on the couch so I covered him up. What would you have liked me to do? Turn him outdoors?"

"And you swear this was the only time he was here?"

"No, I don't swear to any such thing. He has called on several occasions to go through his mail and to discuss my visit to Mr. Gladstone. While you were in Spain I suppose he called three or four times. He did expect to find you on some occasions. I'm afraid he's beginning to think your interest in politics is rather superficial."

Willie began to splutter with rage.

"He dares to criticise me while he makes love to my wife!"

"Willie!"

Katharine's voice was so angry that he had the grace to look a little uncertain.

"Well, doesn't he?"

"I refuse to talk to you in this mood. You're determined to quarrel. Question the servants if you don't mind asking them to spy on your wife. Question the children."

"I have," said Willie, unabashed. "Norah says you're never at home."

Katharine was white with anger.

"I don't believe she says that at all."

"She says you go to London a great deal and come home late at night."

"A great deal? Perhaps twice a week. Wasn't it you who told me I mustn't stagnate in the country?"

"What do you do in London?"

"I go to Anna's, or to the Hatherleys'. Occasionally I go to the Ladies' Gallery of the House, as you very well know. Willie, what is this? I won't be cross-examined."

"Well, word's got around that Parnell has an illicit friendship with a lady and the name mentioned, God forgive you, is yours."

"We have a friendship," said Kate with dignity. "I have the greatest admiration and liking for Mr. Parnell. But," her voice was full of distaste, "I don't like the word illicit. I think you will have to apologise for that."

"Do you know what they're calling you? Kitty O'Shea. How do you think I like that, my wife's name bandied about like a music hall strumpet?"

Kitty O'Shea. A tremor of distaste and apprehension went over her.

"Who calls me this?"

"How do I know where it started? Among the Irish party, no doubt. They're not all loyal followers of Parnell. Some of them call him a damned Protestant. But I'm not interested in his religion. I'm only interested in what he's doing to my wife."

Willie gave the portmanteau another vicious kick.

"That thing there. Evidence, if ever I saw it. Making me a cuckold. I'm going to call him out for it."

Katharine's hand went to her throat.

"You couldn't do anything so crazy!"

"Couldn't I, indeed?" Willie saw her flash of fear and was instantly gleefully sadistic. "My old friend, The O'Gorman Mahon, will back me up in this."

"That braggart," Katharine said contemptuously. "So that's all you're doing. Trying to emulate him."

"No, I am not!" Willie shouted. Her contempt had been a mistake. Now, whether he had meant his picturesque threat or not, he intended to carry it out. She saw that by the lowering dogged look that came into his face.

"Willie, please don't be so foolish. You won't only ruin Mr. Parnell's career, but your own, too."

"Who cares about my career? You? Of course you don't. Not the faintest iota. As for your precious Mr. Parnell— let him get out of this scandal if he can."

Kitty O'Shea, Kitty O'Shea . . . Faint and exhausted after Willie's departure, she lay on her bed and in a half-doze the ribald words seemed to be shouted at her. Kitty O'Shea. A name, as Willie had said, that might belong to a music-hall performer free with her favours. What wicked malicious person had thought it up? Someone in Charles' own party? There had been that day when he was afraid they had been seen as they went into the Cannon Street hotel. He had admitted himself that they suspected he had "a woman somewhere".

What irreparable damage would this threat of Willie's do to him? Almost all of his party were Catholics and under the thumb of their priests, and bishops. Also, apart from religious intolerance, the party, as any political one was, must be full of jealousies and ambition. How many would be glad to see Charles Stewart Parnell topple from his high place? How quickly would they forget what he was doing and would do for their country, more than any other man for a half century or perhaps more than any other man at all.

Ireland. The country that loved martyrs.

Katharine sat up vigorously. Charles Stewart Parnell was not going to take his place in that long tortured line. Not if she could do anything on earth to stop it.

And the first thing to do was to dismiss Miss Glennister with her sly tittle tattle.

"But, Mamma, why must Miss Glennister go?" Norah asked. Carmen, with her gentle heart, had been distressed, but Norah was only deeply interested. It appeared that she had not liked Miss Glennister much either.

"I want to find a more suitable person, my darling." (Who would come to a notorious household?)

"Why isn't she suitable, Mamma?"

"She cried," whispered Carmen.

"Why did you put on your best dress to dismiss her?" Norah asked.

"It isn't my best dress."

"Well, I like it best. And your hat with the ostrich feather. Are you going to London?"

"Yes, but I won't be away very long. Be good girls, and go to bed when Miss Glennister tells you."

"But she'll be packing."

"Since she isn't leaving for a week, I hardly think so."

"Mamma, you do look beautiful. Are you going to see Papa?"

"That's exactly what I am going to do, as it happens."

"Are you going to tell him about Miss Glennister?" Norah tossed her curls. "He won't mind because he doesn't like her."

"He does so," said Carmen.

"No, he doesn't. I saw him pinch her last Sunday on the way to church."

Katharine had not been to Willie's rooms since the night they had dined with Mr. Chamberlain. She was afraid she might find him out, and if so intended to stay until he returned. But he was in. He was even ironically pleased to see her, and looking so well, too. She had evidently taken

129

trouble with her appearance, which was considerate of her since she was only visiting her husband.

"Willie, I've come to persuade you not to be so hasty. When you left, I really thought you intended to carry out that crazy threat of a duel."

"But I do intend to. I've just finished writing a letter to Parnell. Do you want to see it?"

He held it out, and she took it from him and read it unbelievingly.

"Sir,
Will you be so kind as to be at Lille, or at any other town in the north of France which may suit your convenience on Saturday morning, 10th instant. Please let me know by one p.m. today so that I may be able to inform you as to the sign of the inn at which I should stay. I want your answer in order to lose no time in arranging for a friend to accompany me."

Katharine made a movement to tear the sheet of paper up, but he snatched it from her. "If you do that, I'll only write another."

"Willie, you can't do this!"

"Why not?"

"Because it would be a terrible mistake. Are you going to make not only yourself and me and Mr. Parnell, but the whole Irish party a laughing stock?"

"To hell with the Irish party. I'm only interested in my rights. What's mine is mine, and that refers to you."

"Does it?" said Katharine slowly. "Perhaps it also refers to Aunt Ben's money, and the house she so kindly bought for your family. What are you going to do without those things? Support us on your earnings?"

His face had gone a dark red.

"That about fixes it, Kate. This letter goes."

She knew she had gone too far. It was only Willie who made her lose her temper like this. He always had done. She had come meaning to plead and humble herself to him, and instead had insulted him.

"Oh, post your silly letter," she cried, tears of rage filling her eyes. "Indulge in your crazy melodrama. But don't expect ever to set foot in my house again. And it is mine, remember."

She had no idea where Charles was staying. She drove to the Keppel Street hotel to make enquiries, but got such an insolent suggestive look from the man behind the desk that she did not dare go elsewhere. Her very anxiety for his welfare was going to do him harm. He was not in the House of Commons, either. She could do nothing but go home and face a sleepless night.

The scent of roses drifted through her open window, and for the first time since this dreadful comedy had begun she thought of her unborn baby. God protect it, she thought despairingly.

There was no news at all for two days. Forty-eight endless hours. She read to Aunt Ben in the mornings, apparently making sense, for the old lady made no complaint. She gave the servants orders, talked to the children and tucked them up at night, attended to correspondence, paced up and down the garden until it was too dark to see, and waited. She was both hopeful and fearful that Charles would come.

It was Willie who came at last, accompanied by that great white-bearded dissolute old man, The O'Gorman Mahon.

"The fellow's a coward," Willie flung out at Katharine.

"Why?" She scarcely dared to ask.

"He's ignored my letter. I've sent him another."

"Perhaps he isn't in England."

"Oh, yes, he is, I've made enquiries. He's been in Liverpool and now is back in London. Mahon saw him. I've written telling him I find he hasn't gone abroad as I requested."

"But neither have you," said Katharine, as reasonably as possible.

"Don't be a fool. Am I going to cool my heels in France waiting for someone who doesn't come?"

The O'Gorman Mahon, whose twinkling impertinent black eyes had never left Katharine, suddenly gave a roar of laughter.

"I'm thinking you took my advice too seriously, Mrs. O'Shea."

"What advice?"

"I told you to be kind to Parnell, but I didn't expect you to take him quite so much to your heart. Not that I'm en-

131

tirely blaming the poor fellow if you look at him with those fine sparkling eyes that would melt an iceberg."

"May I give you some advice, Mr. Mahon?"

"By all means. I'll be glad to hear it."

"Just don't step over the threshold of my house. It is mine, as my husband may possibly have told you."

Willie went white with rage, but The O'Gorman Mahon threw back his great shaggy head and gave his tempestuous roar of laughter.

"Well, Willie, me boy, we'd better adjourn to the nearest public house and drown our sorrows."

Much later Willie came back alone. He was a little drunk and had lost a lot of his bravado.

"You're cruel to me, Kate. Cuckolding me, and showing me up in front of my friends."

If she had not had to fight so fiercely for Charles she might have relented a little. She didn't dare to. She asked coldly if he meant to go on with his intention to fight a duel.

"If Parnell is man enough to face me. But he's not. He's gone into hiding, the coward."

"Perhaps he is just treating your threats with the contempt they deserve."

"The story will get around. It won't do him any good."

"Nor you."

Willie looked at her with bleary incredulous eyes.

"I believe you think you're the only one who is lily white."

The next development was entirely unexpected. Anna arrived. She had driven down from London and she was very excited, anticipating a drama.

"Kate, what on earth have you and Willie been up to. Charles Parnell came to my house in a dreadful state. He says Willie is making the most absurd threats."

Willie started up. "Why hasn't the fellow answered her letter? Did he tell you that?"

"He says he only got it today. That's why he hadn't answered it."

"Of course," Katharine cried in relief. "You know how he is with mail, Willie. That's why he had most of his directed here. He never opens letters."

"This one was marked urgent and important. I don't see how he could have missed it."

"Well, he obviously did. He says there's some misunderstanding about a portmanteau he left here, and that you want to fight a duel. Really, I don't understand." Anna's wide shocked eyes went from Katharine to Willie. "It can't be because—"

"No, it's not," Katharine said harshly. "Willie is only absurdly suspicious because he found the portmanteau. He thinks Mr. Parnell has been coming here frequently in his absence. He's quite wrong, although I do see him occasionally. As you very well know, Anna."

"Did Parnell tell you to come as a mediator or something?" Willie asked Anna scathingly.

"He didn't ask me to come at all. My own curiosity brought me. Really, Willie! The notion is fantastic. Can't you talk him out of it, Kate?"

Katharine sat down wearily. "You try, Anna."

Anna was still trying when Jane came in breathlessly, sensing excitement.

"Mr. Parnell is here, ma'am. And before Katharine could ask that he be shown in, he was there himself, in the doorway, his grave gaze going from Katharine to Willie. He was not in the dreadful state Anna had described. She must have exaggerated as usual, for he stood there completely self-possessed, instantly dominating the room. In a quiet voice he apologised for his unexpected arrival, but this challenge of Captain O'Shea's, which he regarded as quite preposterous, had better be settled as quickly as possible.

"I must be back for a division which should take place about ten," he said. "I'm sure you'll permit this, Captain O'Shea, before risking my life." His voice was quietly ironic, and Willie lifted his chin belligerently. "I'm quite prepared to go abroad and give you satisfaction at any time you like to fix after tomorrow. I simply can't walk out of the House at this stage of the debate. But it's anticipated it will be finished by tomorrow evening. And, if I may add, I'd be glad of your attendance at the division this evening. We need all the votes we can get."

"You can't get away with that, trying to cloud the issue with politics." The drink Willie had taken had left him baffled and uncertain. It had been all very well to bluster and rage in private, but now faced with his opponent, and his leader, this cool polished man with his unshakable self-possession, he seemed a little surprised at his own temerity. "I don't care a damn for politics at this moment. I only care about my wife."

"If you cared for her, I don't think you'd subject her to this distress. Mrs. O'Shea, how can I tell you how sorry I am? This is all due to my carelessness in leaving my portmanteau behind. I hadn't even missed it. It only contains papers I haven't needed to refer to. But I'll remove it at once if that will undo some of the damage."

"You can't deny this," Willie insisted. "It's all over town that you're seeing my wife. The portmanteau's only final proof."

"Willie, Willie!" Katharine begged.

Charles said in his controlled voice, "I'm sorry it's all over town, but I do acknowledge that it's true. I have been seeing Mrs. O'Shea and I hope to see her again frequently. We must have a medium of communication with the Government, and as you know, she kindly undertook this office. Her first interview with Gladstone was highly successful. Shortly I want to brief her on matters she must discuss with him in a second interview. I trust—if we both survive the duel, of course," his eyes flickered sardonically, "that you will have no objection to my continuing to see her, Captain O'Shea. Not at Eltham if you prefer it, but at least at meeting places in London. If we're seen and our meetings misunderstood, then can't you look on it as a sacrifice you make for your country?"

"A bloody sacrifice!" Willie exclaimed incredulously.

A look of cold calculated ruthlessness, that gave Katharine a twinge of fear, came to Charles' face.

"I'm not interested in anyone in my party who isn't capable of sacrifice."

"But my own wife! You want me to believe that all this talk's got about because you're doing nothing but talking politics to her!" His baffled eyes stared at the cold implacable face opposite him. "I almost do, God forgive me," he said. "You're a cold devil, Charlie Parnell, and that's the truth."

"I have a job to do."

'You make it sound like a religion!'"

"Perhaps it is. Perhaps it is." Suddenly he looked intensely weary. "May I sit down, Mrs. O'Shea?"

"Oh, do, please. Willie—

Anna interrupted by saying forcibly, "Well, I do think you two men are the limit, using Kate like this. Running errands for the Irish party, pulled this way and that. If this is politics, thank goodness my husband isn't in them."

Katharine poured some brandy into a glass and gave it to Charles. Her hand was trembling. She had a moment, with her back to the others, to give him a quick anxious loving look. There was an answering gleam in his eyes. But he suddenly looked so gaunt and strained as if his last ounce of energy had gone into carrying off this scene successfully.

However, when he had swallowed the brandy he was able to say with a flash of humour, "I long ago decided to give my life to Ireland, but I hadn't exactly visualised doing it in this way, being run through with a sword on a beach in France." He put down his glass, and leaned forward with urgent seriousness.

"Can we keep this little matter between these four walls? If we go on with it, it won't only be mine or your death, Captain O'Shea, but the death of the present Irish party. And that would be a great pity. We've gone a long way. We've got a long way still to go."

"For goodness sake, shake hands," Anna implored. "You're both behaving like schoolboys."

"Please, Willie," whispered Katherine, her hand on his shoulder.

Willie looked at her, his eyes beginning to smoulder. Just for a moment she thought she was going to faint. She knew what that look meant. A wave of bitter resentment swept over her. Why couldn't Charles have stood up and shouted that she was his lover, and they were prepared to tell the whole world? But no, Ireland must be saved, that dark old hag who was insatiable in her demand for sacrifices.

So Katharine must go to bed with her husband tonight, and give the Old Woman another sacrifice.

"But don't expect to be welcomed here any more," Willie was saying. "Keep your assignations in another place. And for heaven's sake, don't get talked about. I've been made enough of a fool as it is."

Then, as always, Katharine's resentment changed to relief and love and heartbreak. For Charles, standing up and holding out his hand to her, for he must leave, had an expression of such tormented sadness that she knew he had been aware of all her thoughts, and that he sympathised intensely with them and could do nothing at all about them.

At least she was spared the humiliating necessity of seducing Willie into making love to her, for the agonising afternoon had left him with only one overwhelming desire, to prove to himself and to her without doubt that she was still his wife.

Afterwards, when he lay heavily asleep, she crept out of bed and went to the bathroom feeling so sick that she could scarcely hold her head up.

But it was done, and now she would allow nothing to spoil her pleasure in looking forward to her baby. She could be ruthless, too.

Only one thought nagged at her. If Charles had known about the baby, would he have behaved differently?

She was glad he hadn't been put to such an agonising decision.

Kitty O'Shea! The words echoed in her ringing head. She stared at her haggard face in the mirror. Kitty O'Shea, adulteress!

CHAPTER 11

THEY had left the hansom cab on the corner by the Mortlake brewery, telling the driver to wait, and had walked down to the path beside the river. Katharine had chosen to do this rather than to sit in some depressing hotel, nervous as to who was listening over their shoulders. But it had begun to rain, and it wasn't such a good idea after all being out of doors. Charles held his umbrella over them both, keeping them reasonably dry, but all the same Katharine's skirts dragged in the wet grass, and the river was pewter grey and chilly.

Charles suggested going back to the cab, but she refused. First they must talk. She didn't mind the rain. Everything smelt fresh and sweet. She couldn't breathe inside a closed cab.

"Aren't you well, darling? I believe you are looking pale."

"What do you expect? It's been terrible."

"But surely you didn't think Willie intended to carry out his absurd threat?"

"With that horrible old fireater, The O'Gorman Mahon, urging him on? Certainly he would have."

"Then supposing he had. I believe you underestimate me. I may even have won. I'm a good swordsman, and an excellent shot."

She turned on him vehemently. "Charles, don't joke! It's all too dreadful to think of."

His face became sober, his voice concerned. "What is it, my darling? That little bit of bad opera is over. What are you still worrying about? I don't intend to give up seeing you, if that's what you're afraid of. Nothing in the world will make me do that. We'll manage somehow."

"Charles, I'm expecting your child."

He stopped dead and stared at her. The stillness of his face frightened her. She had quickly to reassure him.

"There'll be no scandal, Willie will think it his."

The bald words were out. She supposed she could have

softened them. But at this moment she was incapable of doing so, and no matter how it was expressed the fact remained.

"So you've done what was necessary." After a long silence
the flat dry words were without expression. Only his eyes
blazing at her out of a white face betrayed his emotion.

"Perhaps we could say that it was I who fought that
duel," she said in a voice that trembled.

Abruptly he left her side and strode away down the path,
some compulsion driving him, his umbrella held aloft so
that he looked a perfectly respectable gentleman out for a
walk in the rain. His tall form seemed gradually to dissolve
in the soft curtain of rain. Presently he turned a bend and
was lost to sight.

She stood appalled, not knowing what to do. Would he
come back? Had he been so shocked he had left her forever? Had he forgotten she had no umbrella and her hat
was wilting round her face, and trickles of rain running
icily down her back? Her wry laugh at her plight turned to
a sob, and her sob to a great wave of anger. How dare he
walk off like that and leave her! Wasn't this predicament as
much his fault as hers? Would he have wanted her—or
Willie—to announce to the world that Mrs. O'Shea was
expecting the child of the leader of the Irish party? And
now what was she to do, climb ignominiously into the waiting cab and drive back to town alone? With the driver
speculating interestedly on her soaking wet condition, and
her desertion by her friend.

Picking up her skirts, Katharine began to run down the
path in the direction Charles had taken. She would catch
him up and tell him what she thought of him. She would
spare him nothing. He had yet to see his dear Kate in a
temper. Well, now he would.

But round the bend in the path she almost collided with
him, coming back.

He dropped his umbrella and wrapped her in his arms.

"Kate, my darling, you're crying."

"No, I'm not, it's only the rain."

"Well, I am."

She saw the runnels of water on his cheeks. His face
looked hollow and haunted, full of an impotent anger and

bewilderment. Her own anger vanished as quickly as it had come.

"Charles, it will be all right. It really will."

"I can't bear him touching you. I told you that once before."

"Don't think of that. Think of the baby."

"Do you want it, Katie?"

"Very much."

His eyes burned through their tears. "You're wonderful, and I love you."

He kissed her, his lips cool with rain, his wet cheek against hers. A small flurry of wind lifted the unfurled umbrella and deposited it on the grey stream of the river where it floated gently away. Now they would get very wet. But they were wet already. It was much too late to worry about that.

A month later she nearly fainted when she was with Aunt Ben, and came back to her senses to see the old lady regarding her speculatively.

"What is it, Katharine? Another child?"

"Yes."

"Does Willie know?"

"Not yet. I mean to tell him on Sunday, if he comes down."

"Do you want it?"

"Very much. Very much, Aunt Ben."

She had spoken with unguarded warmth, and saw the old periwinkle blue eyes on her.

"What will Mr. Parnell say?"

"Mr. Parnell?"

The old lady paused just long enough to observe the colour mounting in her cheeks.

"I thought you were being his intermediary with Mr. Gladstone. I hardly think Mr. Gladstone will be diverted by a pregnant young woman."

"Oh, no, Aunt Ben, I can just see his disapproving stare." Katharine was laughing as she tried to scowl in imitation of Mr. Gladstone's fiery gaze beneath snow-white brows. "I'm to see him next week. I must tell Mr. Parnell to try to accomplish all the business he can in the next two or three months."

"When am I to meet your Mr. Parnell?"

Aunt Ben was full of surprises this morning. Katharine wasn't feeling well enough to parry her.

"*My* Mr. Parnell? The Irish people would have something to say about that. They think he's theirs. But I didn't know you wanted to meet him, Aunt Ben."

"And why not? I'm not in my dotage. I'm quite abreast of the times. Bring him here one afternoon soon."

The opportunity to do this occurred very soon, for Charles wanted to see her about arranging another interview with Mr. Gladstone. The Land Bill had been passed, and now was the time, when the Government was feeling reasonably pleased with itself, to press for the ultimate object of Home Rule. Charles had been making Katharine, on one of their long drives, learn by heart what she was to say. He didn't want to put anything in writing. He didn't trust the English, even the Prime Minister.

But he agreed willingly to take time to call on old Mrs. Wood.

The visit was a great success. Aunt Ben was charmed with her good-looking courteous guest. She liked his appearance, his quiet manners, his soft voice. She took his arm and made him pace up and down the tapestry room as they talked.

"I once met your Daniel O'Connell. That was when my husband was a Member of Parliament. I heard his greatest speech. But I prefer your voice, Mr. Parnell."

After he had gone she looked at Katharine musingly. Finally she said, "Yes, I believe he's a man worth following. Bring him again some time. I've enjoyed my talk with him."

Katharine's next meeting with Mr. Gladstone coincided with news of more outrages in Ireland. Mr. Gladstone was bitterly disappointed. He was no longer the indulgent host greeting a good-looking young woman, but an old man with a tightened face, and furious eyes.

"You must tell your friend, Mrs. O'Shea, that I'm not interested in anything he has to say about Home Rule while he is encouraging this violence. Tell him to stop it. If he arrests the operation of the Land Act then other measures will have to be taken." He took Katharine's arm and began walking her up and down the long room, talking rapidly.

"We've given him a great deal. The Government won't stand for much more. And I keep getting complaints from the Palace. The Queen isn't overfond of her Irish subjects. To tell the truth, no more am I. I got the Land Act through, and now Mr. Parnell seems determined to wreck it."

"He wants a great deal more than a Land Act, Mr. Gladstone."

The old eagle face was turned to her.

"Will he never be satisfied?"

"Yes. He will. One day."

"I doubt it."

"When he attains his object."

"Yes," said the old man thoughtfully. "I imagine he is a man who doesn't rest until he attains whatever object he has in mind, wise or not. Isn't that true, Mrs. O'Shea?"

Katharine kept her eyes downcast.

"You must have discovered his mettle by now, Mr. Gladstone."

Her arm was suddenly flung away.

"Yes, by God, I have, but my patience will come to an end. Tell him to keep his Irish outlaws in check, or I won't be able to keep Mr. Forster in check. Mr. Forster, I might tell you, won't be happy until Mr. Parnell is safely under lock and key."

"You mean he'll be arrested after all!"

Mr. Gladstone looked down at her, then abruptly patted her hand.

"The resources of civilisation are not yet exhausted."

She repeated all of this conversation to Charles next time he was in London, and part of it to Willie.

Willie was completely on Mr. Gladstone's side.

"If you ask me, Parnell's lost control of his people. He's stirred up such a flood of hatred against the English that now he can't stop it. He'll find it will consume him, too, if he's not careful. He's an odd intense fellow, I must say. But you like him, don't you, Kate?"

"You know I do. I like and admire him."

Willie looked at her broodingly.

"Just so long as he hasn't been leaving his things lying

round here again. The O'Gorman Mahon thought I let him get out of that affair too easily."

"The O'Gorman Mahon can look after his own business."

Willie, about to retort, changed his mind, and kissed her good-temperedly.

"I did behave a bit wildly, I suppose. It's a good thing my mother didn't hear anything of it. She'd have been shocked to death. She's never approved of you as my wife, but she's never questioned your morals."

"As you have," Katharine said.

"I told you, I was a bit impulsive. After all, you might like Mr. Parnell, but you're much too conventional to do anything foolish. I should never have mistrusted you. It was only that you were so confoundedly cold to me for so long. But I've scotched those rumours about Kitty O'Shea. You won't hear them again." He was looking at her more closely. "What's the matter? You're looking a bit white."

If only she never heard those rumours again! She was praying silently that they were finished forever.

She put her hand to her forehead.

"I'm all right, Willie. Just a little tired. It's not unusual in my condition."

"Your condition!" he shouted. "What the devil do you mean?"

"There's only one thing I can mean." She was determined to smile. "Norah and Carmen will be delighted. They've been begging me to have a baby for them. I don't know about Gerard. He might feel rather too grown-up."

She had to endure his arms round her and seem to welcome them.

"Well, well, what a secretive puss you've become. Not a word to the person most interested, the jolly old father. When is it to be?"

"Oh—the spring."

He was making a rapid calculation. "Late spring, it must be. Well, that will keep you quiet, eh?"

Formal letters came from Charles from time to time.

"My dear Mrs. O'Shea,
    I had arranged to go to a meeting at Durham today, but was unable to do so at the last moment. I think you have

some books of mine at Eltham which I propose going down to look for on Monday about ten or twelve unless I hear from you that you can't find them for me. Please reply to House of Commons where I shall call for my letters on Monday morning."

She showed them to Willie, diplomatically, and he managed to overcome his dislike for Mr. Parnell very well, by frequently meeting him and discussing political manoeuvres. Willie was beginning to hold his head high and strut about with his fingers in his waistcoat pockets. It seemed that he was beginning to indulge in grandiose dreams about one day being made Chief Secretary to Ireland. He was getting on famously with Mr. Joseph Chamberlain, too, and other members of the Cabinet. It was shrewd and far-seeing to have friends on both sides of the fence. This could not fail to forward the career of Captain O'Shea. Wasn't Kate pleased that he was at last settling down and taking his career seriously? Perhaps one day he, too, would be drawn in triumph through the streets of Dublin.

Reading of Charles' triumphant progress through Ireland, Katharine was not overjoyed but deeply alarmed. He was continuing to do all the things Mr. Gladstone had warned him against. Inciting the people, making seditious speeches. The one he had made at Wexford in October was the culminating one. Standing on an improvised platform in the marketplace, looking down at his intent audience, he said,

"You have gained something by your exertions during the last twelve months, but I am here today to tell you that you have gained but a fraction of that to which you are justly entitled. And the Irishman who thinks he can now throw away his arms will find to his sorrow and destruction that he has placed himself in the power of a perfidious, cruel, unrelenting English enemy.

"It is a good sign that this masquerading knight-errant, this pretended champion of the liberties of every other nation except those of the Irish nation, should be obliged to throw off the mask today and to stand revealed as the man who, by his own utterances, is prepared to carry fire and sword into your homesteads unless you humble and abase yourselves before him and before the landlords of this country. In the opinion of an English statesman, no man is good to Ireland until he is buried and unable to strike a blow for Ireland, and perhaps the day may come when I may get a good word from English statesmen as a moderate man when I am dead and buried.

"When people talk of public plunder they should first ask themselves and recall to mind who were the first public plunderers in Ireland. The land of Ireland has been confiscated three times over by the men whose descendants Mr. Gladstone is supporting in the fruits of their plunder by his bayonets and buckshot.

"Mr. Gladstone admits that the English Government has failed in Ireland, he admits the contention that Grattan and the volunteers of '82 fought for, he admits the contention that the men of '98 lost their lives for, he admits the contention that O'Connell argued for, he admits the contention that the men of '48 staked their all for, he admits the contention that the men of '65 after a long period of depression and of apparent death of all national life in Ireland cheerfully faced the dungeon and the horrors of penal servitude for, and admits the contention that today you in your overpowering multitudes have re-established, and, please God, will bring to a successful and final issue, namely, that England's mission in Ireland has been a failure, and that Irishmen have established their right to govern Ireland by laws made by themselves on Irish soil . . ."

It was after this speech that Mr. Forster wrote to Mr. Gladstone saying that Mr. Parnell must be arrested under the Coercion Act. He would have liked to have arrested every single Irishman suspected of revolutionary practices.

Mr. Gladstone, in an agonising dilemma, summoned his Cabinet, and Mr. Parnell, completely cool and unruffled, seemingly indifferent to the threats of the despised English, said that if he were arrested Captain Moonlight would take his place. The dreaded phantom who struck by night, and in a dozen counties at once. There would be fires and pillaging and death from Cork to Dublin City.

In spite of this threat Mr. Forster continued with his intention. He instructed Sir Thomas Steele, the Commander in

Chief of police in Ireland, that should the Cabinet agree to arrest Mr. Parnell, he would receive a telegram of one word "Proceed."

Katharine, awaiting events in desperate anxiety, received another letter, a secret one enclosed in a formal one.

"My own Katie,
Tomorrow I go to Kildare and shall try to start for London Friday morning, but I cannot be sure of this as 'something' may turn up at the last moment. If I arrive in London Friday night I shall go to same hotel and wait for you.
Always your own Charles."

She answered the letter hastily, begging Charles to be careful and at all costs to avoid arrest. How could she bear it if he were shut up in jail for months, perhaps years? Supposing he were there when her baby was born. Her tears dropped on the paper, and she had to tear it up and start afresh. Though a tear-blotted letter may have done more to dissuade him from his recklessness than a calm and sensible one.

His answer was very tender and loving, but didn't she understand that the turmoil and rebellion he had brought to a head could be better served in Kilmainham Jail than out? And how could she doubt his feelings? *For good or ill I am your husband, your lover, your children, your all. I will give my life to Ireland, but to you I give my love, whether it be your heaven or your hell.*

Suddenly, after an Indian summer, the weather had turned cold and stormy. The trees in the park bent and cracked in a rising gale. Katharine was literally blown across the garden and up the steps to Aunt Ben's door, and when she was admitted the wind swept through the hall and up the stairs. Aunt Ben was sitting in the tapestry room wrapped in shawls.

"How can you let such a draught in?" she asked Katharine peevishly. "Now we will have to warm the house all over again. Well, what's the matter? You're looking pinched in the face. It surely isn't as cold as all that."

"Aunt Ben, what is it like in prison? You've visited

145

prisons when you were helping Uncle Benjamin. I never did with Papa, although I wanted to."

Aunt Ben retreated into her shawls.

"They're not as draughty as this room, I can tell you that. But they're not exactly the height of comfort either. I wouldn't recommend them. Damp, cold, bad food. Which of your friends is a jailbird, my darling? You haven't told me. I would find him interesting."

"Don't tease me, Aunt. You know very well, if Mr. Meredith has read the newspaper to you as thoroughly as he usually does, that Mr. Parnell is threatened with arrest."

"Oh, then that would be an Irish prison. And for an Irish patriot. My dear child, what are you worrying about? He'll be fed on the fat of the land."

"But what about the damp and cold?"

"I'll be surprised if he doesn't get the warmest blankets in Ireland sent to him."

"But his jailors will be English."

"Tut, tut, child. And where did you get the idea that the high and mighty English are above a bribe or two? Stop worrying now and put on a more cheerful face. I don't like you looking glum."

"Supposing it's for years."

"Mr. Parnell in jail for years! Shame on you! And I thought you admired his cleverness."

"You mean he'll find a way to shorten his sentence. How can he? Mr. Forster and one or two others would like to see him dead."

"You're exaggerating," said Aunt Ben placidly. "Being pregnant is making you fanciful. Sit down and wind some wool for me. That's a nice calming occupation. Anyway, I thought Mr. Gladstone was your friend. Why don't you get him to stop such a barbaric act? It won't look well in history."

"Oh, Aunt," Katharine exclaimed in exasperation. "I'm not interested in history. I'm interested in now. And it's no use going to see Mr. Gladstone or anybody. Mr. Parnell wants to be arrested."

"Then whatever are you worrying about?"

"I won't have him being a martyr for his wretched country!" Katharine cried.

146

"I agree it's an extreme way of winning a political point," Aunt Ben agreed. She looked over her spectacles at Katharine. "But the Irish have this tendency to melodrama and I don't imagine Mr. Parnell is any exception. Thread my needle for me, child. I can't see an inch in front of my nose."

In the afternoon Katharine battled her way home against the wind. Her heart leaped as she saw the brougham drawn up outside her front door. But then she recognised the face of Partridge, their coachman. He tipped his cap to her, and shouted above the wind that he had just driven the Captain down from London.

Willie here! There could be only one reason.

She burst into the hall to find Willie doffing his greatcoat. He turned and without attempting to suppress his triumph, said, "Well, they have Parnell laid by the heels."

"He's arrested?"

"This morning, in Morison's Hotel. They've taken him to Kilmainham. They've got Sexton, and Dillon and O'Brien too. Well, it's their own fault. But especially Parnell's. Now he'll have time to reflect on the wickedness and folly of his policy. Condoning violence, alienating the English all the time—it was madness. I tell you, if the Irish question could be left to me and a few others we'd make an infinitely better job of it. I was only discussing it with Chamberlain and Dilke this morning. I've more or less taken it on my shoulders to find some way out of this disastrous impasse.'

Willie's blue eyes were shining with triumph and excitement. Nothing could have pleased him better than the present situation, his great rival laid low and his own opportunity handed to him so fortuitously. Katharine dearly wanted to slap his smug smiling face. She would have liked to have shown him the doorstep. She didn't know how to hide her revulsion for him.

"How long will they keep him in prison?" she managed to ask.

"Oh, months, I expect."

"Months!"

Her dismay was so apparent that Willie looked at her suspiciously.

"What's that to you? You're not going to be shining at

dinner parties, or paying any more calls on Mr. Gladstone for the next few months. You'll be staying decently at home preparing for our child. Mr. Parnell's arrest isn't going to affect your life. Or is it?"

He came close and looked at her so hard that she had to murmur that she was only distressed for Mr. Parnell. His constitution was inclined to be delicate, and the hardships of prison would scarcely help that.

"You worry about my constitution, not his. The gout's been plaguing me again, and I've a cold I can't throw off. Parnell's fortunate, he'll have time to get a rest, and I warrant he won't lack for food. There'll be a brace of grouse, or a side of pork or a fine salmon on the doorstep of Kilmainham every night."

"Yes, the people love him."

"They're daft about him, you mean," Willie said sourly. "What is it about that man that even my own wife is in a state of the vapours about him? However," Willie began to chuckle with malicious glee, "I have one thing he hasn't. A wife. Come and give me a kiss, my love."

"Willie!" Her heart was pounding. "At this time of day!"

"You had no complaints about it being this time of day once. No, don't protest about the children or the servants. If you were a loving wife you'd simply turn the key in the lock."

"But I'm not a loving wife."

"Damn you, you're not. But I'm not standing any more of your ladylike nonsense. Do you hear?" He gripped her wrist, hurting severely. Then he flung it away. "Ring the bell and order tea. And tell Anna we'd like an early dinner tonight."

"You're staying?"

"Do I need permission?"

"Not if you stay in your own room. I'm not feeling well. The baby—"

"Forget that. The others came to no harm. Did they?"

He had had such a boyish good-looking face once, kind and merry. It was difficult to remember it when one looked at what it had become, coarse, reddened, insolent, unhappy. Yes, unhappy . . .

Towards midnight the gale died away and the moon came

out, drifting behind flying rags of cloud. The same moon would be shining over Dublin. Could he see it from his cell? Was he in a cell, lying on a hard bench, comfortless, cold? How did his face look in sleep, pale, too thin, too hollow, with its severity that was almost monk like? Was he asleep, or was he lying wakeful thinking about the bars across the door? As she lay with the bar of Willie's arm across her. Just as completely in prison.

"Kitty O'Shea," she said aloud, her voice dry with contempt.

CHAPTER 12

MR. GLADSTONE, loudly applauded, made an announcement at the Guildhall, "I have been informed that towards the vindication of the law, of order, of the rights of property and the freedom of the land, of the first elements of political life and civilisation, the first step has been taken in the arrest of the man who has made himself preeminent in the attempt to destroy the authority of the law."

And, at Wonersh Lodge, the postman delivered a letter addressed to Mrs. O'Shea.

"My own Katie,
    I have just been arrested by two fine-looking detectives and write these words to tell you you must be brave and not fret. The only thing that makes me worried and un-happy is that it may hurt you and our child. You know, darling, it will be wicked for you to grieve. I can never have another wife but you, so if anything happens to you I must die childless.
    Politically it is a fortunate thing for me that I have been arrested as the movement is breaking fast, and all will be quiet for a few months when I shall be released."

Aunt Ben, too percipient, sent a note to Wonersh Lodge. "Stay home with the children today, Katharine. The weather is much too inclement for you to cross the park." And in the schoolroom, sitting by the fire sewing while the children did their lessons, Katharine was aroused from a brown study by Carmen climbing on to her lap.

"What's this? A big girl of eight wanting to sit on Mamma's lap?"

Carmen said nothing, but laid her head against Kath-arine's breast.

"She thinks you're sad, Mamma," Norah said. "You're not, are you?"

Katharine rested her chin on Carmen's head. The little

warm body pressed against her was comforting and poignant. Her throat hurt, and she had the greatest difficulty in speaking normally.

"I'm just thinking. I have a secret."

Carmen lifted her head, and Norah flung herself at Katharine.

"What's the secret? Tell us, Mamma. Do tell us."

"Shall I?" She smiled at the two pairs of inquisitive blue eyes. "Well, then, I've decided that we'll have another baby in the house."

"Of our own! Really and truly our own!"

Katharine nodded.

"Don't you remember telling me you wanted a baby?"

Carmen began to smile and nod. Norah squealed, "Oh Mamma, you are kind to us. When will it come? Soon?"

"Not immediately. You mustn't be impatient. In the spring."

"Oh, what a long time to wait. Does Papa know? Have you written and told Gerard?"

"Papa knows, and you may write and tell Gerard yourselves. Supposing we go up to the attics, and get out the cradle and the perambulator."

"And the baby clothes!" shouted Norah.

"No, a new baby must have new clothes. But there's your old high-chair and your rocking horse."

So somehow that long sad day passed. When the children had gone to bed that night she was able to write a long almost composed letter. She had never thought she would address a letter to a prison. Kilmainham Jail, Dublin, she wrote on the envelope, and then put on her bonnet and cloak and walked out in the tearing wind to post the letter herself.

The moon was shining again, and one day of her torture had passed. If she had known the number of days ahead she thought she could have faced them with more courage. But political prisoners had been known to rot in jails for years. Could the British Government dare to do this to someone so famous and so revered as Mr. Parnell? She didn't doubt that they could. She had seen the hard cruel glint in Mr. Gladstone's slate-coloured eyes. She knew the

Queen's stubborn irrational dislike for Irish rebels. The great might of Britain turned against one of her detractors could be annihilating.

That was her biggest fear. Her smallest, but also an agonising one, was that no letters would be allowed to come out of Kilmainham, or if they did that they would be censored.

She was ashamed of herself for this fear when Charles' next letter came. She should have trusted his ingenuity.

"My own darling,

Now after we have been all locked up safely for the night and everything is quiet I am going to send you some news. First I must tell you that I sleep exceedingly well and am allowed to read the newspapers in bed in the morning, and breakfast there also, if I wish.

"I want, however, to give you a little history from the commencement of my stay here.

"When I heard that the detectives were asking for me a terror fell upon me, for I remembered that you had told me you feared it would kill you. I kept the men out of the room while I was writing you a few hasty words of comfort and hope, for I knew the shock would be terrible to my sweet love.

"I feared that I could not post it, but they stopped the cab just before reaching the prison, and allowed me to drop the letter into a pillar-box. My only torture during those first days was your unhappiness. Finally your first letter came and I knew that you were safe.

"You must not mind my being in the infirmary. I am only there because it is more comfortable than being in a cell and you have longer hours of association, from eight a.m. to eight p.m. instead of being locked up at six and obliged to eat by yourself. The infirmary is a collection of rooms, and each has a room to himself. Dillon is in a cell, but he is allowed as a special privilege to come over and associate with us during the daytime. I am obliged to invent little maladies for myself from day to day in order to give Dr. Kenny an excuse for keeping me in the infirmary, but I have never felt better in my life. Have quite forgotten that I am in prison and should miss the rattle of keys and slam of doors.

"The only thing I don't like is that the Government insist upon sending a lot of police into the jail every night, two of whom sleep against my door and two more under my window. A very strict watch is kept and I have been obliged to exert my ingenuity to get letters out to you and to get yours in return. They have let us off very easily. I fully expected that we should have been scattered in different jails through the country as a punishment, but they evidently think no other place safe enough for me. Indeed, this place is not safe, and I can get out whenever I like, but it is probably the best policy to wait to be released. And now goodnight, my dear. Promise to sleep well and look as beautiful when we meet again as the last time I kissed your sweet lips . . ."

But it was risky writing these long personal letters to her at Eltham. Occasionally there was a formal one which she could show Willie.

"Dear Mrs. O'Shea,
Thanks very much for your letters and telegram. I was rather indisposed yesterday, but am very much better to-day. I am told that everybody gets a turn after they have been here for three or four weeks. I write you this lest you and other friends should be troubled by exaggerated reports in the newspapers.

"My esteemed friend Mr. Forster has become very disagreeable lately. He refuses to allow me to see my solicitor except in presence and hearing of two warders, so I have declined to see him at all. He also refuses to allow me to see visitors except in the cage, which I have also declined to do, but probably things may be relaxed again after a time.

Yours very truly, C.S.P."

Her own private letters were addressed to Mrs. Carpenter, at a small shop in Soho. Very plainly dressed, she called there once a week, hating her disguise, but longing for the letter that was her reward.

153

"My darling,

Now that everything is quiet and with your own sweet face before me I can give my thoughts up entirely to you and talk to you as if you were in my arms.

"I am trying to make arrangements for you to come and see me. I will ask if I may see my cousin 'Mrs. Bligh who is coming from England'.

"I admire supremely my life of ease, laziness, absence of care and responsibility. My only trouble is about your health and happiness. You must try not to be so unhappy.

"You will be anxious to know what my short illness was about. It was of a very unromantic kind—not the heart but the stomach. However, our doctor by means of mustard and chlorodyne got me all right again. In fact, I have gotten over very quickly the *mal du prison* which comes on everybody sooner or later.

"One of the men in this quarter who has been here for nearly nine months looks after me as if he was my brother. He makes me a soda and lemon in the morning and then gives me my breakfast. At dinner he takes care that I get all the nicest bits and concocts the most perfect black coffee out of berries which he roasts and grinds fresh each day. Finally in the evening just before we are separated for the night he brews me a steaming tumbler of hot whiskey.

"I do not think there is the least probability of my being moved, this is the strongest place they have and they are daily trying to increase its strength according to their own notions which are not very brilliant. My room is warm and perfectly dry. They wanted me to go to another which did not face the sun, but I refused, so they did not persist.

"With a thousand kisses, and hoping soon to lay my head in its old place. Goodnight, my darling . . ."

His ingenuity was never at an end. Someone, perhaps a friendly warder, had provided him with some invisible ink, and the recipe for it, which he sent to Katharine, instructing her to take it to a particular chemist in London. After that they were able to correspond with the greatest freedom, writing their private messages invisibly between the lines of their short formal letters.

"I continue very well and very much contented with the position of things outside. I am told the Government doesn't know what to do with us now they have got us, and will take the first decent excuse which presents itself of sending us about our business. Your letters give me great comfort, but I am in a continual state of alarm lest something may hurt you. Do take care of yourself and our child."

She was going to be forever ashamed of herself, but early in December, after reading in the *Freeman* that the health of the Irish leader in Kilmainham Jail was causing some alarm, she had such a fit of hopelessness and angry despair that she succumbed to the temptation to put all her fears and unhappiness on paper, and to post the letter before she came to her senses.

The next day, before Charles could have received this shameful letter, one came from him, written with his usual thoughtfulness for her anxiety.

"You will see a paragraph about my health in the *Freeman* which may worry you, so I write to say that it is very much exaggerated for the purpose of preventing a change in our rooms to some which are not in any way so nice. I have caught a slight cold which the doctor thinks will pass off in a day or two.

"You must not pay any attention to the newspaper report as it was carefully got up. I don't eat bread, only for breakfast, and D. and I have two raw chops smuggled in daily which we do for ourselves and also make our own tea. We also always have a cold ham in stock.

"But we hope by the row we are making to compel the Government to make the food sufficiently good to satisfy the men."

The reply to her own despairing letter came almost by return post.

"You frighten me dreadfully when you tell me that I am surely killing you and our child. Rather than that you should run any risk I will resign my seat, leave politics and go away somewhere as soon as you wish. Will you come?"

Would she come? With all the resolution of which she was capable she pushed the tantalising prospect from her. She had not, after all, become so sunk in her own unhappiness as to be so selfish and short-sighted.

She wrote, "I have warned you I would not always behave well, but even I did not know how bad my bad behaviour would be. I was feeling so low and hopeless about the future that my pen wickedly ran away with me . . ."

His answer came just before Christmas.

"Your letter has relieved me very much. I have been dreadfully frightened about you for the last week. Do take care of yourself, my darling, and I will also take good care of myself. We have both to live for each other for many happy years together."

Then it was Christmas, and his message, "Many happy returns for Christmas, my own darling."

The thought of him spending Christmas in jail was too much to endure. From then on Katharine lost patience. She bombarded Willie with requests to do more. Willie was doing all he could, but it still wasn't enough. It was all very well to put his head together with Joseph Chamberlain and Sir Charles Dilke, and discuss terms under which the Government could release the prisoners without losing face. Nothing was happening except talk. He must see Mr. Forster in Dublin, he must see Mr. Gladstone, if necessary. Katharine herself wrote to Mr. Gladstone asking for an interview, but he was visiting Scotland and then Hawarden, and in any case it seemed likely that he would have nothing to say to her at present.

Besides, she was now conspicuously pregnant. Willie was shocked at her suggestion that she see Chamberlain. She could do no more than he was doing, and it wasn't seemly for a woman in her condition to go about publicly. What was she worrying about? The political prisoners were being well looked after. Her precious Mr. Parnell was snug and cosy while he, Willie, was doing all the running about in foul weather.

She could only write again to Charles, the bottle of invisible ink at her elbow.

"I don't think I can bear this pretence any longer. When you are released you must promise to come here immediately. But I warn you you must be prepared for my never letting you go again."

His answer was prompt.

"Yes, I will come to you, my love, immediately I am released. There is nothing in the world that I can do in Ireland nor is it likely that I shall be able to do anything here for a long time to come. I am disposed to think that the Government intends to release me shortly before the opening of Parliament.

"Yesterday and today as three of us were exercising in our yard the gates in the adjoining yard were opened twice to permit some carts to come in. A low wall only separated the two yards across which we could have easily sprung. There was no warder in our yard, and only one with his back to us in the next. But trying to escape is six months with hard labour so we have nothing to gain by it."

January went by at a snail's pace. It was February and Katharine knew that her time was getting near. She told Willie she feared the baby was going to be born too soon. He had not expected it until the spring, but it was going to make a February appearance. The doctor confirmed this.

"The sooner the better," Willie said heartily. He never had liked the last weeks of her pregnancy, and had always made excuses to be out of the house as much as possible. Illness, apart from his own, bored him intensely.

After the long waiting and the strain of the last few months Katharine almost welcomed the physical pain when it struck her. It came very suddenly. She had been across the park to Aunt Ben that morning, feeling no warning that her baby would be there before the day was over.

But immediately after luncheon the fierce pain had stabbed her. She had sent Jane running for the doctor, and had scarcely reached her room before the pain came again so strongly and severely that she thought the birth would be a quick one.

She was filled with wild elation. At last something was happening.

Yet for all her welcoming the agony ahead it was not an easy birth. The hours ran away into night. Lamps were lit and shaded from her eyes. Firelight flickered on the ceiling. Now and then she dozed, and thought that Charles was beside her. Then, with pain and exhaustion, her fantasies grew wilder, and she thought that she was being rent in two to give birth to a strange object shaped like the map of Ireland. The sweet stifling smell of chloroform was in her nostrils, and the little country grew and sprouted green and was filled with crying children.

"Mrs. O'Shea! You have a little daughter."

That was the crying she could hear. But it sounded feeble, starved . . .

She lifted heavy eyelids.

"Is she all right?"

"She's fine. A little small. But time will remedy that."

There were echoes of Lucy in that prosaic statement. Dear Lucy who had been there for the birth of all her other babies. Tears filled her eyes. She should be so happy, she had safely given birth to Charles' child. But she only felt terribly lonely. The room seemed too dark. Shadows were pressing on her.

"Doctor—"

"Your husband's downstairs, Mrs. O'Shea. Would you like to see him for a moment."

"No." Her lips trembled with exhaustion. "Just—the baby."

Dark hair, eyes tightly shut, a miniature but beautifully rounded forehead—*his* forehead. A slight blueness about the mouth.

Katharine's eyes flew open in alarm.

"Doctor, is she all right?"

"She's a little small, but she'll do nicely. Now you must rest."

The habit of constant care, constant watchfulness, came

back to her. No one must know she couldn't bear Willie hanging over this baby, making fatuous remarks.

"Tell my husband—I'll see him—in the morning."

"It's morning now, Mrs. O'Shea," said the nurse comfortably. "And a nasty wet stormy one. No wonder baby keeps her eyes shut on this queer old world."

"Can I have her beside me?"

"Well, now—I've just tucked her in her cradle."

"Give her to me, please."

"Well—if you promise to sleep."

She would sleep, she promised eagerly. With this tiny scrap of his flesh against her her loneliness slowly dissolved into peace.

They were all round her bedside later, Willie looking red-faced, as if he had been drinking, Gerard, her tall fair-haired son, home from school, and the little girls starry-eyed with excitement.

She was ashamed that she could scarcely bring herself to share the baby with them. Reluctantly she folded back the shawl to show its face.

The little girls were absurdly disappointed.

"Mamma, she's so *small*. Will she ever be big enough to dress?"

"When will she smile at us?"

"Can we put her in our doll's carriage? She's smaller than our dolls!"

"Mamma, are you sure God meant her to come like this?"

Katharine met Willie's eyes over the commotion. He, too, was disappointed. She guessed he would have preferred a boy, but anyway a man couldn't be expected to go into raptures over such a scrap of human flesh. Wait until she grew a little.

"What about you, Gerard? Are you disappointed, too?"

Being at school had taken her son away from her. Although only twelve he seemed to have entered a man's world. He was not going to show any but the most offhand interest in his new sister.

"I suppose she's all right."

"The thing is," said Willie heartily, "what to call her. Any ideas, Kate?"

Katharine's eyes widened. She drew the baby closer to

her. She had been so absorbed in wanting this child and waiting for its birth that she hadn't thought of all the difficulties ahead. Here was the first one. Willie naming *his* child. And after that the elaborate Catholic christening ceremony.

"No, I haven't thought yet."

"Well, we'll all have to get our heads together. We'll give her a good family name."

The baby stirred, stretching her minute hands, and beginning to cry. She had a weak cry, Katharine thought anxiously. And so far she had refused to suck. Let her get properly hungry, the nurse had said, but she didn't seem to have enough strength.

"She's the first one to take after you, Kate. Brown hair. What colour are her eyes?"

"I think they're going to be dark."

"Well, it makes a change," said Willie cheerfully. "Come along, children. You mustn't tire your mother. There'll be plenty of time to admire your little sister in the future."

The letter came from Dublin.

"I cannot describe to you what a relief your little note was that everything was quite right. I burst into tears . . . You must be very good and quiet until you are quite strong again . . ."

Katharine regained her strength slowly, the baby more slowly. Indeed, all of Katharine's fears were realised. This child was going to be difficult to rear. She took her food badly, she refused to grow, and she cried far too much. The pathetic weak wailing wrung Katharine's heart. She would sit for hours with the child in her arms, hushing and soothing her. Then there was a terrible time when she caught a cold and her little face went blue with her efforts to breathe.

Willie was unexpectedly thoughtful. He stayed home more and allowed Katharine to devote all her time to the baby. She had to tell Charles of her anxiety, and he replied:

"I am very anxious about our little daughter. Is it dangerous?" And, "If you will send me some of our daughter's hair I will put it in the locket with yours. Would Sophie make a nice second name? It is the name

160

of one of my sisters. I am very much troubled about our little daughter's health and hope it will not make her permanently delicate."

He also wrote, "D. is to be released immediately the house adjourns for Easter and after a time when they find nothing happens as a consequence of his release, they will probably take courage and let me out also. Anyway, this Government is not likely to last more than another session."

The baby was eventually named Sophie Claude. Since she was too frail to take to the church, Willie arranged for the priest to come to the house, and there was a quiet baptism ceremony in the drawing room.

For a little while after that the baby seemed to grow stronger. One evening, opening enormous brown eyes she looked up into her mother's face and gave her first tremulous smile of recognition. Katharine had loved all her children, but never one so much as this. She scarcely left the little one's side, scarcely slept.

Willie was working hard, writing long letters to Parnell, and to Chamberlain about the proposed treaty to be made between the Government and the Irish party. It was obvious that the prisoners would have to be released soon.

It was an April morning and little Sophie was eight weeks old.

Willie had gone back to London. Jane, and loyal Ellen, who perhaps both guessed more than they should, rushed into Katharine in her sitting room exclaiming simultaneously, "Ma'am! Mr. Parnell!"

Katharine started up, her heart in her throat.

"What about him? Has there been an accident? Is he ill?"

"No, ma'am, no, he's here! On the doorstep. God be praised!" Ellen added piously.

He was not on the doorstep, he was standing behind the excited maids. Katharine brushed them out of the way as she ran to him.

"It can't be you! Have they let you free?"

"Not quite. I'm on my way to Paris. My nephew, my sister Theodosia's boy, has died of typhoid. They've let me out on parole to go to the funeral."

"Oh, Charles, how sad!"

"Yes, it's a tragedy. He was only twenty-one. But how are you, Kate? The baby?"

The maids had withdrawn. She was able to fling herself into his arms and be held for a few precious moments before she lifted her head to search his face, seeing its thinness and pallor.

"Oh, Charles, how good to see you. I thought it was never to happen again."

"And you, my darling. Tell me how you are. Have you quite recovered?"

"I'm all right, but our baby, little Sophie——" She shook her head. "Come upstairs and see her. How long can you stay?"

"No more than a few minutes. Officially I'm on my way to Paris. But I had to come straight to you." He had her hand gripped so hard that her fingers were numb. "Kate, this must never happen again."

"Then you must stop it," she said passionately. She breathed deeply, trying to smile. "I'm sorry. Don't invite me to say things now that I'll be sorry for later. Come and see the baby."

The cradle stood beside Katharine's bed. She drew aside the curtain and let him gaze on the tiny sleeping face.

"She's like you, Charles. See that round forehead. And her eyes are exactly yours. She smiled at me yesterday. Shall I wake her and see if she'll smile at her Papa."

"No. Please don't. She looks so frail. Is she going to be all right?"

"I don't know. I'm so afraid."

"You're wearing yourself out looking after her."

"I don't care about that if only she will live."

"She's been baptised?"

Katharine nodded, and saw his face tighten.

"But I called her the name you wanted. Sophie."

"Thank you, my darling."

The tears were aching in her throat.

"Willie's in London. He's been working hard on getting you released. He's discussing a treaty with Mr. Chamberlain."

"I know. Tell him I'm grateful, and that I'll come here on

my way back from Paris. I'll wire him. Will you do that, Kate?"

"Then I'm to tell him you were here this morning?"

"Certainly." He lifted his chin. His face had a hard determination. "I somehow don't think I'm going to be quite so secretive in my movements in future. It's beginning to be an impossibility—leaving you all the time. Now I've got to be off again."

"Haven't you time to rest and have some food? You're so pale."

"Yes, my prison pallor. I must take care not to lose it. It's a valuable asset." He bent for a moment over the cradle, then tenderly replaced the lace curtain that shielded the baby's face from the light. "I thank God for you both," he whispered.

He was at the door so quickly that she cried in dismay, "Charles, aren't you going to say goodbye?"

"If I attempted to I would fail too miserably."

Then he had left the room and was leaping down the stairs on his long legs. A moment later the front door banged.

He had gone. It was safe now to cry.

CHAPTER 13

In three days he was back. Willie, having had his telegram, was there to meet him. The two men immediately plunged into a discussion of what was to be called the Kilmainham Treaty. Willie said he had Chamberlain on their side, and was convinced that Gladstone only needed to be presented with some concrete terms to be brought round, too. He proposed making out a document that night which he would mail to Gladstone in the morning.

They spread out papers on the dining-room table, and worked all night. Katharine, who, under other circumstances, would have taken a keen interest in the discussion was scarcely listening. Tenant farmers and arrears of rent, an amendment to the Land Bill, a promise to bring to an end the campaign of violence . . . The words meant nothing to her, for she was desperately afraid her baby was dying. The little thing clung to life by the frailest thread. Now too weak even to cry, she lay giving her fluttering breaths, and Katharine could scarcely bear to leave her side. Even Charles must wait. And he himself giving her enough cause for anxiety, he looked so ill and tired.

At half-past ten she rose to go upstairs. Willie protested.

"No, stay, Kate. Let's have the benefit of your views, too. The more heads the better."

"I'm sorry, but I must go to the baby."

"Isn't she better, Mrs. O'Shea?"

"I'm afraid not."

Willie was less acutely concerned.

"Can't the nurse manage for another hour or two?"

"I want to be with her myself." Katharine scarcely dared look at the brown eyes watching her across the lamplight. She might have begged, *you come, too. Let us watch over our child together* . . . She might have cried desperately, *Let Ireland wait, for once.*

She quietly left the room and went upstairs. The nurse reported that the baby seemed a little better. She had taken a few drops of milk off a spoon, and was sleeping.

"Let me have her," said Katharine.

"Should we pick her up? She seems comfortable."

"If she's to die," said Katharine stonily, "it's to be in my arms. You can go to bed now, nurse."

It was the longest vigil she had ever had. It lasted till daylight. Then, at last, there were sounds of the men coming upstairs. They had worked all night.

She heard Willie saying, "Get some rest, Parnell, before you set off again," and then his footsteps went along the corridor to his room. He hadn't bothered to come in and see how the baby was. Perhaps he thought, by the silence, that both she and the baby slept, and he would not disturb them.

It was another familiar and welcome soft tap that came at the door a little later.

She said in a low voice, not stirring from her chair, "Come in," and Charles entered quietly, crossing swiftly to kneel beside her, and look at the little round head with its cap of brown hair against her breast.

"How does she seem?"

For the last hour Katharine had been listening agonisedly to the scarcely audible breaths.

"I'm so afraid she's sinking."

"Let me see her face."

She turned the baby to let the light fall on her face, and as she did so the eyelids fluttered open for a second. A tiny spasm passed over the paper-white face, and then it was still.

She was dead. She was just nine weeks old.

After a long time Charles said very quietly and tenderly:

"Let me lay her down, Kate."

"Oh, no, no!"

But he took the minute form in his strong hands and laid her in her cradle. It was the first time he had held his daughter, and she was dead.

Then he knelt beside Katharine, putting his arms round her. With his head against hers they stayed silent. A little

165

ash crumbled in the fire. Outside the birds were beginning to sing. It was an April morning, and it might be a fine sunny day.

"Be strong, Kate. I know you can be."

"Must you go back?"

"I must. I'm on parole. But it won't be long now."

"Where—would you like her buried?"

"Somewhere near. I'll be back soon to visit her grave."

Katharine clung to him in an agony of despair.

"How can I let you go?"

His eyes burned in his gaunt face. He thrust her arms away. "Don't make it too hard! I have limits of endurance, too."

Then he lifted her hand, and laid his lips on it very tenderly, and a moment later had gone. She was still sitting there when the bustle of departure took place downstairs, the sound of wheels on gravel as Partridge brought the brougham to the door, and Ellen cried, "Oh, Mr. Parnell, are you leaving us so soon?"

"I must be off to my comfortable cell, Ellen. But not for long this time."

"*Not for long* . . ." The echo of those words was the only thing that kept Katharine above despair. But how could she be as strong as she was required to be? Norah and Carmen wept in passionate grief for the loss of their baby sister. They looked at her, a white doll dressed in her christening gown, and Norah refused to say her prayers that night. It was no use to remonstrate with her and tell her she must ask God to look after little Sophie Claude.

"We would have looked after her just as well," she sobbed.

Willie looked mournful for a day or two, but as he hadn't grown fond of the sickly baby he couldn't pretend too much grief. He had her buried in the graveyard at Chislehurst, and there was a letter from his mother in Ireland.

"Dearest Kate,

Dear little Claude—we shared your grief at losing her, but happy child, how glorious is her existence. What a contrast to ours, we who must struggle on. The Bishop is writing to William offering his tribute of sympathy on the death of your dear baby.

> I remain, dearest Katie, your
> affectionate
> Mary O'Shea."

Mary O'Shea, that rigid Catholic, mourning a grand-daughter who was not hers at all. The situation was ironical, to say the least.

The other letter, from Dublin, was the one she cherished.

> "I have been thinking all day of how desolate and lonely you must be in your great sorrow. I wish so much that I might have stayed to comfort you, but I have indeed every hope and confidence that our separation will not now last long. It is terrible to think that on this saddest day of all others you should have nobody with you . . ."

It was a relief to get out of the house and go across the park to Aunt Ben whom she had scarcely visited during her anxiety over the baby. Aunt Ben showed her rare tact and understanding. She suggested that since it was a fine spring morning it was a great pity to remain indoors. The carriage should be brought round, they would stop at Wonersh Lodge to pick up the little girls who could very well be excused lessons for one morning, and then they would all go for a long drive in the country. The children could pick primroses and bring them back to make a pretty coverlet over the baby's grave. Then they could think of her sleeping among flowers instead of in the cold earth.

Willie was very busy and important about his negotiations to get the prisoners released. The terms of the treaty, to which the Irish party would agree, had now been settled. Willie undertook to send them to Mr. Gladstone, and had a letter in acknowledgement.

> "I have received your letter of the 13th and I will communicate with Mr. Forster on the important and varied matter which it contains. I am very sensible of the spirit in which you write."

They were saying now that at liberty Parnell was a disturbing enough force, but imprisoned there was no dealing with the spirit let loose in Ireland, it had gone from a scourge of whips to a scourge of scorpions. The Land League perpetrated new crimes every day. It was rumoured that Parnell himself was afraid of the intensity of the hate he had unleashed. One of the terms of his release was that he would do his utmost to end this campaign of violence. It seemed that only he would be able to maintain any control.

Whatever his own people thought about him, he had become a distinct embarrassment to the Government. Mr. Gladstone informed Mr. Forster that the peace treaty arranged by Captain O'Shea and Mr. Parnell was acceptable, and Mr. Forster, bitter and angry, resigned his post as Chief Secretary for Ireland. He said sarcastically that if all England could not govern the member for Cork, then let everyone acknowledge that he was the greatest power in Ireland today.

Unperturbed, Mr. Gladstone accepted the Chief Secretary's resignation, and announced in the House his intention to release the political prisoners. There was to be a new Viceroy, Lord Spencer, and a new Chief Secretary, Lord Frederick Cavendish, Mr. Gladstone's nephew-in-law. And again bonfires were lit on every hill in Ireland and shouts of triumph went up for the Chief, the beloved leader, who had once more turned what should have been defeat into an outstanding victory.

Mr. Parnell would be in England very shortly. But first, on the insistence of his family, he had to go to Avondale.

He wrote to Katharine saying he would be back in England on May 4th. Could she be in the House of Commons that afternoon? He was only going to Avondale for a day or two to lose some of his prison pallor and present a respectable appearance in the House. He was taking his favourite dog, the Irish setter, Grouse, and going up to Auvghanagh for a day's shooting. The peace of those lonely hills would restore him, he would come back to her a new man.

It was a full House that afternoon. Katharine, on taking her seat in the Ladies' Gallery, could see everyone but the one person who mattered. Willie sat with the Irish members, the Prime Minister on the front bench was engaged in a whispered conversation with Mr. Chamberlain. Sir Charles Dilke on the bench behind, was interposing his brown beard between them. Mr. Forster, the chagrined Irish secretary, was on his feet making a melancholy speech. He had just got to the words: "There are two warrants which I signed in regard to the member for the city of Cork—" when, with no intention of choosing such a dramatic moment, Mr. Parnell walked in.

As one man the Irish members rose and cheered wildly. A moment later the rest of the House followed suit. The ovation went on thunderously while the member for Cork bowed to the Speaker and then, with head erect, composed as always, walked to his place. The unfortunate Mr. Forster's concluding sentence was drowned. He sat down, and shortly afterwards left the House.

Katharine's throat ached. The tears were slipping down her cheeks beneath her veil. She was thankful she wore a veil to hide her intense emotion. She felt so many things, pride, love, loyalty, anxiety for his pallor unbanished by the soft air of the Wicklow Hills, and the unbearably sad knowledge that this man could never belong only to her. She had known that for long enough, but the wild cheering of a moment ago had confirmed it beyond any possible doubt. If she was to love him well, she must allow him to be completely free, never placing impossible demands on him, never failing him when he needed her. She would need to be a saint, she thought. And the world, perhaps her children, too, would call her a whore.

Someone slid into the seat beside her. She blinked back her tears as Willie's voice whispered, "I saw you up here. You're looking very fetching."

She was wearing the first new clothes she had bought since being pregnant. Aunt Ben had said she had grown deplorably shabby, and had insisted on her being outfitted from head to toe. She had chosen a soft blue for her jacket and skirt, and a hat trimmed with cornflowers and yards of veiling. She had been thinking of only one pair of eyes admiring her. She wanted to remove the image of the last time he had seen her, weeping and distraught after the baby's death.

But here was Willie inquisitively staring at her damp cheeks.

"I've come to take you down to tea."

"But the debate—"

He had risen, and she had to follow him.

"The jailbirds will take care of that," he said, as they left the gallery.

There was a faint insolence, a barely concealed contempt in his voice. She realised, suddenly, that although he had worked so hard on the treaty that had achieved the prisoners' release, he would just as soon have them still locked up. His efforts had been on his own behalf, not on theirs. Captain O'Shea, the member for County Clare, who had worked so assiduously with the Prime Minister and Mr. Chamberlain. Was he a likely fellow for a future post, such as Chief Secretary for Ireland?

She had always known this, of course. But it had never been so obvious as it now seemed to her, following his impeccably tailored figure down the stairs. What did he care for the hungry, the poverty-stricken, the sick, the homeless, so long as he advanced his own career, so long as he was the debonair witty member of the Irish party, the one who knew how to dress and how to behave. He would give lip service to the leader just so long as he remained powerful and could suitably further Captain O'Shea's own career.

Katharine's tears had dried. Her mouth had tightened. She knew exactly what her own plans were, too.

"Well, what do you think of him?" Willie said, over tea.

"Him?"

"Don't pretend to be stupid. You know I mean Parnell."

"I thought he didn't look well."

"He never looks robust. And I don't suppose six months in jail agrees with the strongest constitution."

"No, I'm sure it doesn't. That's why I intend taking him down to Eltham tonight. He needs fresh air and quiet."

Willie's blue eyes stared at her.

"You can't tonight. I won't be home."

"That's a pity. Have you an unbreakable engagement?"

"Absolutely. Chamberlain and Dilke and I are dining."

"Then I shall have to entertain Mr. Parnell alone," Katharine said serenely.

"I forbid this!" Willie exploded. But he remembered to keep his voice low. The good-mannered Captain O'Shea must not be seen quarrelling with his wife. "Do you want to start up that old scandal again?"

"It was you who started the scandal with your ridiculous behaviour. Anyway, that's a minor consideration compared with Mr. Parnell's health. I intend to make it my business from now on to look after it. If people talk, let them. I've never cared about gossip. One should be above it." She returned Willie's stare with a level serene one. "If you don't like this, you must make an effort to be home more often."

"B'gad, Kate, what are you doing?"

"You heard the cheers in there a little while ago. Do you hear them often? No. Only for great men. And great men should be cherished. I intend to do something about it, that's all."

Willie looked round quickly, then leaned closer, his face an angry red.

"I believe you have got a bee in your bonnet about this fellow after all."

"I always have had the greatest admiration and liking for him. But never mind that. I'm only telling you that I intend to invite whom I please to my own house, and that you can't stop me."

"The servants will talk. What about the children? You're mad, Kate. This is a most damnably quixotic thing to do. If Parnell accepts, I hope he's properly grateful."

"Who wants gratitude? I only want—" Katharine stopped, seeing the look that had come into Willie's face, an intensely thoughtful evasive look that indicated the springing to life of some scheme in his mind.

With a complete turnabout he said, "I believe I begin to understand you. You want to have your own share in political life. I must say you have the brain for it. It's not entirely feminine, but you're a curious creature, aren't you, my Kate? Well, for heaven's sake, be circumspect. Cosset him, if you must, but don't let the servants gossip." He leaned forward, whispering, "And if he dares to lay a finger on you I give you fair warning I'll have his name blackened. I'll have every priest in Ireland against him. He'll no longer be riding the crest of the wave as he is at present. But while he is—" Willie suddenly looked bland, "—I believe you may have the right idea, we may as well ride with him."

She drew away, trying not to shudder.

It was so easy to read his clever superficial mind. He had suddenly seen how this friendship, so nearly approaching the scandalous, could be turned to his own benefit. Not immediately, perhaps, but when it was necessary. This situation, much more than conspiring to bring about Parnell's release from Kilmainham Jail, might entitle Willie to large rewards. But it must be kept quiet, decent, decorous. Anyway, he was sure Kate was only suffering from a case of hero worship and a little desire for some limelight herself. With her upbringing and her sense of morals she couldn't possibly be promiscuous. Besides, like every other fastidious woman, she didn't care for sex. And hadn't she just suffered the loss of a child? She wouldn't be in the mood for that sort of thing for a long time, even from him.

But perhaps Willie with his private scheming was no worse than her. She was completely false. And for the very best cause in the world. She was almost in danger of thinking her falseness a virtue. At least, she was able to feel extremely happy and quite guiltless about it.

CHAPTER 14

ALTHOUGH it was May it was chilly enough for a fire. They had had dinner, just the two of them, with Jane waiting on the table and a delighted Ellen putting her head round the door to see if her beloved Mr. Parnell had enjoyed the roast lamb, and one of her best apple pies. He'd have had nothing like that in jail, the poor soul, and him looking as if he needed feeding up for a long time to come.

Katharine had had a talk to the servants before dinner, Jane Leinster, Ellen Murphy, the new governess, Miss Coombe who had taken Miss Glennister's place, and Partridge, the coachman who had driven Charles and her from Blackheath station.

Mr. Parnell would be coming down as frequently as he was able. Between campaigning in Ireland and attending sessions in the House he would need all the rest and quiet he could get. She hoped that the servants would co-operate in this and that she could count on their loyalty. It was important that his visits should not be talked about, as not only could they be misconstrued, but he could also be besieged by unwelcome callers. So would everyone promise to be as secret as she and Captain O'Shea intended to be?

They promised readily, though Jane looked at her feet, and Partridge wanted to know if the master minded his horses being used for the frequent trips to railway stations.

"Certainly not," Katharine said firmly. "Mr. Parnell likes to ride, too. You might saddle up Pilot for him in the morning. That will be all now, and thank you."

There were two other things that could not be achieved so quickly. She intended to give the gardener orders to let the privet hedge in front of the house grow a foot taller so that curious passers-by could not stare in. She also intended to have a room built on next to the conservatory so that Charles could have complete privacy in his comings and goings. It could be a study sitting room. She would use it herself when he was not there. It would be a little home within a home, a place where she could dream that she was his wife and no other man's.

She was making her own laws, she thought, with quiet triumph. The world could say what it would.

After dinner she sat in her favourite position, on the hearthrug, with her head against Charles' knee. She could feel his fingers entwined in her hair. If she moved they tightened, as if he were afraid she would leave him. From the moment he had joined her at Charing Cross station he had not been able to bear her out of his sight.

"Stay with me. I can't stand being alone," he said. "In prison I had a couple of warders sleeping at my door. I was glad of their company, I confess."

"Have you been having nightmares, darling?"

"Sometimes. I won't if you're with me. But we'll have to be careful, if I'm to stay here."

"I know. I told you what I said to Willie."

The face above her was cruelly thin and pale. It had not yet thrown off the shadow of recent events. She knew that her own, too, had changed. They might be gay in the future, they might have times of great happiness, but their faces would remain marked, for the rest of their lives, with the strain and suffering of the last months.

"Willie is the cross we must bear. But we must avoid other crosses, if we can. We'll have to go on being careful about not being seen together. I feel safe here. Isn't that curious? These four walls are a haven. But outside, in the street, in hotels—" he brooded for a moment, his face full of loneliness, "—we'll have to be careful, Kate."

"But do you approve of my plan?"

He put his lips against her hair.

"I don't believe I could go on without it. And I have to go on," he added tiredly. "I'm committed. That's the word they use for sending someone to prison. Well, I'm committed to my own prison. But it'll end one day, never fear."

"How far off is that day?"

"Well, closer since the last six months. The Government's feeling somewhat shamefaced, and that's the time to press home our advantage. I believe we'll have the first Home Rule bill drafted before long."

"I cried with pride when they applauded you today."

174

"Oh, that. Don't trust it too much." He lifted her face. "I want no applause but yours, my Katie." And then, "Am I to have my old room?"

"No. Because of the servants, and anyway it's much too small for a permanent room for you." She saw his disappointment, and laughed softly. "The one you are to have has a door that leads through that little dressing room."

All the lethargy had gone from his face.

"Can we go up? Must we wait any longer?"

In the still dark early hours of the morning he said, "Does Willie know?"

"About this? Oh, *no*!"

"I won't share you."

"My darling, you don't have to!"

"Supposing there's another baby."

Katharine's arms tightened round him. She had the most intense obsessive desire to protect him and shield him.

"I will manage Willie."

"How?"

"I'll find a way," she said stubbornly.

He sighed, relaxing against her.

"I believe you will." Presently he murmured, "I would like you to have another child. I watched your face as you sat with little Sophie. It nearly broke my heart."

"The next one will live."

"But I can't have you go through that awful deception again."

"I told you I would manage Willie."

"He'll have his price."

"I know. Will you be prepared to pay it?"

"I'll have to. Because without you I'd die."

The bleak words struck a chill in her heart. She was so afraid that they were true. The responsibility put upon her shoulders was suddenly alarming. Yet she accepted it readily, with a feeling of exaltation. This, she thought soberly, was her destiny.

Night fears disappeared in the morning sunlight. They breakfasted together, Jane waiting on the table, and stealing furtive glances at the gentleman guest. Anyone could have listened to their conversation. It was full of optimism. Charles thought he would have time for a ride before catch-

175

ing his train. Katharine said that was splendid because she had asked Partridge to saddle a horse and bring it round. She wouldn't accompany him, but later she would go with him in the carriage to the railway station. If Aunt Ben didn't keep her too late she would come up to town this afternoon. She wanted to shop for the children, they were growing out of their clothes. If there was time she would come to the House for an hour.

"Then you may have a dull time," Charles said. "I fancy there will be an unaccustomed harmony reigning."

"I hope there is, if it makes you look as content as you do at this moment."

"That is not entirely attributable to the current state of politics."

He smiled into her eyes, and she remembered afterwards that moment of peaceful happiness. It lasted such a tragically short time.

On the railway station there were a few minutes before the train departed, and Katharine went to the news-stand to buy a morning paper for Charles to read on his journey. He opened it casually, then gave an exclamation.

"What is it, Charles?"

His face was rigid, full of horror. With a trembling forefinger he pointed to the headlines. MURDER OF LORD FREDERICK CAVENDISH AND MR. BURKE.

"The new Chief Secretary!" Katharine could only whisper. "Where did it happen?"

"Where do you think? In Dublin. In Phoenix Park. Practically on the doorstep of the vice-regal Lodge." His voice was the voice of a stranger, harsh, low, terrible. "Whoever did this—God rot their souls!"

He was trembling and frighteningly pale. Katharine made him sit down and got into the train beside him. She felt her rings cutting into her flesh as he unconsciously crushed the hand she had slipped into his.

"I'll resign," he said.

"What nonsense! This is nothing to do with you."

He stared at her unseeingly.

"Just as my work was coming to some sort of fruition. The *accursed* fools! How can I carry on if I am stabbed in the back like this?"

The guard began ringing a bell signalling the train's imminent departure. Katharine had to get out, but when Charles, frowning and still alarmingly pale, went to follow her, she pushed him back.

"You're not a coward. Go and see Davitt and the others. You'll know what to do. But you *must* go."

He sank back as if he did not know what he was doing. She was on the platform and the door banged shut. As the train began to move she walked quickly beside it waving, and trying to smile. The shocked white face looked back at her. Then it was gone. The train rattled off down the track and dwindled into the distance.

"Want to read about the 'orrible murders, missis," came the newsboy's cheerful voice.

She did. She had to. She read how the new viceroy, Lord Spencer, had made his state entry into Dublin accompanied by the new Chief Secretary, Lord Frederick Cavendish. There had been a torchlight procession in Dublin the previous evening to celebrate the release of Mr. Parnell, and the next day the crowd was in a mood to welcome the Lord-Lieutenant, hoping that he heralded a time of peace and prosperity. A polo match was being played in Phoenix Park and Lord Spencer, riding back from the festivities, stopped to watch it. He had continued on his way to Vice-regal Lodge, however, before Lord Frederick Cavendish who had walked from Dublin Castle along the banks of the Liffey, entered the park.

Mr. Burke, the Under-Secretary, had hired a jaunting car, but when he saw his chief walking he stopped the car, dismissed the driver, and joined Lord Frederick. A few moments later the murder gang sprang on them stabbing them to death.

Lord Spencer, the new Lord-Lieutenant, said that he had seen the scuffle from the doorway of the Lodge, but had thought it horseplay. Then he had heard a shriek he would never forget.

"It is always in my ears," he said.

A man had dashed up to the Lodge shouting, "Mr. Burke and Lord Cavendish are killed." Lord Spencer had been restrained from hastening to them lest the information had been a ruse to get him out into that murderous dusk,

177

too. So it was left to appalled passers-by to linger at the scene of the crime and wait to give what scanty evidence they could.

Katharine was appalled, too, as she read. This was surely one of the blackest crimes committed in Ireland. It seemed as if some of these Celtic people took a dark evil pleasure in crime and bloodshed. This was the strain in their nature of which Charles was afraid. He who so hated death. Fresh from his triumph of yesterday, how was he to face today?

She didn't know what to do except send a telegram to Willie urging him to bring Charles down that evening. She was afraid for him if he were alone. She had no compunction about calling on her husband's help. This was a national crisis. He should be as disturbed by it as was Charles.

The two men arrived so late that she had been in a fever of worry, thinking they were not coming.

It was Charles' face, drawn and sad, which she studied with anxiety, but Willie's too, was full of gloom.

"This is a damnable thing, Kate," he said. The crisis had put their personal animosity into the background. Yesterday's scene over tea in the House of Commons was forgotten.

"Is it known who committed the murders?"

"It's believed to be the work of a gang who call themselves the Invincibles. They make a sport of removing obnoxious political people. Apparently they've been after Forster for months, but now he's safe in England they've chosen his successor."

"Then at least the party won't be blamed," Katharine said in relief.

Charles lifted his shadowed eyes. "Oh, everything will be blamed on us eventually. Indirectly, if not directly."

"Kate, you must help me," said Willie. "We've been trying all day to persuade Mr. Parnell not to resign. We've just about talked ourselves hoarse. Tim Healy was practically down on his knees."

"Tim gets hysterical," Charles said.

"Well, aren't you hysterical in your own way, with all this determination to give up," said Willie stubbornly.

178

"Oh, I may be a bit mad. All my family is, I believe. But it doesn't take the form of hysteria. I just feel so confoundedly done, as if all I've worked for has been destroyed by that bloody deed in Phoenix Park last night. Lord Frederick was a young man. He left a young bride. He had all his life before him. I tell you, his blood and Burke's will stain our cause forever."

"Now, you're being as melodramatic as Healy."

"Eat something," Katharine begged. "Willie, fill Mr. Parnell's glass. No great decisions were ever made on empty stomachs."

"Well, I don't intend making any great decision, only a small defeated one. I shall write to Gladstone offering to resign, and abide by his decision."

No amount of persuasion from Katharine and Willie would turn him from this course. The letter was written and posted. At the same time Katharine came to a private decision. She also would write to Mr. Gladstone asking him to meet and talk to Mr. Parnell.

Two gloomy days went by, and Mr. Gladstone's reply came to Katharine's letter. He was afraid it would not be possible for him to see Mr. Parnell, but he would meet her at Thomas's Hotel, if she wished. Perhaps she would give him the pleasure of taking tea with him.

To observers it was a perfectly proper and ordinary thing, the elderly gentleman with the great powerful nose and beetling brows taking tea with the fashionably dressed good-looking young woman.

Their conversation was far from ordinary.

"It's good of you to have tea with an old gentleman, Mrs. O'Shea. I admit that it would be most inconvenient and unwise for me to be in private communication with Mr. Parnell. But he has a very charming intermediary."

"You're not going to allow him to resign, Mr. Gladstone?"

"Good heavens, no. I'll be frank with you. We need the Irish vote if we're to stay in power, and your friend can guarantee that for us, I believe. No, no, he mustn't resign. He isn't being blamed for what happened in Phoenix Park. But those ruffians have set the clock back a bit for Ireland, I'm afraid. There's going to be a devil of a row in the House, and we'll have to return to coercion laws. A great pity. But patience, Mrs. O'Shea."

The old man leaned back. He looked every one of his seventy-three years, but his eyes sparkled with their immense vitality.

"If it's the last thing I do, I'll get this Home Rule Bill through. And Parnell's the man to work with, I believe. He's cool, intelligent, keeps his emotions in control, yet he has this tremendous hold over his people. He's a curious personality, a paradox, a wonderful man. I expect you know his inmost feelings, Mrs. O'Shea?"

The words were shot at her so unexpectedly that she could not prevent her look of pride and pleasure. But she had sense enough to choose her words carefully.

"I think so. I know that he hates the English, and would die for Ireland."

"Yes. He's not a man for half-measures."

Mr. Gladstone continued to regard her reflectively, and she was certain now that he knew the truth about her and Charles. He had suspected it, and now his suspicions were confirmed. But it would never be mentioned between them. There would be politeness, courtesy, and perhaps even sympathy.

"I hope he's grateful for the loyal supporter he has in you, Mrs. O'Shea. Tell him not to lose heart. We've stood against a few storms and we'll stand against a few more."

But there had never been a storm like this.

On Mr. Gladstone's announcement that coercion would have to be resorted to once more, and a new Crimes Bill passed, Mr. Parnell said,

"We have been contending against the Right Honourable Gentleman for two years. We have found him to be a great man and a strong man. I even think it is no dishonour to admit that we would not wish to be fought against in the same way by anybody in the future. I regret that the event in Phoenix Park has prevented him continuing the course of conciliation that we had expected from him. I regret that owing to the exigencies of his party, of his position in the country, he has felt himself compelled to turn from that course of conciliation and concession into the horrible paths of coercion."

This caused Mr. Forster, who perhaps felt the chill breath of the death he himself had so luckily escaped, to make a long denunciation against Mr. Parnell, accusing him of having connived at the murders.

Mr. Parnell, although he looked so haggard and careworn, was equal to this. Perfectly composed, he replied that he was responsible to his countrymen only, and did not in the least care what was thought or said about him by Englishmen.

"By the judgment of the Irish people only do I stand or fall."

The statement, infinitely more effective because it was spoken so quietly, and without histrionics, fell into an absolutely silent House. Everyone listened intently to the man who, still only in his thirty-sixth year, carried tragedy so plainly in his face.

He was all too aware that the murders in Dublin had set alight another outbreak of violence. Buildings were blown up, bailiffs for hated English landlords murdered, and innocent people who may have been compelled to give evidence silenced, too, by way of the dark door of death. A juryman was fatally stabbed for convicting a prisoner, an informer shot in broad daylight in a crowded street in Dublin.

But as to Mr. Forster's attack on him, Mr. Parnell had to say with cutting sarcasm, "Why was the Right Honourable Gentleman deposed? Call him back to his post. Send him to help Lord Spencer in the congenial work of the gallows. Send him back to look after the secret inquisitions in Dublin's castle. Send him to distribute the taxes which an unfortunate and starving peasantry have to pay for crimes not committed by themselves. All this would be congenial work for the Right Honourable Gentleman."

Slowly the acuteness of the tragedy passed. Only Katharine knew that Charles had fought against illness during all those difficult weeks. He would come back to Eltham at night or in the early hours of the mornings and collapse. His nerves were gone to pieces, he said. He also suffered from feverish attacks and had nagging rheumatic pains. He needed a long rest and complete freedom from worry, neither of which things was remotely possible.

Somehow, and due only to Katharine, he said, he kept on his feet.

But the worst of the trouble was over. His manifesto denouncing the murders was out, and he was beginning to work on the Home Rule Bill again, frequently sending Katharine to Downing Street with drafts of amended clauses. Mr. Gladstone would walk up and down the long room, his arm tucked in hers, talking freely, and making her repeat the messages she was to take back to Mr. Parnell.

Construction was taking the place of destruction once more.

In spite of the anxiety, Katharine was conscious of a happiness the more acute for being tinged with sadness and uncertainty. Every morning she found a white rose to tuck in Charles' buttonhole. The blooms would last all the summer and into late autumn. After that he would have to make the best of a non-festive appearance, which perhaps would be a good thing since a prospective father didn't want to look too much like a gay bachelor.

Her casual words startled and dismayed him so extremely that he jumped to his feet and took hold of her.

"Is this true? Are you pregnant?"

"Yes.".

"For how long?"

"Three months. I didn't tell you sooner because you had enough on your mind already."

"Good God!"

She saw that his exclamation was not for her secrecy, but for the new dilemma.

"You are pleased?" she begged. "Tell me you are pleased."

"Oh, Kate. Under these circumstances?"

"You said you would like me to have another baby. Didn't you mean it?"

She had intended to be so calm and in control of this situation, but the agony of doubt in his face filled her with anger.

"Is saying one thing, and doing another?" She certainly had not meant to taunt him, but as he began to pace up and down, frowning heavily, she was determined to make him share her misery. She had been so deeply happy herself that

182

she had enjoyed cherishing her secret, and had shut out of her mind the insuperable difficulties. He had expressed the hope that they would have another child, and that had been enough.

But now, by his expression, he thought her feckless, careless, imprudent. As if it were her fault alone! And yet in a queer way she thought it was her fault for having wanted another child by him so badly.

"Does Willie know?" His tone was so aggressive, that it seemed he might believe her capable of deceiving him as well as her husband.

"No, he doesn't."

"Then you haven't—"

She couldn't let him finish the bald statement.

"No, I haven't slept with Willie, and I never will again! How dare you think such a thing! The baby is going to be mine. And yours if you want it. But not his. If necessary, I'll disappear completely. I won't ruin you. But I *will* have this baby. I deserve it." She was beginning to cry, although she had been determined to show no weakness. "I do deserve it, Charlie."

He put out his hand to touch her, as if he were bidding her farewell. "Yes, Kate. You do deserve it."

Then abruptly he left her. She didn't hear him go downstairs, but a few minutes later the front door banged. She flew to the window to see him, with his top-hat on, and carrying a light coat over his arm, walking briskly towards the gate.

He was going to London. Had he left her? She knew he hated goodbyes, and preferred never to say them. But surely he could not leave her just like that. Had the news of her pregnancy, coming on top of all his other worries, been too much? He was so highly strung, so unpredictable.

But he would be back. He must be back. He had said that only she kept him alive, and, frightening as that fact was, she was afraid it was true. How many times had she calmed him, nursed him, dispelled his nightmares, prepared him for each new ordeal?

He must be back.

But for how long would he leave her in this agony of

183

doubt, and what new solution would he or she eventually find to their new problem?

It was nearly midnight before she heard the sound of horses' hooves, and the crunch of wheels on gravel. Someone called goodnight, the front gate clicked shut, footsteps approached.

Who was it? Willie on one of his unannounced visits, or Charles.

A moment later the soft tapping came at the conservatory door, signal that she, and no servant, was to let the visitor in.

She flew downstairs, not waiting even to light a candle. She flung the door open and was in his arms.

"Katie! Such a welcome! Did you think I had gone for ever?" His voice was calm, tenderly teasing. She was weeping with relief.

"How did I know where you had gone?"

"But you might have guessed. I've been to Albert Mansions."

"To Willie!"

"And who else would I be consulting on this peculiarly private affair? Luckily I found him at home."

She had drawn him inside and closed the door. There was faint moonlight shining through the glass roof of the conservatory. The orange tree she had been tending so carefully all the summer hung its glossy leaves above them. She couldn't see his face, only the gleam of his eyes.

"What did he say?"

"I asked him if he'd be prepared to give you a divorce. He refused completely."

"Did you tell him why?"

"Naturally."

"And didn't he want to fight you."

"If he had had a weapon to hand, I'm sure he would have. But he didn't. He fought me in another way."

She was aghast, and fearful, and yet, contrarily, happy—because Charles, at last, was standing openly by her side.

"What *happened*? Tell me."

"The usual thing. His religion. A divorce was not possible. That was his only reason."

"It's certainly not because he loves me," she said

fiercely. "He thinks of me as his, I admit. But he doesn't love me. He hasn't for a long long time, if he ever did. I think he only ever loved his prospects through me, and my relations."

"I don't know about how much he loved you," said Charles. "But it's true he always thinks about his prospects. Through you and your aunt's money. And now through me. He isn't a fool."

Katharine put her hands over her face.

"What does he want?"

"At the moment, no scandal. At least, that's what he assures me."

"He will want more than that. I know Willie."

Charles gently took her hands from her face.

"Shall we face that when it comes? At present he's prepared to acknowledge the baby."

"As his! Oh, my darling!" she cried tormentedly.

"He thinks he's being generous."

"While he lives on Aunt Ben's money, and expects you to do wonderful things for his career!" Her voice was harsh with scorn.

"My dearest, what can we do? We're the beggars."

"*You* a beggar! How terrible!"

"Why is it more terrible for me than you?"

"Because you're famous, someone above the crowd, someone on a pedestal. It would be better," she said bitterly, "if I had gone to bed with him and deceived him again."

He gripped her so tightly that she cried out with pain.

"I'll fall off my pedestal a hundred times rather than think of that happening. It nearly drove me mad the first time."

"It would have been better if we'd never met."

"Do you really think that?"

His voice was so low and sad, that she went into his arms and laid her head on his shoulder.

"No, I don't think it. Only I'm afraid. I'm so afraid."

"Why should you be? At least Willie will leave you alone now."

"Oh, yes, that. That won't worry him too much. He's always had other women. But if it weren't for Aunt Ben's

185

money, if he didn't think he would have a rich wife one day—" she strained to see his face in the gloom "—I believe he would ruin you. You talk of your pride. What about his? His vanity is the biggest part of him. If that's to be publicly damaged, he would really fight a duel and kill you, if he could. If he doesn't do it that way, he will use slower measures."

"Kate, your imagination!"

She couldn't respond to his gentle chaffing.

"What are his conditions?"

"For now? Why, that we exercise the greatest discretion. That we don't be seen in public together, that I don't stay here unless he is home, that we—the three of us—keep up our pretence of being good friends, that I keep him in my confidence politically, and reward him suitably when the appropriate times comes."

"Charles, this won't work. How can it?"

For the first time his voice lost its warmth, and was ruthless, adamant.

"It must."

"Is it worth it? Will you sacrifice your position? Your country?"

"Do you want to hear me say it? Yes, if I must, I will even sacrifice my country."

But his voice was so harsh, so cold, so inimical, that she shivered violently. She knew that now and again he must hate her and this was one of those moments. Her lips moved, but she didn't speak. She was trying to formulate a prayer that such a thing as sacrificing his country would never be necessary. She was afraid it would kill him.

CHAPTER 15

In the morning Charles left for Dublin, and Willie arrived. Returning from Aunt Ben's Katharine found him there. He was sprawled on the sofa in the drawing room, the brandy decanter beside him. If she had expected him to rage and storm he was going to disappoint her. True, he wore a look of smouldering anger, but beneath it there was a not quite hidden satisfaction that his so superior wife had proved herself capable of human weaknesses after all. Now she could no longer take a high and mighty attitude with him.

But was it more than that? Katharine began to have the scarcely believable suspicion that Willie had envisaged this situation from the beginning. So long as it could be handled without public humiliation to himself it suited him very well.

"So you are *enceinte*, my love," he drawled. "What are you hoping for, a boy or a girl?"

"What is that to you?"

"A great deal, since the little beggar will bear my name. Don't look so angry, Kate. You should be down on your knees with gratitude to me. At least, I must say for Parnell, although I don't like the fellow, that he's been honest with me at last. Much more honest than my own wife. And how did he know I wouldn't shoot him on the spot."

Detesting his hypocrisy, Katharine's voice was icy.

"Because, I imagine, he's much more valuable to you alive. How do you dare talk to me of gratitude when you're determined to squeeze all you can out of this situation! It's you who should thank Charles and me."

" 'Charles and me'. Don't say that, Kate," he said fretfully. "It offends me. And for God's sake be discreet in your behaviour with your lover or I swear I'll make the whole thing public. There are enough rumours as it is. It's only my word that keeps them down."

"So what do you want?"

"At the moment, I'm comparatively content. You might

suggest to your aunt that an extra hundred or so wouldn't go amiss. I'm planning some dinner parties after the summer recess. We've got important work to do. By the way, how long are you going to look presentable? Until Christmas, I hope. I'll want you at these affairs. I thought you might persuade Gladstone to come one evening."

"Are you crazy? If he won't see Mr. Parnell, is he likely to see you?"

Willie's face darkened at the scorn in her voice. But he went on amicably enough, "Then we shall have to make do with lesser fry. Chamberlain won't refuse. Nor will Lord Randolph Churchill. Nor Dilke nor Rosebery nor Labouchere. You might tell your aunt you'll need some clothes. You're still very handsome, my dear." His eyes were on her slim waist. "No one would know you had had four children. And that soon to be five. Well, perhaps your sister Anna will help me out when you're no longer available. Anna's a fine-looking woman. I admire her. Kate, come here."

She stiffened. He gave a brief shout of laughter.

"I'm not going to rape you. I only want to know what it is you see in Parnell. For the life of me, I can't think what it is. He seems far too gloomy and intense." Willie was no longer mocking. His eyes were bewildered and stormy. His vanity had been deeply hurt. "But he must have something to make a nice woman like you kick over the traces. Why are you so obsessed with him?"

How could she explain to him that fusion of body and spirit, so rare, so overwhelming, so inevitable? How could it be explained to anybody who had not himself or herself experienced it?

Anyway, it was not to be talked about, especially to Willie who would bewilderedly try to turn it into his own version of love, a light-hearted romp that did not make too many demands on his time or his memory.

He sprang up, angry again.

"The children are not to be involved, do you hear? Especially Gerard. I'm not going to have a growing boy's morals ruined. You be a decent mother to him."

She flushed with pain. This was the way he could wound her most. It was the most difficult thing of all to face.

"You will have no cause for complaint," she said in a low voice, and went quickly out of the room.

Anna had a habit of appearing when there was any news in the wind. She made a journey especially to enquire after her sister's health.

"Willie says you're having another baby. Do you really want another so soon after poor little Sophie? But I suppose you didn't have much say in the matter. I do think men might be a little more thoughtful. No matter what other sacrifices they may be capable of, *that* seems to be one they can't make."

Anna was forever the elder sister, more sophisticated, more knowledgeable, more worldly, than dear country Kate.

Katharine couldn't help smiling.

"Strange as it may seem, I *do* want this baby. So do Norah and Carmen. We think it will be like having Sophie back."

Indeed, the children firmly believed that God had repented of his cruelty and was giving the actual Sophie back to them. They were highly excited and Norah had said she wasn't going to put any more flowers on the tiny grave in Chislehurst graveyard since Sophie would no longer be there.

Anna seemed a little put out. She had expected to find Katharine worn and tired and peevish at the prospect of another pregnancy. Her own marriage wasn't being very satisfactory and she didn't see why Katharine, with four difficult births behind her and another one approaching, and Willie decidedly drinking too heavily, could look so serene. She looked worn, of course, too pale and with shadowed eyes, but that only added to her looks. With her erect carriage and crown of rich brown hair, her long graceful neck and slim waist, she was, more than she had ever been, a woman to be noticed in a crowd.

She had a look Anna could only define as the look of someone loved. And that was a little mysterious since dear Willie, charming as he was, was far from a perfect husband.

Or was it mysterious? She too had heard rumours. She didn't believe them, of course. She had talked Willie out of that nonsense of the duel. And yet there was Kate with that shining enigmatic look.

"How can you bear to face being cooped up here all winter?" she burst out. "Unless you're planning to have frequent visitors. Or visitor."

"If you mean Mr. Parnell," Katharine said composedly, "he has a permanent room here, as I expect Willie has told you. Though he doesn't want it talked about. People put the wrong construction on things."

"Do they?"

"Of course they do. Even though I'll be beginning to look the size of a house, which is a most unlikely time to be having an intrigue. Anna, be a love the next time you come and bring me some white baby wool. The Scottish brand that Debenhams have. I can't get it down here and I don't seem to have the energy at present to go to town."

"Yes. the House is dull when Charlie Parnell's away."

Even that barbed remark failed to disturb Katharine.

"And you might bring some crimson for Aunt Ben. She likes bright colours. She's making mittens for the two housemaids who suffer from chilblains. By the way, she was greatly taken with Mr. Parnell when I introduced them. She walked up and down quoting Irish history to him."

"It would be better," said Anna a little waspishly, "if you got Willie and not Mr. Parnell to cultivate her."

"You know very well that she and Willie don't see eye to eye. They never have. It's a great pity, but I can do nothing about it. She only pays Willie's debts for my sake."

"All that money," said Anna thoughtfully. "How much is it, actually? Willie puts it at a quarter of a million." And suddenly she added, "Don't be a fool, Kate."

"What do you mean?"

"Just what I said. Don't jeopardise a fortune."

"Why? Do you think that I would then lose my husband?"

"I wasn't suggesting that. Anyway, Willie's religion wouldn't allow him a divorce. Even if you became as poor as a church mouse," Anna said flippantly, "you'd be stuck with him."

"I wonder," said Katharine.

The serenity she had made herself wear for Anna was

not entirely assumed. Some of the time it was genuine. When she was with the little girls, when Aunt Ben and she knitted industriously and companionably, when a letter arrived with an Irish postmark, when she dreamed of the dark-eyed baby she would hold in her arms. And most of all when she thought of the relief it was to have Willie know the truth, though his visits were now twice as frequent and his early euphoric triumph had changed to a sullen vindictiveness and resentment.

For his own pride he would keep silent about the baby. But he was impatient for rewards that were slow to come. In Ireland the new hated Crimes Act was in force and no progress could be made at the present time. Everyone had to have as much patience as Katharine in her state of pregnancy.

Willie gambled, and led a rakish life, and frequently fell into a state of self-pity. He was cold but polite to Charles when Charles came, but kept the conversation to politics, and talked a great deal about what he himself had done for the Irish party. He attributed the Kilmainham Treaty entirely to himself. He plotted and planned ceaselessly. He was imagining himself very clever and powerful, with his influential friends. His conversation was studded with references to "Chamberlain and I", or "my friends and I".

It was a hideously difficult situation. Charles honourably kept to his word about not staying at Eltham unless Willie were home. He thought this wisest until the baby was safely born. Nothing must jeopardise its or Katharine's health.

But their snatched few minutes alone were desperately unsatisfactory. Katharine knew it to be impossible to continue for long in this way. They were reduced again to meetings in small depressing hotels. That, too, could not be done for long as she grew more conspicuously pregnant and Willie objected strongly to her going anywhere except to Aunt Ben's. She would stay at home, like a modest woman, if she could act such an unlikely part, he ordered.

The winter seemed endless. Katharine worried incessantly about Charles' health. He had been in bed at Avondale for two weeks, with a fever, influenza he thought. His sister Fanny had nursed him. But he had never liked talking about his health. There were plenty of troubles in Ireland with the harshness of the Crimes Act giving rise to resentment and reprisals. The invisible, fast-moving, entirely unpredictable Captain Moonlight was at large again, striking here one night, a hundred miles away the next. In addition, there were the inevitable clashes among the widely diverse and inflammable members of the party itself. Sometimes, Charles said, they were more difficult to control than the peasants drunk on poteen.

His eyes, always the most striking feature of his face, now utterly dominated it, and they would haunt Katharine long after he had left with their look of sadness. It seemed as if they didn't have one lighthearted moment during those bitter months.

Aunt Ben grumbled about Willie's extravagance. In spite of her great age she had kept her head for money, and once a month sat at her desk with a pile of bills, examining them minutely.

"Katharine, dear, what is this item? Ten pounds, seventeen and six at Debenham and Freebody's."

'Gerard's new school blazer, Aunt Ben. He had grown out of his old one. He's getting so tall. And he needed new boots and underwear. I'm sorry, but growing boys are expensive."

"That's all right, dear. Be sure and bring him to see me the next time he's home. The last time he gave me a scant half-hour and then was off. He's a good-looking boy, but I wish he took after you more."

"Perhaps the new baby will."

"Perhaps. It seems wrong for children to take after their weakest parent."

"Oh, darling aunt! I'm not a strong character."

"Then how do I tolerate you around me? You know I can't abide weak flabby people."

"But morally—"

"Who was talking about morals? Boring things. Since that German princess sat on the throne of England every woman in the country has been holding her breath and walking on tiptoe. Morals! I wasn't talking of them, Katharine. I was talking of honesty and loyalty and courage. Now what's this item? Twelve privet bushes."

"Oh, yes, I wanted to thicken the front hedge. It looked awfully straggly. People peer through."

"Impertinent. Privacy is one of the human rights. I like to see you taking an interest in that ugly old house. Is there anything else you can do to improve it?"

"I did have a scheme if you didn't think it too extravagant. You know that Mr. Parnell visits us frequently when he's in England. He likes to work down here in peace and quiet. It would be so much more convenient if there was an extra room on the ground floor for his use. I'm sure we would get the price of it back when the house is sold. You wouldn't be throwing money away."

"That will be your affair, my dear, since what I have will be yours one day. If you want to spend some of it in advance, by all means do so. All I object to is an unnecessary extravagance such as your wine merchant's bills. Four dozen bottles of champagne when a good hock would have done just as well."

"Oh, that's Willie, I'm afraid. He was entertaining important people."

"I didn't suppose it was you. You don't need to bolster up your confidence by showing off. Nor, I imagine, does Mr. Parnell. By all means make him as comfortable as possible. It will give me pleasure to know that that's done."

Katharine threw her arms round the soft bundle of shawls, smelling of clean wool and lavender water.

"Dear Aunt Ben! Whatever would I do without you?"

The old lady looked at her with her blandest expression. "I haven't the faintest idea."

CHAPTER 16

IT was Christmas, and Willie spent it at home. He was in an irritable mood. He would obviously have preferred to be with his own chosen company in London, but he was doing his duty as a father, and also perhaps seeing that Katharine didn't have any private celebration of her own with her lover. The position was galling him extremely, but he was stubbornly pursuing the path he had decided on, no divorce but a persistent nagging for his rewards, and a slightly sadistic watchfulness so that if he were not happy neither should his wife be happy. He shared fully the inheritance of the Celts, great charm and wit overlying a melancholy that led him to drink too much, and a vengeful nature.

However, the children enjoyed the festivities. They had so far seen only the best side of their father, and Gerard admired and desired to emulate him. He would like to dress as well, to talk as well, and be as good horseman. The boy fortunately noticed nothing wrong between his parents. He was high-spirited and happy, and when the time came for him to go back to school he kissed his mother with his usual devotion. If the little girls still didn't realise where babies came from, he did, and he told Katharine, with embarrassed tenderness, to take care of herself.

What would her nearly grown-up son think if he knew the truth?

So perhaps it was a good thing that her other visitor arrived after Gerard had gone back to school.

Charles had spent Christmas at Avondale. He had written, but he had not seen Katharine for a month. He had waited until he was sure Willie would have left Wonersh Lodge before he came.

Then, one chilly January morning, he simply strode in as if he owned the place, an Irish setter at his heels.

Katharine dismissed the servants who stood goggling at the invasion, Mr. Parnell, looking so brisk and impetuous, laying aside his heavy tweed travelling cape, and the big red dog running about snuffling at the furniture as if it, too, thought it had arrived home.

"I've come to wish you a happy new year." Looking round to make sure that the servants had gone, he took Katharine in his arms. "How are you, my darling? Are you well? I've brought you your Christmas present."

The colour was high in her cheeks, the day was suddenly sparkling.

"Oh, what? Tell me."

He snapped his fingers. "Grouse! Come here."

The dog obeyed. Charles took it by its collar and led it to Katharine.

"This is your new mistress. You're to obey her and look after her faithfully."

"Charles! But Grouse is your favourite dog!"

"That's why I'm giving him to you. Now why are you crying?"

She couldn't answer. She laid her head against his shoulder, and felt the warm tongue of the dog licking her hand. At last she said, "Only you can make me so happy."

"And so unhappy? Well, let us concentrate on happiness in the future."

"But won't you miss Grouse at Avondale?"

"No, now I shall have two friends to visit here. Besides, you are often here with only women in the house. I'll be easier in my mind if you have a good watchdog. Tell the girls to give him plenty of exercise."

"They'll love him."

"Then let's have them in and make introductions."

It was a merry party, the happiest there had been in that house. She adored Charles when he was lighthearted and gay like this. She didn't suppose many people other than herself and his family had see him this way. Jane and Ellen and Miss Coombe came in, too, and Grouse amiably accepted the petting lavished on him. He always went back to lie at his master's feet, but Charles said he would soon transfer his best allegiance to his new mistress.

"We're having another little sister soon," Norah had always been quite unable to keep secrets. "Will you come and see her, Mr. Parnell?"

"Certainly I will. But little sisters sometimes turn out to be little brothers, did you know that?"

"No, this one is to be a sister," Norah maintained quite definitely. "God has told Mamma. He's sorry for what He did to our last baby. He took her back. By mistake, I think."

"Miss Norah!" exclaimed Ellen. "God never makes mistakes. How can you say so?"

"Well, why's He sending her to us again?" said Norah unanswerably and Carmen added shyly, "Sophie had brown eyes. Mamma said she likes brown eyes best."

"Whatever colour her eyes are," said Mr. Parnell quietly, "you can count on me being among her devoted worshippers."

And of course, after that, the baby could not help but be a girl. She was born in March and was a strong healthy child. Willie stayed away during most of the time that Katharine was confined to her bed, having the grace to display only enough interest in the new baby to allay suspicion among the servants. But they had their own ideas about the master's lack of interest. The baby didn't take after him at all. It was the exact image of its mother, and the master, being a bit vain, didn't care for that. He liked his family to have his good looks. Wasn't that men all over? Lords of the earth, they thought themselves.

But the mistress made up for the master's negligence. She was daft about the new little one. She laughed at her chubbiness, and showed her off to everyone, most of all to Mr. Parnell, when he came. As if a great man like that, and him a bachelor, too, would want to be bothered with small babies. They had to kiss them when they were electioneering, but that was as far as their interest went.

Still, it made the house happy, with little Clare, and her nurse, a bustling apple-cheeked country-girl whom everybody liked, and of course Mr. Parnell's dog that had made itself completely at home. The mistress didn't seem so lonely now. She got back her looks quickly, and was in grand spirits. The shadow of little Sophie's death had vanished at last.

Gradually, because things were quiet in Ireland, and he preferred to leave them so, Charles began to spend more time at Eltham. Willie had gone on one of his periodic trips to Madrid. He had got bored with this quiescent state and was letting the party go hang for the present. He knew that Parnell, through Katharine, was negotiating with the Prime Minister, but the negotiations must necessarily be long and slow before they came to fruition, if ever. It was generally thought that the Liberals would not be in power much longer, and when they went out the Irish party must decide whether it would be better to treat with the Conservatives, or wait patiently for their cool but fairly honest friend, Mr. Gladstone, to return to power.

It was disappointing that the life seemed to have gone out of the attack. Some of the Irish members were agitating for action, and smiling in secret glee when attempts were made to blow up public buildings in England. But their leader advised patience, and himself disappeared from the scene.

Most people could make a pretty good guess where to find him, and the name, Kitty O'Shea, was being bandied about again. Fortunately her husband hadn't come to hear of this, although it was rumoured, too, that he would do precious little about it. He could hardly denounce the woman who was reported to be working so loyally for the party, and was even on friendly terms with the Prime Minister.

His colleagues didn't know of the more immediate reasons of course. Plain hard cash.

Willie's ailing sister had died. To get over this sad event, Willie went once more to Spain and Katharine had a letter from Madrid.

"If Aunt insists on your crossing the park in bad weather you will make yourself ill, Aunt very unreasonable. If she accuses me of extravagance you can truthfully tell her my sister's illness was an immense expense. This hotel is simply ruinous and I never have anything but one-and-sixpenny wine. I must have a sitting room to transact business."

Aunt Ben was grumbling more and more about Willie's constant demands but, after a particularly cold and wet summer, she encouraged Katharine to take a house in Brighton for the early winter, and until after Christmas, if she wished. The children would benefit from the sea air. Carmen had been looking peaky, and Norah was growing too fast. Little Clare was as bonny as a rose but she, too, would enjoy her first trip to the seaside.

"See if you can persuade your husband to join you. It will be much cheaper than all these jaunts abroad. Besides, if he stays with the children you will be able to come up to me occasionally. I don't suppose you want to inhale sea breezes for weeks on end."

The house was on Medina Terrace, with a view of the sea. Katharine took it furnished. There was a resident house-keeper, Mrs. Pethers, and a housemaid, Harriet Bull. She, Norah and Carmen, their governess, the baby and her nurse, and Grouse whom they couldn't bear to leave behind, moved down there in November. Gerard was to join them when school holidays began, and Willie had grudgingly promised to be there for Christmas. But there were four weeks until Christmas.

The last time they had been together in Brighton Charles had sacrificed his beard. That, Katharine wrote, would not be necessary this time. He was to come down as soon as possible. The sea air would do him good, too. He knew how she always worried about his health, but perhaps some vigorous walks on the downs and the fresh air filling his lungs would set him up for the winter. No one would re-cognise them here. They could be out together all day. She would only suggest, as a precaution, that he take separate lodgings. There was just a chance that Willie would arrive unexpectedly. It would be like him to do so deliberately. Not that it seriously mattered, except that scenes were so disagreeable and Willie had been particularly short-tempered lately.

A week of perfect bliss followed. They walked on the downs all day, lunching at small inns, or carrying a picnic lunch that Katharine had prepared herself, since she didn't find the housekeeper, Mrs. Pethers, particularly obliging. With colour in her cheeks, and her hair tumbling down in the wind, Charles said she had never been so beautiful.

"Is your eyesight failing? I'm nearly thirty-seven."

"Thirty-seven, forty-seven, eighty-seven, you'll always be beautiful. Will you remember that?"

"Must I?"

"Yes, in case I'm not always able to tell you so."

She stopped.

"Don't say that."

"It was only a passing observation." He took her hand "Come, don't look so full of doom. If you anticipate it, you invite it."

"It was you who made the remark inviting doom."

He laughed. "Kate! My dearest one! You're even more beautiful when your eyes are stormy like that. What are you worrying about? I'm very much afraid you're going to have me to the end of my life."

She flung herself into his arms. The wind billowed her skirts about his legs, her tumbling hair blew in his face. They were wrapped together like one person on the high cliffs with the grey sea spread beneath them.

"Come back to the house, Miss Coombe has the children out. It will be empty."

"My darling, you're trembling."

"I felt a cold breath of mortality. You know what that feels like."

His eyes grew sombre. "I do."

"Come back to the house, darling."

The wind blew the front door shut behind them. His hand in hers, Katharine led him up the stairs to her bedroom. Within it, she locked the door, and flung her cloak off. He took the remaining pins out of her hair and let it fall loose over her shoulders. Then he began to undo the high collar of her dress. Her throat was too lovely to hide beneath the whalebone and starch, he said. And her shoulders, too. What he especially loved were her breasts covered only by the falling curtain of her hair. His fingers were gentle, expert, making her flesh tingle unbearably. It was always like this, always new, exciting, perfect. Perhaps the difficulties and dangers added stimulation to their love making. Perhaps it was like this because it had to be fairly infrequent. But she didn't think so. If he were her husband and lay beside her every night, she was sure she would respond just as eagerly to his beloved body.

They could not linger behind a locked door for too long. The children would be home. The long-faced Mrs. Pethers with her pinched lips might have an inquisitive ear cocked in the kitchen. As it was, as they came out of the bedroom, Katharine saw a form disappearing into the children's bedroom. It was Harriet Bull, the maid. Katharine recognised her red hair beneath her starched cap. She had moved too quickly, as if she might have been pressed against the wall listening.

Fortunately, Charles had not seen her. This small blot on the perfection of their love-making should not trouble him, at least. An inquisitive maid, an inquisitive housekeeper. Well, Willie would be here soon enough, and there would be nothing for them to whisper about.

Indeed, he arrived a week earlier than he had said he would come, and without warning. It was late afternoon. The children were having tea in the kitchen, the baby was asleep, and Katharine and Charles sat relaxed before a fire in the drawing room.

A few moments earlier Mrs. Pethers had tapped at the door saying she wanted to light the gas, but Katharine told her not to come in. The firelight in the dusk was so pleasant. She was sitting on the hearthrug with her head against Charles' knees. He had disarranged her hair, and she had had to hastily pin it up when Mrs. Pethers knocked. But the woman, with an audible sniff, had gone away, and it was then the front doorbell rang.

Katharine sprang up, her heart pounding. She had been certain in that instant that it was Willie. She scarcely needed to hear his voice to confirm it.

"Good afternoon! I'm Captain O'Shea." He was always hearty with servants. "Is my wife in?"

"Yes, sir. She's in the drawing room."

"Don't disturb her. I'll take my bags upstairs first. I suppose there's a room for me."

"Yes, sir, the one at the end of the passage was kept for you."

Katharine didn't wait to reflect on the scarcely hidden relish in Mrs. Pethers' voice. She only knew that she couldn't bear one of Willie's scenes within five minutes of his arrival. Charles must not be found with her.

"Quick, darling. Go out of the window. You can drop down from the balcony, can't you?"

200

"Easily. But I won't leave you . . ."

"Yes, do, please. It will save unpleasantness. Call at the front door later. The children know you're in Brighton, so Willie will have to be told. But not like this."

Perhaps she was foolish and had panicked unnecessarily. There had been no time to think. She virtually pushed him through the window, and watched him drop safely to the ground. Then she quickly closed the window, drew the curtains, and rang the bell.

When Mrs. Pethers appeared, so quickly that she must have been lurking as Harriet Bull had lurked the other day, Katharine said calmly, "Was that my husband I heard arriving? Then you had better light the gas, Mrs. Pethers. And make some tea."

It would have been all right if Charles had not come back so soon. But he had disliked leaving her, had grown anxious, and was at the front door in too short a time. Why should Mr. Parnell be asking to see Captain O'Shea so soon after his arrival? It was highly suspicious.

Willie could scarcely be civil.

"I didn't know you were in Brighton, Mr. Parnell," he said stiffly.

"Yes, I am for a few days. Katharine—" (he always called her Katharine in that endearingly solemn way to Charles), "—told me she was expecting you. We've been having discussions about our next moves with Gladstone. Your arrival is timely. We'll be able to thresh out the matter."

"Discussion on politics, fiddlesticks!"

"Willie! Keep your voice down," Katharine begged.

"Who've you set talking now? Do you want more scandal than there is already?"

"And there'll be even more if you shout the news to the whole house."

"Don't let's pretend, O'Shea," Charles said in a quiet reasonable voice. "You know the position between Katharine and me. You refuse to give her a divorce, so you condone our love. What more is there to be said?"

"Plenty! Plenty, if I care to."

"Do as you please, my dear fellow. I'll welcome any action."

His complete composure and an almost lordly indifference to public opinion left Willie, as always, baffled and angry. He should have been the one to crack the whip, not his wife's paramour. What was more, the fellow had the nerve to say,

"I only ask you not to distress Katharine too much."

"Distress her! I can hardly endure the sight of her, the brazen hussy!"

"Then perhaps you will undertake to stay here with the children while I go back to Aunt Ben for Christmas," Katharine said, her composure gained from Charles. "I don't like leaving her alone so long. And all things considered, it would be better for the children if we were not together in this sort of mood."

"Do what you like," Willie flung out. "But I won't go on being treated in this fashion. The both of you had better take notice of that."

CHAPTER 17

IT was the first white Christmas for several years. The Lodge was bitterly cold. Aunt Ben wrapped herself in rugs and shawls, and dozed by the fire. She wanted no festivities. The servants could have a Christmas party below stairs if they liked, but since Katharine's children were not there there was no need to have all that nonsense of a tree lighted with candles and too much exhausting excitement.

She listened, however, to Katharine's suggestion that Mr. Parnell should be invited to have dinner with them. He usually went to his home at Avondale for Christmas, but this year he had decided to remain in England.

"Because he enjoys an English Christmas?" The old lady's eyes were too knowledgeable. "I'm afraid you can't deceive me about that, Kate. He has told me he abhors all English customs."

"That's only an attitude he uses politically."

"Well, I'm glad to be assured that we're not among his abhorrences," the old lady said dryly. "By all means, invite him. I shall enjoy his company. But even for him I will not sit up until midnight. You will have to entertain him after ten o'clock."

If Aunt Ben were with company she enjoyed she would willingly sit up until two o'clock, and not look fatigued. Katharine could only realise that with her exquisite tact she was withdrawing from the scene to allow Katharine to be alone with the man she loved. Being perceptive about so many things, how could Aunt Ben not be perceptive about this most important of all situations? She had frequently admired the baby Clare's beautiful dark eyes and smooth golden brown hair. She had pretended to be glad that for once Katharine had had a child that bore no resemblance whatever to her husband, a man who was unworthy of her in every way. Whatever suspicions she might have, she had not mentioned them. She might never do so. They might go with her to the grave.

They dined by candlelight, the three of them, and punctually at ten o'clock Aunt Ben asked to be excused. It was still snowing, and intensely cold, but no doubt this would not deter the carollers who would be along about midnight. Perhaps Katharine would see that they got their usual sovereign, and tell them not to sing too loudly as there were, strange as it might seem on Christmas Eve, some people who wanted to sleep.

Katharine suddenly had the crazy idea that she would like to walk in the snow. Charles quite willingly put on overshoes and a greatcoat, and accompanied her.

It had stopped snowing, and the moon was shining. The scene was eerie and frozen, the leafless trees casting spidery shadows, the stone urns along the balustrade piled with white pyramids. Their footsteps crunched. The frozen snow was slippery and, nearly falling, Katharine clutched at Charles. Her face was nipped with the cold. She felt intensely alive, her mind clear, her lungs full of the sharp clean air.

Voices and the crunch of footsteps indicated the arrival of the carollers. Katharine drew Charles back behind one of the massive elms. Standing close together, his greatcoat wrapped round them both for warmth, they watched the stumbling merry party. A square of yellow light fell on the snow where one of the maids had thrown open the front door. The voices, quavering at first then growing strong, began to sing.

"Hark the herald angels sing . . ."

At this distance, in the still white night, the sound was poignantly beautiful. From the village the Christmas bells had begun to chime.

"Do you believe in God?" Katharine whispered.

"I'm not sure. But I do believe in a personal destiny. I believe certain people are meant to meet and love, and that it's quite useless to fight against that because it's their destiny."

"Us?"

He nodded. "What's more, I believe that if we were born again in another age we'd meet and love again. Simply because sheer longing would bring us together."

The cold was making Katharine shiver. It had been a

night like this when Papa had died. She didn't want to talk of death.

Nevertheless, something in his shadowed face made her say, "You're not afraid of dying, are you?"

"Yes, I am. I confess I've always had a horror of it. Even in my childhood I was haunted by the thousands of cruel and unnecessary deaths in Ireland." He gave a sudden dry laugh, "I gave John Redmond a fright not long ago. I wasn't too well, I'd gone to bed early. I was staying in Morison's Hotel in Dublin, and Redmond came in to go over points of our campaign. We had lit four candles, but one went out, and before I could stop myself I had blown the remaining three out. Redmond was startled, I can tell you. He said we couldn't work in the dark, and that my face, when he struck a match, was like a corpse's."

"Oh, no!"

"Well, that was what the trouble was. There are always three candles lit round a corpse. To represent the Holy Trinity. And I'm a superstitious fellow. I didn't care for that sign or omen or whatever it was."

"It was nothing," Katharine said fiercely. "I suppose the draught blew one candle out."

"A breath from the Almighty?" Charles said. Then he exclaimed penitently, "I've alarmed you. You look as white as the snow."

"I'm only cold. Let's go in."

But to tell the truth she was shivering from more than cold. His face in the moonlight had had an austere ethereal look, a fragile and decidedly uncomfortable look. This walk at midnight hadn't been such a good idea after all. It had called up ghosts.

Willie, too, must have been reflecting on the unsatisfactoriness of affairs, for early in the new year he began talking about his ambitions. Wasn't it time something was done for him? He ought to be made Chief Secretary for Ireland without more ado. It would be a good idea, since she had his ear and, apparently, his admiration, if Kate would suggest this to Mr. Gladstone. Her word would probably carry more weight than Parnell's, since after all she was his wife and would naturally want his advancement.

With the greatest unwillingness Katharine carried out this task, only to meet a frosty stare from the great man.

"Impossible, Mrs. O'Shea. Oh, I understand your feelings. They do you credit." (Did his narrowed and formidably sharp gaze see other reasons behind this request?) "But for one thing O'Shea hasn't shown sufficient abilities yet, and for another, I'm not in a position to grant favours. There'll be another election before too long, and I'm not happy about our chances. I tell you this in the greatest confidence. Your husband, and Mr. Parnell, too, may have to look elsewhere for a while. I'm sorry. I still hope to realise my ambition of getting the Home Rule Bill through. But it may have to wait awhile. And whether I can wait for it I don't know. I'm seventy-seven, Mrs. O'Shea, and I'm very tired."

He added, "Another thing. Would you write me letters about your business in future? I think you're seen coming here too often. It's getting a bit indiscreet."

She would miss the stimulation of their meetings. She liked, admired and trusted Mr. Gladstone. She believed he also admired her. But perhaps his edict was timely, for she was pregnant again. Willie had already guessed this fact. He had a sharp eye for her pallor and the dark stains she got beneath her eyes. That would be why he was agitating for the Chief Secretaryship. But since that wasn't to be his, what else would he want?

However, another scandal was occupying political circles at this time. It was a very shocking one. Sir Charles Dilke, that solid and upright Victorian, a widower who had just become engaged to a most respectable young woman, and who shared equally with Joseph Chamberlain the chance of stepping into Mr. Gladstone's shoes, was being named as co-respondent in a particularly unsavoury divorce suit.

Although his guilt was not proved, the scandal compelled him to resign from politics, and go to live abroad. In one stroke he had lost his career.

It was a tragedy for an exceptionally able man, and Katharine could not get it out of her mind. She became ill, and the doctor, fearing a miscarriage, put her to bed for a couple of weeks. She had to write to Charles, who was in Ireland, telling him this, as she would be unable to keep their next assignation. He was immediately deeply alarmed, and sent a telegram begging her to reply at once telling him how she was.

When he heard, he wrote, "I felt very much relieved by your letter last night. However, it is evident you must take great care." He made no mention of when he would next be down at Eltham, but as it happened it was the very evening of the day she had received his letter.

There was a great commotion downstairs, with sundry thuds, and doors opening and shutting. Katharine rang the little silver bell on her bedside table. No one answered it. She had to ring again, shaking the bell impatiently for a long time, before at last Jane appeared at the door.

"Oh, ma'am, I'm sorry to be so long in coming, but Mr. Parnell's arrived. He's brought—"

"Not a word, Jane," came Charles' voice behind her. "It's a surprise for Mrs. O'Shea. Can I come in, Katharine?"

"Yes, do." She dismissed Jane, and Charles strode towards the bed. She was pleased to see that he looked well, his eyes bright, his colour good. But perhaps that was caused by excitement, for he looked quite boyish in his pleasure at his secret.

"How are you, my darling? Can you get up?"

She lifted her face for his kiss, sighing with happiness.

"Of course. As long as I don't walk too much."

"You shan't walk at all. Put on your robe."

He picked it up from a chair, and held it out for her to put it on. Then, to her complete surprise, he swung her into his arms.

"I'm taking you downstairs."

"Charles! I'm much too heavy! There are two of us, remember."

"All the better. That's what my surprise is for."

And there it was before the fire in the sitting room. A large invalid couch upholstered in pale pink brocade.

Charles laid her on it as carefully as if she were made of glass, then stood back, hugely delighted with himself.

"Is that comfortable! Is that better than spending all day upstairs? But wait a minute. You need pillows and a rug."

He went leaping upstairs again, and by the time he returned Katharine had been able to stop her tears and present a smiling face to him.

"Charles, it's heavenly. It makes me feel like a consumptive heroine."

He laughed with enormous enjoyment.

"Thank God you don't look like one. You look remarkably healthy. Let me see. The pillows slightly more to this side. Your hair displayed so. One hand outside the coverlet. Very artistic." His face sobered as he knelt beside her. "If only I could look after you all the time."

"This is enough for the present. I feel cherished."

"So you are. Is it really all right about the baby now?"

"I think so. the doctor says in another week the danger will be completely past, but it's past now, I'm sure. Especially in the last fifteen minutes. How did you get this large piece of furniture down here?"

"By hansom cab, after some hard bargaining with the driver. He didn't like his cab being treated like a furniture removal van, but when I explained the couch was for a very charming lady who would immediately get well when she lay on it, he relented."

"I expect it was your charm that he couldn't resist, not mine." She laid her hand over his. "Can you stay?"

"May I?"

"Please! Willie's in Scotland shooting. In any case, I'm not worrying about him. Ring the bell, will you? I want to tell Ellen about dinner, and Jenny must bring Clare in after her bath. You'd like to see her, wouldn't you?"

"You hardly need to ask that question."

It was true, for Charles was deeply devoted to his plump brown-eyed little daughter. When the nursemaid brought her in she flung out her dimpled arms to him, and gurgled as his beard tickled her. Grouse had followed, and, as always, went into a frenzy of joy to discover his master there. Although he had settled down happily enough in his new home he had never given his complete loyalty to anyone else. He whimpered with pleasure when the tall familiar form was there before him.

Katharine had to blink back tears again. These scenes were all the more precious for their rarity. She thought that she lived all her life in a tenth of the time that other people had, for she was only truly alive at these times.

But they were not entirely ecstatic. There was always a

208

shadow. This evening it was the tragedy of Sir Charles Dilke.

"And the case against him was not even proved," Katharine said. "That girl, Mary Crawford, may have been lying. So what would public opinion be if the guilt were undeniable?"

"Are you talking about a hypothetical case? Or us?"

"Us," she admitted. "Supposing Willie got vindictive."

"Is he likely to?"

"I don't think so at present. In spite of his tempers, I still think the situation suits him. He was very disappointed about the Chief Secretaryship, but he knows that's not your fault. No, I don't think he will do anything. But if he did—"

"Kate, there's something I want to tell you. Not long ago I consulted my solicitor, Mr. Inderwick, as to whether there was any country in Europe where you could live and retain custody of Clare and the new baby. He hasn't given me an answer yet. He was going to look into the matter."

Katherine was sitting bolt upright.

"You mean that we're to run away?"

"Wouldn't you like to?"

She ignored his question. "Charles, you're *never* to do this! Never! We've talked of this before and I suppose we'll talk of it again, but my answer will always be the same. I won't allow you to run away."

"Even if it came to the question of being another Dilke?"

"No! Even then you would face your enemies and fight. I know you would. Because otherwise you would die. You would be eaten up with contempt for yourself and die."

"Katie, my dearest, we're talking about you, too."

"Oh, I have a long neck. I can hold my head high on it."

He bowed his own over her hand, lifting it to lay his lips on it, and holding it there for a long time.

"So tell Mr. Inderwick to do nothing more about the matter."

"I would so much like you and my children to myself."

"But our house, wherever it was, would be full of phantoms." Her voice was wry. "I suppose the Irish are better at haunting than anyone."

"Yes. They do that to me even now." He suddenly sprang

up as if trying to shake off a burden. "Curse this ambivalence of mine! Curse this obsession I have for my country."

"And curse mine for you," said Katharine. "But I don't mean that any more than you do. Sit down, my darling. Read to me."

He obeyed slowly, the tension still in his body.

"What?"

"John Donne, please. '*Take heed of loving me. At least remember I forbade it thee*'."

The slow quiet voice, the flickering fire, the gaslight turned low, were infinitely peaceful, unbearably sad.

"*Yet, love and hate me, too. So, these extremes shall neither's office do ...*" "*To let me live, O love and hate me, too ...*"

CHAPTER 18

In August 1885 Parliament was dissolved preparatory to the General Election to be held in 1886.

In November, when the lilac-coloured mists were hanging about the trees in the park and the first frost powdered the grass, Katharine's baby, another girl, was born.

She was named Frances, and nicknamed Katie. All the women in the family welcomed her warmly. Willie, to Katharine's relief, stayed away, and Charles had time for only the briefest visits since he was deep in his election campaign. It was important to return the Liberals to power, though he was fairly certain that the Conservatives wouldn't be too opposed to a Home Rule Bill. Whichever party was elected, the Irish Nationalists, eighty-six strong, could hold the balance of power. The position was heady and exciting.

Not, however, for Willie. Mr. Gladstone and his party were re-elected but, far from getting the Chief Secretaryship, Willie found that he could not even get re-elected to his own seat, County Clare. He had always been unpopular with the Irish party, which was not surprising since he openly despised and derided them for their uncouth manners and haphazard way of dressing.

It was no use for Parnell to point out their cleverness. Willie merely said that he could rejoice in but not sit with unvarnished genius. Indeed, one of the exasperated members who returned Captain O'Shea's contempt in full measure, lay in wait for him one night in the lobby of the House, intending to kill him. But the silly fellow had been inflaming his anger with too much Irish whiskey, and in the end was too drunk to be of harm to anybody. Which event might have gone to support Willie's condemnation of the unbalanced behaviour of his fellow party members if he hadn't been just as stubborn and foolhardy himself in an entirely different way.

He refused to take the party pledge.

It looked as if he shared the feelings of the Queen, who, after the election, wrote acidly in her *Journal* :

"Mr. Gladstone continued to say that one could not doubt the opinion of Ireland when eighty-six members were returned by the Irish people in favour of Home Rule. I observed that these were mostly low disreputable men who were elected by order of Parnell, and did not genuinely represent the whole country."

Willie certainly did not count himself one of the "low disreputable men" but the fact remained that he was without a seat, and he intended to make trouble until he had one. It was true that, with Lord Richard Grosvenor's and Mr. Gladstone's help (Katharine had written to both of them) and with Mr. Parnell campaigning for him, he had stood for one of the Liverpool divisions, but had been defeated. So he must be given another opportunity elsewhere. The great and powerful Mr. Parnell must get an Irish seat for him, even without his taking the party pledge.

He went down to Eltham to make this known to Katharine. He sprawled in a chair in front of the fire, the port decanter beside him, and said, not without satisfaction, "Well, the time has come, Kate. Parnell must do something for me."

"How can he, if you ruin your own chances?" Katharine asked hotly. "You won't take the party pledge, you make yourself unpopular with the other members."

"No, I don't. I'm a popular fellow," Willie said in a hurt voice. "Talk to Parnell for me. Use your own kind of persuasions. They'll be effective enough, if I'm not mistaken."

"Willie, I beg you, don't worry him now. The election has been an enormous strain on him. He's exhausted. Let a few months go by. Let things settle down."

"And go about with my tail between my legs? I have no intention whatever of taking your advice, my love. I want something done for me now. Now!" He pounded the table several times, making the decanter and glasses rattle. "Otherwise I might turn out to be just as awkward a customer as some of my fellow countrymen. Chamberlain, I might say, is behind me in this. I've got a letter from him here. I'll read it to you."

He took the folded paper from his breast pocket, and opened it.

"In the present condition of affairs it is more than ever unfortunate that you have not found a seat. Is there any chance of your standing for one of those now vacant by double election in Ireland? Surely it must be to the interest of the Irish party to keep open channels of communication with the Liberal leaders? Can you not get Mr. Parnell's *exequatur* for one of the vacant seats? It is really the least he can do for you, after all you have done for him."

Willie stopped reading and replaced the letter in his pocket.

"There. Tell Parnell that, will you?"

"Which seat is he referring to?" Katharine asked reluctantly.

"Galway. O'Connor was elected to it, and also to one of the Liverpool divisions. He's taking Liverpool, so Galway stays vacant. I'd like it. If you see Parnell before I do, tell him this conversation. Don't leave anything out. Don't try to protect his feelings. Because this is something I expect him to do for me. Do you understand, my love?" He smiled, his blue eyes cold. "I'm sure you do."

It was a terrible dilemma. She knew the harm it would do Charles in his own party if he showed this sudden strange partisanship for such a discredited member as Captain O'Shea.

If only she could have found an answer to the problem without worrying Charles with it. But there was none. She had to welcome him with the news when he came down to Eltham a few days later.

It was a great pity because he was in such good spirits. They had talked of the nuisance it was that he had no good horse to ride when he was in England, and after a discussion with Aunt Ben the arrangement had been made that he should bring his own over from Ireland and keep it in the stables at Wonersh Lodge. Partridge could take care of it along with the children's ponies.

Charles arrived with the news that he was having not one but three horses shipped over, Dictator, President and Home

213

Rule. He couldn't wait to take Kate driving with Dictator. She would find him the fastest horse she had ever been behind.

"But what's the matter, Kate? Aren't you pleased?"

"Of course. I'm delighted. But we have another problem, I'll have to talk to you about it at once. I can't stop worrying about it."

He listened closely as she related the conversation between herself and her husband. A frown deepened between his eyes. Otherwise he betrayed no emotion. When she had finished, he said quietly, "I had anticipated this. I'm afraid it's something we'll have to face."

"But it will do you so much harm."

"If I have to do it, yes. What's more, the residents of Galway may be less easily managed than my own party. Twisting politics to serve the ends of an individual is bad. Even the most uninformed will see through that. But perhaps I can talk Willie out of this. Get him down. We must have a meeting."

He walked up and down, his frown deepening.

"What I do know is that there must be no scandal until the Home Rule Bill is passed. After that, you and I can be happy in the sight of the world. But until then I fear these English hypocrites. If your husband chooses to be difficult now, the whole thing can come tumbling down like a house of cards."

"It's what I've always been afraid of. Willie's cunning. He's been waiting for an opportunity like this."

Charles stopped in his pacing to stand over her and smooth out the lines in her brow with his fingertips. But the gesture was perfunctory. It was one of the moments when he felt her like a stone round his neck. She knew it. She was agonisingly unhappy.

"Get Willie down as soon as possible. We must get this settled once and for all."

But for once Katharine's courage deserted her. She felt she couldn't face the painful scene that there would have to be. She put off writing to Willie for three days, and eventually a peevish impatient self-pitying letter came from him.

"Dear Kate,

I have kept my temper more or less well so far. Mr. Chamberlain, with his knowledge of what I did at various times for Mr. Parnell, considers the latter—well, he thinks very ill indeed of him. Chamberlain says that if he had any feelings, any spark of honour, he would have told his party that he was under an obligation that my seat must be secured, or he would resign his leadership.

"I am not going to lie in a ditch. I have been treated in a blackguard fashion, and I mean to hit back. Parnell won't be of 'high importance' soon.

"I wonder the little girls have not written to me. No one cares a bit for me . . ."

So there was nothing for it but to face the inevitable without delay.

They met at Wonersh Lodge one late afternoon. Willie greeted Charles in an offhand insolent way.

"Well, I hope you haven't brought me down here for nothing."

"I hope to talk you out of your wild notions, and that's a fact. Even if I got you nominated for Galway how do you know the people will accept you?"

Willie coloured darkly.

"I'm very popular in Ireland."

"Well, you're scarcely popular with the party. You won't even sit near them in the House."

"I should be sorry to be liked by that rapscallion crew."

Charles gave a small shrug of futility.

"That attitude scarcely helps matters. You're not being adult about this, O'Shea. You won't take the party pledge and yet you expect me to put you forward as a sincere and honest candidate. You scorn the dress and the speech of your fellow members. You make fun of their accents behind their backs. Don't deny it. I've heard you at it. You act the grand gentleman. You want a seat in Parliament because it's a social asset. It gives you the entrée into such fashionable houses as your friend Chamberlain's."

Willie, about to make an indignant rejoinder, was silenced with a wave of the hand. Charles, with withering scorn, continued: "You're playing at politics, O'Shea. Oh,

I admit you had a hand in the Kilmainham Treaty because it suited you to, it was an opportunity for you to get some serious attention from the friends you so admire. But let me warn you, those same friends may not be so trustworthy as you think. I personally don't trust Chamberlain one inch. And I assure you that I won't be blackmailed into anything by him. If I help you over Galway, it will be to suit my own interests, not because I'm afraid of any politician, from the Prime Minister down."

At last Willie had his opportunity to sneer.

"The three of us in this room know what your interests are very well indeed. But the rest of the world doesn't. Yet."

"Willie—"

Willie paid no attention to Katharine.

"I fancy I know who will get the sympathy when it does. The higher you've climbed, Parnell, the further you'll have to fall."

If Willie went red with anger, Charles went white. His mouth was hard. His eyes were black in his blanched face.

"Be careful, O'Shea. I may take you at your word and let the whole thing go. Which I hardly think would suit your schemes. I would dearly like to lay down this burden. But I've got so far. It would virtually be a betrayal of my people. So, if we can keep our tempers, let's talk about this sanely. Will you take the party pledge?"

"No, I will not."

"Then God knows how I'm to get you accepted."

"You might mention they owe me some gratitude for getting their chief out of jail."

"Willie, if Charles goes this far for you, surely you can put aside your scruples, whatever they are, and take the pledge."

But Katharine could never say anything to suit him now. He automatically contemptuously rejected her arguments.

"You're prejudiced, Kate. And you damn well should be. I hear I'm even stabling Parnell's horses now."

"*You* stabling them! However can you have such flights of fancy? That would amuse Aunt Ben. And you do little enough to amuse her, I assure you."

"Well, I won't have my son riding any of those brutes," Willie said sulkily.

In a low, very tired voice, Charles said, "This is irrelevant, O'Shea. If you won't take the party pledge, all I can ask is that you give me your word to behave with discretion. Try to get yourself liked a bit, especially by your constituents. I can fill their ears with advice, but I can't guide their hands when they fill in their ballot papers. Now can this interview be ended?"

He looked so pale that Katharine was alarmed. Willie, looking less triumphant than he might have felt, said: "You're a fine one to talk about discretion, I must say. I don't understand you, Parnell. How can you let a love affair ruin you?"

"I quite see that it's beyond your understanding. I didn't take your wife from you, O'Shea. You never had her." In an almost inaudible voice he added, "Thank God."

But Willie didn't remain to hear that. He snatched up his hat and strode out, And Katharine flew to Charles.

"Are you all right?"

"A little dizzy. Will you get me a glass of water?"

She did so, and was relieved to see him looking less shaken after he had drunk.

"Charles, are you ill?"

"No, no, I get these turns occasionally. I've been at it too hard, I expect. And now I'll have to begin again in Galway. There'll be the fiercest opposition. But I'll run O'Shea and I'll get him returned. I'll force him down their throats. It will cost me the confidence of the party, but I'll be done with his talk of pledges and ingratitude."

Then he began to smile, the tenderness in his eyes.

"Don't look so tragic, Katie. No one's being cast to the wolves. Well, not yet, at least."

But he so nearly was. The two most formidable members of his party, Biggar and the headstrong ambitious Tim Healy, bitterly opposed what they regarded as the outrageous nomination of Captain O'Shea, and threatened a revolt within the party, even though Healy unctuously gave out that he still "declined to believe that our illustrious leader" was really supporting O'Shea.

Mr. Biggar was much more outspoken. He stood up at a

public meeting in Galway, and made the shattering announcement that the lamentable truth was, Mr. Parnell had chosen Captain O'Shea to be their representative because Mrs. O'Shea was his mistress. He did even more, he prepared a telegram to be sent to Mr. Parnell stating bluntly, "Mrs. O'Shea will be your ruin." Healy interposed and suggested more discretion. The wording was changed to "The O'Sheas will be your ruin", and the gossip, beginning with a talkative post-office official, spread like wildfire.

They began to be afraid of what they had done, the stolid Biggar whose own personal life was far from being above reproach, and the mercurial Healy who was always torn between love and hate for his leader, although of latter years the black side of hate was winning. When they heard that Mr. Parnell was coming to Galway to quell the riots, Healy, in a fine state of nerves, asked what should be done. "Mob him, sir," answered Biggar unhesitatingly.

But the people took this decision out of his hands, for they gathered of their own accord outside the railway station, a large restless muttering mob who were capable of anything, even lynching.

Mr. Parnell had asked the retiring member for Galway, Mr. O'Connor, to accompany him. It required considerable courage on Mr. O'Connor's part to do so. He knew what the temper of the mob would be. Whether Mr. Parnell knew or cared, he could not have said. Certainly the man didn't turn a hair. On the journey to Galway he talked of every subject except the important one, the coming election and the controversial candidate, Captain O'Shea. He might have been going to a reception where he knew that flags would be waving and people cheering for him.

Not Galway under a sullen stormy sky with an enormous crowd waiting to rend the man whom they thought had betrayed them.

As the train came to a halt the roar of the crowd was alarmingly menacing. Mr. O'Connor bit his lip and lost his colour, but Mr. Parnell opened the door of the compartment and stepped out, an erect figure, his fine head held high, his authority so hypnotic that after a surge forward, the roaring of the crowd died away, there was a brief almost shamed silence. Then one wavering cheer rose, and

218

suddenly they were all cheering. And Mr Parnell stood there completely composed bowing in acknowledgement as if the cheers were entirely expected.

It was only when the unfortunate Mr. O'Connor emerged that pandemonium broke out. The mob had gathered to take vengeance on somebody. If it couldn't be their beloved leader—how could they ever have imagined it could be him?—then they would turn on their late member, Mr. O'Connor, who had deserted them for an English constituency.

The poor man was thrown to the ground and would have been in danger of being trampled to death if he had not been rescued by the man who had been meant to be the victim, Mr. Parnell himself.

The Irish certainly had a habit of turning their deepest affairs to farce, their lightest sometimes to tragedy. At least there were no half-measures.

For when Mr Parnell, later, stood on a platform in the market square and addressed them they listened in the most obedient and reverent silence.

"I have a Parliament for Ireland within the hollow of my hand," he said, the passion breaking through his voice. "Destroy me and you take away that Parliament. Reject Captain O'Shea, destroy me, and there will arise a shout from all the enemies of Ireland, 'Parnell is beaten; Ireland no longer has a leader!' "

For a moment the silence was complete. Then one lonely voice spoke. Mr. Biggar's. "Sir, if Mr. Lynch (O'Shea's opponent) goes to the poll, I'll support him!"

But then the cheers broke out, and his voice was drowned. It was drowned again when, meeting his colleagues in the hotel, Mr. Parnell said, "A rumour has spread that I will retire from the party. I have no intention of resigning my position. I would not resign it if the people of Galway were to kick me through the streets today."

This time the subdued cheers were led by the effervescent Mr. Healy. Perhaps his admiration for a great and courageous performance had temporarily made him forget the facts. At least no one now had the temerity to mention the name, Kitty O'Shea.

Mr. Healy made the announcement: "I retire from this

219

contest and Captain O'Shea becomes, I suppose, the member for Galway. It is a bitter cup for you. God knows, to me it is a cup of poison, but even so let it be taken for the sake of the unity of the party we love."

After that, it was a foregone conclusion that Captain O'Shea should win his seat in Galway by an overwhelming majority.

All the same the seed of doubt had been planted. The party's confidence in its leader had been badly shaken. From now on the warring factions would be difficult, if not impossible, to control.

It was to be hoped that Captain O'Shea would do something to make himself more popular.

CHAPTER 19

AUNT BEN was failing. She frequently spent the morning in bed, half the time dozing, although she liked Katharine to be with her so that she could see her as she woke.

In the silence of the comfortable bedroom where the fire now burnt constantly, and the heavy curtains were drawn against the bright light, Katharine had too much time to think.

News had come of Willie's success in Galway, and of its accompanying difficulties for Charles. She had heard of that shameful telegram, and echoes of the shouted name "Kitty O'Shea" seemed to come to her here, so far away.

They were talking of her as if she were a street girl, a common and shameless baggage. She supposed they would be considerably surprised if they saw her as she was now, a woman over forty, with lines in her forehead and at the corners of her eyes. She had taken a long time to recover fully from the birth of her last baby, and this, added to the constant tension and strain, had given her a gaunt look, her eyes too large, her cheekbones too prominent. The skin beneath her jaw was beginning to sag slightly. Her throat was still smooth and white, and her mouth kept its soft warm curve, the corners tilted upwards, but her face was the face of a middle-aged woman. If those people who shouted her name so mockingly were to see her they would certainly wonder what it was that made her so irresistible. And especially to a man who was beginning to show alarming signs of his own mortality, although he was still comparatively young. Young indeed compared with the seventy-seven years of his Prime Minister.

But sometimes Mr. Gladstone, with his flashing imperious eyes, showed more vitality than Mr. Parnell, although Mr. Parnell, when whipped to the height of his emotion was more vigorous and dynamic than anybody.

Katharine was deeply worried about his health. She was afraid he was seriously ill. She intended to persuade him to see a specialist when he was next in London. This last trouble with Willie and the Galway election would have drained all his frail reserves of energy. She couldn't rest until he was back so that she could see for herself what had happened to him.

She sat in Aunt Ben's quiet bedroom, the only sound the gentle snoring of the old lady in the bed, and clenched her fists, wishing Ireland at the bottom of the Atlantic. She had never seen it and never wished to. It loved and it crucified.

But don't you do the same yourself, a voice in her head said. Aren't you both between you, the calm English woman and the old hag in blood-draggled skirts across the Irish Channel, tearing this sensitive man to pieces?

"Katharine!" That was Aunt Ben's voice from the bed. "Why are you looking so sad?"

"Am I, Aunt Ben? I was only thinking."

"But it has turned out all right, hasn't it? Willie will be happy now he has his seat in Parliament again."

Aunt Ben was constantly amazing. Her body might be failing, but her mind seemed, in compensation, to have grown doubly acute and intuitive. One must be careful what thoughts one indulged in, in her presence.

"Yes, I hope he will."

"But you're worrying about what this might have done to Mr. Parnell? He's a strong man. He'll bear it."

Katharine came to stand by the bed.

"You know, don't you, Aunt Ben?" and for one blessed moment she felt as if, in making this admission, she had dropped her burden.

"My dear child, what do you take me for? I was never stupid, and I'm not yet blind. I'm only sorry that you're being hurt so much. It makes me begin to dislike all men."

"Oh, no, Aunt Ben. It's my fault as much as his. I hurt him, too. Terribly."

"Then I can only say he must think it worth it. And I suppose if you work that out, it comes to the fact that that's the only kind of love worth having."

"How long have you known?" Katharine asked.

"Long enough. You're very foolish, Katharine, but brave. You're the daughter I always wanted. Someone who's not afraid to be a real woman. But I won't always be here to protect you, even in my small way. I can make you financially independent, no more."

"Aunt Ben, don't talk like that."

The old lady was pursuing her thoughts.

"But I fancy that will suit your husband rather too well. I must think about this. Our laws need revising. A husband shouldn't have so many rights over his wife. It takes away a woman's dignity."

Especially when that husband stooped to blackmail, Katharine thought privately. But a good wife, of course, would not find herself in a position to be blackmailed. Willie had most legitimate grievances. Or so the world would think, the world not having discovered his failings as a husband.

She was remembering suddenly that pretty frivolous hat she had worn on her wedding day, and her apprehension when the minister had said, *"From this day forth . . ."*

"Have those privet bushes grown thick enough?" Aunt Ben asked abruptly.

"Yes." Katharine didn't add that people still peered through the hedge, sometimes breaking branches in their destructive curiosity. But they saw little enough. Old Benson cutting the lawn or the children playing. Norah and Carmen, big girls now, were very sweet with their little sisters and loved them dearly. It would be a great shock to them if their home were broken, and they found that the babies were to be separated from them. But this must not be allowed to happen. Willie had Galway. What else would he want? Aunt Ben's death, and a fortune to play with?

"Mr. Parnell enjoys having his horses here. He goes for long rides down the country lanes. It does him good after all the strain he goes through. People don't need to look through the hedge to see him," she added. "He doesn't try to hide."

"What an extraordinary situation! It can't go on."

"It must until the Home Rule Bill is through," Katharine said vehemently. "After that—we can face mere scandal. I believe Charles will give up politics. He will have done what he set himself to do. But until then—and it won't be long now—"

"Are you so sure the Bill will go through?"

"It must!" Katharine's voice was low and intense. "Because neither of us can go on like this forever."

Charles came home from Ireland. He was nervous, thin, drawn in the face, preoccupied. He spent almost all his time in the new room off the conservatory working on clauses for the Home Rule Bill. He didn't want to talk about what had happened at Galway, and when Katharine mentioned Willie he said that they must only be thankful he was staying away from Eltham. Apparently, having got what he wanted, he was going to relax for the present. There were more important things to worry about than the state of Willie's temper. It looked as if the Home Rule Bill would be introduced during the present session of Parliament. Nothing must now stand in its way.

Katharine must write letters to Gladstone constantly with amendments, new clauses, propositions. It was a pity the old man still thought it unwise to see her, especially at this vital stage, but letters would do as well. The long, long road Charles had travelled seemed at last to be coming to an end.

One April morning Mr. Gladstone's private secretary arrived at Wonersh Lodge with a letter for Katharine asking her to telegraph the one word "Yes", if he was to introduce the Home Rule Bill that night. Charles said briefly, "This Bill will do as a beginning." His eyes were burning with controlled excitement. "Send him the word, Kate. Will you be up?"

"If I can leave Aunt Ben. She's quite poorly." Because Jane was hovering with his hat and coat she could do no more than squeeze his hand and whisper good luck. Then he was gone, and she had nothing to do but wait.

Mr. Gladstone's speech on the Bill lasted three and a half hours, a *tour de force* for such an old man. He, and the Irish leader sitting listening so intently and impassively, were both on the verge of realising their ambitions.

But a wearying debate lasted for sixteen days, and the second reading of the bill did not take place until the middle of May.

By this time Mr. Chamberlain had shown his hand. He did not intend to support the Bill. He threatened to split the ranks of the Liberals. This was exactly what happened, for when the division over the Home Rule Bill was finally called in June, the Bill was defeated.

All the efforts had been in vain.

Led by Chamberlain. the Conservatives leapt from their seats and cheered. Gladstone seemed to shrink in his seat. He was suddenly very old, very alone, bewildered by failure. In vain the Irish members (with one important dissident, Captain O'Shea, who had refused to vote—was not Chamberlain his friend and mentor?) stormily and noisily applauded the defeated Prime Minister. With their lack of inhibitions they turned on the sallow-faced imperturbable Chamberlain and shouted, "Judas! Traitor!" But what was the use now? There was the whole thing to do all over again, and who now had the strength for it? The aged Prime Minister whose Government would be compelled to resign? Their own leader who seemed to have expended his last strength and sat with a ravaged face and burning eyes, contemplating the ruin of his hopes.

But Mr. Parnell continually surprised. On the first reading of the Bill he had said those memorable words, "No man has the right to set a boundary to the onward march of a nation," and on the day after the defeat (and after a sleepless night about which only the woman who loved him knew), he sprang to his feet, and full of fire and nervous energy made one of his most poignant speeches.

"During the last five years I know there have been very severe and drastic Coercion Bills, but it will require an even severer and more drastic measure of coercion now. You have had during those five years the suspension of the Habeas Corpus Act. You have had a thousand of your Irish fellow subjects held in prison without specific charge, many of them for long periods of time without trial and without any intention of placing them upon trial, you have had the Arms Act, you have had the suspension of trial by jury. You have authorised your police to enter the domicile of a citizen of your fellow subject in Ireland at any hour of the day or night and search any part of this domicile, even the beds of the women, without warrant. You have fined the innocent for offences committed by the guilty, you have taken power to expel aliens from the country, you have revived the curfew laws and the blood money of your

Norman conquerors, you have gagged the Press, and seized and suppressed newspapers, you have manufactured new crimes and offences and applied fresh penalties unknown to your law for these crimes and offences. All this you have done for five years and all this and much more you will have to do again . . .

"I am convinced there are a sufficient number of wise and just members in this House to cause it to disregard appeals made to passion, and to choose the better way of founding peace and goodwill among nations, and when the numbers in the division lobby come to be told it will also be told, for the admiration of all future generations, that England and her Parliament, in this nineteenth century, was wise enough, brave enough and generous enough to close the strife of centuries and to give peace and prosperity to suffering Ireland . . ."

He did not wait for the applause to end. He did not even resume his seat. He simply turned and walked out of the House to Katharine, who was waiting.

She had the carriage, and Partridge on the box. He had orders to drive to Harley Street. She had at last persuaded Charles to see Sir Henry Thompson about his failing health.

They talked very little on the way. They were both too dispirited.

Finally Charles said, "Don't look so mournful, darling. We haven't given up."

She turned to him despairingly.

"This is killing you. How can you begin all over again?"

"If Gladstone can do so, who am I to complain?"

"But there's going to be another election. The Conservatives are bound to win."

"We can work just as well with the opposition. That's our strength. Eighty-six members of the Irish Nationalist party, and the Government has to woo them for their vote. We'll keep them constantly on the jump."

Katharine bit her lip.

"I was dreaming of being able to forget politics."

"You wouldn't expect me to give up with my task half-done?"

She hated his cold surprised voice. Couldn't he see that

any other man in his position would retire on the grounds of ill health? Any other man, not Charles Stewart Parnell . . .

"Do you expect me to sit at your deathbed?"

He faced her with blazing eyes.

"Never say that! Never say that!"

Her lip trembled. "I'm sorry. You know I didn't mean it. But will you take Sir Henry Thompson's advice? If he tells you you must retire, will you do so?"

"No."

He seemed to realise his cruelty for after a moment he took her face and turned it to him, making her look into his eyes.

"You know me, Kate. You know I have to go on to the bitter end. Try to put up with me, if you can."

"And if I can't?" she managed to say.

"Then I shall have to try to survive without you, and that is presenting me with an impossibility. Ah, Kate, have patience."

"Patience!" she whispered. Reluctantly she said, "You know I will never leave you."

He looked so moved that he had to be a little flippant.

"That's capital, because Gladstone's already talking of the next Home Rule Bill. He has invited me to go up to Hawarden."

"Oh, Charles! And he never has before."

The carriage was coming to a halt. They had drawn up outside one of the tall Harley Street houses. Partridge leapt off the box and opened the door. Katharine got out, and waited for Charles to alight. The Home Rule Bill had vanished from her mind, the more immediate worry was with her. The man beside her was so gaunt, so thin. He trembled as he stood. His nerves seemed to have gone completely. She thought of their conversation with incredulity. As if she could ever leave him!

They were ushered into a well-furnished room and told to wait. The maid seemed doubtful whether Sir Henry Thompson would see them. He was at his dinner. What name should she give?

They had decided on this beforehand.

"Mr. Charles Stewart," Katharine said.

She looked anxiously at Charles who had collapsed into a chair as if all his strength had forsaken him. She made a quick decision.

"Let me see the doctor first. I'll explain your case. It will save you the energy."

He opened his eyes and made an attempt at a smile.

"Forgive me, Kate. It's reaction, I think. I held up in the House to finish my speech. It about finished me."

And yet he intended to begin again.

The maid came back to say that the doctor would see them, Katharine followed her into the consulting room, and saw the elderly man with impatient face behind his desk.

"Sit down, Madam," he said curtly. "Is this an urgent case? I hope it is, since you've interrupted my dinner. Look at the clock!"

"I'm sorry, doctor. but—"

"Well don't waste my time now. I understood it was a Mr. Stewart I was to see. Who is he? Your husband? Why doesn't he come in?"

Katharine's heart sank. She knew that Sir Henry Thompson was a famous man but she hadn't anticipated his abrupt irritable manner. He would get nowhere with Charles this way. Charles would simply walk out of his room.

She had to make a swift decision.

"I had better tell you the truth, doctor. We thought it wise to come under another name to avoid publicity. The patient waiting to see you is Mr. Parnell, and he is too ill to be received in this manner."

Sir Henry sprang up, his face changed.

"But my dear lady, why didn't you say so at once? Mr. Parnell! Poor fellow. Let me do everything I can for him. Can you tell me a little about his illness?"

Katharine related what she could about the fevers, the sleeplessness, the rheumatic pains.

"I'm afraid he doesn't tell me everything, doctor. He dislikes talking about his health."

"Then I'd better see him myself."

There was no question now of a spoilt dinner, for Sir Henry was closeted with Charles for nearly an hour. Katharine waited with what patience she could, anxiety making her body ache with tension. When at last the two men came in to her, she wondered how they could possibly be smiling. She had begun to expect the most dire news.

"Well, here he is, Mrs. O'Shea." (So Charles had told Sir Henry who she was, or had he guessed. Did everyone in London know?) "Make him follow my advice completely. He will tell you what it is. And don't hesitate to get in touch with me at any time. At any time at all." He shook hands with them both, and Katharine, encouraged by his now friendly manner, asked impulsively:

"Have you advised him to retire from politics, Sir Henry?"

"I hope I'm too good a doctor to prescribe a death sentence, Mrs. O'Shea."

"Yes. It was foolish of me to even ask. I see you understand him already."

In the privacy of the carriage again, it was now Charles' turn to reassure Katharine.

"It's nothing serious, Kate. My circulation is bad, I'm always to keep my feet warm. And I mustn't drink any wine but Moselle. My kidneys seem to be a little affected. Sir Henry has written out a diet that's going to be a bit tiresome. You know how I never notice what I eat. And of course I am to rest."

"And you shall, election or no election," Katharine said grimly. "For once I'll have my way. You shall simply disappear. Your friends can whistle for you."

He laid his head on her shoulder.

"Very well, my darling," said his tired voice.

229

CHAPTER 20

THE election was over, the Conservatives were in, led by Lord Salisbury, and Ireland had no Home Rule. Not that Mr. Gladstone had given up the fight. He had merely retired to Hawarden to work on a new Bill. He called it a "mischievous and painful struggle" and was as dogged in his efforts as was Parnell.

Parnell followed his example and for a great part of the time disappeared from public view. No one knew exactly where he was, though most people could make a good guess. Rumours that he was mysteriously ill spread. There were also whispers about his family's history of mental instability. He would accept invitations to meetings or parties, and then frequently not appear, either because he had forgotten about them or had been too lethargic. He was terse and autocratic with the members of his party, and developed an idiosyncrasy of not wanting to be recognised when he walked in the streets so that he muffled his face with a scarf. His habit of seldom reading or answering letters became worse.

But for all this he retained absolutely his grip on his party. He was never too ill to be present at an important issue. There was no question of his being a spent force.

Though only Katharine knew how ill he had been, and the intensely worrying time she had had when he had been unable to read even a newspaper, unable to put pen to paper or rouse himself to any mental effort.

There was another annoyance, slight but persistent.

Willie had begun writing offensive letters to Katharine saying that his day would come, and that if Parnell continued to visit Eltham when he had been especially asked to keep away, there would be a way of revenge. It seemed as if his bitter jealousy of Parnell, not only as the man who had taken his wife's affection, but as a man of exceptional distinction and importance, had turned to hate.

Katharine was alarmed and afraid. She hated the scenes

Willie made in front of the children. Once, after he had gone, she found Carmen in tears, and Norah, very flushed, saying: "Why does Papa have to be so horrid? Does he really hate us?"

"Not you, my darlings," Katharine said sadly.

Carmen lifted a tear-streaked face.

"Mamma, we don't really have to go to a horrid boarding school, do we?"

Katharine felt a small chill.

"I didn't know anything about this. Is that what Papa has been saying?"

Norah, less volatile and emotional than her sister, said aloofly, "He said we were getting too big to be at home. He was going to make enquiries about boarding schools." But Carmen, in a flood of tears, flung herself at her mother. "He said we ought to be away from you, Mamma. Why must we? We'd *die* at boarding school."

"Clare and Katie would miss us," Norah said. "Could you manage without us, Mamma?"

Her daughters were growing up. They were pretty girls. It was almost time they were out of school frocks and pinafores. Soon they would put their hair up and go to parties. Thinking back to her own girlhood, so sheltered, so correct, Katharine had a pang of dismay. Was Willie right this time? Should the girls be taken from her and brought out by someone thoroughly respectable? Could she, a notorious woman (oh yes, that was true, much as she refused to believe it), launch these charming innocent budding creatures into society? What black harm was she doing her family?

It was so long ago since she had protested that she would not have her children hurt. But the irresistible events had swept her on, and here she was with the love and trust of Norah and Carmen so precariously retained. On his last holidays Gerard, too, had been less friendly. He had made comments about the new horses in the stables, and had admired Dictator's speed, but had not attempted to ride any of them, preferring the elderly pony which was now too small and slow for him. All the children, by an unspoken law, avoided the room where Charles worked.

Clare and little Katie toddled after him, and Grouse always lay at his feet. But the older children held him more in awe than affection. They were not his. They had not experienced his tenderness.

Reassuring her daughters that they would not under any circumstances be sent away, Katharine forced herself to take a calm detached look at the situation. Had the time come to sacrifice Charles and her own personal desires for the children?

But it took only the sound of wheels in the carriageway, the familiar knock at the door, and his voice, "Kate, where are you?" for the old obsession to sweep over her. She might as well fight against a tidal wave. The children, she told herself, would soon enough grow up, marry, make their own lives. But Charles—those dark eyes so anxious until they saw her, the hand that sought hers—she knew that she never would nor could forsake him.

The climax came after a mischievous report in the *Pall Mall Gazette*. Charles, returning late from London, had had a slight accident. Too slight to have been mentioned if, unfortunately, he had not been recognised.

The paper reported: "Shortly after midnight on Friday evening Mr. Parnell while driving home came into collision with a market gardener's cart. During the sitting of Parliament the Hon. member for Cork usually takes up his residence at Eltham, a suburban village in the south-east of London. From here he can often be seen taking riding exercise round by Chislehurst and Sidcup. On Friday night as usual his carriage met him at the railway station by the train which leaves Charing Cross. As he was driving homeward a heavy van came into collision with Mr. Parnell's conveyance, damaging it, but fortunately causing no serious injury to its owner."

Willie happened to read this report, and wrote one of his furious letters to Katharine saying that although he knew well enough that she was ignoring all his requests, it was intolerable that the whole world should know of her behaviour.

Willie, since Mr. Chamberlain's desertion of the Irish cause, had been in an unhappy position. He had refused to vote for the Home Rule Bill, and went on refusing to co-operate with his party. He was extremely unpopular, and this heightened scandal must have been galling to him.

Katharine had one of her rare moments of feeling sorry for him, and tried to reassure him.

She wrote, "I should say the paragraph has been put up by Healy and Co. to annoy you. Charles says it is better to put up with a great deal of abuse rather than retaliate for it is ill fighting with a chimney sweep. I advise you to hold on to your seat for I am sure you will annoy the sweeps most by doing so. I am sure there is no end to their spite after your Galway success."

Whether Willie accepted this explanation or not, there was worse to come.

Gerard, home for the Christmas holidays, had been taken by his father to see the great Jem Mace in a boxing tournament.

All the next day he was so quiet and subdued that finally Katharine asked him whether he were feeling ill.

"No, Mamma. I'm perfectly well."

"Then is something worrying you, darling? You have such a frown."

The boy coloured furiously and burst out, "Is it true, Mamma, what Papa read to me in the paper last night? He asked me if it was and I said no, because I had to. But is it true?"

Again the chilly feeling was touching Katharine.

"How can I answer you until you tell me what you're talking about?"

The boy's eyes were on his boots.

"The paper said that Mr. Parnell was always here in this house."

"And you denied it?" Katharine said softly.

"I had to! How could I let Papa think that about you?"

The tormented blue eyes begging for her own denial were almost more than she could face.

"It's true, as you know, that Mr. Parnell often comes here to work and rest. I myself have always been deeply interested in Mr. Parnell's work and thought it of first importance and that talk by foolish people scarcely mattered. But if it is going to hurt and worry you, then I promise to see that he makes other arrangements. So you see that although Papa was speaking the truth, in his way, so were you in yours. And there's nothing for you to be upset about."

Although Gerard seemed satisfied, she was sure that he was only partly so. His father's conversation (had it been deliberate, to turn her son against her?) had had a severe effect on his adolescent mind.

That, and Willie's constant abuse, and Charles' health finally made up her mind for her. She would find a suitable house in London within easy reach of the Houses of Parliament for Charles. She would establish him there with a housekeeper, and then visit him frequently. It was the best she could do. The present situation was becoming intolerable for everybody. Even Aunt Ben had commented on it, for Mr Meredith had inadvertently (or had he, too, a liking for gossip?) read her the article in the *Pall Mall Gazette*, and she had made one of her indirect but penetrating comments about the dividing line between love and self-indulgence.

The house was in Regent's Park, and for discretion Katharine rented it in the name of Mr. Clement Preston. She said she was Mr. Preston's sister. She was able to find a good capable couple called Harvey to look after the house, and Charles, acknowledging its eminent suitability, agreed to move in.

On his first evening there she took charge herself. She supervised his unpacking, asked Mrs. Harvey to cook a small but appetising meal for two, saw that fires were lit in all the main rooms, and then disappeared to change.

When she came downstairs Charles, in his comfortable smoking jacket, was sitting before the fire in the drawing room, relaxing quietly before dinner. He sprang up at her entrance, then gave an admiring exclamation.

She had dressed for this first meal in the new house in a pale grey gown ruffled at the neck and sleeves. She had also done her hair in an elaborate style on the top of her head, the coiled weight of it held by a Spanish comb. She had on high-heeled velvet slippers, and carried a fan.

She was the lady of the house come down for an informal dinner with her husband.

"Kate, you're lovely. Have I seen this gown before?"

"No. I kept it for tonight. We must celebrate our new house. I hope you are enjoying it, Mr. Preston."

234

He gave his small courtly bow.

"From this moment, immensely."

She laughed, taking his hand.

"Mr. and Mrs. Preston were the happiest. That's why I chose their name."

Charles Stewart had been less happy, he had had to visit the Harley Street specialist. Mr. Fox had written letters from Kilmainham Jail. Mr. Campbell had kept her waiting a very long time in a small depressing lodging house in Bloomsbury. But the fates had always been kind to Mr. and Mrs. Preston.

"Kate, part of you is a child still." He leaned towards her. "Will you grow up sufficiently to be kissed?"

His cheek was warm from the glow of the fire. His hands were firm through the thinness of her gown. The familiar touch of his lips was excitingly unfamiliar, as if this new adventure had made him partly a stranger. She felt that she was a little strange to him, too. His hands sought enquiringly.

"Do you have to go back to Eltham tonight? Say no, please. You can't leave me here alone."

She leaned against him.

"I am at Anna's—officially. Just for tonight. No, I couldn't leave you here alone."

There were distant sounds from the kitchen. "Are you Mrs. Preston?" he asked.

The solemnity of his tone made her giggle.

"No, I'm your sister. Mrs. Steele. I used Anna's name. Mrs. Harvey has prepared two bedrooms since I told her I would be staying. She and Mr. Harvey have a room in the basement, of course. And yours faces the park. You'll be able to hear the owls. You will be happy here, won't you?"

"On occasions like this, yes. Otherwise, no. But never fear, I shall be very comfortable and make the best of it. You've done well for me, as usual." Suddenly his face worked. "Katie, what would I do without your thought, your care, your love? I would be a lost man wandering in the wilderness."

"Hush! You have my love and care always. You know that without my telling you again. But what you also need

235

at this minute is your dinner. It's time we tested Mrs. Harvey's ability as a cook."

He let her go reluctantly. During the whole of dinner his eyes admired her, sitting across from him, her ruffled sleeves falling gracefully from her wrists, her head poised charmingly and attentively as he talked.

"I really do believe you're the loveliest woman in England, Kate."

She laughed merrily. "You're romancing. I'm over forty."

"Well, so am I, and I still expect to look a handsome fellow."

She studied him critically.

"Your hair's getting a little thin, my love. And mine's beginning to go grey."

"Where are the grey hairs? Can't we pull them out?"

His voice was so urgent that she realised she had roused his never quite dormant fear of old age and death. It was not something he could be laughed out of. His thoughts had to be coaxed away from the haunting spectres.

"It would be a major operation, and we haven't time if we are to thoroughly test the comfort of our bedrooms."

His eyes were twinkling again.

"The first point is taken and approved. To the second I make an amendment. Since there is only one room with a view of the park, and since we both enjoy such a view, the solution is to share the room."

It couldn't always be like this. Aunt Ben was now so feeble that Katharine worried if she was out of reach. She couldn't spend many nights in London. She must pay frequent short visits to the Regent's Park house, sometimes for dinner, sometimes for tea, and once even for breakfast after she had had to spend one night at Thomas's Hotel to attend one of Willie's functions.

But mostly she was not there, and the plan that had seemed so good was no longer quite such a happy one. At Wonersh Lodge Katharine found that her habit of sitting up late in case Charles drove down from London persisted. She couldn't settle to sleep before midnight. She played parlour games with the children, and then worked late at her sewing in the hope of encouraging drowsiness.

On one particular night she was so restless and wakeful,

that at one o'clock she made up the fire, and at two o'clock replenished it. It would be useless to go to bed. She would never sleep. She must walk up and down trying not to think, trying not to weep.

How could it be so lonely in a house full of people?

She was getting so wrought up and fanciful that she thought she could hear the familiar sound of a horse trotting, and cab bells jingling.

She strained her ears. Had she imagined it? Was that the sound of footsteps on the side path? It couldn't be.

But yes it was! For a moment later there was the gentle tapping at the window, and he was there, his figure tall and dark in the moonlight, his face pressed against the window-pane.

She flew to the door, opened it and was in his arms.

"Oh, my love, you must never leave me again!"

"Neither I shall. I was so lonely in that damned house in Regent's Park I thought I would go mad . . ."

"*Never leave me again* . . ." What miracle did she think could happen?

Carmen came home from dancing class in tears. Katharine finally managed to extract her woebegone story. Some girls had been singing a bad song about someone called Kitty O'Shea. They said it was her mother. They said you were Kitty O'Shea, Mamma . . .

Gerard, who had trusted in her promise that Mr. Parnell should not come to the house, heard his voice in the sitting room. He said nothing to her, but switched his bewildered loyalty to his father and wrote him a letter.

"Dearest Father,

Although my news may not be pleasing to you, yet it must be told. On my return from London this evening I came in by the back way and as I came past the window of the new room that was built last year I heard the voice of that awful scoundrel Parnell talking to a dog—Grouse, I suppose. So I asked my mother if it were and she says that he has come to dine and will be gone presently. Perhaps I ought to have gone in and kicked him, but I am anxious to avoid unpleasant scenes with my mother. And I also think that it is better for you to know

237

about it before giving him a thrashing, as you, of course, understand more about these things than I do. However, if you wish me to kick him you have only to say so and it shall be done on the first opportunity.

Your affectionate son, G. H. O'Shea."

Willie telegraphed saying that he had had a letter from Gerard and would be down the next day.

Katharine braced herself for the inevitable quarrel. She caught a glimpse of her face in the mirror and was shocked by its look of hardness and determination. Where was the graceful woman who had sat in the ruffled teagown and smiled at her lover? Was she two people?

But Willie was unexpectedly calm. Indeed, his calmness unnerved her more than his usual blustering rage. He startled her to begin with by saying he was resigning his seat and getting out of politics.

"After all the trouble there was to get Galway for you!" she said incredulously.

"I'm *sick* of the whole business. I have no respect for any of them, least of all their leader. Am I to take orders from the man my own son calls a scoundrel? I refuse to be picked out as owing a seat in Parliament to Parnellite terrorism."

Katharine winced. Willie had shown her Gerard's letter and it had struck her to the heart.

"Has it occurred to you that the Irish party might despise you as much as you despise them?"

"What do you care about the Irish party, Kate? You're not even Irish. You're English. You don't care a damn whether Ireland sinks or swims. You don't care if every peasant starves to death or drowns in the everlasting rain. You're a hypocrite."

"That's not true. I do care."

"Yes, for the man. Not his country."

"For people," she insisted.

"Then why never for me?" he demanded. "Why am I always the one to be kicked out?"

"I never kicked you out. You left. You left when you started having other women and remembering me only when it suited you. I didn't love Charles until whatever

238

there was between us was completely dead. You're the hypocrite for refusing to admit that."

He brushed that aside. "Let's not argue about old history. I came down to settle more immediate things. I've got Gerard with me in London and Anna has agreed to have the girls."

"Anna! My own sister!"

"Who happens to be a much more suitable person than their own mother."

Katharine froze. "The girls stay here. And I hope you will allow Gerard to come home so that he can get on with his studies." She added, "What have you said to Anna?"

He gave a short laugh. "I didn't need to say much. She knew. Everyone knows. I tell you, it's an intolerable situation."

"Charles isn't here now," she said in a low voice. "He has a house in London. He only comes down to dinner occasionally. Gerard knows this. I promised it some time ago, for his sake. And I certainly won't have my daughters taken from me because I entertain a friend to dinner."

"I want you to see your solicitor."

Her head shot up.

"What do you mean?"

"I want you to go and see Pym. I've talked to him myself. He knows the position."

"But whatever for. Unless—"

"Unless I'm at last planning a divorce?" His eyes narrowed cruelly, "No, it hasn't come to that yet. But I intend having a talk with Cardinal Manning."

Katharine looked at him in despair.

"Why didn't you do this years ago? Now it's too late. They would make it so dirty."

"What do you care about dirt? You've asked for it, haven't you? What about that woman in Brighton where you rented a house?"

"What woman?" she asked patiently.

"The housekeeper. Mrs. Pithers, Mrs. Pethers, whatever her name was. She said you used to come in late at midnight with your hair all flying. Imagine a servant being able to talk of my wife like that!"

"Imagine you listening to a servant like that!"

Her contemptuous voice at last roused the tell-tale colour in his cheeks.

"That's what you've reduced me to. But I'm not going to stand it any longer. If you don't go and see Pym I'll know what to do next."

She could fight with just as sharp weapons as he could.

"It will be a pity to have to give up your comfortable rooms in Albert Mansions. You won't much like living on a mortgaged estate in Ireland among the people you so despise, will you? What will your mother say when her famous son comes home a failure? And if you take the children from me, how are you going to support them? How is Gerard to be started in a profession? Are Norah and Carmen not to have a coming out? I know you don't need any more help in your career from Mr Parnell since you've decided to throw that away. It was a pity you backed the wrong man when you backed Chamberlain. But you'll still want to be the man about town, won't you? You'll still hope to enjoy good food and wine. I'm sure you'll still want to entertain feminine company occasionally. I don't suppose you've ever thought that my aunt might not be the golden goose forever."

His face had gone dark. "Kate, you've turned into a shrew!"

The shock in his voice turned her cold deadly anger into a weak hot dissolving spot inside her. She must not at this stage burst into tears. But he had spoken the truth. She was becoming a shrew. Somehow she managed to say:

"If you fight, I will fight, too. You won't emerge from this any better than I will. And one thing you won't do, you won't destroy Mr. Parnell. You can't."

"We'll see about that when the time comes." She could not have said anything more calculated to inflame his anger. "The man isn't a god. He's simply a clever unscrupulous fellow who sneaks into another man's house when his back is turned, and makes love to his wife. Oh, I can destroy him, never fear."

"But Willie, you agreed to all this. You encouraged him to come to the house. You knew that Clare and Katie were his. We had conversations."

"With no witnesses."

240

She saw the trap, and cried passionately, "Will you be believed more than me?"

"Yes, I will. Because I'm the injured party, and because you're a woman who will be a disgrace to her sex." He picked up his hat. He was jaunty again, his confidence restored. "Take my advice, Kate. Go and have a long talk to Pym."

It was unfortunate for Anna that she chose to come down that afternoon, after Willie's departure.

Katharine, bruised and sore from the worst encounter she had ever had with her husband, turned on her sister angrily.

"Have you been conspiring with Willie to take my children from me?"

"We haven't been conspiring, Kate. We've only been discussing the desirability of it. Don't look at me like that. I was the last to believe in all this talk. But I have to now. It's an open secret. You might as well face it."

Anna was looking remarkably handsome. She had always dressed well, and was now wearing a maroon jacket and skirt, with a dashing little hat with a curling feather. She was a little plump, but that made her face nicely rounded and smooth. It suddenly occurred to Katharine that Willie might find it not only comforting but enjoyable having her as a confidante. He had always admired her. It was very probable that had Anna been unmarried when they had first met it would have been she and not Katharine whom he would have chosen. She had always been more worldly and amusing, qualities Willie liked in a woman.

These thoughts made Katharine say in an intense voice, "I will not have you and Willie take my children from me. I haven't harmed them, and they still love me. I'll fight for them, in court if necessary."

"Now, Kate, don't get so fussed. Be practical. How can you bring Norah and Carmen out? Do you want them listening to whispers about their mother's reputation? Or worse still, being ostracised? Why should they be punished? I beg you, do have some sense."

Katharine had felt the colour draining out of her face. She felt prickles of gooseflesh on her arms. She was cold, cold.

"They're much too young to talk about coming out. Wait until that time comes."

"And what then?" Anna asked implacably.

Her defences were down.

"I don't know. Don't ask me. I just don't know."

"Kate, what is it you see in this man? Do tell me. I'd dearly like to know how a woman can ruin herself for a man. Is it worth it? When he kisses you, do you forget the whole world? Can you? I'm sure I couldn't. I'd be thinking of the winks and the skirts drawn out of my way. I'd begin to hate him for what he had done to me. But perhaps you're too noble to do that. Perhaps you only hate poor Willie."

Katharine had her fingers in her ears.

"Stop!" she whispered. "And never come here again if you're going to talk like that. Find someone of your own to fall in love with if you're so anxious to experience love."

"Kate, how dare you! I've been happily married for years."

Katharine looked at her with dry exhausted eyes.

"Then why do you ask *me* what love is like?"

Anna departed in a huff. Katharine watched her go, realising that she had alienated even her own sister. It was ugly, ugly, ugly.

But she would go and see Mr. Pym, who had been hers and Aunt Ben's solicitor for years. Things were getting too difficult to manage alone. She was resolved only that Charles should know nothing about this development. The obsession to protect him was almost stronger than the obsession to love.

Mr. Pym was dry and quiet and apparently impossible to shock. He listened to her protestations of innocence, giving no sign whether he believed them or not. But he did agree wholeheartedly that it would be a bad thing to remove the children, especially the girls in early adolescence, from their mother whom they loved.

He agreed to write a letter to Willie.

"My dear sir,

I have seen Mrs. O'Shea and laid before her your wishes. She most indignantly and emphatically denies that you have or ever had the least ground for the very

242

unworthy suspicions you have chosen to affix to her credit. The particular friend you alluded to has been a rare visitor to her house, and he only became a friend of the family on your introduction and by your wish. She must decline to peremptorily close her doors on the few visits this friend is ever likely to make . . ."

Somehow the storm blew over. Probably it was because Willie had no fancy to leave London and reside permanently in the cold draughty neglected much-mortgaged and tumbledown mansion on his estate in County Limerick. Besides it would not even be safe. He was one of the hated absentee landlords, more English than Irish. He might have been murdered in his bed. It was better to condone his wife's infidelity than face that dismal prospect.

CHAPTER 21

AUNT BEN had sent for her solicitor, Mr. Pym, to come down. There were one or two changes she wanted to make in her will. Katharine imagined they were to be legacies to the servants and thought no more about it. Although later she did remember that Aunt Ben had already made gifts to the servants who had been with her the longest. She had bought a cottage for old James, the gardener and coachman, and had distributed some pieces of jewellery among the women in the house.

Mr. Pym and his clerk, William Buck, were closeted with her a long time. Then young Mr. Buck came out requesting that two of the servants should be sent in to write their names as witnesses. Sarah, the cook, and Maryann, one of the housemaids, did this. Maryann came out wiping her eyes. Wills always upset her, they were as good as a death warrant. Katharine, walking restlessly up and down the tapestry room, could not laugh at this superstition, for Aunt Ben was like a puff of thistledown waiting for the first breeze to carry her away.

Katharine was wiping her own eyes when Mr. Pym came briskly out, carrying his brief-case.

"Your aunt would like you now, Mrs. O'Shea."

"How is she?"

"Good gracious, as lively as a cricket. In my experience making a will gives the old a new lease of life. It's one of their few remaining pleasures. A compulsion, like taking to drink. How are you getting on yourself? Did your husband accept that letter I wrote for you?"

"In the meantime, yes."

Mr. Pym patted his bag, seemed about to say something, then changed his mind. Had it been going to be about the new will? Was there something in that that would change the position? Perhaps Aunt Ben would tell her.

But the old lady said nothing. She had got up and dressed for Mr. Pym's visit, and now sat erect wearing her best lace cap, her jet beads, and the large gold mourning brooch that held a lock of her husband's hair. She said she was not at all tired, and would take a short walk along the terrace if Katharine would take her arm.

On the terrace Katharine looked down at the tiny creature on her arm.

"I don't know what you've just done, Aunt Ben, but I'd like to say now how grateful I am for all you've done for me already." She felt the warning tightening of the grip on her arm, and went on determinedly, "I must say it now because the time will come when I can't."

With all her feeble strength the old lady thumped her stick on the ground.

"I don't want your gratitude, my dear one. I only want your happiness. How that is to be accomplished, I'm not sure, but I have done what I can. I hope you won't mention this subject to me again."

Happiness . . . It came and went. It seemed as if they no sooner entered a peaceful time when all seemed well than another shock came to remind them that there could be little prolonged peace for two people leading lives such as theirs.

Charles had come down to Eltham for the weekend. It was springtime and exceptionally warm for early April. Too nice to stay in London even though his house did have a view of the park.

He was having his breakfast on Monday morning, preparatory to leaving for London, when Katharine casually opened *The Times* newspaper and saw the headlines.

It wasn't another murder although at first it appeared to be one. The article was headed "Parnell and Phoenix Park Murders" and appeared, from Katharine's quick scanning of it, to be accusing Mr. Parnell of having been secretly involved in them. A letter had come into the possession of *The Times*. It was signed "Chas. S. Parnell" in the handwriting that Katharine knew so well. The contents of the letter were quite damning.

"15th May, 1882.

"Dear Sir,

I am not surprised at your friend's anger, but he and you should know that to denounce the murders was the only course open to us. To do that promptly was plainly our best policy. But you can tell him and all others concerned that, though I regret the accident of Lord F. Cavendish's death, I cannot refuse to admit that Burke got no more than his deserts. You are at liberty to show him this, and others whom you can trust also, but let not my address be known. He can write to the House of Commons.

Yours very truly,

Chas. S. Parnell."

Katharine glanced quickly at the unaware face opposite her. She quietly folded the paper, and poured more coffee.

"Darling, you haven't finished your ham and eggs. Ellen will be upset."

"Ellen must think me to be two people, at least. What's in the paper this morning?"

"Will you have some marmalade with your toast? No? Then at least drink your coffee."

"Kate dear, I am more than adequately nourished. Now what are you hiding from me in the newspaper?"

Reluctantly she showed him. She watched him studying the article intently, his face showing no emotion.

Then he said quite calmly, "Wouldn't you hide your head in shame if I were as stupid as that?"

"Then someone has made up this letter and forged your name? Who could be so wicked?"

"Oh, I have plenty of enemies. I've no doubt more than one has a gift for forgery."

"How can you be so calm? This is going to harm you terribly."

He stopped to kiss her.

"Who is going to believe it? No one in their senses."

"But this is *The Times*!"

"My darling, that doesn't make it the Bible. What Irishman is going to believe what is printed in an English paper?"

It was no use his being flippant, she couldn't stop worrying.

"Will you come back tonight and tell me what has happened?"

"Of course. Ask Partridge to meet the seven-thirty. I'll be on it without fail. And stop looking so worried. I'm not about to be assassinated."

"I believe they would assassinate you if they could," Katharine muttered, and he gave her a sideways look.

"Who is they?"

"I don't know. Your enemies."

Neither of them mentioned the name that was in both their minds. Captain O'Shea. The disappointed politician. The vindictive husband.

"I tell you, no one will take this seriously. It would take some stretch of the imagination to believe I had anything to do with those horrible murders. My own men know me better than that. Can I say goodbye to the babies?"

Katharine could not help but think this significant. Although Charles was very fond of his little daughters, he was considerably forgetful of them. His mind was always too occupied. But this morning he was particularly affectionate, kissing their rosy faces and rumpling their dark hair. Their innocence seemed to please him. He looked at them wistfully for a full minute. Then abruptly he put them aside, and was ready to leave. The copy of *The Times* protruded from his overcoat pocket. He was not as indifferent as he had pretended to its threat.

He was not on the seven-thirty that evening, nor the train that came in an hour later. Partridge arrived home with an empty brougham. He had not thought it necessary to wait any longer. Mr. Parnell must have been delayed in the House.

So there was trouble, Katharine thought worriedly. It had been a hideous day altogether, for when she had left the house to go across the park to Aunt Ben, she had found copies of *The Times'* letter cut out and pasted to the front gate. All day there had been more sightseers than usual. The hedge was not yet tall enough or thick enough to shut out the peering eyes.

If Willie were responsible for this latest outrage she thought that she could kill him.

It was useless to go to bed. Norah sat up later than usual, making the excuse that she wanted to finish the water-colour she had begun that day. She and Carmen could not have failed to see those horrible letters pasted to the front gate. Norah didn't mention them, but her frequent anxious glances at her mother showed that she was concerned. She was growing up, this eldest daughter, her face losing its round childishness. Less volatile than Carmen, she had deeper affections. She was intensely devoted to Clare and little Katie, and took them in her charge completely during Katharine's absences. What she thought of either her mother's or her father's absences, Katharine had never asked. She would not be held on trial by her own children, much as she loved them.

"You must go to bed, Norah. It's after ten o'clock."

"Yes, Mamma. Are you coming up?"

"Soon, darling."

"Mamma—"

"Yes, my darling?"

For answer Norah suddenly crossed the room and flung herself down, her head in Katharine's lap.

"Mamma, I will always stay with you even if Carmen and Gerard don't."

Katharine lifted the flushed, tear-stained face.

"What is this? My sensible Norah in tears? No one is going to leave me, you, Gerard or Carmen. Except, of course, to get married one day."

Norah shook her head violently.

"I shall never get married. I don't think it's a very happy state."

Katharine's own eyes filled with tears.

"Oh, darling, have Papa and I made you feel like that? We do quarrel, it's true. But all married people don't. I'm sure you won't. You'll find the most delightful young man for a husband. Now off to bed with you. And don't do your growing up too quickly."

After that, she was even more alone and heavy hearted. The hours dragged. It was eleven o'clock. Then twelve. And still no sound but the falling ash in the fire.

She tried to do a little embroidery. She tried to read. Finally she just sat with her hands in her lap.

It was two-thirty before she heard the distant jingle of cab bells. Charles had told her that he had found an obliging cab driver called Sam Drury who was always prepared to drive him down to Eltham late at night. Obviously Sam had been persuaded to do the journey once more, for presently the crunching wheels came to a stop, and Katharine, wings to her feet, was at the door flinging it wide to the figure which had alighted from the cab.

"Charles, how could you have been kept so late? I've been out of my mind with worry."

"Oh, I have to fight this thing." She had never heard his voice so weary. "It's a terrible nuisance. I've seen George Lewis. He's going to get the letters from *The Times* and study the handwriting."

"But what was said in the House?"

"You mean, what did I say? I told them it was an audacious and unblushing fabrication. There were questions asked late this evening, and I thought the sitting would never end. I got up and said that politics are coming to a pretty pass in this country when a leader of a party of eighty-six members has to stand up in the House of Commons at ten minutes past one in order to defend himself from an anonymous fabrication such as that which is contained in *The Times* this morning."

"What else was said?"

"Among my own members? I should say they wouldn't have the temerity to believe such a thing of me. But are we to stand on the doorstep all night? You waited up for me. You always wait, don't you my dearest?"

She drew him in. "I have the kettle on the hob. I'll make you a hot drink."

"No, I'll just go to bed if you don't mind. I'm done. But this will blow over. Everything eventually blows over—if one lives long enough."

The next day, under a heading "Parnellism and Crime" *The Times* published another of the obnoxious letters.

"9th January 1882.

"Dear E,
    What are these fellows waiting for? This inaction is inexcusable. Our best men are in prison and nothing is being done.

    "Let there be an end to this hesitency. Prompt action is called for. You undertook to make it hot for old Forster and Co. Let us have some evidence of your power to do so.

"My health is good thanks.
Yours very truly,
Chas. S. Parnell."

The letter had a frighteningly authentic ring, especially regarding the curt comment about Charles' health. He had never liked enquiries about it.

But after seven hours' rest, he had recovered his composure and his sense of humour.

"I have always prided myself on my spelling. I wouldn't have misspelt 'hesitancy'. And I never made an 's' like that since 1878."

"Who is this addressed to? 'E'?"

"Egan, I imagine. He was the treasurer of the Land League at that time. This is obviously meant to suggest a nice conspiracy between us. Well, nobody's going to believe it, so why do we worry?"

"But all English people believe what's in *The Times*. It's so utterly respectable."

"Not any longer, as far as I'm concerned. They've allowed themselves to be hoodwinked. Well, it will be a nice bit of sport getting an apology out of them."

But it proved to be far from sport. For the Prime Minister, Lord Salisbury, himself believed in the authenticity of the letters. He made a speech at Swansea saying that it would be impossible, in the history of the British Government, to find another instance of a man in Mr. Gladstone's position accepting as an ally a man "tainted with the strong presumption of conniving at assassination". Mr. Chamberlain with every evidence of delight talked about the letters being Parnell's death warrant.

The damning articles continued to be published, but Mr. Parnell was dissuaded from his intention of taking action. A London jury, he was told, would probably find him guilty. Certainly no English jury would be likely to find against *The Times*.

The Irish members demanded an investigation by a committee of the House of Commons of the charges made against their leader, but this was refused. It looked as if the matter would never be cleared up.

In vain Katharine and Charles, and their solicitor, George Lewis, studied the handwriting in the letters, comparing it with that of any possible suspect. Katharine knew that from start to finish Charles suspected the letters to be Willie's handiwork, if not written by him, at least at his instigation. He went to great lengths to prove this, even spending the entire day in a tobacconist's shop waiting for a woman to come home who might have evidence incriminating Captain O'Shea.

When, finally, the Government was forced to appoint a commission to enquire into the matter of the letters, and the business of the Land League itself, months had gone by, and months more were to go by before the Commission began its long weary weeks of sitting.

Counsel were formidable, the Attorney-General, Sir Richard Webster for *The Times*, Sir Charles Russell assisted by Mr. Asquith for Mr. Parnell. The list of witnesses was endless. There were peasants from Kerry, women in scarlet petticoats who were more accustomed to being barefoot in the bog than in shoes on London pavements, a convicted murderer brought in custody from Mountjoy prison, witnesses who could speak no English, journalists, professional rioters, landowners who related outrages in immeasurable detail, priests. Everyone but a culprit.

Captain O'Shea, in the witness-box, deplored the attempt to drag him into the matter, but since "the unfortunate question was asked, he should say he believed that the letters were all written by Mr. Parnell".

Then at last Pat Egan in Dublin, who had been similarly incriminated by the forged letters, provided a clue. He remembered once having a begging letter from Richard Pigott, an impecunious Dublin journalist, who had spelt "hesitancy" in exactly that way, with an "e" instead of an "a".

No time was wasted in having Mr. Pigott served with a subpoena. He came to London as bold as brass and stood in the witness-box, full of bravado. He wasn't even intimimidated by such brilliant and famous counsel, especially since Sir Richard Webster began so gently.

251

"How old are you?"

"Fifty-four."

"What are you?"

"A journalist."

"Have you been connected with journalism a great many years?"

"Yes."

"In February 1868 were you prosecuted for an article written on the Manchester executions?"

Mr. Pigott was still jaunty. "I was."

"Were you the proprietor of *The Irishman*?"

"Yes."

Sir Richard mentioned the meeting that had taken place between Pigott, George Lewis, and Mr. Parnell.

"Did the name of Captain O'Shea crop up?"

"Yes. Mr. Lewis asked me to say whether or not Captain O'Shea had anything to do with procuring the letters. I said distinctly not. He said it was a matter of great relief to him because he had been convinced that Captain O'Shea had and so had Mr. Parnell."

"Did you go to Ely Place at five o'clock on 26th October?"

"Yes."

"Who were there?"

"Mr. Parnell and Mr. Lewis."

"What passed?"

"Mr. Parnell proposed to ask certain questions. I told him I declined to be cross-examined. His manner was exceedingly threatening. After repeating his assurance that I had forged the letters he said they were in a position to prove that I had committed other forgeries."

This comparatively innocuous questioning went on for some time. Mr. Pigott, a plump balding amiable little man, was perfectly composed and seemed to be enjoying himself. His answers came out easily, without hesitation. If he was nervous, he managed to hide it. It would not be the first time his tongue had got him out of a tight spot.

But when Sir Charles Russell, defending counsel, began his cross-examination, things were not so easy.

"Mr. Pigott, would you be good enough to write some words on that sheet of paper for me?"

Mr. Pigott sat in the witness-box, took the quill pen

handed to him by a clerk, and wrote the words dictated. "Livelihood. Likelihood. Hesitancy." And finally his own name. He wasn't quite so sure of himself now. He suspected a trap.

"Mr. Pigott, I put it to you, did you not communicate with Lord Spencer as far back as 1873?"

"No."

"Offering, I will remind you, to give valuable information for money?"

"No, I have no recollection of that."

"Did you write to any Home Secretary offering to give any information for money?"

"When?"

"I am asking you."

"No, I did not."

"Will you swear you did not?"

"I will not swear."

"Will you swear you did not to several?"

"I will swear."

"To two?"

"No, not to two."

"To one?"

"To none, as far as I can recollect."

"Did you write to Sir George Trevelyan offering to make a revelation?"

"Not a revelation."

"Well, to give information."

"No, neither one or the other."

"What did you write about?"

"As far as I can recollect I wrote to him asking for some pecuniary help."

He was floundering now, visibly shaken. He didn't know whether he had misspelt those words he had been asked to write, and hadn't expected Sir Charles Russell to have copies of letters he had written to Archbishop Walsh, when his conscience had been bothering him. Mr. Lewis had asked the Archbishop for copies of the correspondence but he had declined to send them on the ground that the secrecy of the communications was secured by the seal of the confessional. And now this adamant man persecuting him with questions had the revealing letters after all. And was being sarcastic about the seal of the confessional.

"You are a Catholic, are you not?"

"I am."

"That must have amused you, I suppose."

But Mr. Pigott indignantly denied that he had been amused by thinking he could shed his sins and have his secret kept.

Sir Charles was reading another part of that wretched confessional to Archbishop Walsh.

"What do you say to that?" he rapped.

"It proves to me clearly that I had not the letters in mind."

"Then if it proves to you clearly that you had not the letters in your mind, what had you?"

"I have no idea."

"Can you give their Lordships any clue of the most indirect kind?"

"I cannot."

"Or from whom you heard it?"

"No."

"Or when?"

"Or where?"

He was an automaton now, repeating words. "Or where."

"Have you ever mentioned this fearful matter, whatever it is?"

"No."

"It is still locked up—hermetically sealed—in your own bosom?"

He had lost the sense of what was being said. He twisted his hands and got out desperately, "No, it has gone away out of my own bosom."

Charles came home that night with a bottle of champagne. It was all over bar the shouting, he said. Tomorrow that deplorable seedy scoundrel Pigott would tell them how much he had been paid for forging the letters, and who had paid him. So another enemy had been removed.

But Katharine was wary now. Nothing ever went right for very long, especially in politics. It was Pigott today, who would it be tomorrow?

She had written to Willie after his open declaration of

254

enmity when he had been in the witness-box, and told him that he was never to attempt to set foot in her house again. If he insisted on seeing the children she could not refuse, but they must go to him. She would never open her door to him again. She was not much more civil to Anna who had now taken Willie's side completely. She was getting too old and too tired for conciliation. Her obsession to love and protect Charles, and accept all his enemies as her own, was now overpowering. Only her children, and dear Aunt Ben who was now completely bed-ridden, occupied the rest of her heart.

"*The Times* will owe you an apology," she said.

"Don't you remember I said I would get one from them eventually. Isn't it something to have proved the infallibility of that English institution? Perhaps I'll be remembered for that, if nothing else."

Katharine had been tense for too long to be able to relax so easily.

"Are you sure Pigott will confess tomorrow?"

"If you had seen him this afternoon you wouldn't have been in any doubt. Sir Charles had him reduced to incoherence. Poor devil. He's got a family in Dublin he's feeling conscience-stricken about. He'll say he did it for them, of course."

"If they take after their father it would be better to let them starve," Katharine said bitterly.

"Kate, that's not like you, being vindictive."

"Look what he's done to you!" she flamed. "A whole year of this suspicion. Dirt flung at you from all sides. How could I feel any sympathy towards him or anyone belonging to him?"

Charles' eyebrows went up in mock distress.

"Oh dear, and I had thought we were going to have a party. Shall I put the champagne away for a more suitable occasion?"

As always, her hot temper faded and she was filled with remorse.

"I'm sorry, don't let me turn into a shrew."

"You! I know better than that."

The very quietness of his voice dispelled her vindictive mood, and the evening was not a disaster, after all. The champagne made them feel confident and optimistic, and they talked of the future, a thing they seldom dared to do. When Aunt Ben died, as she must do very soon, for she had had her ninety-seventh birthday, Katharine had decided to sell Wonersh Lodge and buy a house in Brighton. She had always liked Brighton and being near the sea. There was an excellent train service to London. If they could find a house at the far end of the town near the downs there would be few passers-by, few to stare.

"Then I am to be with you, Kate?"

"Of course you are. Aren't I your wife? Aren't we as married as two people ever could be?"

He said only, "I'll be very glad to leave Regent's Park. That house was never a home."

"And Willie will never darken our door," Katharine said, following her own trend of thought.

"I think you've been reading Mrs. Henry Wood, my love."

"And Ireland will get Home Rule, and we'll live happily ever after."

"Do people ever live happily ever after?"

"I don't know. We'll find out."

Nothing ever did go smoothly, however, for the next morning the witness, Richard Pigott, failed to appear. For a little while it looked as if the mystery would be unsolved after all.

The President of the Commission said, "Where is the witness?"

The Attorney General replied, "My lords, so far as I am concerned I have no knowledge of the witness's whereabouts. I am informed that Mr. Soames sent to his hotel and that he is not there and has not been there since eleven o'clock last night."

Sir Charles Russell, defending counsel, said, "My lords, if there is any delay in his appearance I must ask your Lordships to issue a warrant for his apprehension immediately."

The President replied that he would direct it to be made out.

But before this was done, information arrived that Mr. Pigott, in the presence of Mr. Shannon, an Irish Sergeant of Police, had made a statement at his hotel the previous evening. The wretched man admitted that the letters had been forged by himself.

He had not been able to resist the bait offered by an Irishman, Mr. Houston, secretary to the Irish Loyal and Patriotic Union, who had been collecting proofs of Nationalist complicity in crime. He had compiled a pamphlet called *Parnellism Unmasked* and had suggested to his old friend Richard Pigott, an ingenious fellow and then in dire poverty, that he would be well paid for any evidence he could produce against Parnell or the Nationalist party. He would pay especially well for any documents. So, after collecting a considerable number of guineas for travelling expenses, Mr. Pigott decided to set the scene in Paris, and intimated to Mr. Houston that he had discovered incriminating documents in a black bag, probably left in mistake by some of the Invincibles (who had been responsible for the Phoenix Park murders). Among these documents were letters signed by Parnell and Patrick Egan.

Mr. Houston, in his eagerness, accepted the letters on their face value. He paid Mr. Pigott six hundred pounds, a fortune for that impecunious scoundrel, and took his booty to England.

The astonishing thing was that the manager of *The Times* accepted the authenticity of the letters almost without question. He discussed them only with *The Times'* solicitor, and a hand-writing expert, and then proceeded to make a deadly attack on a man so famous and eminent as the leader of the Irish party.

It was a squalid story, and the mighty *Times* didn't much relish making the stiff apology which appeared in their columns the next day.

"We deem it right to express our regret most fully and sincerely at having been induced to publish the letters in question as Mr. Parnell's."

A few days later the flight of Mr. Pigott was found to have ended in Madrid. He had shot himself miserably and sordidly in a hotel bedroom.

And Mr. Parnell became, temporarily, a national hero in England, the country he professed to hate. Wherever he went he was cheered. When he next rose to address the House of Commons he received a great ovation. The whole of the Liberal party rose to do homage to him. Mr. Gladstone turned and bowed to him particularly, an open indication to the whole house that he was still firmly with Parnell and the Home Rule Bill. Mr. Gladstone, it was true, was still only leader of the Opposition, but that would not last forever. The Conservatives were likely to lose the next election, and then the old man, over eighty now, but still indefatigable, would be back.

All this must have been in Mr. Parnell's mind as he listened to the cheering. But if it was he gave no sign. He stood erect among the standing crowd, waiting patiently for them to resume their seats. The incident for which they applauded him was over. Now they must get on with more important business.

Composed, self-confident, exuding his extraordinary magnetism, he waited. And when at last the clapping died away he began to speak in a quiet calm voice:

"Is there anyone here who will get up in his place, or, sitting in his place, by a shake of his head, or a nod, or a word, will venture to say he believes that there is any doubt whatever as to the forgeries of these letters which have been alleged to have been written and signed by me?"

The loud cheering broke out again, and when it quietened the ebullient Tim Healy was on his feet saying that for himself he had cared nothing for *The Times*' charges. Let the Irish party go on as their fathers had gone on, and let those who had slandered John Mitchell, Smith O'Brien, Emmet and Wolfe Tone go on with their slander and moral assassination and do their worst, while the Irish party, standing safe in the confidence of their fellow countrymen, would go on raising the flag of Irish nationality and would keep it untarnished.

He added that he did not doubt before a month some Conservative member would come forward and say that the letters had been conclusively proved and that Pigott had been assassinated in Madrid by the Honourable member for Cork.

There was tolerant laughter, more tolerant than an Irish member usually was granted. Then the long weary business was all over, and Katharine, sitting in the Ladies' Gallery, her veil hiding her tears of immense pride and emotion, wondered how long the adulation would last. Particularly the changeful Mr. Healy's.

She was very tired and for a moment the figures before her seemed to blur into a black mass, like crows, squabbling, fighting, ready to pick a weaker one to pieces.

CHAPTER 22

It was strange, it showed their intense mental closeness, for when Katharine said, "Aren't you proud and happy? I never heard such an ovation before." Charles answered:

"They'd be at my throat in a week, if they could. Their cheering reminded me of the howling of a mob I once saw chasing a man to lynch him." And she knew that he had had exactly the same thoughts as hers.

Involuntarily she shivered.

"Don't think of things like that. Enjoy your popularity."

"I shall enjoy it and be amused by it, but I won't be taken in by it. They're only feeling guilty because they made a mistake about me. The English worship laws. I'm glad Ireland has a religion, there's so little hope for a nation that worships laws."

"Well, at least, you acknowledged the applause with great dignity. I was proud of you."

He smiled, pressing her hand.

"I'm happy to have you proud of me. But don't be too pleased with their clapping. I've a presentiment you'll hear them another way before long."

"Why do you say that?" she asked intensely.

"I have no reason except that I don't trust this present happy marriage. I'm being besieged with invitations. They want me to talk at the Eighty Club. I suppose that's an honour, though it's one I could do without. I'm accepting simply because it's an opportunity to make them listen to me. There's a great charm about a captive audience."

"And what else do you have to do?"

He said, a little reluctantly, "Sir Charles and Lady Russell are giving a reception for me. I wish I could refuse to go, but I can't. Sir Charles conducted a remarkable case for me, especially in his cross-examination of Pigott. So I shall have to show my gratitude."

He kissed her lightly, his eyes begging her not to mind. It was galling that she could share none of his triumph. Almost everyone knew of her position in Mr. Parnell's life, yet she must be kept out of sight, ignored. No one must be offended by the presence of a notorious woman.

This situation had not arisen too much in the past because of Charles' refusal to take part in a social life. But now he had his moment of lionisation forced on him. Katharine must wait quietly at home until he returned from gatherings at which her own relations were present. Her brother, Sir Evelyn Wood, might be there, or her aunt and uncle, Lord and Lady Hatherley.

She tried not to show that she minded. When she was alone, waiting for him to return, she wondered how long they could go on living this unnatural life. She would sit stitching at her embroidery and thinking of the carriages drawing up at the lighted house, the doors wide open, footmen on the steps, and the rustle of silk and taffeta as the ladies stepped out of the carriages, their jewels glittering. She scarcely knew what was the latest fashion. The leg of mutton sleeves which she thought hideously ugly were very much in favour, and bustles were smaller, sometimes no more than a sweeping curve from a small waist.

This summer she must get herself some pretty gowns even if just to wear at home in the evening. What did she care about elaborate receptions and balls? She had had plenty of them in her youth and what did they consist of but meaningless chatter, empty politeness. Men looked at her askance if she wanted to discuss serious matters, and the women with their restless fans, their coquettish smiles, their endless artificialities, bored her to death. She much preferred the quiet evenings with Charles.

But not these evenings alone when he was at some festivity. That was when she felt ostracised and unbearably lonely. Yet when he arrived home, flinging off his cloak and top-hat and exclaiming how he hated a social life, how he had done nothing but look surreptitiously at his watch to see the earliest moment when he could leave to come home to her, she was happy again, all her doubts vanished. She even thought with pity of all the animated smiling women at those parties who were endlessly seeking the happiness that she had.

One thing for which she was thankful that spring was

that Willie left her alone. Although he wrote his endless complaining letters, as he always had, he did not attempt to see her. So long as he got some money occasionally he had the decency to stay out of her sight.

But the hand of fate showed itself again. Aunt Ben was dying at last, and the family was gathering round, Willie among them. Aunt Ben was rich. Everyone, beneath formal expressions of concern, was wondering what was in her will.

Katharine, her constant companion and the only person she still loved in the world, never left her side.

The thistledown head on the pillow in the great four-poster looked so frail that it might take flight. But the old lady's remarkable mentality had not deserted her, even in the hour of death.

The curtains had been drawn back because she wanted to see the sky, the pale blue serene sky that heralded summer. There were flutterings on the window-sill because the owls were nesting there again. Maryann, Aunt Ben's faithful maid, had said that the owls' nesting was an omen, the dear mistress must be going soon. It was no use for Katharine to point out that the owls had nested there for the last seventy years. Maryann merely said stubbornly that time would show.

Time, indeed, was the enemy. For now it was obvious that the servants must be summoned to make their farewells.

Solemnly they filed past dear Mrs. Ben's bed. They had loved her. She had sent them to church on Sundays and made them learn the collect off by heart and recite it to her afterwards. She had been sympathetic in their illness, their family affairs, their marriages and the births of their babies. She had stood no nonsense and although of late years she had moved only from her bedroom to the tapestry room, or, on a mild day, gone for a short drive, she had known everything that had gone on in the house. She had been a good mistress of the kind that was slowly disappearing. They paid their sad farewells, the younger ones sniffing, old James, the coachman, with tears running unashamedly down his cheeks.

Then the room was silent again, and Katharine stood by the bed, holding the tiny dead-leaf hand.

"You do believe, don't you, my swan?"

"Yes, I do."

"I'm glad. I wish you could come with me."

Did Aunt Ben think that Katharine's troubles would be too much for her to face? Or was she herself suddenly a little afraid of the dark unknown road she must travel alone?

It was too late to ask, for without even a sigh the tired eyelids had fallen shut forever.

Too late . . .

And so much trouble.

The will, made a year ago and witnessed by the cook, Sarah Elizabeth Russell, and the housemaid Maryann Elizabeth Allam, with Mr. Pym and his clerk William Buck in attendance, disclosed that Anna Maria Wood widow of Sir Benjamin Wood had left her entire estate valued at about one hundred and fifty thousand pounds to her beloved niece Katharine O'Shea. None of her other nieces or nephews had been mentioned. More significant still, there was a clause excluding any control of her fortune by Katharine's present or any future husband. Katharine was also the sole executrix, and if she had predeceased her aunt the estate was to have gone to her children to be invested in British or Indian Railway company debenture stock.

They were furious, all of them, her brother who was now General Sir Evelyn Wood, her sisters, Anne, Emma and Clarissa. Particularly Anna, and more particularly Willie, her husband. After the reading of the will Willie had got up and left the room, banging the door in the most marked manner. Naturally he was devastated. He might be estranged from his wife, but he was not legally separated so he had expected to have control of her fortune. Wasn't that the particular right of a husband? Hadn't he put up with a very great deal just to maintain this right?

It was useless for Katharine to protest that she had known nothing that was in the will. She kept hearing the words "undue influence" and seeing the hostile faces of her brothers and sisters.

They were all against her, she realised with dismay. Perhaps it wasn't only because of this vast inheritance, perhaps it was because they had so much resented her becoming a notorious woman, shaming the family. Imagine someone in the highly respectable Wood family having her name bandied about in music halls and drinking houses. What would their father have said?

Willie had not attempted to speak to her. He had only glowered at her across the room. She had been shocked by his appearance. The dandy had vanished. His clothes had been badly cut, his linen none too white. His eyes were bloodshot, his face bore unmistakable marks of dissipation. The gay debonair Captain O'Shea had gone forever. All his little intrigues, and ambitious scheming had brought him to this shabby failure.

Somehow that frightened Katharine much more than had he been his usual jaunty menacing self. He could have blackmailed her for money had she been able to get immediate possession of Aunt Ben's fortune. But since the will was to be contested, this would be tied up for a very long time. It looked as if, for Captain O'Shea, the golden goose was really dead.

Katharine could not bear to stay at Wonersh Lodge and look out of the upstairs windows over the park with its familiar footpath to the Lodge. It was too painful to see the distant white house so empty now that Aunt Ben lay at rest beside her husband in the churchyard.

One wise thing Aunt Ben had done was to have this ugly Victorian house put in Katharine's name. So it at least could be sold immediately, and she could carry out her plan to move to Brighton.

Although Wonersh Lodge had been home for the last ten years, and although three of her children had been born there (one of them the frail beloved Sophie), she had no regret about leaving it.

Charles said, "Whatever you say, my love, I shall always have the fondest memories of your little boudoir. It was my dearest prison."

For a moment she was still, remembering the intensity of her first love. It seemed long ago now. She seemed to have been so young. She supposed the first true love in her life must always make a woman feel young, even though she were over thirty and seemingly mature. What was more, true love made one retain an illusion of youth even ten years later. For here she was, a middle-aged woman with grey in her hair and lines deeply scored about her eyes, looking forward eagerly to the new house in which they would live like any married couple. A house that had never been lived in by Willie.

She only forgot the unpleasantness of the legal squabble that was beginning over Aunt Ben's will, and her secret fear about Willie, when she was deep in the upheaval of moving.

She had found exactly the house she had wanted, at the end of the town with cornfields at one side, and the sea in front. It was quiet, isolated, not too far from the railway station. She had also found stables to which the horses, Dictator and President, could be moved. Home Rule had been sent back to Ireland. So the trap would be taken down and they could go driving perhaps now without curious people staring.

The moment Wonersh Lodge was empty people surged in destructively to get souvenirs from "the house where Parnell lived".

Ellen the cook, elected to come with them to Brighton, but Jane Leinster had decided to leave. Katharine found another maid, Phyllis Brown, who was already devoted to the younger children, and to her. A new children's nurse would have to be found for the little ones. Norah and Carmen had outgrown the need for a governess. Norah was seventeen and Carmen sixteen. Katharine was considerably worried about their future. Norah should be coming out, but the sisters were so devoted that it was only sensible that they should come out together. But how was this to be done?

She hadn't moved from Wonersh Lodge before this problem was solved for her. Willie, unseen but threatening, was beginning to act. He wrote to his daughters saying that they were to spend the summer with their Aunt Anna, and Anna who had been particularly incensed by Aunt Ben's will, but who also had never forgiven Katharine for being so shamelessly happy in her illicit love, was triumphant about carrying out Willie's request.

She arrived in her carriage for the girls. She looked them up and down as they stood there in their good grey worsted coats and skirts and said, "Well, you poor little country mice." She turned accusingly on Katharine, "Are those the best clothes they have? They look like schoolgirls."

"They are schoolgirls," Katharine said.

"Nonsense! They're grown up. Really, Kate, how much longer were you going to let them look like that? With all Aunt Ben's money—" Anna couldn't stop being spiteful now.

"But none of you are letting me have all that money, are you? Dear Aunt Ben has bought the children's clothes all her life, but she isn't being allowed to do so any more because my own family won't let her. My own family who knows I've had a husband who never provided for me. If you're unhappy about Norah's and Carmen's appearance you'd better ask their father to do something about it."

"Kate, really—"

Katharine turned away angrily.

"Oh, Anna, I'm sick of your hypocrisy. I believe I'm the only one in our family not to be a hypocrite."

Anna coloured furiously, her face tightening.

"Better a hypocrite than some things I could name."

Katharine's voice was icy.

"If you're going to take the girls, at least let me say good-bye to them properly." She held out her arms, trying to smile, hoping she wouldn't remember Norah's tears dried on her desperately unhappy white young face, or the spark of excitement Carmen couldn't quite conceal. Gerard was in London and Carmen adored her brother. It might be much more amusing there than with Mamma who had a habit of shutting the drawing-room door when Mr. Parnell was there, and saying that she did not wish to be disturbed. There was no doubt that Mr. Parnell would be in Brighton too. So perhaps London would be more fun.

"Mamma, remember to tell the new nurse that Clare can't eat porridge. It makes her s-sick—" Norah's tears started afresh, and Katharine, kissing her lovingly, said, "Yes, my darling. I'll remember. But you're not going to London forever. Carmen, angel, be good. You really are only a schoolgirl, in spite of what your aunt says."

The carriage rolled away. They were gone, her grown-up children. But she still had Clare and little Katie. Clare was precociously intelligent. Her head with its cap of smooth brown hair was heart-breakingly like her father's. Katie was a plump bundle of mischief.

Really, Katharine told herself sternly, a woman was never satisfied. Why should she grieve for the three who had left her? It was natural and right that growing children should leave home, and she still had the two babies who were her dearest loves.

The incandescent happiness came back when they were settled in the Brighton house. Now they really felt married. Charles had his study, a room at the back of the house overlooking green fields, and the big double bedroom, facing the sea they shared. For who was there to hide things from now? The servants were loyal, the babies too small to understand. And Willie never came here. Neither did Gerard. It had been clear for a long time that Gerard uneasily favoured his father. This was one of Katharine's deepest sorrows. And Norah was writing homesick letters.

But all the same she was happy. The crowning achievement of that year came when Mr. Gladstone at last kept his promise and invited Charles to Hawarden. Charles returned saying that the visit had been immensely successful. Mr. Gladstone had expressed his determination to see the Home Rule Bill passed in his lifetime. It really looked as if all the years of work and struggle were going to be rewarded.

"And then we will take Clare and Katie and live abroad," said Charles. "I will be done with politics. Will you be glad?"

Katharine looked at the worn face, the deepset dark eyes that less often lit up now.

"I'll be *so* glad. Once I was afraid you would never come out of all this alive."

"Oh, I'm not so easy to kill as that."

"I only hope the Irish people are grateful to you."

"I expect they'll put up a monument to me one day. But who cares for monuments? I shall have seen that my country gets fair laws in future. There'll be more to eat than the everlasting potato. The children will be taught to

267

read and write and have shoes to wear in the winter. There won't be mothers giving birth to babies in ditches. No one will have to lie out in the rain dying. The emigrant ships won't take all the youth. I have a recurring dream of women weeping on the quay at Cork. I wake up with their wailing in my ears. But there'll be no more of that. Paddy and Johnnie and Mike will be able to stay home and marry their sweethearts and look after the old people."

"You make it sound like a Utopia."

"No, not a Utopia, only a decently governed country. Anyway, I don't believe there could be a Utopia unless there were no people in it." He smiled. "Except you and me, perhaps."

Katharine smiled too and said, "It will be very strange for Parliament to have no Irish question. What will they debate in future?"

"That won't be our concern, my darling. But that's looking into the future and I've never dared do so until now. I was never optimistic enough."

And even now his optimism was premature. For the day before Christmas when a December gale was whipping up the Channel and flinging foaming glass-green waves against the sea wall, the front door bell rang, and a man stood on the doorstep with a legal-looking document in his hand.

It was a petition for divorce, O'Shea versus O'Shea and Parnell.

Katharine was too stunned and dismayed to be able to wait until the evening for Charles to return home. She took the afternoon train to London and, knowing he was attending the afternoon's debate, sent in a message to the House of Commons asking him to come out and see her.

This was an ironic repetition of their first meeting, but in what different circumstances.

As soon as Charles saw her face he asked, "What's the matter? Is it one of the children?"

She took his arm. Even here, in the quiet Palace Yard, people were watching.

"Can we go somewhere to talk? Charles, Willie has done it at last! He's suing for divorce."

For a moment he was completely still. Then he said:

"You had me alarmed, Kate. I thought it must be one of the children had an accident."

She looked at him in astonishment. "Don't you mind?"

"Why should I mind? Isn't it what we've always wanted?"

She stared at him, trying to read the face she knew so well. He actually did look pleased and excited. But was there a wariness, a reserve, beneath his excitement?

"Wait while I get my coat and bag. We'll go home. We can talk on the way."

Driving through the streets gay with Christmas decorations, and then waiting for a train at Victoria, Katharine's head began to ache. She still imagined everyone was staring. She imagined eyes could penetrate her handbag and see the document inside it, Petition for Divorce, O'Shea versus O'Shea. She had always held her head high when she and Charles were together in public. Now her neck ached with the effort.

At least they were able to find an empty compartment on the train. Immediately the door was closed and they were alone she began in great agitation.

"Charles, what will happen to you? Will the scandal ruin you and your work? How will the Irish accept a leader who has been co-respondent in a divorce case?"

He gave her the tender gaze that could nearly break her heart.

"Bless you, Katie, you're only thinking of me. Think of us and Clare and little Katie."

He hadn't even begun to answer her question.

"Isn't almost everybody in Ireland a Catholic? The priests and bishops will be your bitter enemies, and you can't imagine the people not doing what the priests tell them. This can't be allowed to happen when you're so near to success. In another year it might not have mattered." Her voice grew intensely bitter. "I have no doubt Willie realised that perfectly."

"Do you think that's why he has overcome his own scruples about his religion?"

"Scruples! He doesn't even know what that word means. He hates you and would dearly like to ruin you. I believe he would have done this long ago if he hadn't found it too convenient to live on Aunt Ben's money. He was furious when he found out what she had done in her will. He never thought I could get free of his demands. Even now," Katharine said thoughtfully, "I'm quite sure he could be bought off if the money was available. But it isn't, and it's not even certain I'll ever get any. Or enough to keep him quiet."

"Kate, I won't have you talking like this. You now have the opportunity to get free of this man forever, and you're to take it. If you had a million pounds I wouldn't let you give him a penny. What's he living on now, by the way?"

"I haven't an idea. Perhaps Anna is keeping him. She's always been sympathetic towards him, and she has Norah and Carmen. I think Gerard is there a great deal, too."

"But Anna isn't rich. Certainly not rich enough for a man of Willie's expensive tastes."

Katharine looked at him sharply.

"What are you thinking?"

"I don't know. I could wonder if there are under-currents here. It always puzzled me why Chamberlain cultivated a man like O'Shea unless he saw in him a weapon to bring me down."

Katharine was horrified.

"You mean Chamberlain might be paying Willie to bring the divorce!"

"Well, that's a thing I don't suppose we'll ever know. And if he is," Charles took her cold hand between his own, "I insist that he's doing us a good turn."

"We can defend it," Katharine said feverishly. "We can prove connivance, collusion, whatever they call it. Before I ever met you Willie begged me to be nice to you. Use your charms on him—that was his expression. What did he care for me? I can find, if I try, a dozen women who have been his mistresses."

"No, Kate."

"No, what?"

"Don't do that. Let it be."

"Let it be!" she exclaimed incredulously.

The train had stopped at a station, the door of the compartment opened and two women with bundles of holly and a great many parcels struggled in. They subsided in the seat opposite Katharine and Charles, and began to stare.

At least Katharine was convinced that they did. Their sharp eyes scrutinised unmercifully the middle-aged couple holding hands (for Charles wouldn't let her draw her hand away). Presently one or the other would recognise them and there would be surreptitious winks and nods.

Their urgent discussion had had to be cut off in the very middle, and her head ached furiously. She couldn't believe it when one of the women opposite nodded asleep, and her companion took out some knitting and became absorbed in it. They were not staring after all and she and Charles were not yet quite as notorious as she had thought. But that would only be a matter of time.

He mustn't be destroyed, she thought passionately. No matter what he said, she would fight this divorce with every weapon she could find. She would sink to any depths to protect him.

In the house at Walsingham Terrace it was as if nothing had happened. Dinner was ready, but before it was put on the table Clare and Katie, bathed and in their nightgowns, expected to be kissed goodnight by Mamma and Papa. A splendid fire roared up the chimney in the dining room, Grouse stretched in front of it. The curtains were drawn, the stormy night shut out. Only an occasional hail of spray on the window-panes reminded them that the gale still blew. It almost seemed as if the elements could be shut out of this cosy room.

Charles poured two glasses of Moselle.

"Come, Kate. Stop brooding. We want the divorce, and divorce or not I shall always come where you are."

Her lips trembled.

"How can you be so calm? Why aren't you as frightened as me?"

"Now, love, that's very contrary of you. We've been longing for this freedom all these years and when it comes you're afraid! I shall go on giving Ireland what it is in me to give. But my private life doesn't belong to a country. It belongs to you."

"I have hurt your work."

"No, you have not. You've kept the life in me, and the

will to go on. I truly believe I would have died without you. The stones that have been flung and will still be flung are no matter. We were destined to love each other. This had to be."

His eyes were so compelling, his face so alive with warmth and sincerity that, with a great sigh, she let him take her in his arms, surrendering to his comfort.

"Think, Katie, we can be married."

She stirred in assent.

"You have always been my wife, but now you can have my name. I've always longed for you to have that."

No more Kitty O'Shea, she thought with silent gratitude. No more Mr. Fox, Mr. Carpenter, Mr. Preston, Mr. Stewart. They could all be buried in the same grave.

"But I still intend to see George Lewis immediately after Christmas," she said stubbornly. "If you think I'm going to let Willie stand in court posing as the innocent and injured husband, you're mistaken. We must defend ourselves. We must!"

He had drawn away from her. Although she could still put her hand out to touch him he suddenly seemed an infinite distance away, his face proud and withdrawn.

"My people will stand by me. Do you imagine I care what the English think?"

"The majority of your people are Roman Catholics who will do what their priests tell them to."

He nodded slightly. "Yes, the Church will be against me, but do you really think the people will listen to it to that extent? I have been their hope for too long. I'm a much more visible and practical hope in this life than their Heavenly Father who seems to have turned a remarkably blind eye on their sufferings for a very long time. And if that sounds like blasphemy, then I'm a blasphemous fellow." He stretched himself wearily. "Let's go to bed, darling. I'll read you to sleep."

The tensions of the day had exhausted her, and little as she expected to, she did fall asleep. She was awoken in the early hours of the morning by Charles twisting and turning beside her. He was in the grip of one of his nightmares. He had not had one for a long time. She thought he had completely outgrown them.

272

She had to shake him awake, and he opened his eyes saying in great distress, "They thought I had deserted them."

"Who thought that?"

He turned and came fully awake.

"Kate? What is it? Did I have a nightmare?"

"Yes, tell me what it was."

"I don't know. It's gone." He buried his face against her shoulder. "Let's go back to sleep."

But she knew his nightmare hadn't gone, and she knew what it was. He had been lying to her all evening. He cared desperately about his people in Ireland and the harm that might come to them through this new scandal. Through her, Kitty O'Shea, the woman whom they would like to see burned on one of their bonfires, or with a stake through her heart.

CHAPTER 23

KATHERINE waited only until Christmas Day was over before putting on town clothes, her fur-trimmed cape and bonnet, for it was very cold, and making a journey to London to call on her sister Anna.

She did not expect a cordial welcome. The sisters' estrangement at the time of Aunt Ben's death had continued. Katharine's visit today was not going to lessen it, for she had come to take Norah and Carmen home. It was her first move in the fight ahead.

Anna showed surprise when she saw her visitor. Her manner was guarded.

"What brings you here, Kate? If it's to plead with Willie I can tell you at once that you're wasting your time."

"To plead with him is the very last thing I intend to do!"

Anna, who might have been expecting tears and humility, was put out by this.

"Really, Kate, if I were in your position I would be hiding my head, not behaving like a duchess. If this is that man's influence—"

"That man, as you call him," Katharine interrupted swiftly, "knows nothing about my coming here. I've called for my daughters."

"I don't think you can do that. I'm perfectly certain Willie won't allow them to go."

"I'm not asking Willie's permission. I'm simply telling you I want Norah and Carmen home. Why are you looking at me like that? Do you think I will contaminate them?"

"I don't know, Kate, but you and Charlie Parnell behave as if you're right and the rest of the world is wrong. I've never known anything so blatant as the way you two have gone on for the last year." Anna shook her head, her eyes full of an entirely affected wonder. "And then you want two innocent young girls whom their father is trying to protect to go back to your household."

Katharine's voice was icy. "I'm not asking your permission either, Anna. I didn't come here to argue. I came for my daughters. Will you send them to me or must I go and look for them? I still remember my way about your house, I think."

"You don't need to be sarcastic. But one way and another—you've got round poor old Aunt Ben in her dotage, you've practically ruined poor Willie—"

Katharine interrupted again.

"You can't lecture me any more, Anna. I expect that's why you're angry with me, because you can't. If Willie's so unhappy, and you're so sympathetic towards him, you'd better comfort him." Her eyes widened in startled comprehension as she saw Anna's rising colour. "If you haven't already," she said slowly.

Before Anna could answer—and what would she have said?—the door flew open and Norah came bursting in.

"Mamma, I heard your voice." She was in Katharine's outstretched arms. "Oh, darling Mamma, why haven't you been to see us for so long? How are Clare and Katie?"

Over Norah's head Katharine saw Carmen enter the room, her welcome much more guarded than her sister's. Indeed, it wasn't a welcome at all, it was a quick automatic curtsey and a wary glance towards her Aunt Anna.

"The babies are very well, and waiting to see you. Clare has done nothing but ask for you since I told her you were coming home."

"We're to come home?" Norah said thankfully. "Oh, Mamma, we thought you were never going to want us again."

"I've wanted you all the time, silly child. Carmen? Aren't you going to kiss Mamma?"

Carmen came reluctantly to lift her face.

"You've both got your hair up!" Katharine exclaimed. "That's why you look so different."

They also wore dresses Katharine had never seen before. It must have come as a change to Willie to have to clothe his children, but he seemed to have done very well. With Anna's guidance, no doubt. The girls looked sweet and young with their starched organdie collars and neatly tucked waists. But Norah's face was too thin, and Carmen —her sensitive Carmen who had always hid her face at

275

trouble—wouldn't quite look at her. The blue eyes slid away not with shyness but with embarrassment.

How terrible that her own child should be embarrassed by her mother's presence!

Katharine's face tightened and hardened. Her hands clenched. This she could fight, too.

"Well, go and pack your bags, darlings. I have a hansom cab waiting."

Anna stepped forward, her eyes glinting.

"If I were you, Kate, I'd ask them first if they want to go. I don't think you can order them to. They're not infants, so even a court of law has no jurisdiction over them. They will be free to choose which parent they want to be with."

"You've been briefed already, I see," said Katharine bitterly. "Willie is really thinking of everything now, isn't he? I expect a little bit of adversity has sharpened his brains. But he won't have everything to his liking. I intend to fight the divorce in every possible way." She flung up her head, her eyes blazing. "Did he think I wouldn't? Did he think I would allow him to bring down one of the greatest men in England? Has he no sense of honour or history?"

Anna's mouth was wry.

"I don't think Willie cares about history. He only sees the man who has stolen his wife."

"Oh, Anna, you can't believe *that*! Then he really has got you under his spell." She looked at her sister, again seeing the tell-tale flush in the plump face. A feeling of utter revulsion seized her. She twitched her skirts sharply round her as she turned to leave.

"Run along, girls, and pack. Just put in the things you brought with you when you came here. I'll be waiting in the cab. Be as quick as you can."

Anna took a step forward.

"For goodness' sake, Kate—"

Was she worrying now that someone would see her sister waiting in a cab outside her door? Would that be another scandal? Such little things she bothered herself with when perhaps the fate of a nation lay at stake.

Waiting in the cab Katharine deliberately made her face grow serene. She looked in her little hand mirror and saw

276

that although she was very pale her mouth had softened and she was ready to smile when the girls came out.

But when the door opened only Norah appeared, and she was crying.

"Mamma, Carmen won't come. You see, Gerard was to take us to a party this evening, and she wants to go. She says if we live with—I mean down in Brighton, we'll never go anywhere."

After a moment Katharine said very quietly, "Then isn't she going to come and say goodbye?"

"Yes, of course she will. She was only afraid . . ."

"Tell her not to be afraid. I won't persuade her against her wishes. But what about you, Norah?"

Norah smiled radiantly, through flowing tears.

"Oh, I don't care for parties. I'm a social failure, Aunt Anna says. I only want to be at home with you and the babies."

She picked up her skirts and hurried back inside, re-appearing a few moments later with Carmen who now forgot her reserve, and flung herself into her mother's arms.

"Mamma, do you really not mind? It's only that Gerard would be so disappointed. He says I'm not bad for a sister, and he has a friend—"

"I understand, my darling. But tell Gerard I'd like a visit from him, too, when he can spare the time from his studies and all this social life."

"Yes, Mamma, I will. He often speaks of you."

"Kindly?" She had to ask the question.

Carmen hesitated, then said reluctantly, "It's only Mr. Parnell he dislikes."

Katharine bit her suddenly trembling lip. The cabman had poked his head round to grumble that his horse was getting cold. How much longer did they have to wait?

They could go at once, Katharine said, and waved to the daughter she was leaving behind. Her errand hadn't quite failed nor had it quite succeeded. But it was a beginning. Now she could safely leave the little ones in the care of Norah while she consulted her solicitor, Mr. George Lewis, and made frequent trips to London in the months to come.

Willie and Anna? she was thinking, and her mouth

tightened again. She could have no sentiment now. She had to use every stick to her hand.

They went over it every time Charles was back from Ireland. Katharine had all the evidence Mr. Lewis had advised her to get, evidence of Willie's cruelty, of his collusion in the way he had encouraged them to be together, of his hopes of reward, and, if that evidence were not enough, of his own affairs with women, conducted privately but not privately enough. She had a list of those women, all able to be called as witnesses. Including her sister Anna.

She no longer cared what her family thought of her. What did they care for her, anyway, with their long-drawn-out litigation over Aunt Ben's will? They had accused her of everything possible, lying, treachery, greed. They had turned her devotion for Aunt Ben into a nasty grasping scheming. So what did adultery matter?

Not one of them had imagined her true feelings. They would never have dreamed of calling her behaviour loyalty. She was black to the soul. Did it matter if she starved?

But she could scarcely believe her ears when Charles, too, turned against her. Or that was what he seemed to do. For suddenly, although he had consulted George Lewis, and allowed him to brief Sir Frank Lockwood, he announced that he intended to withdraw his defence, and would be obliged if she would do the same.

The case was due to be heard in a week's time.

Katharine thought the long months of strain must have affected his mind.

"But how can you do this? You've assured everyone that when the facts were known you wouldn't be blamed."

"My people won't turn against me, whatever happens. The English . . ." he shrugged. "Let them think what they like. It won't concern me."

"But Charles!" She didn't know how to cope with this new problem. "Supposing they decide to believe Willie? What else can they do if we say nothing? Then you'll be ruined."

He shook his head reflectively, as if he had scarcely been listening to her.

"No, they won't believe Captain O'Shea in preference to me. They remember him as the man who made fun of their manners and their dress, and wouldn't take the party pledge. They won't have any sympathy for him."

"Nor for me, as his wife," Katharine said in a low voice. "I'm Kitty O'Shea to them. They can't wait to fling stones at me. You trust them too much. What about Tim Healy who loves you one day and would strike you down the next? What about Mick Davitt who is practically a monk? What about Sexton and Justin McCarthy, and Colonel Nolan? And surely—surely you're not going to forget the voice of the Holy Roman Church?"

"Kate, I don't like you when you're like this."

She put her hands to her face, shocked.

"What do I look like? A shrew again?"

His gentle smile reassured her.

"No. Only bewildered, as if you were being a woman you were never meant to be."

Then suddenly he had snatched her into his arms, and buried his face in her hair. "Let Willie have his way. Let the divorce go through. I'm only so afraid something might stop it, even at this late hour. What does it matter what people say about us? We'll face it together. I'll at last be able to make you my wife. Isn't that worth keeping silent for?"

She had to push him away from her to look at his face. It was so worn and transparent. She had been so wrapped up in her bitter search for evidence to defend themselves that she hadn't noticed how frail he had grown. Had he the strength to stand all the trouble ahead?

"It's worth it to me," she said at last. "But would it be worth it to you if you had to give up Ireland?"

"You're determined to under-estimate your importance in my life," he said, smiling quizzically. "And mine to the people of Ireland. Well, I'm optimistic enough to think that we'll all come through. Kate, will you promise me to withdraw your defence?"

"Must I?"

"I found that you'd even brought in your own sister."

Her chin went up aggressively. "She deserves no better. And you know that I would do anything to protect you."

"I must refuse to be protected in this way. It doesn't do either of us credit. The divorce will go through whether we smear other people or not."

279

"But Willie will smear us. You wait until he starts giving evidence!"

"Then let us refrain from reading it. And six months from now, in the spring . . ." It was her turn to bury her face against his shoulder, sobbing convulsively.

"Now, Kate, my love."

"You have made me remember Papa's favourite text. *And now abideth faith, hope and charity.* I haven't thought of it for so long."

"Then think of it now, and let me see my gentle Katie again."

He wouldn't tell her what had made him change his mind about defending the case. He said he had been coming to that idea for a long time, it would be the best way, she would see.

Perhaps he was right, for that evening she found Norah in tears. When she went to comfort her, saying, "This isn't *your* trouble, my darling," Norah began laughing and crying at the same time.

"I am only so relieved, Mamma. Mr. Parnell says that now Carmen and I won't have to appear in court. We were dreading it terribly, especially Carmen."

"You and Carmen! In court! Why didn't you tell me?"

Norah hung her head.

"I couldn't bear to talk about it. Papa wrote some time ago saying we would have to do this. It was our duty to testify. If we refused we could be put in prison for contempt of court."

Katharine's voice was harsh.

"And what were you to testify, pray?"

Norah's cheeks flamed. She couldn't meet her mother's eyes.

"Nothing very much, really."

"What?"

"Only that you were not to be disturbed when you had a visitor. That the sitting room door was shut. That—that the servants knew this, too."

For so many years, Katharine thought in agony. How could she not have realised how her children felt about the door shut against them?

"And Gerard? Was he to be called, too?"

280

Norah nodded mutely.

Katharine clenched her hands, unable now to see either right or wrong. She so wanted to vindicate Charles and herself. But at the expense of her young daughters' distress, at the public spectacle they would have had to make of themselves?

For the first time she was thankful that Charles had taken the decision from her. They could stay safely at home, shut from the sight of the gloating public, while Willie had it all his own way in that court room.

Charles had advised her to stop *The Times* coming, or at least to refrain from reading it while the case was being heard. He might as well have told her not to stir from a house that was on fire.

She had to pore over the long report that took up far too much space and relegated to the back pages of the newspaper news of far more vital interest to the nation.

Her face flushed with anger and shame as she read evidence given by servants, Jane Leinster, and that sly Miss Glennister, who both identified Charles from a photograph, said he was often at the house, and sometimes the door of the sitting room was locked; Esther Harvey, the housekeeper at the house in Regent's Park, who said that Mrs. O'Shea often came to visit the gentleman who lived there; Samuel Drury, the cab driver who frequently drove Mr. Parnell down to Eltham at night; that infamous pair at Medina Terrace, Brighton, Harriet Bull who testified that she had seen the respondent and co-respondent coming out of a bedroom together, and Mrs. Pethers who said that often Mrs. O'Shea came in late at night, her hair all flying, she didn't look respectable, and there was that queer episode when Captain O'Shea arrived unexpectedly, and Mr. Parnell hurriedly left the house by the fire-escape. Even dear old Partridge, the coachman, was brought in to say reluctantly that he had looked after the horses, Dictator, President and Home Rule, that Mr. Parnell had brought over from Ireland, and that he often took the brougham to the railway station to meet Mr. Parnell late at night.

As for Willie, he had turned himself into a model of injured innocence.

How he must have glowed with relief when Mr. Lockwood Q.C. stood up to say, "I appear with my learned friend Mr. Pritchard for Mrs. O'Shea, the respondent in the case, and I desire to take this opportunity of stating on her behalf that I do not intend to cross-examine any witnesses, to call any witnesses nor to take any part in these proceedings."

This did not, however, prevent Sir Edward Clarke from putting his client in the witness-box and extracting his damning evidence of the shameless infidelity of his wife.

It was his wife's wish, and the wish of her aged aunt, Captain O'Shea said, that he lived at Albert Mansions while she lived at Wonersh Lodge. But he visited her frequently, and their relations were always amicable. It was not until the Galway election that he began to hear the rumours about his wife and Parnell. Since then he had written to her frequently, and entreated her on many occasions to give up the friendship. There were many letters as exhibits to prove this, including one written by his son Gerard stating in schoolboy fashion that he would thrash Mr. Parnell if his father wished him to. He had advised his wife to consult Mr. Pym, her solicitor, and this she had done. There was another of those damning letters to prove this.

But she hadn't kept her promise to break with the co-respondent, even after the damaging publicity of the article in the *Pall Mall Gazette* about Mr. Parnell's slight accident on his way to Wonersh Lodge.

The hearing lasted for two days. At the end of the first day Katharine could not bear inactivity any longer. She put on a cloak and went out, intending to walk along the sea-front until she was physically tired. The wind would blow away her nightmares. She would begin to think of the happy future rather than letting her mind dwell constantly on the unseen courtroom in London, on Willie committing perjury with every word he said, his face bearing its familiar look of righteousness and injury.

What irremediable harm was being done to Charles in that courtroom? She must shake off her unhappy prescience of troubles ahead and return to him with a calm face. Already, the bracing air and her quick purposeful walk was clearing her head.

But she had not thought to wear a veil. That had been a

mistake. For, although there were few people about on this cold stormy day, she was recognised. A young lout lounging on the seawall pointed a finger, his face lighting with evil glee.

"There she is herself. There's Kitty O'Shea!"

Two women passing stopped to stare. "Fancy showing herself!" Their voices were loud, intending to be heard.

The youth had two companions. The three of them began to walk behind Katharine as she quickened her step. Above the wind and the crash of the waves she could hear their mocking footsteps, their coarse adolescent laughter.

It should not have worried her. They were young, idle, ignorant. They would learn better one day. She would not allow them to drive her off the front. She continued to walk quickly, with dignity, hoping they would tire of their silly game. When they did not, her exacerbated nerves made her whirl round to face them. She cried out, "You are molesting me! Pray stop."

She had an impression of wind-reddened grinning faces, and then before she could pick up her skirts to pass them, one of them stooped, straightened, and the mud was flung.

It spattered her face and her cloak. She stared at it in shocked astonishment. The three youths began to laugh uproariously and although she wanted to berate them for their intolerable behaviour she saw that other passers-by had stopped to stare, that she was a spectacle with her splattered face and muddy cloak. She couldn't face the wretched scene. She had to hurry away, trying not to run, trying to keep her dignity and hold her head high. She remembered saying once to Charles, "I have a long neck. I can hold my head high on it."

It was easier saying than doing. And it was also unfortunate that Charles should be in the hall when she returned. She averted her face, murmuring that it was so cold, the wind had made her eyes stream. But how could she hope to escape with that excuse? He had seen her dirt-streaked cheeks.

"Kate, that isn't tears, that's mud." His face became stone. "What happened?"

She had to tell him, making light of the unpleasant adventure.

"I'd like to have them whipped," he said with quiet ferocity. "Why did you go out?"

"Am I to hide? Am I to be a prisoner?"

"You've tortured yourself reading that damned newspaper. Now you're putting yourself in the way of insults. And after me keeping you out of the witness-box, sparing you all that distress."

Then suddenly he gathered her into his arms.

"Oh, Kate, Kate, I'm not angry with you. But to see your dear face smeared with muck—" he had taken out his handkerchief and was wiping away the stains "—I'm in the mood to break a few necks, beginning with those louts."

In spite of this exacerbation of her feelings, Katharine read *The Times* again the next day.

It was all over then.

Mr. Lockwood, in asking for a decree nisi to be made absolute in six months, also asked with complete confidence for the custody of the children under age to be given to his client.

How could they be refused to him? Clare and Katie were registered as his daughters and the Judge, whether or not he was taken in by Captain O'Shea's air of injured innocence, had no alternative but to uphold the law. Minors were never left in the care of the guilty party, and since there was no defence, the respondent in this case admitted her guilt. As for the co-respondent, he could only describe him as "the man who takes advantage of the hospitality offered him by the husband to debauch the wife".

Katharine walked up and down, the newspaper crushed in her clenched fists. She was talking out loud without knowing it.

"There was no fire-escape at Medina Terrace! Oh, that wicked woman! She's invented that or someone had told her to invent it, because it makes a better story. How they'll lampoon Charles! Mrs. Pethers knew he merely discreetly went out the back way to avoid one of Willie's terrible rows, and it was I who made him do it." Her eyes filled with tears of rage. "And Jane, who I trusted. And reading out Gerard's letter, that he only wrote in innocence, poor boy. And poor Partridge. *Was* my hair flying wild like that? What do they

284

know about it, any of them? They've never been in love, poor wretches."

The door opened and Charles came in.

"Good morning, my love. Aren't we to have any breakfast?"

"Charles, he's even got our children, too!"

"But you have your divorce, at last." He kissed her trembling lips gently, then with passion. "Didn't I tell you again not to read that newspaper?"

She pulled herself away from him.

"Don't you *care* about Clare and Katie? How can Willie possibly have them? He knows they're not his."

"Then he won't have them. That's just a legal direction he doesn't need to carry out."

"But he will do it to spite me. He and Anna. Anna stood up in court declaring her innocence, and wondering how she could wound me next."

"I always told you you made a mistake in bringing Anna into this."

"But so did you make a mistake in dropping your defence. Have you read the leader?"

"I told you not to look at that paper."

"Then I had better read it to you. Listen."

She read in a slow articulate bitter voice,

"The result of the O'Shea divorce case has taken Mr. Parnell's constituents completely by surprise. All along they were led to believe that he would be able to clear himself of the charges made against him and vindicate his moral character. The people are so deeply committed that they are reluctant to raise any cry against him, but they consider that if he had made any defence at all they would have had some excuse for sticking to him. There being now no room left for that excuse, the opinion is that he cannot much longer remain as leader . . ."

Phyllis knocked at the door.

"Shall I bring in the breakfast now, ma'am?"

Katharine looked at Charles' silent form slumped in a chair by the fire.

"Yes, Phyllis. Bring the large coffee pot. We'll want plenty of coffee this morning."

She went to kneel beside him.

285

"Darling, didn't you know this would happen if you refused to defend yourself? Didn't you wonder what Mr. Gladstone would have to say? Or the Queen? I know the Queen is a narrow puritan but she sets the fashion. I don't think even Mr. Gladstone would dare to take a stand against her. He might in politics, but not in morals."

At last he lifted his head.

"A moment ago you were only worried about Clare and Katie. Now it's Mr. Gladstone and the Queen."

"It's you," she whispered, "I only get into rages because I worry about you."

"And then you think that I ought not to match your loyalty."

"But it's so different for you. You have three million other people on your conscience as well as me."

"You are not on my conscience." He laid his hand on his breast. "You are here, in my heart. And we'll find a way about the children. We must appeal against the Judge's ruling. If that fails I suppose Captain O'Shea is quite likely to have one of his financial crises before long."

"You mean—buy them back!"

"Not back, because we'll never part with them. But we might buy his signature to a document relinquishing them. I shall sell Avondale, if necessary. Now where's that coffee? And I hope Ellen has done some kidneys and bacon. I shall need to feel strong today. I'll have to call a meeting of the Irish party and I've no doubt everyone will be in a fine spate of words. Not that they're ever anything else."

Katharine, pleased for the small mercy that he was ready to eat, for his lack of appetite worried her a great deal, said hopefully, "Perhaps they'll be with you. You *are* their leader still."

"No, they'll be at my throat. But I'm confident I can still manage them. I certainly have no intention of resigning at this critical stage." He sat at the breakfast table. "And what will you do today?"

Katharine looked at the grey sea, whipped by a sharp wind, remembered yesterday's incident on the front and shivered.

"I shall stay indoors with the children. I don't intend to let them out of my sight."

And wait for you to come home, she added silently.

Later in the day she sent Norah out to buy all the newspapers she could.

After that came the distressing task of assessing their opinions. Not opinions, as it turned out, but one unanimous opinion.

"Retire into private life . . ." "Neither clergy nor laity in America would have anything more to do with him . . ." "His career is closed . . ." "Is there a man in the wide world who would now accept Mr. Parnell's word about anything, however insignificant . . ."

To add to her distress, she read of taunts of "Kitty's petticoats" and jokes about the lamentable fire-escape story. More seriously, a series of outrages had been begun in Tipperary, houses were burnt, and escaping moonlighters shot a bailiff dead. The calming voice of their leader had faltered. What were they to think? What were they to do?

Katharine rang the bell violently and when Phyllis came she thrust the papers into her arms and told her to burn them in the kitchen stove.

"Yes, ma'am. But won't you go upstairs and rest, ma'am. The master won't be home for a long time yet."

The master . . . Phyllis had never called him that before. A small stubborn glow began within her, and would not be put out even when it had gone ten o'clock and Charles was still not home. He would come. He always did.

CHAPTER 24

IF she had regained her calm, he had lost his.

He came at last at nearly midnight, his eyes burning in his white weary face.

"We've got to fight, Kate," he said, and fell into his chair by the fire, his body flat with exhaustion.

"Damn their miserable hypocritical souls," he said with quiet intensity.

"Why does it matter to them now?" Katharine asked indignantly. "They've known for long enough."

"They're afraid of shocking Mr. Gladstone. We're public reprobates now, and he's a devout churchman."

"Even Mr. Gladstone . . ." Katharine began, only to be interrupted by his weary, "Oh, yes, I expect he knew, too, but while there was no public scandal he could turn a blind eye."

Katharine came to sit beside him.

"Tell me what happened today."

"We had a meeting to elect a chairman."

"They did re-elect you?" Katharine cried.

"Oh, yes, they did. They even cheered me. I was elected unanimously."

"How could they not after all you have done?"

"It wasn't I who influenced them so much as the messages coming in from Ireland. Dublin, Limerick, Clonmel, Ennis, all sent pledges of loyalty and confidence. They said they wouldn't submit to dictation, they'd have no leader but me. And O'Brien and O'Connor in America paid me the compliment of being the greatest Parliamentary leader the Irish had ever had. Even Tim Healy made a flattering speech for me in Leinster. I have it here. Listen. 'For Ireland and for Irishmen Mr. Parnell is less a man than an institution. We have under the shadow of his name secured a power and authority in the councils of Great Britain and the world such as we never possessed before.' "

"It's all true."

"Well, as you know, I don't trust Healy too far."

"But after all this, what happened? What went wrong?"

He looked at her with his hollowed tired eyes.

"Gladstone has killed us."

The flat statement sent a tremor of fear through her. She remembered all too well the veiled cruelty in those slate-coloured eyes even when Mr. Gladstone had been at his most affable.

"I was afraid of this," she whispered. "How did he do it?"

"He wrote a letter to John Morley. It's been published in a special edition of the *Pall Mall Gazette*. Here it is." He pulled a crumpled newspaper from his pocket, and stabbed with his forefinger at the place. Katharine began to read, then pushed the paper away, unable to concentrate on the formalised language.

"Tell me what it means."

"Morley told Justin McCarthy about the letter just before the meeting. McCarthy told me, but I had no alternative at that late hour but to stick to my guns. I intend to go on doing so. I won't have the Grand Old Spider defeat me. Briefly, Kate, he says that it would be a great embarrassment to him if I continued as leader of the Irish party. It would render his retention of the leadership of the Liberal party, based as it has been mainly upon the presentation of the Irish cause, a nullity."

Katharine bowed her head.

At last she said, "Was it such a crime—loving a woman?"

His fingers worked in her hair.

"He's a coward. He's afraid of public opinion. Probably, as you guessed, he's afraid of the Queen."

"He's an old man," she said fiercely. "He'll die."

"Not soon enough. I know he's eighty-one, nearly twice my age. But at this moment he seems younger than me. And he's got the whip-hand. He's the one man in the British Government who can get the Home Rule Bill through."

"Without you?"

"I believe my party may think so."

"So he must be placated."

"At any cost."

Katharine looked at him, knowing what that cost was.

"What will you do?"

He stirred. "Begin on a new manifesto."

"Now?"

"There's no time to be lost. We've called a meeting for next week. Everyone will be there except those on sickbeds and poor Patrick O'Brien who's still in jail. Most of them," he added, "out for my blood. So I must have a plan of campaign. Don't wait up for me, Kate. I don't feel like sleeping yet. I'll begin work."

She looked at him in dismay, allowing herself to worry only about his look of exhaustion. Later the other thoughts would come. The realisation that he was still, for all his protestations of happiness, deeply, irrevocably involved with his country. If it now, in all its histrionic cruelty, destroyed its most dedicated leader, he would die, as surely as if he had been assassinated.

But it wouldn't be Ireland, it would be she who had killed him. By adultery.

Not only Mr. Gladstone would be responsible.

An edict that no Irish bishops or priests would dare to disobey was bound to come from Rome. The people might struggle against it. But they would begin to remember that the leader they had loved so wildly and trusted so much was not a Catholic like themselves. And the powerful yeast of their religion would begin to work in them.

All Catholics, Katharine thought, turning on her pillow to look at the high cold moon riding over the dark sea, had the death wish. If Parnell were dead they would have a great glorious orgy of grief. But alive, and tarnished because of the woman at his side, they would be as unremittingly cruel as ignorance and emotional frenzy could make them.

She had always known these things, but Charles had almost convinced her that they didn't matter, that it was she only who mattered.

Now, as she thought of his tired gaunt face bent over the papers on the lamplit table downstairs, she knew better. He had not won a victory over his two-sided self after all. He was forever committed to both sides. It was a situation too harrowing to be endured.

But she must endure it. She got up and went downstairs and made coffee. Sitting in the chilly kitchen waiting for the water to boil she thought of those other nights now so long ago when she had cooked midnight meals over the fire in her bedroom and they had sat in the firelight making the first exquisite discoveries of love.

Looking back, that time seemed to have been a time of perfect happiness, all its anxieties and separations forgotten. She remembered their stolen drives by the river, the white rose she had dropped and the dried remains of which she had found years later in an envelope in the breast pocket of his jacket, their secret meetings in hotels, his private signal to her across the floor of the House of Commons. Even their vigil over the dying baby now had its aura of poignant happiness.

And now they were back to this, the unending fight, and both of them ten years older, and exhausted by the constant tension of their efforts to be together.

But they were still together. She smoothed her hair, and made herself look alert and sympathetic as she carried the tray into the study.

He looked up.

"Why aren't you in bed asleep?"

"You know I never sleep well without you. Have some coffee now. I see you've written a great deal."

"Yes. I expect I'll discard most of it. I'm feeling my way. Stay down here with me, Kate. Sit by the fire."

"Grouse is here." She touched the sleeping dog with the toe of her slipper."

"Grouse does his best, but doesn't stop me from being lonely." He sat back and regarded her. "It's only you who has ever been able to do that. Isn't that wonderful, Kate? That I should find the one person in the world who can do that for me?"

"And yet you leave her to sleep alone."

"Don't scold me at this hour in the morning. But you're not. I can see that naughty twinkle in your eye." He flung down his pen. "I believe neither of us will stay down here, after all."

So she had won again for a few hours, although she had not gone downstairs meaning to win. But with the dear heaviness of his head on her breast, and the blown spray on the windows heightening the comfort of the warm bed, she had her familiar feeling of victory, of being saved once more, of their happiness being strong enough to stand the coldest winds.

The meeting in Room 15 of the House of Commons began the following week.

The effect of Mr. Gladstone's letter on the Irish Nationalist party, most of whom were men who had fought long and painfully served jail sentences for their cause, had been devastating. They had felt duped, deceived, humiliated. Victory had been in sight and now it had been snatched away from them. Home Rule, possible only through Mr. Gladstone's Bill, was receding like a mirage. And it was all the fault of their leader with his fatal flaw, his obsession for a woman.

Not that many of them led perfect lives themselves. Mr. John Morley had made an acid comment. "Why don't the Irish members go into their constituencies to speak about improvident marriages?" But they were not fools enough or great enough to risk their entire future for a woman. They had listened to and sympathised with Mr. Parnell's earnest comment, "Life is not supportable without the friendship of a woman. Even the saints needed them. You would never have got young men to sacrifice themselves for so unlucky a country as Ireland only that they pictured her as a woman."

But the virtue was in not being found out.

Mr. Parnell had been found out. So he must be sacrificed.

They used his manifesto to defeat him. They debated it and argued about it hour after hour. Tempers rose. There were heated objections to a reference to "English wolves" which Mr. Parnell flatly refused to remove. The chameleon Mr. Healy shed emotional tears at one stage, he was still torn between love and hate for this man who had influenced him so deeply. But eventually hate triumphed.

He was an orator trained by Parnell himself, and he could not resist the cut and thrust of brilliant wounding argument.

The long trial in Room 15 went on all the week. They swayed back and forth in their emotions. Redmond was always strongly with Parnell.

"Who is the man to take his place? Who is the man who, when the Home Rule Bill comes to be settled, can discuss its provisions on an equal footing with the leaders of the English parties? There is no such man."

But Healy was having none of this any longer.

He turned to his leader, his eyes glittering, and made a long peroration, finishing with the words:

"If you, sir, should go down, you are only one man gone. Heads of greater leaders have been stricken on the block before now for Ireland."

"Not by their own friends," Colonel Nolan interrupted, but Healy, contemptuously ignoring the interruption, went on, "And the Irish cause remains. The Irish people can put us down, but the Irish cause will always remain."

He dropped from this noble level, however, when Mr. Parnell, still somehow retaining his composure, said that he was the chairman of the party until he was deposed.

"Allow me to depose you," retorted Mr. Healy.

From the turbulent discussion that ensued Mr. Redmond's sane voice emerged, "Mr. Parnell is the master of the party."

As quick as a flash came Mr. Healy's spiteful, "Who is to be the mistress of the party?"

Pandemonium broke out. Mr. O'Connor appealed for order, and over the confused shouting, Mr Parnell's voice rang out, incisive, full of a deadly cold anger.

"Better appeal to your friend," he said to Mr. O'Connor. "Better appeal to that cowardly little scoundrel there who in an assembly of Irishmen dares to insult a woman!"

That was the end. There was a desultory effort to restore order and continue discussions, but Mr. Justin McCarthy rose and said he thought the time had come to close the debate. He stood a moment looking round the assembled company, then turned fatefully to the door, and forty-four of his colleagues rose to follow him.

Mr. Parnell was left in the disastrously emptied room. Only twenty-six had remained with him. The king was dethroned. The Irish Nationalist party had committed suicide.

But Mr. Parnell refused defeat. He said that he would retire only if Gladstone said in writing that he would give the Irish Parliament control of the police and the land. And if ever the letter was written he advised its being kept in a glass case.

Dr. Walsh, Archbishop of Dublin, probably finding him now too much of an embarrassment in a Catholic country, urged him to retire, but this plea also he ignored, saying that a time came sooner or later when a priest had to choose between Rome and Ireland and he would always choose Rome.

The immense strain of those weeks told severely on his health. He was suffering from acute rheumatism in one arm and Katharine rubbed it with firwood oil and packed it with wool.

That made it feel a little better, and he pronounced himself perfectly fit to travel. He would need to be in Ireland a great deal over the next few months, he said. He intended travelling backwards and forwards twice a week.

Katharine couldn't bear it. He was growing old visibly, his hair greying, his face deeply lined, his eyes sunken. Why couldn't he give up? Why didn't he acknowledge that the fight was hopeless? They would be free to marry in midsummer. Why couldn't they then go abroad and live quietly and peacefully as Sir Charles Dilke had done?

He listened gravely to her arguments, but only said that it was now too late. He would be a coward to desert his post when the difficulties were at their greatest.

"Be patient, Kate. It will all come right."

How *could* he still be optimistic?

"You're not only killing yourself, you're killing me."

His face tightened with pain, and she, as always, bitterly regretted her impulsive words.

"The children scarcely ever see you. They think of Papa as someone who lives on the Irish mail steamer."

"One couldn't exactly call it living," he said with a flash of his old dry humour. "I do understand, Kate. After the Kilkenny election I'll try to be home more."

The Kilkenny election was another bitter blow. The Parnellite candidate was defeated. The Church was showing its strength. There were priests at every polling booth. The people who in a Dublin Square had shouted hysterically, "We will die for him," now showed that they had not the courage to disobey their Church. They found it easier not to die for Mr. Parnell after all lest they should endanger their immortal souls.

294

But they still longed to love him.

At Kildare, Portarlington, Maryborough, Ballybrophy, Thurles, and Limerick he was cheered wildly, at Mallow he was called a ruffian, a coward, a renegade, but at Cork, his own constituency he spoke to a crowd of fifty thousand. He stood on the platform, the wind lifting a lock of hair on his forehead, his dark eyes blazing in his pale dedicated face. He looked frail and ill, his clothes hanging on his gaunt frame. If the wind got stronger he might very well be in danger of blowing away. But there was nothing weak about his voice.

It rang over the complete hushed crowd.

"Men of Cork, I come before you with a proud and confident heart. Without you I am nothing. With you we are everything . . . I don't pretend to be immaculate. But never in thought, in word, or deed have I been false to the trust that Irishmen have confided in me. I have fought for you for sixteen years . . ."

When he stopped there was a brief silence, an isolated voice called "Kitty", then like an avalanche the cheering began. Women sobbed, lifting their black shawls to their faces, men waved their caps and shouted themselves hoarse. This was tremendous. This was what they admired, a brave man pitting his strength against a hostile world. They were for him completely in that moment. Indeed, they were so carried away with their enthusiasm that they hardly noticed the brave man being assisted from the platform, and taken into an hotel to be revived with brandy. Nor did they know how often this happened on that strenuous tour.

But he came safely back to England in time for Christmas.

CHAPTER 25

APART from the joy of having Charles home, Christmas held another pleasure for Katharine, a visit from Gerard and Carmen.

They arrived with gifts for her and Norah, and lollypops for the little girls. Best of all, they were able to reassure Katharine that they didn't think their father intended to exercise his rights under the Court's ruling and demand custody of Clare and Katie. At least he didn't intend to do so at present for the simple reason that he had no permanent home. Children at that tender age needed a nursery, nursemaids, and a governess, all requirements which Willie would find much too expensive.

But he would enjoy holding over her head the threat of removing them from her, and in one of his bitter revengeful moods he could very well carry out that threat. She would never be easy until a legal arrangement was made giving her custody. As Charles had said, there was only one way to get Willie's consent to that. A considerable bribe. She could only pray that when the litigation over Aunt Ben's will was finished she would be left with sufficient money to do this. Her solicitors assured her that she must succeed in at least half of the estate. She had to cling to that hope, and never leave the children too long out of her sight.

But for all her preoccupation about this, and about Charles' health, it was a happy Christmas. There was roast turkey, and brandy flaming on the plum pudding, the little girls shrieked with delight when the candles were lit on the Christmas tree and later the servants came in and they all sang carols round the fire. Katie nodded asleep on her father's lap, and he looked rested and contented and less gaunt. Although that might have been the trick of the firelight.

Later Katharine tucked the little girls in bed, and Clare

296

said in her grave voice, "Isn't Katie a baby, she went to sleep on Papa's lap."

"I did not," Katie protested. "I couldn't because his watch hurt my ear. I could hear it ticking in his pocket."

"Well, Papa almost went to sleep. Is he home to stay, Mamma?"

The two pairs of brown eyes looked at her. She had met that identical eager attentive gaze so often across the House of Commons, on railway stations, across the fireside, and from the pillow beside hers. Something in her heart said, "Whatever happens I will have some part of him." She pushed the thought away and said briskly:

"He is here until Saturday, and after that he will always be home once or twice every week. Isn't that enough when he's such a busy man?" She lit the night light, and bent to kiss each round brow. "Remember he always loves you," she said.

In Ireland the people still said that they would not submit to the dictation of the Church, but more and more became afraid to defy their parish priests. Especially when at Mass one priest remarked that he noticed several Parnellites in the congregation, and that the loyal flock would know what to do with them when they got them outside. A young boy who dared to cheer for Parnell was knocked senseless by his village priest. The tenacious hand of the Church was tightening its grip.

Matters were not helped by the variety of ribald songs sung about Kitty O'Shea. An element of hate, as uncontrolled as had been their love, was rising in the assembled crowds. Sometimes Parnell could not make his voice heard above the rude interjections. Michael Davitt, living up to his reputation for saintliness, offered to share his platform, saying that in this way Parnell would be sure of a quiet hearing.

Mr. Parnell replied with his immense dignity and arrogance, "Tell Mick Davitt that I have never asked for his permission to speak where and when I pleased in Ireland, and I will not do so now."

But the battle was slipping away from him. His candidates in Sligo and Carlow were both defeated. And worst of all, physical violence began. Stones and mud were flung at him. In Kilkenny a bag of lime, thrown at him in the dark, burst in his face and blinded him for several days.

He came home to Katharine wearing dark glasses, and with a bandage still over one eye.

"Charles, what has happened?" she cried in alarm.

"Only a devilishly uncomfortable accident. I got lime in my eyes and they became inflamed. I was blind for two or three days. But Doctor Kenny assures me the injury isn't permanent."

"That horrible country!" she said with intensity. "I'm glad I've never set eyes on it."

"Now, Kate. You know very well you would be seduced by it as everyone is. A few hysterical people aren't going to make me hate it."

"Far more than a few! I read the papers."

"Then stop reading them," he said equably.

"Oh, my love! Supposing you'd been permanently blinded."

"Yes, that would have been a calamity. I wouldn't have been able to see you on our wedding day. Do you realise we have only four more weeks to wait?"

"Charles, stay home until then. I beg you. I'm so afraid."

He removed his glasses and looked at her with his one good eye. It was deeply sunken and the bones of his skull were disturbingly prominent. He looked old and tired and ill. How could she not be afraid?

But he was smiling as if her fears were completely groundless.

"I assure you that nothing is going to kill me before I stand at the altar with you. Not any bishops or priests or a pack of unruly peasants or the English Government or the Archangel Gabriel himself."

And at last it was mid-June and her wedding day.

She wore a dress of dove grey silk, and a little turban with violets. Norah helped her to dress, and scolded her when she took too long.

"Don't you keep poor Mr. Parnell waiting. He's been walking up and down the hall for the last half hour. He's as nervous as if he were a young man."

"Well, believe it or not," Katharine said, dabbing her

flushed cheeks with rice powder, "I feel like a young girl, too. Does that seem ridiculous to you?"

Norah answered judicially that she expected she would feel the same if she were getting ready for her own wedding.

"And you won't make the mistakes I did," Katharine said vigorously.

"But I would never be able to love one man as you have," Norah said, a little wistfully. "Sometimes I have hated Mr. Parnell. But it must be wonderful to be loved like that."

"Yes," Katharine breathed. "It is."

"Oh, Mamma, you're not crying!" Norah exclaimed. "You mustn't. You'll spoil your looks."

Katharine drew Norah to her, holding her closely.

"Have I been such a bad mother to you and Carmen and Gerard?" she asked intensely. "I never meant to be."

"Sometimes—" Norah began, then cried warmly, "But we *always* loved you. And now do hurry. Don't keep Mr. Parnell waiting. You see, I do care about his feelings. And you look beautiful, Mamma. Like a bride."

Charles, waiting impatiently at the foot of the stairs, said, "Come along, Kate. It's time to be married."

But as she descended slowly, he smiled, his eyes burning with all their old remembered brilliance. "Here is your bridal bouquet." He showed her a white rose, touched it gallantly to his lips, then pinned it at her breast.

The servants, with Norah and the two little girls, had gathered in the doorway. They called their good wishes, and Charles, taking Katharine's arm, led her out of the house.

The fast horse, Dictator, was harnessed to the phaeton outside. There was also a growing crowd headed by several journalists. Newspapers were interested in this belated marriage of a pair of notorious lovers.

Charles helped Katharine into the phaeton, climbed in himself, took the reins from the groom, and whipped up the horse.

He was smiling broadly. "Listen, they're after us," he said. "They won't catch Dictator."

Katharine, her father's daughter, was deeply grieved that they could not be married in a church. But the registrar's

299

office at Steyning was decorated with bowls of summer flowers, and the registar's manner grave enough to have graced a pulpit. Katharine seemed to hear an echo of her father's beloved voice, and had a conviction that the church's blessing was with them, although she could never be married in a church. She held out her hand for the ring to be slipped on her finger, and in that moment her lips trembled uncontrollably. She and Charles had always belonged to each other, but now they did so by law, and, she thought stubbornly, looking round the little registry office, that had no altar, no candles, no air of reverence, in the sight of God.

They drove back to Walsingham Terrace with the sun on their faces. Charles had to hold the reins with one hand, for his other was in hers. This would be their most familiar gesture of love until they were old, she thought. Its comfort would stay with them long after their most passionate embraces were finished.

The crowd outside the house had grown. They stood a moment to acknowledge the few ragged cheers. As the newspaperman pressed forward Charles lifted his hand.

"Let my wife go. I'll come out and see you presently."

My wife ... Katharine's cheeks were flushed with the colour of girlhood. They went into the drawing room where Norah and the little girls waited, and where faithful Ellen had laid out a feast. The room was full of flowers, and there was a pile of letters and telegrams. So many good wishes, Katharine thought with gratitude and humility. She had done a great deal of damage to Ireland and the Irish cause, but all these people could still forgive her.

She let Norah take off her smart hat with the gay knot of violets, and then sank on her knees to gather Clare and Katie to her.

"Mamma, you have wet on your cheeks," Katie complained, and Clare said severely, "You shouldn't cry in your good dress, Mamma."

Phyllis knocked at the door and came in, flustered.

"Mrs. O'Shea, could you come down for a minute. There's one of those newspaper men in the hall insisting on seeing you."

Charles rapped out, "What do you mean, Phyllis? *Who* is

Mrs. O'Shea?" and suddenly everyone was laughing uproariously, and from then on there were no more tears.

Mrs. Parnell ... It had come true at last. Long after Charles had fallen asleep that night, Katharine lay listening to his quiet breathing, acutely conscious of his form beside her as if it were for the first time and she didn't know every bone, every muscle of his body. Its familiarity seemed suddenly strange and exciting. Was this because a few words had been said over them, and a ring slipped on her finger? Perhaps it was. She was more deeply conventional than she had realised.

But there were soon more separations. Charles was off to Paris to see Irish exiles, and then back to Ireland. Ireland, Katharine thought, was like a disease that was eating him up as surely as the famine killed so many peasants. But he was doubly thoughtful of her now. She had been so distressed by the incident of the lime in his eyes that he sent a telegram to her every day. Not that they were always cheerful messages, they merely indicated that he was still alive. "Town of Sligo hostile, the priests against us," he reported, or "good friendly minority". Then there was the day when he said sadly, "O'Kelly has gone, too." O'Kelly had been one of the closest to him. The scar from his wounding stayed on one eyelid. On her questioning he had to admit that the name Kitty O'Shea was still screamed derisively at him. "They don't know your real name, my Katie."

It was August, the summer heat was beginning to wane, and the wheat in the fields behind the house had turned golden. September came in with rain, and leaves were beginning to turn rusty. It was an early autumn. It looked like being an early winter.

Charles was ready to catch the Irish mail again.

"I'll send a telegram from Dublin."

"Darling, you look so tired."

He was so taut, so preoccupied, that he was beginning to find even her solicitude irritating.

"Now, don't tell me again to give in, because I would rather die than do that." He saw her look of hurt and added belatedly, "I will only if you insist."

She turned away, biting her lip.

"You must do what you think right. I've packed plenty of warm underwear and socks. You will remember to change if you get wet. How can you expect your rheumatism to get better if you sit in damp clothing?"

"Yes, Kate, yes."

"And promise to ask Doctor Kenny for a sedative if the pain is bad."

"You don't need to worry. Kenny watches over me like an old woman." He was gone from her already, his eyes brooding over troubles ahead, his face set. "I'll be back by the weekend, I hope. I'll telegraph."

The autumn in Ireland was beginning to be more like winter. At Creggs where Mr. Parnell was due to make a speech the lowering sky touched the treetops, and before his speech was half finished a drenching downpour had set in. He had never let bad weather stop him. Scorning shelter, he continued to speak in spite of his audience slowly drifting away. Once they would have been indifferent to the rain, too, when they had their beloved chief to listen to. Now the cold was deeper than that brought by the bad weather.

When at last Mr. Parnell consented to go into the hotel and changed into dry clothes, he was shivering with fever and his joints were so stiff and painful with rheumatism that he had difficulty in moving.

Nevertheless, in spite of Doctor Kenny's advice to rest, he travelled back to Dublin and spent three days working on plans for starting a new paper. One of the most recent and hardest blows had been the defection of the loyal *Freeman's Journal*. It had turned to the seceders, it was echoing Tim Healy's sentiments, and could not be allowed to do so unopposed.

Mr. Parnell's remaining friends were deeply worried about his health. His cheeks burned with fever, his eyes were sunken, at times he seemed half-delirious. But he drove himself on. He must be back in England for the weekend, he had promised his wife. He would be obliged if he could be got a cabin on the boat so that he could lie down during the crossing. That rest and a few days at home would set him up capitally. He would be back in Dublin the following Saturday.

He stood on deck waving goodbye to Mr. Kelly and Mr. Clancy. It was still raining and the sea was grey as the mail-steamer edged out of the dock. The watching men could see that the tall figure remained on deck for as long as the boat was visible to their eyes. It seemed as if he were taking a long farewell of the land he loved.

Katharine had not expected him home that day, and was delighted to see him. But her delight changed to alarm when she saw that he was ill. It seemed as if he had had only sufficient strength to get to the doorstep, and now was on the verge of collapse.

"It's only a chill," he managed to say. "I stopped in London to take a Turkish bath. Perhaps that was foolish. It has made me feel extremely weak."

Katharine helped him off with his coat. Fortunately the fire in the drawing room had been lit an hour ago, and the room was warm and cosy. Charles eased himself, with a sigh, into a chair drawn up close to the blaze.

"It's my confounded rheumatism again. At times I can hardly move. Getting wet through in Creggs didn't help. I had three days in Dublin when I was almost incapacitated."

"That miserable Irish rain!" Katharine burst out. She had to vent her anger and fear on something. She had never seen him look so ill.

He gave a half-smile, a barely visible lift of his shoulders. "Yes, it's as uncontrollable as the British Government."

Grouse, an old dog now and almost as stiff as his master, had come to wag his tail and sniff at the remembered hand. Then he stretched at his master's feet contentedly. Katharine shovelled more coal on the fire, and knelt to unlace Charles' boots.

"No, love. I'll do that."

"You'll sit quite still. I'm going to the kitchen to make you a hot drink."

"I couldn't drink it. Don't go. Don't leave me."

She looked up at him, trying not to show her fear.

"What did Doctor Kenny prescribe?"

"Champagne."

"Then I'll open a bottle."

His fingers were in her hair. "Not now. Later. Stay where you are. I like to feel you there."

303

So she sat in her familiar place on the hearthrug with her head against his knee. She couldn't relax. There were more practical things she could be doing for his illness. But this was what she wanted. Perhaps he was right, for he seemed to doze, although at intervals his fingers stroked her hair as if to reassure himself that she was there.

Norah looked in and stopped short. Katharine signalled to her to go, and she went at once, quietly closing the door. Grouse shuddered and whimpered in his sleep, and the other sleeper stirred and murmured something about famished children. "Hungry. In rags. And it's raining. Winter's begun. Must do more for them . . ."

Katharine stood up and gently shook his shoulder.

"Darling, you're falling asleep. You must come to bed."

When he opened his eyes there was no light at all in them. They were dark extinguished hollows that struck a chill in her.

"I'll help you. Can you get up?"

He moved painfully. "If I could travel down from London, surely I can climb the stairs to bed."

But he had to grip her arm, and at the stairs she had to call to Norah to come and take his other arm.

Norah was alarmed, and wanted to know if she should go for the doctor, but Charles answered her himself.

"No, no, I don't need a doctor. It's only cursed rheumatism. A day or two of rest will put me right."

When he was undressed and in bed Katharine made him drink a glass of champagne, and prayed that it would make him sleep. She lit a night-light and turned out the gas. But he moved restlessly and said that he would not sleep until she was beside him.

She went downstairs to reassure Norah and the servants.

"He'll be better by morning, I hope. If he isn't we must send for Doctor Jowers whether he likes it or not. Now I'm going up to stay with him."

"But, ma'am, your dinner!" Ellen protested.

"If I want anything I'll come down in the night. I'll probably be making hot drinks for Mr. Parnell."

"Mamma, you will call if you need me?" Norah asked.

"Of course, darling. Don't look so alarmed. This illness isn't serious."

She spoke firmly, the statement almost reassuring herself as well. But during the night her fears mounted.

For Charles talked continually through the long hours. The dimly-lit room seemed full of the spectres of Irish peasants who had died of famine, for they haunted him unceasingly.

His weak voice went on and on about the poverty, the potato blight, the half naked and shivering children who must have learned to hate the world before they were five years old, the dark damp cabins, the evictions, the old people who died in open fields with the rain falling on their faces, the humiliating queues for a crust of bread or a bowl of lukewarm cabbage water, the long degradation of poverty that finally conquered their spirit.

"They suffer in silence," the weak angry voice beside Katharine said. "That's the terrible thing. When an Irishman loses his gift of speech he's lost everything. They're a nation of song-makers and story-tellers. They have the proudest heritage of learning and poetry in Europe. It's being crushed out of them. Their voice is being killed. I've got to save it, Kate. I've got to loose the stifling grip of England. This great powerful country with its mean little vice of keeping Ireland down . . ."

"Forget it now," Katharine urged. "Try to sleep."

"Hold me in your arms."

But even when she did so his wandering voice went on:

"I see their white dumb faces. They look up at me with their sad pleading eyes. A mother holds out her baby to show me. It's too weak to cry. It's wrapped in a bit of old shawl. Their hands pluck at me. They ask so much. They need so much. I have to try to give it to them. They're suffering. Their pain never ceases."

He was half-delirious. She realised that these starving faces were in front of his eyes. The pain he spoke of was his own physical pain transmitted to them.

"Charles darling, you're here with me."

"Thank God for you, Kate. Don't leave me."

By morning, to her intense disappointment, his fever had not gone down. On the contrary it seemed to have risen. He was flushed and his eyes were now much too bright and glittering. He scarcely dared move for the pain in his limbs.

Thoroughly alarmed, Katharine wanted to send to London for the Harley Street specialist, Sir Henry Thompson. But the idea seemed to worry Charles too much. He said if there must be a doctor old Jowers would do. Surely he would be perfectly capable of treating a chill.

Doctor Jowers came, diagnosed a severe rheumatic chill, and said that little could be done that Katharine was not already doing. Rest, warmth, plenty of liquids and above all no worry.

"Make him relax his mind, Mrs. Parnell. He suffers very much from an over-active mind. The fever must run its course. It's likely to get worse before it gets better. I'll look in again this evening."

The long anxious day went by, and by evening Charles did seem a little better. A saner quieter look had come into his face. When Grouse clambered on to his bed and settled down he would not allow the dog to be removed.

"Let him stay." He moved his painfully stiff hand to pat Grouse's head, then felt for Katharine's hand.

"My friends," he said.

He slept a little better that night although his body beside hers was burningly hot. When he woke in the morning she would give him a sponge bath in an attempt to bring his temperature down. He must also take some of the chicken broth Ellen had made. All day yesterday Ellen had been preparing beef tea, beaten up eggs in milk, and barley broth in the hope of tempting the invalid's appetite. Katharine found the faithful old creature in tears when her offerings were rejected.

"Ma'am, he's got to get a drop past his lips if he's not to starve to death like all those peasants he's forever fretting about."

"Yes, Ellen, tomorrow he will. Tomorrow he'll be better."

But by the next morning the alarming temperature was higher than ever. Doctor Jowers hummed and hawed, said it looked as if an improvement could not be hoped for for a day or two, but there was not yet cause for serious alarm. The patient would presently begin to respond.

It was raining that day, the sea lead-grey, the fields denuded of their summer harvest turning into the quenched beige of winter. The wind lifted spray and flung it against the windows so that the panes were continually weeping. It was difficult to shut out the damp and draughts.

It had perhaps been a mistake to buy a house so close to the sea, Katharine thought. If Charles' rheumatism persisted they had better plan to move inland. They no longer had to evade curious stares and gossip. They could take plenty of time finding a house in the most attractive surroundings. In all her married life she had never had a house of her own to furnish as she wished. It would be a labour of love.

She made herself dream of this while the slow hours ticked by. She had to fill her mind with hopeful thoughts of the future, otherwise Charles, who was sleeping more today, might wake to find her weeping. She refused to leave the bedside although Norah was getting worried about her look of exhaustion.

"You'll be ill, too, Mamma," she whispered, but Katharine merely shook her head and signalled to her to go away.

Once there was a subdued scuffling outside the door, and she opened it to see the large-eyed faces of Clare and Katie. They stood there in their white pinafores and their buttoned boots saying that they wanted to see Papa and wish him to get well.

Katharine shook her head.

"Not today, my darlings. Papa's asleep and we must let him go on sleeping. Tomorrow he'll be able to talk to you."

They went away obediently, their two dark heads so like the one in the bed that Katharine couldn't stop her tears. She was so intensely lonely. The form in the bed might have left her, too, it was so uncommunicative, so remote.

She stood in front of the mirror smoothing her hair, and putting on a freshly starched fichu. She had been shocked by her haggard and dishevelled appearance. Charles must not see her like that when he woke.

In the early evening Doctor Jowers came again. This time he shook his head portentously and ventured the opinion that if Sir Henry Thompson would consent to come down it might be a good idea to have a second opinion. If the fever did not drop soon the strain on the heart might become serious.

"Then he must be sent for at once," Katharine said agitatedly.

"Don't be too alarmed, Mrs. Parnell. The morning may tell a different story." He added that if it didn't she must engage a nurse. Otherwise she would be in danger of collapse herself.

Katharine didn't waste time arguing about that. She had no intention whatever of leaving her husband's bedside until all danger was over.

It occurred to her to wonder what Charles' precious political friends who had deserted him would think if they could see him now. She wished that they could. It would do them good to suffer some remorse. For they had put him on this sickbed. They with their ears turned to their priests. And other people, too, such as the cruel old eagle Gladstone with his non-conformist conscience, and Chamberlain who had betrayed him long ago, and Willie, the go-between, the dupe, who had turned so meanly vindictive. And herself, too. For the simple fact of her existence. For the terrible strain this man had borne for so long, torn between the woman he loved and the country he loved.

She put out her hand to grope under the covers for his, and he stirred and miraculously opened aware and intelligent eyes.

"Kate," he said with pleasure.

"Is the pain better?"

"A little, I think."

"Could you take something? A spoonful of broth?"

He turned his head feebly.

"Come and lie beside me. That's all I want."

She had to stir the sleeping Grouse who reluctantly got off the bed and ambled to the fire. She lay beside Charles and took his hand in hers. Its heat frightened her, but her clasp was returned. His fingers lay in hers as they had done so often, every time they sat side by side, at every farewell.

She made herself smile at him calmly and lovingly, and his lips moved in response.

"Kiss me," he said. "Then I will try to sleep."

She did so very gently. His eyelids closed, the long dark feminine lashes lying on his sunken cheeks. He breathed very quietly. She wasn't sure whether he slept or whether he had slipped back into a coma. She didn't even hear when his breathing stopped. She only felt the clasp of his fingers loosen, his hand fall away.

She sat up with infinite care, afraid of disturbing him, totally unable to believe that the last separation had begun.

EPILOGUE

So they had come to her at last, those dour implacable men with their stubborn grief-stricken Celtic faces. This was Kitty O'Shea, the woman they had maligned and hated. After all, she was no scheming strumpet, no wicked sorceress, but a middle-aged woman worn with weeping and defenceless.

They realised then that she had always been defenceless. If she were the unwitting cause of Ireland's rights being delayed for many years, if she was to have a great deal of bloodshed and violence on her conscience, she was still curiously innocent.

They would have liked to say this to her now, for they were Irish gentlemen. But it was too late for remorse. They could only tell her clumsily what Mr. Gladstone had said that day that one of the very noblest hearts in England had ceased to beat.

And make the blunt announcement, without apology, that they had come to take their dead chief home.

He had promised he would be back in Ireland on Saturday, they said with merciless logic. He had always kept promises. She, of all people, must have known that.

So she had to stand by the white calm face, so familiar and yet now so strange, and say her farewell. The envelope containing a withered white rose dropped long ago in Palace Yard lay on his breast, the ring with its intertwined K and C was on his finger. Those two things, and her heart, he would take with him on this last journey he would ever make across the Irish Sea. She wished he could have known that she had capitulated at last, that she was letting Ireland have him. The Irish earth would cover him gently, and she would never lie beside him again . . .

Dorothy Eden on Never Call it Loving

How did I come to write this book? I wanted to write a Victorian cause célèbre, but when the story of Parnell and Kitty O'Shea was suggested I thought it just another story of rather sordid intrigue and put it out of my mind.

However, it happened that I made several visits to Ireland, and became deeply interested in its history, beginning to see it as the poets did, this dark sad quiet country with its ruins of old castles, its ballads, and its voluble people, especially the now ageing patriots with their obsessive love for their country. To them, ironically, Ireland's freedom has been its death—or the death of the old vital quarrelsome poetic tragic land. It has no enemy any longer, it no longer demands martyrs, so life has become flat, dull and commercial.

But I caught something of the patriots' dream, and that was the beginning of my book. The next step was even more significant. I came upon Katharine O'Shea's memoirs which I hadn't known existed.

Katharine has told her story guardedly, with a great deal left out. It has been suggested by other historians that this book was written with her son, Gerard O'Shea, holding her back from too many admissions. So one has to read between the lines.

From the moment of reading that book the missing and vital information became brilliantly clear to me, and I knew that the story must be written again, this time in full.

Perhaps I have misinterpreted, perhaps in some incidents I am wrong, but I have the strongest feeling that I have scarcely erred, that poor unhappy Katharine has been at my shoulder all the time.

And I am sure the brown-bearded gentleman who followed me into the library one day was Mr. Parnell himself! And when I went to Somerset House to find Aunt Ben's will, and saw on the old parchment the signature of Anna Maria Wood and the unformed hands of the servant witnesses, I had the strangest feeling of looking into a dusty grave.

Yet there is very little visible evidence left in England of Parnell's or Katharine's existence. Eltham is now a busy suburb of London, the house in Brighton where Parnell died has been pulled down and a block of flats built in its place, Thomas's Hotel in Berkeley Square has long since gone. So has the Westminster Palace Hotel and the Ladies' Gallery in the Houses of Parliament. Only the soot-grimed Victorian railway stations where the two so often met remain practically unchanged. Even the National Portrait Gallery has put the portrait of Parnell (which should hang in the room where Queen Victoria is surrounded by her ministers) in the basement.

In the end, perhaps Katharine's greatest grief was that Parnell was taken to Ireland for burial. She never went to see his grave in Glasnevin cemetery, the place that is famous for its graves of Irish patriots. The last bones to be interred there were those of Sir Roger Casement, recently removed from a prison yard.

Katharine wrote that she heard Parnell's grave was untended, with grass growing over it, and that she would have looked after it lovingly if it had been in England. Thirty years after Parnell's death, when she herself lay dying, looked after by her faithful daughter Norah, she called constantly for her lover. "It was Parnell, Parnell, Parnell, all the time," Norah wrote in a letter to one of Parnell's last loyal supporters.

Katharine is buried at Littlehampton, and Norah lies beside her.

I think one of the most eerie experiences of the researcher is reading about one's subject in old newspapers, facts written down as the news happened, and unaffected by the hindsight of history. Old storms in the Houses of Parliament, old outrages perpetrated in small towns or villages in County Cork, County Limerick, County Kildare, eloquence and tears and violence of long ago. The Times, the English Bible of those days, had a long column headed "Ireland" every day. No other of Britain's widespread colonies had a tenth of the space given to small unruly Ireland. When the commission sat on the enquiry into the

Pigott forged letters and the Land League whole pages were devoted day after day to reporting evidence. The O'Shea divorce case occupied several columns for two days. Then the comments, the criticisms and arguments went on for weeks. Charles Stewart Parnell must have been a godsend to English journalists.

But it all came to an end. And one of the saddest ends that could possibly be written. I put off writing it for days, then wrote it in one long session and could not alter a word afterwards.

Perhaps I have been too kind to the lovers. This, I do not know. I wrote only as intuition told me. And anyway, why not be kind? Their debt to society, if they owed one, has been paid long ago.

Afternoon for Lizards

DOROTHY EDEN

On arrival in Australia, Abby found the man she had grown to love and come to marry so very different from the man she had known in England. Once gay and sparkling, now taciturn and withdrawn, Luke seemed tormented by fears he could not disclose.

Abby felt so alone, so powerless. And as she tried to understand, everything around her began to play on her mind; from the kookaburras laughing at her, to the neighbours forever watching her. Then suddenly her world exploded, and she opened her eyes to violence and crime, and beyond these to the man, her husband, who would not let even his love drag him from the path of bitter revenge.

CORONET BOOKS

Siege in the Sun

DOROTHY EDEN

MAFEKING—THE PLACE OF STONES

Isolation, hunger, disease and death—these were the things that hovered in the air along with the flesh-craving vultures, and enveloped Mafeking during its siege in the Boer War.

But Colonel Baden-Powell and his small army of brave men were not alone in their hell-hole. And among the dust-covered prisoners there were two women who viewed the siege with completely contrasting eyes.

On the one hand there was Alice Partridge, whose fatalism led her into the gulf of despair. And on the other there was Lizzie Willoughby, whose eagerness and determination to live went side by side in her love affair with a man whom she could never marry.

'A good read—at any level' _Catholic Herald_

CORONET BOOKS

The Vines of Yarrabee

DOROTHY EDEN

Set in Australia in the early years of colonization, this is the story of Yarrabee, a vineyard, and of the people whose lives it dominated.

Gilbert Massingham, master of Yarrabee, whose obsession for the land threatens to destroy his marriage. *Eugenia*, his sensitive English bride, who is thrust against the rawness of pioneer life. *Molly Jarvis*, the convict servant who shares Gilbert's bold dreams and who becomes the secret mistress of Yarrabee. And *Colm O'Connor*, a passionate young artist who reveals to Eugenia a kind of love she has never known.

The vitality of life in a strange, violently beautiful land provides a compelling background to Dorothy Eden's superb new bestseller.

'From the first page of all her books Dorothy Eden never fails to intrigue'   *Books and Bookmen*

CORONET BOOKS

Whistle For The Crows

DOROTHY EDEN

To Cathleen, ghosting the history of a poverty-stricken Irish family, the main interest seemed to lie in the private lives of the present brood of the tribe. But at every turn, past scandals threw gloomy shadows into her path.

What was the mystery surrounding the death of the eldest son? And how authentic were the wild-sounding rumours concerning his wife and child?

When she heard a baby crying at the dead of night, she investigated—only to find her safety threatened in return. For Cathleen was quite alone in the world. After the tragic deaths of her husband and baby daughter, she had come to Ireland to try and make a new life for herself. Little did she know of the hidden dangers that would surround her at Loughneath Castle.

CORONET BOOKS

The Pretty Ones

DOROTHY EDEN

Nothing would upset the first dreamy days of marriage for the beautiful Emma—or so she thought.

But then she began to hear the unpleasant rumours: that her husband had an ex-wife, whereabouts unknown; that pretty Sylvie, the governess, had disappeared without cause or explanation.

When a lonely grave was discovered in a nearby rain-sodden field, suspicion and foreboding gave way to cold fear, as Emma fought desperately to keep her grip on life.

'No-one can suggest an eerie atmosphere and the sinister trifle better than Miss Dorothy Eden'

The Guardian

CORONET BOOKS

Listen to Danger

DOROTHY EDEN

In the shadows of the night, a veiled woman lurked in the garden, staring at the house, watching, waiting . . .

It all started with a mysterious telephone call that plunged Harriet Lacey into a suffocating atmosphere of terror. With no-one to help her, she was forced to turn to Flynn, the brilliant but bitter writer, whose past was already interwoven with hers in a tapestry of sudden death.

It was an odd assortment of people who lived in the narrow brick house. Aloof, wary, they hugged their secrets to themselves. But one of them was a prowler in the dark, bent on destroying Harriet and everything she held dear . . .

'Miss Eden's particular talent is to blend the horrid and the cosy'   *Times Book Review*

CORONET BOOKS

OTHER NOVELS BY DOROTHY EDEN
FROM CORONET